Shatrujeet Nath has sold ice-creams, peddled computer-training courses, written ad copy and reported on business as a journalist and assistant editor at *The Economic Times*. *The Karachi Deception* is his first book. He has also written *The Guardians of the Halahala* and *The Conspiracy at Meru*, the first two volumes in the epic fantasy series on the legendary king, Vikramaditya. Shatrujeet is also the co-founder of JokerStreet, an IP & content-creation company.

PRAISE FOR THE BOOK

'…an interesting addition to the growing corpus of spy and crime fiction.'

– The Express Tribune

'Pacing is an important element in thriller writing. And Shatrujeet seems to know the nuts and bolts of it.'

– The Hindu

'In one fell swoop, Nath has proved himself as the South Asian equivalent of Robert Ludlum.'

– Newsline

'Shatrujeet Nath has hit a bull's eye with this amazing debut. And for all the lovers of spy-thrillers, *The Karachi Deception* is a must read.'

– The New Indian Express

'For all those who have been pining for an infiltrate-Pakistan-and-take-out-a-target thriller, here's your dream come true.'

– Livemint

THE KARACHI DECEPTION

SHATRUJEET NATH

RUPA

To

Amma, Appa, Nessie and Woo baby.
You light up the four corners of my world.

Published by
Rupa Publications India Pvt. Ltd 2016
7/16, Ansari Road, Daryaganj
New Delhi 110002

Sales centres:
Allahabad Bengaluru Chennai
Hyderabad Jaipur Kathmandu
Kolkata Mumbai

ISBN: 978-81-291-3974-0

Second impression 2020

10 9 8 7 6 5 4 3 2

The moral right of the author has been asserted.

Typeset by Saanvi Graphics, Noida

CONTENTS

PROLOGUE

May 7. Commune III, Bamako, Republic of Mali

Le dessert est servi.

Oumar stared at the message that had just been delivered on his cell phone, his eyes adjusting to the screen's brightness in the darkened interior of the car. For a moment he sat still, allowing the significance of the message to sink in.

Dessert had been served at Le Cercle d'Or. In under a quarter of an hour, the man he had been hired to kill would emerge from the hotel. Oumar and his partner Youssouf would have less than a minute to finish the job.

Kill number twenty-eight.

Oumar dropped the phone on the empty seat beside him, drew a deep breath and cranked up the car's air conditioning. As blasts of cold air surged through the vents, he sat upright and gripped the steering-wheel with both hands. Knitting his brows, he squinted down Route de Guinée towards the Bamako Imperial, where dessert had just been served.

'You'll get only one chance, so give it your best shot.'

Oumar wasn't sure if the rasping, sun-dried voice on the other end of the phone had chuckled at the pun. But he knew there had otherwise been little mirth in the voice as it went through the routine one last time, late last night. The owner of the voice hadn't introduced himself, but Oumar guessed he was talking to Algerian warlord Musa Zawawi. Though why Zawawi had picked English over French or his native Kabyle was beyond Oumar.

One thing was certain, though. Zawawi personally overseeing the assignment meant the stakes were much higher than Oumar had previously imagined.

Not that he laboured under any illusions about his target—Irshad Dilawar.

The man was wanted by the Interpol for organized crime, counterfeiting, and the shipment of narcotics to the United Kingdom and Western Europe. There was evidence that he was in close contact with the Taliban in

Afghanistan and Pakistan-based terrorist groups like the Lashkar-e-Taiba. The dossier said that he had even established links with al-Qaeda's charismatic leader Osama bin Laden. The United States Department of Treasury had designated the man a global terrorist, and he also headed a list of most wanted men issued by the Indian government.

Oumar didn't know who wanted Irshad Dilawar dead or why. He never bothered asking. Indiscreet questions didn't take one far in his line of business, and Oumar had travelled quite a distance. Twenty-seven people killed in cold blood in fifteen countries across three continents. What mattered was the money, and Zawawi and Olaf were prepared to shell out astronomical sums to have the man, presently having dessert at Le Cercle d'Or at the Bamako Imperial, eliminated.

'Accept this job and there's no going back,' Olaf had growled darkly, as they stood leaning on the railings of the wind-blown Pont des Martyrs and gazing at the broad sweep of the Niger River. 'And even if you succeed, you might not come out of this alive to enjoy the things all this money will buy.'

That was four months ago, and now as he sat hunched in the car, Olaf's words suddenly took on an ominous, prophetic ring in Oumar's ears. Soon, the waiter at Le Cercle d'Or would send his second message, and minutes later it would be over, one way or the other.

Oumar leaned back and glanced at the rear-view mirror. Down the sunny street, a grey Citroen was parked unobtrusively in the shade of a giant baobab tree.

If those idiots were slow off the block, Oumar knew he and Youssouf didn't stand an ice-cube's chance in hell.

* * *

La cible se déplace.

The second message from the waiter at the Bamako Imperial had just come in. The target was on the move.

Starting the engine, Oumar threw the car into gear, took a deep breath and pressed the accelerator. As the car nosed up the empty street, Oumar looked briefly at the grey Citroen drawing away in the mirror and sent up a quick prayer. The first time was always difficult. Then it got easy, they said. Oumar had learnt that it never did.

Umpteen dry runs had shown that at a leisurely pace, the 400-metre drive to the parking lot of the Bamako Imperial would take him under two minutes. In forty-five seconds, Oumar was at the hotel's main gate, and after a perfunctory security check, the guards lazily waved him in.

Oumar eased the car past the fountain in the courtyard and manoeuvred into the parking lot. Taking care not to pick a space too close to the exit, he parked the car and stepped out. In his light grey suit and matching grey Ray-Ban Highstreet, Dell laptop bag in his left hand and a bulky business daily in his right, Oumar could have passed off as one of the many local businessmen or mid-level corporate executives who frequented the hotel.

Retracing his steps towards the hotel entrance, Oumar transferred the newspaper to the hand carrying the laptop, reached into his pocket and pulled out his phone. Flipping it open, he punched a couple of keys and held the phone to his ear. Meanwhile, his eyes took in the sight of a black limousine drawing up to the hotel's door. A dark green Toyota Land Cruiser followed the limousine closely.

'*J'ai besoin d'argent,*' Oumar spoke into the phone, before switching to English. 'If you do not make the payment in the next two days, I will not be able to source the computers for you. And that will mean more delay.'

Walking slowly, Oumar pressed the lifeless phone to his ear as he took stock of the situation outside the lobby. He observed a hotel employee drive an electric mopper into the courtyard from the opposite direction, their eyes meeting briefly. Youssouf was in position. Turning slightly, Oumar saw the grey Citroen slowly approaching the hotel gates.

The large revolving door of the hotel slowly spun around, discharging five men into the courtyard. Oumar's eyes instantly locked on the man he had been hired to kill. Irshad Dilawar, standing less than five-and-a-half feet in height, stocky, a thin black moustache covering his upper lip. Even at this distance, Oumar could see the distinguishing scar that ran down his left cheek.

Watching Youssouf slowly begin manoeuvring the mopper towards the limousine, Oumar nodded and spoke into the phone.

'Merci. I shall wait for two days. *Bon jour, monsieur.*'

Snapping the phone shut, Oumar deposited it into the inside pocket of his jacket. Youssouf was just twenty feet away from the group in the courtyard. Their target was still some distance from the limousine, smiling at something one of his associates was saying. His guards were spread around, but two of them were already moving towards the Land Cruiser.

Oumar saw Youssouf unhitch a hose attached to the machine and slowly point the nozzle in the general direction of the guards. Breathing in deep, Oumar began moving towards the group, the fingers of his left hand feeling the contours of the lightweight Kel-Tec PF-9 nestling in the folds of the newspaper. Oumar turned one last time to glance casually towards the gates of the hotel.

His jaw dropped and his heart skipped a beat.

A large, yellow refrigerated truck stood rumbling at the gate. Two security guards were methodically shoving the large mirror under the truck's carriage, while a third was talking to the truck's driver and writing something in a long notebook. The grey Citroen was barely visible behind the bulk of the truck.

The truck, which was clearly making deliveries to the hotel, had somehow swung into the gate ahead of the Citroen, and Oumar and Youssouf, intent on getting into position, had failed to notice this development. Oumar cursed and looked frantically at Youssouf. His partner had his back to the gate and was oblivious to the truck blocking the Citroen's path.

With eyes widening in dismay, Oumar saw Youssouf raise the hose and point it at the men closest to the Land Cruiser. Oumar was acutely aware of the sweat running down the back of his neck and the emptiness in the pit of his stomach. There was no way he could warn Youssouf about the truck without drawing attention. And there was no way the Citroen was going to make it to the courtyard in time.

* * *

The first two shots that Youssouf fired from the hose attached to the specially designed electric mopper hit one of the guards standing right next to the Land Cruiser. The next two went wide, one hitting and shattering the Land Cruiser's window, the other smashing into the car's door.

The group by the limousine instantly swung into action. Three of the guards moved between Youssouf and the target, using their bodies to shield their boss, even as they pulled their guns free. The other guards began scattering in all directions, making it hard for Youssouf to decide where to fire. He randomly fired another volley, hitting one of the guards.

Oumar, his mouth dry as sandpaper, looked at his target. The man was running quickly towards the limousine, his body bent at the waist. Oumar realized that all the guards were looking at Youssouf, their backs to him. He also saw that his target would be inside the limousine in a matter of seconds. As the guards opened fire on Youssouf, Oumar heard Olaf's voice in his head.

'Musa has staked his reputation on this one. Botch it up and he will make sure you run out of places to hide. And once he finds you, death will be sweet mercy.'

Oumar reached into the newspaper in his left hand and his fingers wrapped around the grip of the Kel-Tec PF-9. Pulling the gun loose, Oumar raised his arm, aimed at Irshad Dilawar and pulled the trigger. As the gun bucked gently in his hand, Oumar stared in surprise. Instead of hitting the target, the bullet had been intercepted by one of the guards who had chosen to climb out of the limousine at that very moment. As the guard toppled forward, dead before he hit the ground, Irshad Dilawar lunged through the limousine's open door into the car. Oumar rapidly fired two more rounds at the car's window, but he knew it was futile. The bullet-resistant glass would ensure the target got away.

Awake to the new source of threat, some of the guards swivelled towards him as the limousine's engine roared. Oumar turned and broke into a run, zigzagging towards the parking lot. The nearest car was ten metres away. He fired twice over his shoulder, desperately hoping to keep the guards down. He heard the squeal of tyres and knew the limousine was making a getaway.

Musa Zawawi would be extremely pissed, Oumar thought idly.

The protective bulk of a Honda Accord was just two metres away when Oumar heard two shots go off behind him. Almost immediately, he felt a searing pain in his lower back, just to the right of his spine. He also felt a warm fuzziness in his head as he felt himself being lifted and hurled towards the Honda Accord.

The last image to register in Oumar's mind was a light shower of blood splattering the shiny, silver hood of the car. Then, as he cannoned into the car head first, darkness descended.

PART ONE:
THE WAY OF THE ASSASSIN

CHAPTER 1

24 June. Bijwasan, New Delhi-Gurgaon Border

The sprawling farmhouse, located three kilometres off the busy Mehrauli–Najafgarh Road, was abuzz with activity. Its massive wrought-iron gates were wide open, and a couple of security guards were marshalling a steady stream of cars under its well-lit arch, elaborately decorated with multicoloured tinsel and the words 'Vishwas Weds Alka'.

Beyond the gate, the cobbled driveway branched out across the farmhouse's extensive lawns and landscaped gardens, all strung with colourful paper lanterns bobbing gently in the night breeze. A wedding mandap erected in a gazebo stood to one side of the lawn, which was already teeming with guests standing in clusters, chatting idly. Waiters in waistcoats and bow ties scuttled frantically among the guests bearing fast-emptying trays of starters and beverages, while kids and teenagers fluttered in and out of the main two-storeyed building, shouting and chattering excitedly.

The buoyant atmosphere was, however, conspicuously absent in a large, soundproof room situated deep in the basement of the building. In stark contrast to the floodlit lawns outside, the room was steeped in shadow, a solitary lamp in one corner providing a dim source of light. The only sound to be heard was the faint hum of the air conditioner.

In the centre of the room was a set of comfortable leather sofas, arranged at right angles around a coffee table on a rug. Four squat glasses of amber-coloured liquid sat on the table, while four men sat brooding on the sofas. From their sombre expressions and the taut silence that stretched between them, it was obvious that they were far removed from the festivities outside.

One of the men finally reached forward and picked up his glass. Dressed in a navy-blue blazer and grey trousers, he was in his early fifties, clean-shaven, with short salt-and-pepper hair and tired eyes. He resembled most moderately successful Delhi businessmen, but then Major-General Tushar Dixit didn't habitually look and behave like an army man. Authority was something he wielded with discretion.

Lifting the glass to his lips, General Dixit took a long, slow sip of the Scotch. He used the opportunity to observe the other three men over the rim of his glass. To his left sat a fair man in a shiny grey suit. Not a day older than forty, he had a thick mop of hair and a black moustache. His eyes twinkled merrily when he smiled, crow's feet crinkling the corners of his eyes. Colonel Surinder Mohan was one of the best marine commandos and intelligence and counter-insurgency specialists India had ever produced. He was also the chief architect of Unit Kilo.

The colonel suddenly raised his head and glanced at General Dixit, who inclined his head and gave a small reassuring nod. Nearly a decade ago, the general had hand-picked the enthusiastic young officer to start putting Unit Kilo together, and the colonel had responded admirably. In a way, this meeting was a culmination of Colonel Mohan's work; its outcome, a litmus test for Unit Kilo.

It was the man seated to the general's right who would ultimately determine the outcome of this meeting. Chandrakant Upreiti was short and dark, with shrewd, suspicious eyes. It was easy to tell that he was from a civilian background, but General Dixit was aware that Upreiti was also the most influential man in the room. An IAS officer from the 1980 batch, Upreiti had spent his entire career collating and analysing intelligence data, and had risen to the position of under-secretary at the Joint Intelligence Committee. The general knew that if what he and Colonel Mohan had just proposed stood any chance of getting a go-ahead, bringing Upreiti round to their point of view would be imperative.

The challenge to that sat directly opposite General Dixit, in the form of Inspector General Jagdish Rawat of the RAW. In his early fifties, Inspector General Rawat was of considerable girth, yet there wasn't an ounce of fat on him. A flat nose and heavily-muscled forearms told of a life spent in the boxing ring. A shock of iron grey hair matched the thick moustache, and beady eyes gazed out combatively from under bushy eyebrows. His mouth, set in a perpetual sneer, made the entire package quite unpalatable.

Given a choice, General Dixit would have preferred revealing his plan to Upreiti in private, but being a stickler for protocol, the under-secretary wouldn't have approved of that. The Indian Defence Ministry had given its consent to the creation of Unit Kilo on one condition: every blueprint of every mission conceived by the unit would first have to be whetted *jointly* by an under-secretary of the Joint Intelligence Committee and a senior officer attached to the Directorate of the RAW. Only then could any plan be put into action.

Normally, this wouldn't have been a problem with General Dixit, but his distrust of Inspector General Rawat ran deep. A China expert and staunch RAW loyalist, the inspector general had been assigned to oversee and clear Unit Kilo projects just six months earlier. The man's reputation of being an obstructionist and contrarian was legendary, but for some unfathomable reason he had, from day one, shown an exceptional dislike for Unit Kilo.

The general had already had a couple of run-ins with the man, the most recent one involving a plan to infiltrate Neelum Valley in Pakistan-occupied Kashmir to assassinate three Jaish-e-Mohammed commanders. It had taken Upreiti's backing for the operation to finally get cleared—which had only fuelled the RAW man's antipathy towards Unit Kilo. General Dixit knew Inspector General Rawat was smarting from that defeat, making him a worrisome adversary. He now feared that the inspector general would stonewall his latest proposal out of sheer vindictiveness.

As General Dixit leaned forward and placed his glass back on the coffee table, Upreiti raised his head and looked from the general to Colonel Mohan with troubled eyes. Sighing deeply, he shrugged and finally spoke.

'I don't know, Dixit saab. What you are suggesting is… you know… very difficult. I can't see… how…' Upreiti gave up groping for words. Shaking his head, he pursed his lips and lapsed back into silence.

General Dixit felt his heart sink. Upreiti had veto power over anything that Unit Kilo brought to his table and, at the moment, it looked as if the under-secretary was preparing to spike the proposal.

The general darted a glance at Inspector General Rawat. The man was nodding forcefully, a glint of triumph lighting his eyes as he smelled an opportunity to show the general his place. But before the RAW man could press home the advantage, General Dixit leaned forward and addressed Upreiti.

'But sir, it's for operations like this that we created Unit Kilo five years back. What is the point of having Unit Kilo if we are not going to use the unit for surgical strikes deep inside enemy territory?'

'I know very well why Unit Kilo was created,' Upreiti said levelly. 'Yes, I admit Unit Kilo has had a couple of successes to its credit. But those have been operations just across the border, maybe five or ten kilometres inside enemy territory. And all those involved killing insurgents hiding in remote places. This is different. You are talking of sending commandos to a large city like Karachi… to kill Irshad Dilawar!'

A dismissive snort emerged from Inspector General Rawat's lips. As General Dixit and Colonel Mohan exchanged glances, the RAW man picked up his glass, leaned back in his sofa and surveyed the general mockingly.

'That's going to be easy,' he sneered. 'Probably the most well-protected man in Pakistan. His security staff includes well-trained, ex-Pakistani army officers and ISI agents. His security arrangements are directly overseen by the ISI. Virtually impossible pinning him down to one location as he constantly shifts between a dozen known safe houses scattered across Pakistan. And you propose to walk into Karachi, ask for Dilawar's whereabouts, knock on his door and kill him?' The inspector general paused, drained his glass and chortled. 'Sure, if you ask nicely enough, I'm sure the famed Pakistani hospitality will work to your advantage.'

Noticing Colonel Mohan's face flushing with anger, General Dixit spoke quickly.

'We know it won't be easy, Rawat saab,' he said. 'But we have drawn up a detailed plan to infiltrate Pakistan, locate Dilawar and assassinate him. The men for the operation have been identified, and their entry and exit routes charted out. We have even worked out contingency plans.' Turning to Upreiti, he added, 'Mohan and I have been on this for the last two months. We will share everything with you, sir.'

There was a momentary pause and Colonel Mohan immediately pounced on it. Looking at Upreiti, he spoke earnestly, his voice rising.

'Everyone knows that Irshad Dilawar's underworld network is the unofficial spy network of the ISI in India. It is also a lifeline for almost every terror and insurgency outfit operating in our country, supplying information, logistic support and even equipment and operatives to militant groups from Kashmir to the Northeast to the tribal belts of Andhra, Maharashtra and Madhya Pradesh. We also know that the 1994 Royale Cinema bomb blast that killed over 250 people was directly organized and financed by Dilawar. Every time terror has claimed innocent lives in India, Irshad Dilawar has somehow been involved.'

All four glasses were empty. As the colonel made his impassioned pitch, General Dixit walked over to a low wooden cabinet on which rested a half-empty bottle of Johnnie Walker Red Label and an ice bucket.

'Sir, we have irrefutable proof that Dilawar is hiding in Pakistan—even the Interpol has corroborated India's position,' Colonel Mohan continued.

'Yet, the Pakistanis deny any knowledge of his presence in their country. We routinely hand over evidence of Dilawar's complicity in terror attacks to the Interpol, the CIA, the FBI… to whoever may care to listen. But no one seems to have the wherewithal or the inclination to pressure Pakistan into deporting the gangster to India. And Dilawar and his ISI masters continue to thumb their noses at us and fuel terrorism. How long are we to sit here wringing our hands in anguish like old women?'

Fetching the bottle and ice bucket, General Dixit shovelled ice-cubes into the glasses and poured a measure of the Scotch into each. Handing the glasses out, he looked at Upreiti entreatingly.

'Mohan is right, sir. It's time we stopped running to the Interpol and America for help and settled these old scores ourselves. We have to act, sir. And I assure you that Unit Kilo is capable of pulling this off.'

The under-secretary placed his glass back on the table without taking a sip. With his elbows on the armrests, he steepled his fingers and stared up at the ceiling. When he spoke, the indecision visible in his eyes came through in his voice.

'Maybe, maybe not. But the other thing that concerns me is the political fallout of entering Pakistan and killing Dilawar. Irrespective of whether we succeed or fail, will this blow up in our faces and create a diplomatic and political embarrassment for the Indian government?'

'I agree with Upreiti saab totally,' Inspector General Rawat butted in. 'I doubt if Unit Kilo can pull this off. But that aside, when the Mossad went after Palestinian terrorists hiding in other countries, Israel had the blessings of America and its NATO allies. We don't have such luxuries. World opinion will turn against us. We will be seen as the aggressor and that will only benefit Pakistan.'

'It's not as if we are going in with placards announcing we're from India and leaving visiting cards behind once we're done,' Colonel Mohan interjected sarcastically.

General Dixit winced. He was pleased to see the inspector general getting it right back, but he also knew that antagonizing the man wasn't in their interests. Whether they liked it or not, Unit Kilo would have to work with the RAW in the future, and a lot depended on the RAW's continued cooperation.

'Rawat saab, I appreciate your genuine concern about India looking shoddy in the eyes of the international community,' the general said gently, hoping to assuage the anger that Colonel Mohan's caustic remark must have caused. 'But no one will be able to point fingers at the Indian government for any of this.' Once again addressing Upreiti, he continued, 'Yes, the assassination might be linked back to India, but it will never get officially linked to the Indian state machinery.'

'What makes you so sure?'

'Sir, our target does not "officially" exist in Pakistan for anyone to "officially" blame the Indian state for his death there. What can the Pakistanis say? That India sent commandos into Pakistan and assassinated a man who, as far as Pakistan is concerned, has never been in the country? They would end up looking like fools.'

'That wouldn't stop the Pakistanis from raising a hue and cry,' Inspector General Rawat growled adamantly. 'All they need is an opportunity to raise a bogey about India. Through this operation, we'll be handing them that opportunity on a platter.'

'You speak of the Mossad assassinating those Palestenian terrorists,' Colonel Mohan cut in, his voice on edge. 'But Israel maintains that its agencies had no role in any of the Palestinian and Arab killings. The Americans have shown that if you vehemently deny the truth often enough, people come round to believing you. With Dilawar and the ISI, Pakistan has learnt that art as well. Similarly, once Dilawar's death comes to light, we will insist that Indian agencies had nothing to do with it.'

General Dixit took a swig from his glass. 'Correct,' he said reassuringly. 'And even if fingers are pointed at India, we can always link the killing to the underworld rivalry between Dilawar and his many friends-turned-foes like Vasantrao Guru or Babloo Kasim. If it sounds plausible, the media will lap it up.'

Upreiti digested this thoughtfully. Suddenly, he looked at the faces around him with interest. His gaze finally settled on Inspector General Rawat.

'That reminds me… Any information on who was behind the bid on Dilawar's life in Mali last month? Your department got anything on that yet?'

'We're still following leads,' the RAW officer said brusquely.

Upreiti nodded, a ghost of a smile playing on his lips. The bureaucrat had spent enough time in this business to understand that 'following leads' was a dignified way of admitting utter cluelessness. Raising an eyebrow, he looked from Colonel Mohan to General Dixit.

'Had that attempt succeeded, it would have saved you and Unit Kilo a lot of trouble, right?' he asked.

Without answering Upreiti directly, the general said, 'That job had the hallmark of someone totally inept in the art of assassination. We'll just have to finish what someone else started.'

Upreiti stood up, stretched his arms and took a small walk around the room, his head bent in thought. 'How much will we achieve by killing Dilawar?' he asked suddenly, wheeling around. 'His network will still be very much in place, and will continue to offer support to terrorists and their ISI masters.'

A look of absolute pleasure spread across Inspector General Rawat's face. 'That's a very important point,' he said, wagging a finger at the general and the colonel. 'You believe killing Irshad Dilawar will really solve our problems?'

Seeing his gloating, officious face, General Dixit was overcome by an irrational desire to get up and punch him. They said you could choose your friends but never your family. The latter held true for the people you ended up working with as well, the general decided.

Smiling calmly, he addressed Upreiti. 'The moment Dilawar is eliminated, his network will start imploding. As our friends in the RAW will confirm, Irshad Dilawar is the only reason the network is still holding up. You must be aware that there is a power struggle brewing within Dilawar's empire, with his brother Feroz and his loyalists on one side and his trusted lieutenant Munna Riyaaz and *his* foot soldiers on the other.'

'I know of this tug-of-war,' the under-secretary nodded, a look of comprehension dawning on his face. 'Dilawar has tried his best to divide operations between the two. He wants to keep both Feroz and Munna Riyaaz happy, but neither is satisfied. Each sees himself as the true successor to Dilawar's empire and wants to sideline the other completely.'

Upreiti returned to his sofa. Raising his glass, he swirled it around, staring absently into the liquid sloshing inside. When he spoke, his voice was muted, meditative. 'According to Intelligence Bureau and Crime Branch reports, both factions have been passing on information about the other's members and their activities to the police in many Indian states. So, the house is divided and waiting to fall. We kill Dilawar, his empire plunges into a battle for supremacy, and the network comes apart.'

The general sat back, pleased to see that Upreiti had connected the dots. He glanced at Colonel Mohan, who looked back at him hopefully. Inspector General Rawat glowered across the table.

Upreiti took a small sip and put the glass down. 'You both have obviously thought this through, general saab,' his tone was appreciative. '*Idea mein dum toh hai*. But you still have to convince us that Unit Kilo can do something as ambitious as eliminating the number one enemy of the Indian state. Kyun Rawat saab... correct?'

General Dixit felt relief flooding through him as the under-secretary turned to Inspector General Rawat. Upreiti's sudden warming to the proposal had taken the RAW man by surprise, and he mumbled hurriedly, his voice a trifle petulant.

'*Haan haan… theek hai*. But we shall not approve any of this until we have seen the detailed plan of the operation.'

Realizing that the inspector general had grudgingly conceded the first round, General Dixit thought it best to pamper his ego a bit. 'Bilkul, Rawat saab. Your and Upreiti saab's experience and judgment will be critical in ensuring that the plan we have drawn up is watertight.'

The general picked up a small leather briefcase that sat unobtrusively beside his sofa. He opened it and began pulling out a set of thin cardboard files. Upreiti leaned back and examined his fingernails thoughtfully.

'If this has to work, you'll need a crack team led by the best man at your disposal.'

General Dixit nodded as he shuffled through the files. Selecting one, he handed it to the under-secretary. 'Here's the team that we have put together for this operation. The team will be led by Major Imtiaz Ahmed, the best and most experienced commando in Unit Kilo.'

26 June. Oud-Zuid, Amsterdam

The apartment was located on the third floor of a block of buildings just off Willemsparkweg, a two-minute walk from the famous Museumplein. Its many balconies and terrace gardens overlooked the lush green environs of Vondelpark, but for the time being, all windows were drawn tightly shut to keep out a nippy draft.

The apartment was spacious, but even so, its drawing room was disproportionately large, its size accentuated by a high ceiling from which was suspended an exquisite Murano glass chandelier. The cedarwood floor was mottled with islands of rich Persian rugs, while a Goya on the wall and antique Biedermeier furniture nicely rounded off the air of tasteful indulgence.

Three men occupied the room, each a study in contrast. A white man, incredibly fat and in his late forties, sat on one of the large sofas. A pink, chubby face and curly blonde hair lent him a cherubic look, but there was nothing angelic about his eyes, which were cold and hard as pebbles behind a pair of rimless glasses. He wore a workmanlike black suit, which bulged in all the wrong places. One bulge in the coat, however, was distinctive. It had less to do with lard and more to do with a Smith & Wesson tucked into a shoulder holster.

The second man was in his mid-fifties, short and dark, with thinning hair and a sharp protruding chin. Dressed in a shabby brown corduroy jacket and khaki slacks, he looked completely out of place in the room, an expression of perpetual unease highlighting that fact.

The third occupant of the room was thin, tall and aristocratic, a broad forehead and aquiline nose adding to the distinguished air about him. His brown clean-shaven face revealed little about his age, though the brooding eyes behind the gold-rimmed Savile Row spectacles spoke of experience that only comes from having seen plenty of summers. Attired in an immaculate, pearl-grey Armani suit and brown Oxford full brogues, the man seemed completely at home in the classy drawing room—which wasn't entirely surprising, considering he was the one who had rented the expensive apartment.

Musa Zawawi was a man given to living in elegance. At that moment, though, Zawawi's mind was far removed from the display of material wealth and sophistication that surrounded him. The only thing that mattered was the two men sitting in front of him. He needed to convince them, somehow.

Zawawi assessed the two men, wondering which of them would be more pliable. Zeb Kirkland, ex-paramilitary operations officer with the CIA, stationed extensively at Peshawar during the Soviet invasion of Afghanistan. He knew Kirkland from a long time ago, much before the obesity had set in, when Kirkland had trained countless batches of Afghan mujahedeen on the use of explosives and Stinger missiles. Kirkland had been a tough nut, and looking at him, Zawawi concluded that despite all that fat, age hadn't softened the American one bit.

That meant his best bet was Loya Pathan, retired Pakistani Army officer and erstwhile operative of the Joint Counter-intelligence Bureau of the Inter-Services Intelligence. Like Kirkland, Pathan had worked extensively with the Afghan resistance—in fact, the two men had collaborated on quite a few occasions during Operation Cyclone, and had made handsome contributions to the losses that the Russians had suffered at the hands of the mujahedeen.

'Loya sahib... please. I ask for only one more chance. You know that in so many years I have never let you down.' Zawawi's harsh, nasal voice was at odds with the rest of his genteel persona.

The Pakistani merely drew his jacket around him tighter and shifted uncomfortably in his sofa. Kirkland spoke instead, a dry smirking drawl in his tone.

'If you haven't let us down, how do you explain the ham-handed job in Bamako?'

'It was a mistake and I apologize for that.'

'In this business, no one takes kindly to mistakes. You make a blunder, you pay for it for the rest of your life. Sometimes, you even pay for it *with* your life. You've played the game so you should know the rules, Musa.'

Zawawi fought to choke the anger that was suddenly rising inside him. In general, he disliked Americans for the way they addressed people by their first names. But this one had gone a step further and made a veiled threat. Not trusting himself to look at Kirkland and stay calm, he addressed Pathan.

'I take responsibility for what went wrong and now I want to fix it, Loya sahib,' he said stiffly. 'I'm a man of honour and that's the only way I choose to be known.'

Pathan looked at Kirkland uncertainly. Zawawi knew that the American would take the final call, but he hoped the Pakistani soldier would pitch in for him in some small way.

'Tell me, Musa, is it the money we're offering this time?' Kirkland asked suddenly.

'I… don't understand,' Zawawi's eyes narrowed suspiciously.

'Come off it. You know we've doubled the bounty on Irshad Dilawar's head. You don't want to miss out on that, do you?'

'You think it's about the money,' Zawawi smiled sardonically. He waved his hand around the room. 'By the grace of Allah, I have plenty of that already. More than I can ask for. Money…' As he shook his head, a wave of anger washed over him. 'I will do this job for free, Mr Kirkland,' he said haughtily.

'And why would you do that?'

'My reputation is most precious to me. I will not have people talking poorly of me. I accepted the job to kill Irshad Dilawar, and for one reason or another, I failed. I want to make good, and I'm prepared to do it for free.'

A moment's silence followed. The man from Langley drained the Glenlivet he had been offered, and Zawawi quickly replenished his glass. He looked at Pathan, a teetotaller.

'Some more kahva? Or Moroccan tea, perhaps?'

Pathan declined, shaking his head.

As Zawawi settled back in his chair, Kirkland looked at the Pakistani.

'Dilawar isn't scheduled to travel abroad anytime soon, so it'll have to be in

Pakistan, right?' As Pathan nodded, Kirkland turned to Zawawi. 'You think you could take him there? Kill the dragon in its own lair?'

Zawawi felt the elation ripple through his body. 'Sure,' he shrugged. His voice was flat. 'I'll do the job anywhere as long as I know when and where to get him.'

'Like always, that's Loya's job.'

The Pakistani nodded thoughtfully, stroking his chin as if playing with a non-existent goatee. 'It'll have to be in Quetta, roughly a month from now. Not later than that.'

'I'll leave it to you guys to work out the details. Just keep me posted.' Kirkland glanced at his watch. 'Gosh, it's getting late. We gotta go.' He knocked his drink back and stood up. Pathan and Zawawi also rose to their feet.

As Zawawi gripped the CIA spook's fleshy hand, he said, 'Thank you for putting your trust in me, Mr Kirkland.'

'You asked for one more chance and you got it, Musa,' Kirkland looked up levelly. 'I normally wouldn't have done it, but this is for old times' sake. Don't let me regret it.'

7 July. Sector 37, Noida, National Capital Region

Colonel Mohan stood in a small balcony that overlooked the Noida golf course, a cup of coffee steaming in his hand. The night air felt cool and clean, washed by a sudden thunderstorm that still hung in the sky to the south, revealing itself in intermittent flashes of sheet lightning. It was well past one o'clock, but sleep eluded the colonel.

Sipping the hot but weak brew, he stared at the dark shapes of the treetops, his mind going over his conversation with General Dixit earlier that evening.

'They're still sitting on it,' the general had sounded vexed. 'I'm sure it's that prize ass Rawat who's responsible. We should never have agreed to let the RAW interfere with Unit Kilo.'

It was nearly two weeks since they had first pitched the plan to assassinate Irshad Dilawar to Upreiti and Inspector General Rawat, but so far, no decision had been taken on their proposal.

'We're running out of time, sir. Dilawar will be in Karachi in just twenty days. If we don't start putting the team together…'

'Yes, yes, I know that,' General Dixit had snapped. 'I'm doing everything possible to hurry things up.'

'Any ideas on why the delay, sir? I though Upreiti sounded pretty convinced that day.'

'I don't know. They're not saying anything. Maybe Rawat has sowed fresh doubts in Upreiti's mind,' the general voice's was dark with suspicion. 'Anyway, I'll call them again tomorrow.'

Colonel Mohan breathed in the fresh night air a few more times before turning and walking back into the mid-sized bedroom adjoining the balcony. He went over to a study table and sat down. A thick folder made of blue cardboard lay on the table, the light from the table lamp falling across its cover, highlighting the words 'Project Abhimanyu' and 'Classified' printed in red ink. Two similar folders existed, one in the hands of Upreiti, the other in the office of Inspector General Rawat at the RAW headquarters at Lodhi Road.

Drawing the folder towards him, the colonel put on a pair of reading glasses. Opening the folder, he flipped through the pages inside till he came to one titled 'Maj. Imtiaz Ahmed'. He stared at the recent passport-size photograph glued on the top right-hand corner of the page.

The man in the photograph barely resembled the young captain of the 3rd Battalion of the Assam Regiment, whom the colonel had recruited into Unit Kilo four years ago. The face in the photograph looked tired and drained, the cheeks pinched, and there were dark circles under both eyes. The eyes, though, retained their youthful sparkle.

Looking at the photograph, the colonel understood what four years of living on the edge had done to one of the most promising commandos to have come out of the Counter Insurgency and Jungle Warfare School.

'Cross-border ops, urban warfare, counter-terrorism and sabotage, surgical strikes... Wow, if that's what Unit Kilo does, I would love to be a part of it, colonel.'

Colonel Mohan had pitched the idea of Unit Kilo to Imtiaz as they had walked down one of the empty roads that snaked through the pine forest that surrounded the Regimental Centre of the Assam Regiment in Shillong, and the captain had responded heartily. 'Joining Unit Kilo would be an absolute honour, sir.'

'More than an honour, Unit Kilo is a responsibility. One that you will take with you to the grave,' the colonel had replied sombrely, huddling into his woollen blazer to keep out the cold, bracing wind. 'Unit Kilo is an extremely secret force that very few people will ever know of. Officially, it doesn't even exist within the Indian army. So you will never speak of it to anyone. Not even to your mother Syeda Begum, who loves you more than anything in this world. Not even to that smart lawyer sister of yours who's making quite a name for herself in the Allahabad High Court. Not to anyone who is not already a part of Unit Kilo, clear?'

Imtiaz had nodded quietly, assimilating whatever he was being told.

'There's another thing you must realize. Unit Kilo is and will always be a lonely and thankless place. We will never march down Rajpath on Republic Day and be seen on TV. There will be no public honour for whatever you may achieve, no Param Vir Chakra or Ashok Chakra or Kirti Chakra, no matter how great your bravery was. No one will know what you did for the country, and you will tell no one. The only reward you will get for a job well done is the opportunity to do more.'

Colonel Mohan closed the folder and pushed it away, recalling his words to the young captain that clammy afternoon. 'The life that you are about to embrace is not that of a soldier or a commando. It is the way of the assassin.'

* * *

The colonel awoke with a start. He blinked and squinted, his mind taking a second or two to orient itself with its surroundings. He sensed bright sunlight streaming in from a crack in the heavy drapes, its yellow beam falling languidly over and across his shoulder like the hand of a lover. The table clock resting at the base of the lamp showed it was twenty minutes past nine.

Peering at the clock once again, the colonel cursed and swung out of bed, blinking rapidly to dispel the sleep from his eyes. Sleep had taken a long time coming the previous night, and as a result, he had overslept. Now he was going to be terribly late getting to office.

He was about to shuffle into the bathroom when the loud, polyphonic jangle of his mobile phone erupted from the study table. The colonel grabbed the phone and saw that the call was from General Dixit. He cleared his throat and took the call, hoping the wooziness in his voice won't be too obvious.

'Hello, sir.'

'*Hello Sunny, kahan ho tum?* Anywhere near office?'

Colonel Mohan's brain was immediately on alert. The general's voice had sounded neither jovial nor excited, but he had addressed him as 'Sunny' and not 'Mohan'. 'Sunny' was reserved for times when the general was at peace with the world.

'Sir, I'm sorry, but I've got a bit delayed. I was sitting up late…'

'*Theek hai, theek hai*,' General Dixit brushed off the colonel's apology. 'Never mind. I called because I just heard from Upreiti. It seems they debated our proposal till very late last night.'

Colonel Mohan virtually stopped breathing, all his faculties focused on the general's voice in his ear. This was make or break.

'Upreiti says the decision was unanimous,' the general continued. 'Project Abhimanyu has been given clearance. The official notification will reach us by this evening.'

'Oh, that's wonderful news, sir.' The colonel felt the relief wash over him.

'Yes, it is.' The colonel could tell that General Dixit was grinning. 'Now get yourself to office fast. We have lots of work to do.'

9 July. Beşiktaş, Istanbul

The room was enormous, cleverly lit to accentuate the sense of space. It was tastefully decorated, with minimal furniture, and gave out on to a well-lit marble patio accessed through huge French windows. These windows stood wide open to admit the cool breeze blowing in from the Bosphorus, which lapped the shoreline just fifty metres from the room.

Five black leather sofas were in the middle of the room, spread around a glass-topped coffee table, above which hung an ornate Baccarat crystal chandelier. A low divan, upholstered in black and cobalt blue velvet, was pushed against one wall, on which was mounted a stunning oil on canvas by Bahram Alivandi.

The man who sat on the divan was at odds with the refinement of the room. He was wearing faded blue jeans, a bright blue baseball jacket with white stripes and the word 'Dodgers' scrawled in white across its front, and a pair of old Nike sneakers. A big head with short blonde hair rested on a thick neck, and the roll of the shoulders under the jacket spoke of more muscularity. His icy-blue eyes were set deep in an oafish face.

These blue eyes were, at that moment, apprehensively following Zawawi as he paced the length of the room, hands clasped behind him. The Algerian was nattily dressed in a charcoal grey Versace suit and black Versace patent leather loafers.

Stopping mid-stride, Zawawi turned to the man on the divan. Feet planted slightly apart, his hands still behind him, he looked like a soldier standing at ease in front of a superior officer. But his words, and the tone in which he said them, left no doubt about where authority was vested in that room.

'By the grace of Allah, we have been given one more chance to redeem ourselves. One more chance.' There was a calculated pause during which the man on the divan squirmed uncomfortably. 'I hope you understand that there is no more room for foolishness here, Olaf.'

Olaf nodded and looked down penitently. 'I understand, Monsieur Zawawi,' he mumbled.

Zawawi commenced pacing the room again. However, having taken five steps, he whirled around to face the divan again.

'I really had to persuade Kirkland and Loya sahib to give us a chance to make amends. They had doubled the money they were offering, and were talking to both Eric Yeung in Hong Kong and one of the Turkish syndicates—I'm not sure which, but I suppose it was one of the Anatolian gangs. I told Kirkland we would do the job for free as we have a reputation to salvage, and they finally gave in.'

'We're doing it for free?' Olaf looked incredulous.

'No.' Zawawi gave him a withering look. 'But I insisted we get only the original price that they had put out for the contract. I couldn't accept one dollar more. Not after what happened in Bamako.'

Silence pervaded the room as Zawawi stood looking out of the French windows at the darkness beyond the patio. Olaf knew better than to intrude upon Zawawi as he basked in his inflated sense of virtue. Finally, Zawawi turned, walked back and plonked himself on a sofa. Producing a packet of Benson & Hedges from his pocket, he proceeded to light a cigarette. Inhaling deeply, he watched the smoke rise lazily from the smouldering end for a while, before speaking.

'We have plucked the job from the Turks in their own den, so the men you have put together this time… they had bloody well better be professionals who know how to complete a job. I will not have any more bungling fools like that Oumar, whom you recommended so highly last time.'

'No, Monsieur Zawawi. Not at all,' Olaf answered hurriedly, keen to allay all doubts. 'I can assure you we are not taking any chances this time. The team I have put together has some of the best people money can buy.'

'Now isn't that wonderful,' Zawawi scoffed. 'If these are the best people money can buy, what were we doing with Oumar and company the last time round? You weren't thinking of saving us a few million dollars by hiring a bunch of kids with water-pistols and peashooters, were you?'

Olaf turned red at Zawawi's words. Clearing his throat nervously, he said, 'No, monsieur. It's just that being an Algerian, Oumar knew Bamako…'

Waving the hand holding the cigarette dismissively, Zawawi cut Olaf short. 'Oh, please. I don't want to get into that. Just tell me who's in this group you have now assembled. Who are these men?'

'They are some of the most dangerous, ruthless and tenacious fighters to be found in this part of the world,' Olaf spoke quickly, eager to placate Zawawi. 'Men who have collectively delivered more death than anyone would care to remember. We have five veterans of the Soviet–Afghan War, men trained in the art of guerrilla warfare by the Americans. Then there are a couple of Iraqis, both of whom have done their bit to add to America's ongoing nightmares in Iraq. And leading the team is Hossam Al-Kamil, an erstwhile Hezbollah commander from Beirut.'

'Hezbollah commander?' Zawawi raised an eyebrow. 'Hossam...?'

'Al-Kamil, monsieur.'

As Zawawi mulled over the name to see if it rang a bell somewhere, Olaf dropped his voice to a conspiratorial murmur.

'Monsieur, if rumours are to be believed, Al-Kamil has the scalps of over thirty Israeli soldiers whom he killed in Lebanon. It seems the Israelis stationed in West Beirut had a special name for him: Katzav. It means butcher in Hebrew.'

Zawawi took a final drag from his cigarette before stubbing it out in an ashtray. 'Are all these men familiar with Pakistan?'

'All eight are experts in urban warfare and all are quite familiar with Pakistan, monsieur. They can be depended upon to get the job done. There won't be any mistakes this time. You have my word.'

'Good. Otherwise, I shall have your hide,' snapped Zawawi. After a short pause, he asked, 'So when am I meeting this... butcher... Hossam Al-Kamil?'

'He will be arriving in Istanbul tomorrow evening, monsieur.'

'Bring him here as soon as he lands at the Atatürk International.'

Without waiting for a sign of confirmation from Olaf, Zawawi stood up and walked out of the room, signalling that the interview was over.

CHAPTER 2

10 July. Central Ordinance Depot, Shakurbasti, Delhi

The huge pilkhan lay right across the road, its broad trunk tapering into a profusion of heavy branches, some of which had snapped during the crushing fall and now lay scattered all over the ground. At the other end of the tree, thick mud-caked roots were sticking out stiffly in the air. Men in uniform were milling around the fallen tree, figuring out a way of moving it and restoring vehicular traffic.

Captain Shamsheer Suleiman took in the scene with his coal-black eyes and realized that he would have to go the rest of the way on foot. Dismounting from the jeep, he walked towards the tree, marvelling at how such a majestic specimen could have been blown down by what had seemed a perfectly average thunderstorm that had swept Delhi earlier that afternoon. He was about thirty, tall and lean, with a dark, clean-shaven face that was heavily lined.

Stepping over the broken branches and avoiding muddy puddles, he skirted the tree and made his way towards a building fifty metres further down the road. A flat, nondescript structure, it was one of many such buildings within the Central Ordinance Depot's expansive grounds, and practically no one paid it any attention. This suited Unit Kilo just fine, for it served as one of the unit's six bases in and around Delhi. It was, in fact, one of Colonel Mohan's favourite locations for briefing his commandos, second only to the base within the Southern Naval Command Headquarters on Willingdon Island, Kochi.

Entering the building, Shamsheer found himself in a small anteroom, roughly the size of most waiting-rooms at neighbourhood doctors' clinics. The room was bare except for a metal table that occupied much of the space. A soldier sat at the table, an open register in front of him. Identifying Shamsheer's rank from his epaulettes, the soldier stood up and saluted.

'ID dikhaayenge, sir?' he asked decorously.

Shamsheer produced his identity card for verification. The soldier glanced at the card, then ran a finger down a list of names in the register till he came to Shamsheer's name. Satisfied, he returned the card and pointed towards a closed door covered by a faded green curtain.

'Jaaiye, sir.'

The room that the door opened into was fairly large, well lit and empty. There were a couple of comfortable sofas and four armchairs, all pointing towards a television that was tuned into a Hindi movie channel, set at mute. At the far end of the room stood a small trolley table, next to which was another door, firmly shut.

Shamsheer sat down on one of the sofas and looked at his watch. It was ten minutes past five. He was early. He liked it that way.

For a few minutes, he sat staring at the television, watching Jeetendra romance Asha Parekh with much enthusiasm and no sound. Getting bored, he scouted around for the remote control, but there didn't seem to be one in the room. So he pulled out his mobile phone and checked it for new messages. Then, with nothing left to do, he began playing a game of Tetris.

The door from the room outside opened and Shamsheer observed another soldier walk in. He was a lieutenant, not much older than twenty-seven, of medium build, with short, wavy hair. There was a cheekiness in his eyes, and the set of his mouth suggested that a smile was never far from his lips. As if to corroborate this, the man smiled brightly at Shamsheer. Acknowledging the smile with a faint nod, Shamsheer continued clearing rows of stacked-up bricks.

'Are you also here for the five-thirty meeting?' the lieutenant spoke suddenly.

Shamsheer didn't want to respond. Such questions between strangers were never encouraged at Unit Kilo. Yet, the question had been put so directly and frankly, he had no choice but to answer.

'Yes,' he said tightly, making sure he didn't smile.

'Oh, good,' said the lieutenant. Immediately, he came over to Shamsheer, his right hand outstretched.

'Lieutenant Rafiq Mehmood, sir,' he introduced himself, his eyes twinkling.

Instinctively, Shamsheer reached for the lieutenant's hand. But even as their hands met, he cursed inwardly. Not only was the lieutenant systematically demolishing established Unit Kilo rules, he had made Shamsheer return his handshake. Bloody idiot!

Shamsheer stiffened, determined not to speak. But when he tried to tug his hand free, he felt the lieutenant's grip tighten. Looking at his face, Shamsheer saw a friendly expression.

'*Aur aap, sir?*' asked Rafiq.

In spite of himself, Shamsheer replied. 'Captain Shamsheer Suleiman.'

The lieutenant gave his hand one final shake before releasing it. 'Pleased to meet you, sir,' he smiled.

Shamsheer did not respond. He wasn't feeling particularly pleased about anything now. He slouched in his sofa and returned to his game, hoping that his reticence and poker face would put off the young officer. A couple of minutes lapsed, and when there were no further overtures from the lieutenant, Shamsheer began to relax.

The door from outside opened again. Shamsheer raised his head and looked at the man who had entered the room. The man, who was dressed in civilian clothes, was in his early thirties. Though of average height, he had an athletic build, the toned muscles of his arms showing from under the blue bush shirt he wore. His closely cropped hair was prematurely streaked with silver, but his keen greyish-green eyes sparkled with youth and intelligence. When these eyes met Shamsheer's, the captain saw a small flicker of recognition in them—but the next instant, the man's face was expressionless.

Shamsheer returned his attention to his phone as the man walked quietly to one of the sofas. Sitting down, he crossed his legs, flicked a speck of dust off his knee and turned towards the television, as if it was the only object of any interest in the room. Shamsheer stole a quick glance at Rafiq and hoped the fool would keep a check on his natural curiosity. The man who had just walked in would brook no nonsense from Unit Kilo commandos. Fortunately for everyone, the lieutenant kept to himself.

A minute later, the soldier who had been in the room outside entered, bearing a tray with three cups of tea and a plate of Monaco biscuits. He set the tray down on the trolley table and wheeled it to the centre of the room. He then handed a cup to each of the three men, and passed the plate of biscuits around.

The soldier was about to leave the room when the man who had walked in last asked him the way to the restroom. The soldier answered that it was situated outside the building. The man thanked him, placed his teacup on the table and made his way out of the building.

The moment the door closed, Rafiq turned to Shamsheer, his eyes shining eagerly.

'You know that man, don't you? And he knows you. I saw that you recognized one another. Who is he?'

Shamsheer had to concede that the lieutenant was extremely observant. He also realized that the young officer was going to be in the same meeting, and that he would learn everything anyway. He might as well answer the question.

'That is Major Imtiaz Ahmed.' After a short pause, he added, 'Whatever we're here for, we're lucky to have him for company.'

* * *

Colonel Mohan, Imtiaz, Shamsheer and Rafiq were seated at a massive wooden table that completely dominated the room. The table was spotlit by a row of low-hanging lights, the kind usually found over pool tables, which threw the rest of the room into shadow. The room itself was sparsely furnished, with just a few empty chairs and two old steel almirahs pushed against a wall, giving the table company.

Three large maps lay spread out on the table. One was a detailed physical map of Pakistan, while another was a physical map that covered the region from the Pamirs and southern Tajikistan in the north to the Rann of Kutch and the Gujarat coast in the south, and Herat in western Afghanistan in the west to the Indo–Pak border in the east. The third map was that of the city of Karachi, and looked like a cross between a map and a satellite photograph. A squat digital projector sat on one end of the table, connected to a laptop. On the wall opposite the projector hung a white projection screen; on it was the image of a tree-lined avenue, in what looked like a tony residential suburb.

The men sat pensively, none seemingly inclined to break the silence. Colonel Mohan carefully studied the three commandos over his reading glasses, waiting for one of them to speak. Beside him, Imtiaz was leaning back in his chair, arms folded, staring up at a point where the wall met the ceiling. On the opposite side of the table, Shamsheer sat chewing his lower lip absent-mindedly as he studied the image on the screen. Rafiq sat doodling on the table with his finger, his eyes averted from the colonel's, looking like a schoolboy who was hoping he wouldn't be called upon to solve a tricky algorithm.

'Sir, this operation… is scheduled to begin in twelve days.' Imtiaz finally addressed Colonel Mohan.

The words hadn't exactly been framed as a question, so the colonel didn't reply. He just looked at the major.

'With due respect, sir, neither Shamsheer or I have ever been so deep inside Pakistani territory before,' Imtiaz continued. 'And if I am right, this is Rafiq's first cross-border assignment?'

The colonel nodded, detecting a hint of disapproval in Imtiaz's voice when he spoke of Rafiq.

'Twelve days from now, the three of us are to enter Pakistan and make our way to Karachi. Once in Karachi, we will have to start closing in on Irshad Dilawar immediately.' Imtiaz frowned and shook his head doubtfully. 'It would be good if we had more time for acclimatization, sir.'

Taking off his reading glasses, Colonel Mohan pinched the bridge of his nose. 'Unfortunately, we do not have the luxury of time,' he said. 'Intelligence reports say that in seventeen days, Dilawar will be in Karachi to meet some of his Saudi Arabian business associates. He will be in the city for just three days before returning to one or the other of his many hideouts in Pakistan. Honestly, we have no idea which one he will move to next. So those three days are the only window available to get him.'

'Do we have to get him in Karachi? I mean, if we planned this thoroughly, we could do the job anywhere. Islamabad, Peshawar…'

'When it comes to Irshad Dilawar, facts are few and far between,' the colonel said with a thin smile. 'So it's in our interest to act on whatever little facts we have. This time we have definite information that he's going to be in Karachi in seventeen days. Next time, who knows…?'

Colonel Mohan stood up and stretched his stiff back muscles. 'Karachi is also ideal for this operation because our intelligence network in that city is more reliable than anywhere else in Pakistan. You stand your best chance of completing this job in Karachi. Secondly, Karachi is a big port city with a large floating population. There are fewer chances of anyone noticing three new faces in a city of that size. Outside Karachi, the possibility of detection rises significantly. Lastly, because of its coastline, the city is best suited for a quick escape by sea, once the operation is over.'

Imtiaz digested this thoughtfully. 'We three get just three days together in Karachi. And a lot of that time will be spent in reconnoitring and surveillance,' he said.

'Don't forget that you will have Saadat to help you,' the colonel interjected, taking his seat again.

'Correct, sir, but ultimately it's the three of us who have to go in and kill Dilawar,' Imtiaz countered. 'Everything hinges on how well we three plan and coordinate things inside Pakistan.' He paused for a fraction of a second. 'When do we begin the project orientation, sir?'

'In twenty-four hours.' The colonel gave a theatrical pause. 'At noon tomorrow, you guys will leave for the Unit Kilo facility in Panchkula. There, for the next eight days, you will undergo intensive preparation for Project Abhimanyu. We will furnish you with detailed inputs on police and paramilitary deployment across the Pakistani cities you will travel through. You will have access to as much information we can provide on Irshad Dilawar's movements in Karachi, the kind of security cover he has, the nature and pattern of police force deployment in the city, etc. You will study and familiarize yourselves with the layout of Karachi through photographs, satellite pictures and video recordings. You will acquaint yourself with the city's arterial roads, the distances between landmarks and major localities in Karachi, and also with the key entry and exit points. And you will go through each and every aspect of the operation at least three times a day, tightly coordinating the critical aspect of timing.'

A brief silence ensued as the men took all of this in. Finally, Shamsheer spoke.

'Sir, according to this plan, we are to enter Pakistan separately, from three different directions, and then work our way into Karachi, where we rendezvous with Saadat. Wouldn't it be better if we three went as a group? We could use our time together to review plans and strategies.'

'One stranger in an alien land attracts far less attention than three strangers travelling together,' the colonel explained. 'So till you reach Karachi and are in Saadat's hands, you guys are better off alone. Also, if you go in together and get caught, the entire operation comes apart. But if you go in separately and one gets caught, the other two can still carry out the assignment.'

'The three of us will have no contact with one another till we reach Karachi, right sir?' asked Imtiaz.

'Correct, and there should be nothing on any of you that can be linked to the others. In fact, there should be nothing on you that can be traced back to India or to Saadat in Karachi. No phone, no phone numbers, no addresses, nothing. You will commit Saadat's address and contact numbers to memory and go by that alone. And you will not get in touch with Saadat till you are in Karachi. And come what may, you will never call India directly. We will talk only through Saadat, clear?'

The commandos nodded solemnly. Imtiaz looked at the colonel again.

'Sir, what if one of us gets caught by the Pakistani authorities? How will the other two come to know of this and change their plan accordingly?'

'Each one of you will be given a watch that you are to wear constantly till the time you meet Saadat in Karachi,' Colonel Mohan explained. 'Each watch has an extremely small but exceedingly powerful GPS tracking unit embedded in it, which is linked to Unit Kilo via satellite. These GPS units will be monitored round-the-clock to track your progress. Should any one of you run into serious trouble with Pakistani authorities on your way to Karachi, find a way of destroying the GPS unit immediately. Two reasons: one, we don't want prying eyes to find those high-tech GPS units concealed in your watches. Two, the moment we stop receiving signals from any of the units, we will assume the worst and immediately relay the information to Saadat. Saadat will then inform the others about this when they reach Karachi. In such an eventuality, you are to abandon Plan A and set Plan B in motion.'

Nearly a full minute elapsed in silence. Assuming they were done for the time being, the colonel was preparing to conclude the meeting when Imtiaz spoke again.

'Sir, it seems we are relying a lot on Saadat for this operation. He's our point man in Karachi for information, supplies, logistics support, and even arms and ammunition. We're putting so much trust on one person—how reliable is he?'

The colonel smiled and nodded. 'You are risking your lives here. You have the right to know something about the man who will be your only lifeline in Pakistan.'

Taking a moment to compose his thoughts, the colonel spoke again. 'Saadat Fakih has been an operative of our army intelligence for over twenty years now. Originally from Barmer district in Rajasthan, Saadat started as a small-time smuggler of heroin and fake currency across the Indo–Pak border. He was, however, smart and completely impartial and business-like as far as his loyalties to India and Pakistan were concerned. He cultivated local politicians and policemen on both sides of the border to guarantee him immunity, and he quickly became a fairly powerful don running a largish operation. But as his business prospered and expanded, his operations began clashing with one faction of Irshad Dilawar's gang, which was enlarging rapidly on the Pakistani side. Both gangs wanted access to the same contraband and the same lucrative territories and routes.

'Following a few bloody confrontations that left men on both sides dead, Saadat appealed to his Pakistani benefactors to broker a deal with Dilawar's faction. Meanwhile, Dilawar had already become Pakistan's blue-eyed boy, proving extremely useful in furthering Pakistani interests by smuggling arms and ammunition into India. So, at the negotiating table, Saadat ended up getting a raw deal, losing a huge chunk of his territory to Dilawar's gang under duress from the Pakistani authorities.

'Saadat had no choice but to accept this decision and the matter should have ended there. But seeing Saadat's willingness to make peace as a sign of weakness, and meaning to avenge the earlier loss of some of their men, members of Dilawar's faction killed Saadat's younger brother.

'That proved to be the turning point. Knowing that Saadat was bitter with Pakistan and Dilawar, we approached him with a deal. Six months later, the Border Security Force intercepted a big consignment of heroin loaded on camels owned by Saadat, while the Rajasthan police raided his house and uncovered a cache of fake currency. Saadat himself was absconding, so an arrest warrant was issued in his name. Two days later, under cover of night, Saadat slipped into Pakistan, never to return to India. Using his network of old contacts and large sums of money that we had provided, he first moved to Hyderabad, before going on to Karachi and settling there.'

'Amazing!' Rafiq looked wide-eyed. 'We set Saadat up in Karachi to act as our spy.'

The colonel nodded. 'Saadat now runs a tour and travel agency with branches in six Pakistani cities. He also owns a shipping agency in Karachi, and supplies unskilled manpower in various parts of the city, including the port. The businesses he is in are ideally suited to gather the kind of information we need, and over the years, Saadat has proved to be one of our most valuable assets in Pakistan.'

'How do we know his loyalties are still with us?' Imtiaz's tone was matter-of-fact.

Colonel Mohan scratched his chin as he considered the question. 'Let me put it this way. Saadat nurses a very deep grudge against the Pakistanis for the way they shortchanged him and put him out of business. And the way the Pakistanis mollycoddle Dilawar, whom he hates intensely, fuels his desire to get even with them. For Saadat, the steady flow of Indian money into a private account was never the biggest incentive to work against Pakistan.'

The men had listened to the colonel's account keenly. Now they leaned back in their chairs.

'Any more questions?' the colonel asked.

Imtiaz looked enquiringly at Shamsheer and Rafiq. They shook their heads.

'I guess not, sir,' said Imtiaz. 'But if any of us do have questions after we leave for Panchkula, who do we put them to?'

'Absolutely no one other than me,' Colonel Mohan said. 'The last three days you are at Panchkula, I will be with you to review everything about Project Abhimanyu. That's when I shall answer all your questions.'

The colonel stood up, and the commandos followed suit. The colonel looked at the three men and drew a deep breath.

'All the best, boys. Like the heroic Abhimanyu, you three are setting out to break through the impenetrable chakravyuha, get to its heart and destroy the enemy from inside. Prepare well for what lies ahead.'

As the men filed out of the room, Imtiaz's mind dwelt on Colonel Mohan's allusion to the legendary warrior of the Mahabharata. Sure, the heroic Abhimanyu had broken the chakravyuha. But he hadn't made it back alive.

10 July. Soami Nagar, Delhi

General Dixit picked up the remote control lying on the coffee table and idly began surfing channels. The Hollywood movie that he had been watching had ended, but he wasn't prepared to retire for the night just yet. Maybe there was something else on air that might be worth watching.

As he switched between channels, he distastefully eyed a half-empty can of Diet Coke sitting on the coffee table. He once again wished he could have a glass of whisky-soda instead. But he knew he couldn't.

The general, dressed in a light blue pyjama and an incongruous red T-shirt with a Che Guevara print on it, was lounging all by himself in the drawing room of his daughter's house. His daughter, eight months into her pregnancy, was asleep in the bedroom. His son-in-law, a vice-president at a multinational consumer electronics firm, was in Bangkok, attending a four-day regional conference.

A widower for the last three years, General Dixit lived alone in a large house in Hauz Khas Enclave, but had offered to stay with his daughter till his son-in-law returned. In his magnanimity, the general had, however, overlooked one thing. His daughter's in-laws were staunch followers of the Radhasoami Satsang, and his daughter, out of respect for their sentiments, had forbidden consumption of alcohol and non-vegetarian food in her house. So the general had to be content with Diet Coke, a really lousy substitute for alcohol, in his opinion.

It was while surfing through the block of news channels that something arrested the general's attention. It was a news ticker, running at the bottom of the screen on Headlines Today. '...press for Irshad Dilawar's extradition:

Home Minister' is all he managed to read, before the newscast was interrupted by an ad break.

The general sat upright. He suffered a dozen inane commercials with patience, waiting for the newscast to begin. He knew that once the loop had run its course, the piece of news would reappear on screen.

It was a full five minutes before the news item that he was interested in came up. Reading through it, he understood that the Indian government had presented the US with fresh evidence of Irshad Dilawar's complicity in acts of terrorism in India, and that the gangster's extradition would be high on the agenda when the United States' national security advisor would visit Delhi and Islamabad in the first week of August. The general also noted that the Indian Home Minister seemed confident of putting India's point across, and getting the US to lean on Pakistan to help in the extradition process.

Switching off the television, General Dixit leaned back in his sofa and stared blankly at a jade Laughing Buddha on the mantelpiece. It was time to put the suspense and uncertainty to rest permanently, the general grimaced as he mulled over the news report. For that reason alone, Project Abhimanyu had to succeed.

10 July. Beşiktaş, Istanbul

Zawawi applied a few more delicate strokes of paint onto the canvas before taking a step back to survey his efforts. The painting was only half done, but there was enough on the canvas to see that a desert bazaar was in the making. Zawawi, a connoisseur of art, found painting to be deeply relaxing—even though he knew that he was, at best, merely competent with the brush.

Heaving a deep sigh, he looked at his watch. He was tempted to return to his painting, but he knew it was already quite late in Pakistan. Loya Pathan would be expecting his call.

He put down his palette and brushes, unbuttoned and discarded his stained smock, and made his way to the bathroom adjoining the studio. Five minutes later, he was stretched on a chaise longue next to a mid-sized indoor swimming pool, an encrypted mobile phone pressed to his left ear. After a few rings, his call was answered.

'*As-salāmu alaikum, Loya sahib.*'

'*Wa'Alaikum as-salām,*' came the reply. 'I have guests at home, so I can't talk much. Just tell me how the meeting went.'

'Very nicely. I'm proud to say that I have found the perfect man for the job.'

'Mm-hmmm!' Pathan was being his usual self. Cautious, noncommittal.

'Very impressive guy. He understands his business and doesn't give or take any bullshit.'

'What about the rest of the team?'

'All are his men. Five of them are Afghans who fought the Russians. Who knows, you and Mr Kirkland might even have trained some of them.'

'Oh! Did Hossam also train with us and fight the Soviets?' Zawawi detected concern in Pathan's voice. It was natural. Pathan was a man with many secrets, and one could never say which two secrets would conspire to bite you in the arse.

'No, no. He was busy slaughtering Israelis in Lebanon,' Zawawi spoke quickly, wanting to put the Pakistani at ease. 'That's why the Jews named him Katzav. Apparently it means butcher.'

'Oh, okay.' Pathan paused for a moment before speaking. 'Look, I have to go. The guests are waiting. I'll talk again tomorrow.'

'Sure.'

Before disconnecting the call, Pathan spoke again. 'I hope you're right about this Hossam Al-Kamil being the perfect man for the job. Time is running out, and we have to get Dilawar this time.'

Zawawi put the phone down, but continued lying on the chaise longue, his mind on the meeting he'd had with Al-Kamil earlier that evening.

The moment he had set eyes upon Al-Kamil, Zawawi had known that his search for an assassin was over. The chilling determination in the man's cruel eyes had instinctively appealed to Zawawi, and in a matter of a few minutes, both men had realized that they shared the same emotional orbit. In fact, the two had got along so well that Zawawi had even shed some of his feudal superiority and remoteness and begun treating Al-Kamil with the courtesy and respect he usually reserved for equals.

Although the meeting had only been preliminary, Al-Kamil had given adequate evidence of being an exceptional strategist. And Zawawi was more than pleased to see that the seven men who were to accompany Al-Kamil to Pakistan were all known to him and had worked with him in the past. Zawawi strongly believed that a bunch of average soldiers who knew each other were infinitely superior to a crack team of fighters who had been thrown together for the first time. And by no stretch of imagination was this bunch average.

The meeting had ended on a high note, and as he had risen to walk Al-Kamil to the door, Zawawi had put a question that he'd wanted to ask all along.

'Is it true that when you were a Hezbollah commander in Beirut, you killed and scalped more than thirty Israeli soldiers?'

Al-Kamil had stared at Zawawi for a moment, an amused smile playing on his lips for the first time that evening.

'I wish it were true, but it's not wholly correct. I have the scalps of just eight Israeli soldiers. The remaining twenty-eight, unfortunately, are only of those belonging to militiamen of the South Lebanon Army that sided with the Israelis against us. However, those who told you of those thirty-six scalps failed to add that I also have the scalps of twenty-one other people. Men I have killed ever since I left the Hezbollah.'

They had reached the door and Al-Kamil had turned to Zawawi. 'You see, I no longer work for the love of money alone. I already have enough for my family to live comfortably for years to come. Nowadays I work for the joy that comes with the job. These scalps... they are part of that joy.'

He had paused for a moment, before reaching out and shaking Zawawi's hand. 'Insha'Allah, I will help myself to a few more scalps in Pakistan. *Ma'a-as-salāma.*'

Zawawi smiled to himself as he rose from the chaise longue, took off his bathrobe and slid silently into the pool for a preprandial swim.

Katzav—butcher. He liked the name. He looked forward to working with Hossam Al-Kamil.

CHAPTER 3

15 July. Chandimandir Cantonment, Panchkula

Shamsheer and Rafiq stopped to admire the black buck that stood in the middle of the clearing, grazing on some leaves. The antelope instantly turned and considered the commandos with a mixture of suspicion and curiosity. Then with a toss of its head, it walked away towards the trees on the far side, the two men no longer worthy of its attention.

The commandos were in the middle of a 20-acre deer park that stood at the periphery of the Chandimandir Cantonment, on the northern outskirts of Panchkula. Since the day they had arrived at the cantonment—which also served as the Headquarters of the Western Command of the Indian Army—they had stayed indoors at the Unit Kilo facility, which lay in a detached corner close to the deer park. For five days, they had undergone non-stop orientation for Project Abhimanyu, the routine broken only for strenuous, three-hour combat workouts at the specially equipped gym.

That afternoon, however, Colonel Mohan had asked Imtiaz to join him for a private meeting, and granted Shamsheer and Rafiq 'a well-deserved break' for the afternoon. After a few games of squash and a quick shower, the two commandos had decided to take a stroll around the adjoining park.

Once the black buck disappeared behind the trees, the two soldiers renewed walking. A small pond lay slightly ahead, with a couple of geese and a mandarin duck paddling on the water's surface. Jacaranda, ritha and pipal trees grew in profusion, the larger among them obscuring the overcast sky overhead. Between the trees, the men caught glimpses of the Morni Hills, which formed a part of the foothills of the Shivalik range. Dark grey clouds shrouded the hilltops.

Halfway to the pond, Rafiq glanced at Shamsheer quizzically. Scratching at the five-day-old crop of beard that now adorned his chin, he spoke.

'You seem quite confident about this operation. What makes you so sure it'll be successful?'

Shamsheer, who was still clean-shaven but had started sporting a bushy moustache clipped at the corners of his lips, considered the question before replying.

'There's no surety about anything in life, much less an operation such as this one. But if I had to bet on this, I would fancy my chances of winning.'

Rafiq shrugged. 'You still haven't said why.'

'I think it'll work because it has been planned in great detail. And it's being led by Major Ahmed.'

'You have immense respect for the major,' Rafiq raised his eyebrows. '*Un mein aisi kya khaas baat hai?*'

'I've never met a man with as much determination and as high a sense of duty as Major Ahmed. Once he makes up his mind about a job, he will get it done, somehow or the other.'

'You've obviously worked with him before... Tell me about it, sir. *Please, bataaiye na.*' The lieutenant's eyes shone like a child's, eager to listen to a new story that he has long been promised.

Shamsheer couldn't help smiling. Over the last few days, he had begun liking this boy for his unbridled enthusiasm and innocence. He pointed to a wrought-iron bench that sat by the edge of the pond, next to the weeping willow drooping over the brooding green waters.

'Let's sit.'

Shamsheer looked around to make sure they were not being overheard. He needn't have bothered. Being a weekday, the park was practically deserted. Even the young couples who usually patronize such parks, locked in the embrace of lust and passion, appeared to have given this one's mid-afternoon seclusion a go-by.

'Have you heard of Operation Black Cobra?'

'Black Cobra,' Rafiq said slowly, as if savouring the words. 'I've heard it mentioned during advanced training. Isn't that one of the missions Unit Kilo undertook in Myanmar against the Kachin Independence Army for assisting the Naga and Assamese insurgents?'

'The first against the Kachins... In fact, Black Cobra was the first ever Unit Kilo operation.' Shamsheer looked up at the darkening sky, wondering when it would begin raining. 'The mission was to destroy a KIA camp that was being used by the ULFA as a base for coordinating their campaigns in Assam.'

'And you and Major Imtiaz were part of it?' Rafiq gazed at the captain in open admiration.

'There were six of us, and the major was leading the team.' Shamsheer nodded. 'It was one of the trickiest missions I've been involved in. Trekking through the isolated Hukawng Valley for two days through thick jungles and soaking rain… we almost lost one of our men while crossing the flooded Tawang river. And what leeches, snakes and scorpions! By the time we located the KIA camp, we were half-dead with cold and fatigue.'

'What happened then?'

'Well, as expected, the KIA was sharing the base with the ULFA. But there was a problem. According to our intelligence reports, the camp shouldn't have had more than twenty to twenty-five guerrillas defending it—that was the number we had come prepared to deal with. But in reality, there were about thirty-five to forty men in that camp.'

Rafiq let out a silent whistle. 'Almost double the number! What did you do next?'

'There was nothing to do but retreat. No question of just the six of us taking on those forty.'

The lieutenant frowned. 'The mission was abandoned?'

'Almost, but then something happened,' Shamsheer smiled as he recollected the day. 'I was observing the camp through my binoculars, and I saw Loknath Rajkhowah walk out of one of the buildings. Loknath Rajkhowah was the chief commanding officer of the ULFA's dreaded 28 Battalion, and at that time he was one of the most wanted militants by the Indian Army. The funny bit is that Indian intelligence had absolutely no knowledge of where Rajkhowah was—but I was looking straight at him that evening.'

'Then?'

Low thunder rumbled from the direction of Morni Hills. Surveying the clouds above them, the captain got to his feet. Rain was imminent.

'I told the major about what I had seen, and he immediately changed his mind about aborting the operation,' Shamsheer continued his narrative. 'He was clear that we had to hit the camp and kill Rajkhowah. We knew Rajkhowah's death would break the spine of the ULFA 28 Battalion, but we couldn't see how we could take on six times the number of men. So we tried our best to reason with the major, but he was adamant. I'll never forget his words—if we allow Loknath Rajkhowah to get out of that camp alive, will we be able to sleep peacefully the next time innocent lives are lost in Assam?'

'But there were just the six of you…' Rafiq's expression clouded with doubt.

'Precisely our point, but the major said the rebels in the KIA camp didn't know that, so we could use their ignorance to our advantage. At eleven-thirty that night, we launched our attack. Fragmentation grenades, flashbangs, booby-traps, guns… we used everything in a shock-and-awe strategy, moving in from three sides, shooting at the disoriented men. The attack was fierce and we managed to create a perception of superior numbers. In five minutes, Operation Black Cobra was over.'

Just as Shamsheer and Rafiq had exited the park, a fine spray began falling. The two commandos quickened their pace, heads bent to keep the mildly stinging droplets from striking their faces. The Unit Kilo facility was still a hundred metres away.

'Remarkable,' Rafiq's tone was filled with awe. 'How many rebels did you manage to kill?'

'It's hard to say, but I counted some twenty-two dead bodies, both inside the buildings and outside. Maybe we got about thirty of them.'

'Remarkable,' Rafiq said again, as if practising the word. 'And you got Rajkhowah?'

'He was found lying at the edge of the camp with a clean, black hole at the base of his throat,' the captain nodded. 'We also found the bodies of three other senior commanders of the ULFA 28 Battalion, and those of two top KIA commanders as well.'

'That means Operation Black Cobra was a big hit.'

'Yes. Immediately after, the Indian Army had a series of major successes against the ULFA in Assam. And two months later, intelligence sources got news of the KIA refusing ULFA and Naga insurgents any cooperation in Kachin State.'

'Just six Unit Kilo commandos achieved so much,' Rafiq's face glowed with pride. '*Kya baat!*'

Shamsheer smiled softly. 'What we achieved that day was ultimately because of Major Ahmed. In spite of our reluctance, he pushed us to attack the camp. He convinced us that Rajkhowah could be killed, and he showed us how to do it. As team leader, he could have walked away from the responsibility by citing the safety of his men, but he didn't. He always puts the larger interest above everything else. That's what I admire about him.'

They had almost reached the building that housed Unit Kilo and were about to go under the bougainvillea arch near its entrance, when Shamsheer sensed that they were being watched. He looked up sharply at a row of windows on the building's second floor and saw Imtiaz at one of them.

* * *

Imtiaz watched Shamsheer and Rafiq duck under the bougainvillea arch and hurry into the building as the shower gained in strength. He then looked up towards the deer park, a troubled expression clouding his face, the lower half of which was now covered by a thick beard and moustache.

The thing had been bothering him ever since the first meeting they'd had at the Unit Kilo base in Delhi. It had started as a small niggling thought, but had rapidly burgeoned into a full-scale preoccupation over the last five days at Panchkula.

There was something about Lieutenant Rafiq Mehmood that somehow didn't quite fit in.

'Pardon me for putting it bluntly, sir, but it just doesn't make any sense.'

Imtiaz turned to face Colonel Mohan, who sat on a chair facing the window, a glass of Royal Challenge whisky resting on a small table to his right.

'And why not?' The colonel crossed his arms and shrugged.

'Because, on the one hand, you say this is the most critical operation that Unit Kilo has undertaken in its short history, and that Unit Kilo's future will be largely determined by its success. Yet, on the other, you have included an absolute rookie in the team, a clown who can't stop smiling like a kid with a new cricket bat.'

'You have a problem with Rafiq's smile?'

'I have a problem with Rafiq being in this team,' Imtiaz answered, a trifle hotly. 'Shamsheer and I have been part of Unit Kilo operations inside Myanmar and Pakistan. We have the experience to handle the pressure of pulling off this job. Rafiq has no such experience, so I don't see how he has found a place in this team.'

'You have seen both plan A and plan B of Project Abhimanyu,' the colonel spoke calmly. 'You know the role that technology is going to play in this mission, and Rafiq is probably one of the best tech guys we have in Unit Kilo.'

'He may be a tech wizard, sir, but I know enough commandos in Unit Kilo who can do what Rafiq is supposed to do in this mission. And all those men have experience in operating inside enemy territory. Rafiq has none, so he can easily be replaced by any one of them.'

The colonel took a long gulp from his glass before answering. 'You forget that you too were once an inexperienced rookie. Today, you're one of the best men Unit Kilo has, but you wouldn't have got here if someone had raised objections about you being too green to be a part of some team. Everyone needs to be given a chance to prove their worth.'

'I agree, sir. But given its importance, I seriously doubt whether Project Abhimanyu is the best proving ground for Rafiq. And I don't think Shamsheer and I can afford to babysit and potty-train him once we're inside Pakistan.'

'You are assuming he needs babysitting and potty-training,' said Colonel Mohan. Seeing Imtiaz maintain a surly, stubborn silence, he sighed.

'What do you know of Rafiq for you to have formed such a strong opinion of him?'

Imtiaz shrugged. 'You're the expert, sir.'

The colonel let the slight pass unnoticed. 'Okay, I'll tell you. Today, urban warfare is as much about technology as it's about bombs and bullets. And when it comes to information technology, there's hardly anyone more proficient then Rafiq in Unit Kilo. However, Rafiq is no geek. In fact, he is one of the best commandos to have been inducted into Unit Kilo in recent times.'

Stopping to take another sip of whisky, Colonel Mohan continued. 'You spoke of combat experience… Over the last year, Rafiq has been involved in three major counter-insurgency operations, one in the Northeast, one in Bhutan to flush out the ULFA and Bodo militants hiding in that country, and one against the Naxalites on the Jharkhand–Orissa border. If Rafiq wasn't in Unit Kilo, by now he would have been decorated with one gallantry award or another.'

Imtiaz looked at the colonel with cautious interest.

'I am not exaggerating when I say this guy is good. Till Rafiq joined Unit Kilo, you had the best performance scores across all the training programmes that our commandos attend. Now Rafiq has the highest scores in three of these programmes, including the one you undertook on urban warfare in Germany.'

Imtiaz turned back to gaze out of the window. The knowledge that the young lieutenant had begun outshining him in Unit Kilo was both unsettling and humbling.

The colonel joined Imtiaz by the window and stood staring into the rain. 'Does all this make him a better commando than you? I don't think so. You have a vast experience in real urban warfare, while much of his skill has only been tested in a controlled environment. You have proved your worth to us many times over. He is yet to demonstrate how good he really is. All I am saying is that he has the talent to make a great commando. What he needs is the experience of working under a professional like you. You can actually help him shine.'

There was a brief silence as Imtiaz mulled the colonel's words over. Seeing the effect his persuasions were having, the colonel turned to face Imtiaz. In a rare show of familiarity that was reserved for friends, Colonel Mohan placed his hand on Imtiaz's shoulder.

'I trusted you because I knew you were good. I trust Rafiq for the same reason. Don't you have faith in my judgment?'

Imtiaz looked at the colonel's earnest face for a moment. Then, taking a deep breath, he pulled himself erect.

'I do, sir.'

19 July. South Coast of the Persian Gulf

The Viking Motor 75 bobbed gently in the shallow blue water, its nose pointing in a northeasterly direction. A stiff breeze blew in from the east, sending strong ripples along the sea's surface, but the air was still comfortably warm, with well over an hour to go before sundown.

Zawawi stood on the prow of the luxury yacht, the breeze tearing at his spotless white Versace suit. Behind him, on the yacht's main deck, preparations for a party were underway. Two of his guests, a ruddy-faced German diplomat and a Shylock-like Ukrainian banker, had already started depleting a stock of fine Chilean chardonnay, and the boisterous laughter of the German suggested that inebriation wasn't far away.

Zawawi's mind, however, was not on the shenanigans of his guests, an eclectic mix of individuals of various nationalities, bound by a common thread of avarice and the willingness to satiate it by breaking every conceivable law in any conceivable fashion. Instead, he was occupied with the thoughts of the men on another boat which, at that moment, was somewhere to the northeast, heading towards the Strait of Hormuz and the Gulf of Oman, en route to the Iran–Pakistan frontier.

That boat, a humble fishing trawler, couldn't compare with the classy Viking he was in, nor could the men it was transporting match the crowd he was hosting in terms of net worth and sophistication. Yet, at that particular moment, Zawawi would willingly have traded the Viking and its occupants for the safety of the trawler's payload.

For at that particular moment, the relative usefulness of Al-Kamil and his men was far greater than anything else to Zawawi. Everything depended on their reaching Karachi and killing Irshad Dilawar, and the Algerian knew that they were up against some very stiff odds.

Yet, as he gazed at the haze on the horizon, Zawawi felt strangely at peace. There was something immensely reassuring in Al-Kamil's cold, savage personality…

'Monsieur Zawawi, what are you doing there by yourself?'

Zawawi turned to see the German diplomat, a near-empty flute glass in one hand, lurching towards him, undone by the undulating sea and the liquids that he had been so freely imbibing.

'You are the host,' the German slurred slightly. 'How can you neglect your guests so badly?'

Zawawi smiled and walked quickly towards the drunken man. Holding him by his elbow, he first steadied him, then gently propelled him towards the safety of the main deck.

'I am always at your service, Herr Scheigel,' he said obligingly.

Inside, the Shylock lookalike sat on a deck chair, nursing his glass. Next to him was a Filipino, the owner of a fleet of commercial ships. Zawawi stopped to exchange a few pleasantries with them, but he had barely uttered a few words when a skinny blonde in a burgundy gown with a plunging neckline waltzed up to him, a bottle of Krug in one hand.

'I've been looking for you all over the place. Where have you been?' she twittered in a thin reedy voice richly layered with a Bostonian accent. Before Zawawi could reply, the woman stared at his empty hands and tut-tutted, 'You haven't had anything to drink, I see. Come, you poor dear, let's get you something nice, shall we?'

Zawawi let the woman take his hand and lead him to the bar, his eyes going over the young East Asian girl in a short, tight skirt mixing cocktails and serving the drinks. He would permit himself a lot of pleasures that evening, he decided.

But first, there was a spot of work still to be dispensed with. Zawawi accepted his mojito, excused himself politely and made his way to his cabin below deck.

It was time to update Loya Pathan about Al-Kamil's departure to Quetta.

19 July. Pragati Maidan, New Delhi

Haider Nazir hurried out of the main door of Hall No 2, then stood uncertainly for a moment, wondering what to do next. He glanced at the Nescafe stall on the opposite side of the open courtyard and made up his mind. He needed a coffee. And some time to think in peace.

He walked across to the stall and bought himself a cup of instant coffee, before absent-mindedly scouting for a place to sit. All the open-air tables were occupied, so he finally sat down on a flight of stairs nearby. Taking a sip of the beverage, he glanced at his watch. It was just past seven.

Nazir grimaced and cast his eyes around. He could see people flocking about the many exhibition halls that made up Pragati Maidan, Delhi's largest exhibition centre. And to his left, a steady stream of visitors was entering Hall No 2, which was hosting the inaugural edition of the South Asian Cottage Industries Trade Expo.

Nazir cursed inwardly, wondering what drew the general public to such exhibitions and fairs like magnets. Personally, he hated trade fairs, but as a press attaché with the Pakistani mission in India, his job involved conducting public relation exercises for Pakistani business houses and industries participating in trade fairs.

Seven o'clock, and Delhi's populace was still pouring in through the gates of Pragati Maidan.

At this rate, it would be at least an hour—if not more—before the show wound down for the day. Then the customary niceties and conventions of diplomacy would follow, which meant that he wouldn't be back inside the premises of the Pakistani High Commission in Chanakyapuri before nine.

The problem was that he had to get on the line to Pakistan as soon as possible. The information that he had just received from his contact was explosive, and Nazir knew his bosses in Islamabad had to know of it without delay.

He drained the coffee, crushed the plastic cup and stood up. To hell with the expo! The Pakistani stalls inside Hall No 2 could do without him for the rest of the evening. He dumped the cup into a trash can and was about to make his way towards the parking lot when he saw a woman of about forty approaching him.

'Mr Haider Nazir?' she asked tentatively.

'Yes. How can I help you?'

It turned out that the woman was a senior journalist with *The Economic Times*, and she wanted Nazir's assistance in interviewing some Pakistani businessmen for a story she was doing on Indo–Pak trade relations.

Nazir sighed. Etiquette and protocol demanded that he agree to the journalist's request. So he smiled and politely led the woman back into Hall No 2.

The call to Pakistan would have to wait.

19 July. Chandimandir Cantonment, Panchkula

Imtiaz carefully examined the old, dog-eared passport he was holding. It was green in colour, the words 'Islamic Republic of Pakistan' and 'Passport' printed in gold on its cover in both English and Urdu. It was in the name of Imtiaz Ahmed Khan, and had been issued in Gilgit five years ago. According to it, Imtiaz Ahmed was a resident of Skardu District in Pakistan's Federally Administered Northern Areas.

The photograph inside, though taken less than seventy-two hours ago, was a fair reproduction of what Imtiaz must have looked like five years earlier. The lush Shenandoah beard that now covered his jowls was visibly grey, but the one in the passport was jet black. Further, the face in the photograph had a moustache to go with the beard, a cultivation that Imtiaz had carefully shaved off hours after the photo had been clicked. The picture was the clever handiwork of the touch-up artists in the basement of the Unit Kilo facility. The passport itself was the painstaking result of the efforts put in by a research and simulation team.

Imtiaz shut the slender booklet and placed it inside an old but hardy khaki haversack, which was already packed with three pairs of Pathan suits, a scruffy white-going-to-yellow taqiyah, a copy of the Qur'an, and a bundle of genuine Pakistani currency wrapped in thick polythene.

The haversack also contained a watch, a cheap Taiwan-made digital thingamabob, already set to Pakistan Standard Time. For the next fortnight or so, this would be the only means Imtiaz would have of telling time accurately. While for the tracking team at Unit Kilo, the GPS unit inside the watch would be the sole source of information pertaining to Imtiaz's movements.

After buckling the haversack, Imtiaz folded a grey blanket made of coarse wool and stuffed it into a second bag. A large camouflage jacket and a pair of rough leather khussas, their soles worn by regular use, joined the blanket, and Imtiaz straightened.

He was all set for his journey from Skardu to Karachi.

Imtiaz went through his pockets one last time, checking to see if there was anything of value in them. They showed up empty. His watch, mobile phone, keys, wallet—even his army identity card—were all in a small box that would stay in Panchkula till he returned from Pakistan. For now, his only means of identification as an Indian Army officer was a special, all-purpose pass signed by Major-General Dixit. It would grant him entry into the brigade headquarters at Jammu, Srinagar and Baramulla.

He would burn that pass before crossing the Line of Control into Gultari in Baltistan.

In less than a minute, Imtiaz was standing in what passed off as the drawing room of the Unit Kilo facility. Outside, a jeep was waiting to transport him to Jammu, where he would join an army convoy heading for Srinagar.

Colonel Mohan, Shamsheer and Rafiq had stood up the moment Imtiaz walked into the room. The four men looked at one another in silence, realizing that the moment of truth was finally upon them. At last, Colonel Mohan walked up to Imtiaz and held out his hand.

'All the best, major. May God be with you.'

'Thank you, sir,' Imtiaz responded to the colonel's grip with a warm shake.

Shamsheer stepped up to Imtiaz and proffered his hand. 'I'll see you in Karachi, sir,' he said softly, the calm sincerity mirrored in his eyes. '*Khuda hafiz.*'

Imtiaz nodded and smiled, glad to have Shamsheer by his side.

Once Shamsheer withdrew, Rafiq came forward, his eyes shining eagerly.

'I'll see you as well, sir,' he said, pumping Imtiaz's hand. 'I'm really looking forward to working with you on Project Abhimanyu. All the best till we meet next, sir.'

'All the best,' the major replied, his eyes scanning Rafiq's face.

Five minutes later, the jeep nosed out of Chandimandir Cantonment and joined the concourse of evening traffic making its way into Chandigarh.

19 July. Pakistan Aeronautical Complex, Kamra, Pakistan

Second-lieutenant Gul Nawaz was reclining in his chair, his feet propped up on a second chair, hands locked over his ample midriff. His eyes were shut, but his mouth hung slightly open and his head listed to one side, a gentle snore rounding off this picture of repose.

On one table in the cramped room sat a large radio transmitter-cum-receiver, which was linked to a large dish antenna on the roof of the building. Another table was occupied by a large computer, a series of codes in machine language scrolling lazily up the monitor's screen.

There was nothing remarkable about the room, and very few people working at the Pakistan Aeronautical Complex, the third largest aircraft assembly plant in the world, knew that it and the three adjoining rooms served as a hub for the Joint Signal Intelligence Bureau of the ISI. The JSIB specialized in intelligence collection along the India–Pakistan border, and the Kamra hub was one of its reporting centres.

Suddenly, a low but sharp beeping noise disturbed the silence of the room. The second-lieutenant snapped awake instantly. Sitting upright, he reached for the Thuraya SO-2510 satellite phone that lay next to the radio transmitter. The SO-2510, unlike other Thuraya handsets, didn't have the dual-mode feature that allowed operation in GSM terrestrial mobile networks as well. Given the added security it offered, this satellite-only model was the preferred mode of communication between JSIB operatives.

'Hello,' Gul Nawaz spoke into the phone. 'Foxtrot three zero five, receiving.'

Holding the phone between his left shoulder and ear, the second-lieutenant opened a scribbling pad. As the caller began talking, the soldier quickly began making notes in shorthand.

Suddenly he paused, pen quivering above the pad.

'Are you sure about this?'

He listened, interjecting with brief questions now and again, his voice rising in excitement.

'Any idea how many commandos are being sent?'

'How are they entering Pakistan?'

'I see. I see…'

'You're certain about the target?'

'Okay. Okay. Keep us posted. *Khuda hafiz.*'

Gul Nawaz stared at the notes he had jotted down, his eyes widening as the implications dawned on him. He looked at his watch. Eleven-forty. His replacement wouldn't be in before midnight.

He wondered if he should call up his superior and relay the communiqué, but he discarded the idea immediately. The nature of this message was such that it had to be conveyed in person—the Indians were sending a team of commandos into Pakistan to kill Irshad Dilawar!

He began pacing the cluttered room impatiently, waiting for his replacement to come.

PART TWO:
THE BEST-LAID PLANS

CHAPTER 4

21 July. North Coast of the Gulf of Oman

The water lapping against the hull of the fishing trawler was oily black. For that matter, everything around the boat was black as well, and the men on the deck worked silently in pitch darkness.

Two inflatable rubber dinghies had already been lowered to the sea's surface and were nudging the trawler, buoyed by the swell of the tides and the refreshing breeze blowing inland. One of the dinghies sat low in the water, weighed down by the four men in it. The second was still in the process of being loaded, a man on the trawler's deck transferring heavy bags down to another, who stood in the dinghy with his legs braced.

Hossam Al-Kamil leaned against the trawler's railings and watched his men. After a while, he raised his head and looked at the silhouette of land on the northern horizon. The Iranian coast lay just over two miles away, and in a matter of hours, they would be in the Bahu Kalat district in the Sistān va Balūchestān province of Southeastern Iran. Over the next few days, they would head north through Bahu Kalat, before turning east towards Turbat in Pakistan's Balochistan province.

It wasn't the easiest and most obvious route to Quetta, and Musa Zawawi had pointed out as much. Zawawi's suggestion had been that they cross into Pakistan from Kandahar, and slip back into Afghanistan once the job had been completed. Al-Kamil, however, had argued that owing to the Taliban conflict, the Afghan–Pakistan border would be under close scrutiny by both Pakistani and US forces. In his reckoning, an entry through Iran was a safer bet as that border was poorly patrolled in comparison. Once inside Pakistan, they would take a roundabout route to Quetta through the sparsely populated hinterland of Balochistan.

As the second dinghy was being loaded, a door leading to the trawler's hold opened, emitting a faint yellow glimmer from deep within the boat's belly. A figure emerged from the door and exchanged a few quiet words with

Al-Kamil, their murmur dying quickly in the wind. Al-Kamil nodded, strode to the door and climbed down a steep iron ladder.

A lone lantern, burning low, illuminated the dank hold. The odour of fish was overpowering, but Al-Kamil could smell something over that—the scent of terror. He peered into the far recesses of the hold and made out four sack-like shapes lying on the floor. He walked slowly to the lantern and turned its nob up. As yellow light flooded the hold, the shapes came into sharper focus and four pairs of eyes stared back at Al-Kamil wildly. The trawler's four crew members lay trussed up, hands tied behind them, their mouths gagged.

As Al-Kamil approached them, one of the men uttered a low moan, his eyes raised pleadingly. Al-Kamil stared down at the men before finally kneeling beside the vessel's skipper, a man of around forty-five. When he spoke, the words were chillingly soft.

'You shouldn't have threatened to turn us over to the Omani coast guards yesterday. And the thought of extracting more money from us should never have crossed your mind. Now you will have to pay for your greed.'

The boat's master moaned and gurgled an incoherent petition for mercy, his body jackknifing in anguish and dread, his head rocking from side to side. It was just as well, for he didn't notice the large knife which had materialized almost magically in Al-Kamil's right hand.

In one smooth motion, Al-Kamil grabbed the captain by his hair, jerked his head backwards and upwards and slit his throat.

As he stood up, the three surviving men stared at him, sheer horror on their faces. One of them, a boy of around twenty, had wet himself, a dark stain spreading down the front of his pyjama. Al-Kamil inclined his head towards the skipper who lay drowning in his own blood.

'He was greedy and he meant us harm. But you three…' He paused, using the knife to draw a triangle in the air. 'You were just doing your job. I have nothing against you.'

The three men were silent, the unforeseen prospect of surviving this ordeal lighting up their eyes. Suddenly, Al-Kamil bent and grabbed one of them by the arm. Seeing the knife arc towards his shoulder, the man let out a shriek and screwed his eyes shut, his body taut in anticipation of the agony to come.

But Al-Kamil merely wiped the blade clean on the man's shirt, the dead captain's blood leaving dark smudges on the fabric. As he straightened, he grinned sadistically at the man now convulsing in terror and relief. He then picked up the lantern and walked to the foot of the ladder. Extinguishing the light, he climbed back to the deck and closed the door tightly behind him, leaving the three crew members in the dark hold with a dead body for company.

Twenty minutes later, the two dinghies were on the verge of entering the deserted Gwatar harbour. Although it was still dark, the men in the rafts could clearly make out the ruins of a colonial Portuguese castle rising into the night sky ahead of them. But behind them there was nothing to show of the trawler they had just vacated. All was a uniform inky blackness.

Once day broke, however, the boat would be visible and someone was bound to notice it.

Al-Kamil tapped one of his men on the shoulder. The man merely nodded in response, reached into one of the bags and pulled out a small radio transmitter. Six radio-controlled explosive devices had been methodically placed in six different corners of the trawler. Now, as the man flicked a switch on the radio transmitter, a firing pulse was triggered in each of them.

Al-Kamil noted the sound of the detonation with great satisfaction. In the morning, the only evidence of their arrival on Iranian shores would be lying in itsy-bitsy fragments on the sea-floor.

And, of course, in the charred remains of the two rubber dinghies, which would be burnt as soon as they set foot on land.

21 July. ISI Headquarters, Khayaban-e-Suhrawardy, Islamabad

The drapes had been drawn tight to keep the blazing morning sun out, and the digital display on the air conditioner showed the temperature within the room to be 19 degrees, exactly half of what it was outside. However, the atmosphere in the room felt a great deal colder to Brigadier Abdur Rauf Razavi as he shifted uncomfortably in what was otherwise an extremely comfortable chair.

'This information was delivered to us nearly thirty-six hours ago, yet you bring it to my notice only now? What made you assume that this was anything less than top priority?'

Brigadier Razavi looked furtively at the man who had posed the question. Seated on the other side of the heavy rosewood desk, the man was in uniform, his gaunt face bearing an uncanny resemblance to the picture of Quaid-e-Azam Muhammad Ali Jinnah, which adorned the opposite wall. The man's face, however, was dark with anger as he went through the slim file that lay in front of him, his sharp eyes examining every word for every ounce of information that it might conceal.

Brigadier Razavi swallowed hard. As the director of the ISI, Lieutenant-General Tauseef Rehmat wielded the kind of power that could make or break practically anyone living within the borders of Pakistan. The man could, if he so wished, not only cripple Razavi's career prospects, but also render him a virtual pariah within the Pakistani Army establishment.

'My sincere apologies, sir, but by the time we sifted through all the information that had been coming in and isolated this one as high priority, it was late yesterday evening,' replied a thickset man in uniform seated next to Brigadier Razavi. 'The moment it came to my notice, I instructed Brigadier Razavi to prepare the report and fixed the meeting with you, sir.'

The brigadier glanced at the man who had just spoken and heaved a small sigh of relief at having escaped immediate censure. Major-General Naeem Anjum Dar was the chief of Joint Intelligence X, which coordinated between all the departments of the ISI and processed and prepared reports. He was also Brigadier Razavi's immediate superior, and the brigadier knew that Major-General Dar could easily have pinned all the blame on him. He had, after all, been tardy, and had sat on the communiqué virtually all through the previous day.

Lieutenant-General Rehmat looked up from the file and fixed a baleful eye on the major-general.

'This is not the kind of response time I expect from Joint Intelligence X. You need to do a lot better than this.'

The major-general's large face, which had a peculiar leathery quality to it, was impassive. Yet, Brigadier Razavi could sense that his boss was seething with rage and would tear him to shreds the moment they were alone. For the moment, though, Major-General Dar was keeping a stony calm.

'I'm really sorry for the delay, sir. But ever since the Americans began turning the heat on the Taliban, there has been a lot more data and information to sort through. My men are working almost round the clock, trying to keep abreast of everything.'

'Humph!'

The snort came from the fourth man in the room. Dressed in a grey shalwar-kameez and matching grey qaraqul that covered a receding hairline, the man was slightly built. His thin pointed face ended in a sharp chin, which had a scrubby goatee on it. He wore a reproachful expression, which wasn't surprising, considering Retired Lieutenant-General Wajid Ali Khan Niazi was directly responsible for the security of Irshad Dilawar. As an old ISI hand and close friend of the gangster, it was a role that he took very seriously.

Waving his hand dismissively, Lieutenant-General Niazi continued speaking. 'You people have begun relying more on technology and less on your intelligence. There was always lots of data and information to sort through. If it is America and the Taliban today, once it was America, the Soviets and the Afghan mujahedeen. Nothing's changed. It's just that you guys don't work hard enough.'

'*Aap aise kaise keh sakte hain, sir?* You can't just accuse us…' Major-General Dar began protesting hotly, but Lieutenant-General Rehmat cut him short.

'Enough!' The director's voice scythed through the room. 'While this delay is costly and unacceptable, we're wasting precious time arguing about who is to blame. We've already lost two days. Let's focus on the problem.'

Having stamped his authority over the situation, Lieutenant-General Rehmat leaned back in his chair and folded his arms. 'The first question is how reliable is this information?' Leaning forward, he opened the file again. 'Our source, Haider Nazir…'

'He's one of our mid-level operatives in Delhi, sir. Press attaché at our mission.'

Lieutenant-General Rehmat frowned. 'He was involved in the Tajikistan incident, right?'

'Yes, sir. That was a bit of an embarrassment for us—but that was also quite a few years ago. He's gotten better with time, and he's become fairly reliable with his information. In fact, it was Nazir who first tipped us off on the meeting between the RAW chief and the head of Afghan intelligence about using the Riyast-i-Amniyat-i-Milli facility in Kabul to train Baloch separatists against Pakistan.'

'Interesting… Yet there's very little in this report to go on. Don't we have any more information? After all, this came in thirty-six hours ago.'

'We have sent a message asking for more information, but so far we've had no luck. Hopefully' we'll have more details in a day or two.'

'In situations like this, we don't have a day or two,' Lieutenant-General Niazi scowled.

'That's right,' Lieutenant-General Rehmat concurred. 'So while our source tries to find out more, we'll have to start planning our defence.'

'For all we know, it could be a false alarm,' Major-General Dar frowned.

'Maybe, but I doubt it. The Indians have been after Dilawar for years now. They know he is here with us and they've tried every trick in the book to get him. So we can't take any chances.' Turning to Lieutenant-General Niazi, he asked, 'Where is Dilawar right now?'

'Quetta.'

'Please arrange to have him moved to Saidu Sharif or Miramshah or Parachinar immediately.'

'But… why do we need to move him from Quetta?' Lieutenant-General Niazi's expression was a mixture of confusion and resistance.

'The Indians are working on some information and we don't know what it is. The best we can do for now is to start shifting goalposts. Just make everything harder for them. Also, appraise Dilawar and all your men guarding him about this new threat. I want everyone protecting him to be on their toes.'

'I know the drill, janaab,' Lieutenant-General Niazi looked and sounded distinctly unhappy.

'Perhaps we should increase the number of security personnel around him.'

'That won't be necessary,' Lieutenant-General Niazi said sharply. 'We have enough men to tackle any situation.'

Lieutenant-General Rehmat sighed. As head of security for Irshad Dilawar, the responsibility of protecting the fugitive ultimately lay on the retired soldier, and Lieutenant-General Rehmat suspected that the man was touchy about letting someone else have a say in the matter.

'I'm sure you do, but one can never be too careful after the Mali incident.'

Lieutenant-General Niazi clenched his jaw. He knew that the man sitting across the table was capable of digging up old graves if it suited his purpose. 'That was a minor hiccup and we've taken corrective measures,' he said tightly.

'If you say so… But keep me posted on everything that has to do with Irshad Dilawar—at least till this threat has been resolved. I don't want to be kept in the dark only to have fingers levelled at me later saying I don't do enough to protect him.'

Seeing the retired soldier nod sullenly, Lieutenant-General Rehmat turned to Major-General Dar. 'Okay, send an alert to the chiefs of the Intelligence Bureau and Military Intelligence immediately. Let them know that there is clear and present danger of an infiltration by Indian commandos into Pakistan.'

'Sir, do we tell them the nature of the threat and who the intended target is?'

'Not right now. We don't have enough information to send out a detailed briefing. This report may ultimately prove to be totally incorrect, and we'd have people laughing at us for having cried wolf. So keep the alert vague for now.'

Major-General Dar looked up from the notes he was hurriedly making. 'What about our section heads in India? Shouldn't we tell them?'

'Yes, but again, no details. Tell them to keep their ears open for any reports on planned infiltration bids into Pakistan. Announce rewards for any such news. Meanwhile, instruct Haider Nazir not to share anything related to this report with anyone but us. Establish a protocol whereby all further updates from him are patched directly to us and no one else.

'Next, alert the Sindh and Punjab Rangers to watch out for infiltration bids along the border,' the director continued rattling off his laundry list. 'Inform the coast guards to intercept and search any suspicious vessel in Pakistani waters, especially around Karachi port. Get the police to increase surveillance across the country. The Indians will have to depend on some local support, so they'll need to check if any large arms purchases have occurred recently. They'll need to find out if anyone is hosting a group of strangers anywhere, or if such a group has rented a house of late.'

'Sir, the police would want to know how many people we are looking for.' It was the first full sentence that Brigadier Razavi had uttered through the course of the meeting, and the three senior officers stared at him for a moment, as if suddenly conscious of his presence.

'That is a problem because Haider Nazir doesn't have exact numbers,' said Major-General Dar. 'All he says is that it's a small group of commandos.'

Lieutenant-General Rehmat considered this for a moment. 'If I were to stage an operation of this sort, I'd say it would need eight to ten people. So that's a number we should work on for now. Look for groups of four or more people moving suspiciously.'

Lieutenant-General Niazi shifted in his chair and frowned. 'I think we need to be a lot more focused in our search for these Indians. The infiltration is from the east, so let's just watch the eastern border and the coastline closely. Why spread ourselves thin on the ground? More eyes should be watching the right places rather than the wrong places.'

'You have a point, Niazi sahib,' the director conceded. 'But that won't help if the Indians have already crossed the border and are inside Pakistan. Till we know for sure, we have to increase surveillance everywhere, with a focus on Quetta and possibly Saidu Sharif, Miramshah and Parachinar.'

For the next ten minutes, the men sat working on the finer details of their course of action. Finally, Major-General Dar and Brigadier Razavi stood up, saluted their senior officers and took their leave.

Lieutenant-General Niazi waited for the door to close firmly and the footsteps to recede before he turned to face the director.

'Tauseef mian, what's the latest score on Dilawar?'

'Matlab…?' the director stared back in confusion.

'You know what I'm talking about. Dilawar won't leave Pakistan as long as we army men have our way. But our civilian government—will they be able to withstand the pressure to have him sent back to India? The Indians keep pumping the US with proof of Dilawar's involvement in terrorist activities, and every time some US official comes to Pakistan, he or she presents fresh evidence against him to our government. And now that we are supposed to be part of this war against terror, the US keeps piling the pressure on the government. *Tail-ender batting kar rahe hain… Wicket kab tak bachi rahegi*?'

Lieutenant-General Rehmat sighed, fully appreciative of the other's concern. But before he could reply, the other man leaned forward and spoke bluntly.

'I hear that the national security advisor of the US is visiting Islamabad next month, and that one of the things he is going to discuss with the President and the Prime Minister is Dilawar's extradition to India?'

The two veterans stared at one another for a moment, before the director nodded lamely. Lieutenant-General Niazi immediately shrugged, spread his hands and shook his head.

'See?'

Lieutenant-General Rehmat sat in silence for a moment. Then, looking at the man sitting across him squarely in the eye, he tapped the thin file in front of him.

'This has changed everything.' There was a steely resolve in the director's voice. 'The Indians are planning to get Dilawar by hook or by crook. So whatever happens, we will now do everything to prevent him from falling into their clutches.'

21 July. Avrupa Otoyolu, Istanbul

The black Bentley Arnage was cruising down the O-3, heading west for the city of Çorlu. Inside, in its plush back seat, Zawawi reclined and watched a recording of the previous day's EPL match between Arsenal and Chelsea. He already knew that the Gunners had won by an odd goal, so he didn't mind the fact that Chelsea was leading with ten minutes to go for full-time.

It was immediately after Arsenal had scored the equalizer that Zawawi's phone rang. He reached into his pocket irritably, intent on cutting the call, but when he saw the name flashing on the screen, he stopped and stared. It was barely past ten in the morning in Istanbul, and this call wasn't scheduled till later in the night.

The match quickly forgotten, Zawawi raised the phone to his ear with a strong sense of foreboding.

'*As-salāmu alaikum, Loya sahib.*'

'Musa, there's a problem here,' Pathan spoke without preamble. 'You have to get in touch with Hossam immediately and stop him from coming to Quetta.'

'Why? What happened?'

'Irshad Dilawar is being shifted from Quetta.'

Zawawi stopped breathing for a second, too stunned for words.

'Shifted? Where is he being shifted?'

'Miramshah. And later, Parachinar.'

'But how come this… all of a sudden?'

Zawawi listened in silence as Pathan spoke for a few minutes. Finally, he nodded. 'I see. So what's the next plan of action?'

'Let me speak to Zeb first. Meanwhile, you stop Hossam.'

Zawawi put the phone down and stared out of the window, his mind going over everything that Pathan had revealed. It had all sounded so fantastic that he could hardly believe it could be true. But the ISI seemed to be taking it very seriously, and that meant Al-Kamil wouldn't get his man in Quetta. It also meant that Al-Kamil and his men could run into serious trouble with Pakistani security.

Loya Pathan was right. Al-Kamil had to be warned from going to Quetta.

But Zawawi's problem was that he didn't have a way of getting in touch with Al-Kamil directly. Citing risks of exposure, Al-Kamil had insisted that he was not to be contacted during the course of the mission, and that he would call Zawawi once the job was done.

Zawawi picked up his phone and dialled Farez Nizamuddin's number. His agent-cum-point man in Pakistan, Nizamuddin was to furnish Al-Kamil and his men with the weapons they needed to complete the assignment.

And he was the only one who could relay the warning to Al-Kamil.

CHAPTER 5

22 July. Karakoram Highway, Gilgit–Baltistan, Pakistan

Imtiaz jerked awake inside the cramped and smelly interior of the customized Bedford TJ that he had boarded at Skardu. The lack of motion and the silence told him that the bus had come to a halt, and from where he sat, he could see rows of shapes slouched in their seat, deep in slumber.

Imtiaz tried to peer out of the grubby window, but he could see little through the smeared glass. With some effort, he pushed the window open and stuck his head out, the cold night air stinging his face, driving the vestiges of sleep from his eyes. Screwing his head around, Imtiaz noticed the bulk of another vehicle in the darkness behind, while ahead of him, he could make out the dark shapes of four trucks lined up to a bend in the road. He concluded that the bus was either stuck in a roadblock or was part of some convoy that was forming.

Pulling his left hand free from under his blanket, Imtiaz pressed a button on the side of his digital watch. A pale yellow light lit up the dial and showed that it was just past 3.30 a.m. For the last seventy-two hours he had travelled virtually non-stop, resting for just two hours each at the brigade headquarters in Srinagar and Baramulla. Whatever sleep he had managed to catch had been during the course of his journey from Jammu to Srinagar, and from the minute he had left Baramulla to the time he had reached Skardu via Gultari, he had battled fatigue and kept sleep at bay.

According to the plan they had drawn up at Chandimandir Cantonment, he was to switch buses at Chilas and journey to Abbottabad, from where, depending on the time of his arrival, he would catch a train or another bus to Rawalpindi. If all went well, he would then catch the Awam Express from Rawalpindi to Karachi, failing which, he would have to rely on one of the other long distance trains than ran between the two cities.

Imtiaz sat in the darkness, wondering what was causing this unscheduled halt. Not only was it an irritant in a well-oiled plan, he also found it mildly disturbing. For in all his briefings, there had been not a single mention of such stoppages along the Karakoram Highway—definitely none in the middle of the night, miles away from civilization.

As he was mulling this over, the bus's conductor got into the bus and switched on two lights located on the bulkhead separating the seats from the driver's cabin. Instantly, some of the sleeping passengers stirred. The villager seated next to Imtiaz also awoke and peered out of the window. He then grunted something at the conductor which, to Imtiaz's untutored ear, sounded like Balti but may well have been Shina.

The conductor replied in a loud and clear voice, obviously for the benefit of all the passengers. Imtiaz didn't understand what was being said, but he did catch one critical word repeated twice: police. At the same moment, he heard the sound of the trucks ahead starting up, and almost immediately, the bus's driver climbed back behind the steering-wheel and fired the engine.

Imtiaz frowned. The conductor had said something about the police. Something was amiss.

Fifteen minutes later, his suspicions were proved right when the bus crawled to the checkpoint swarming with policemen, many of whom were armed with more than bamboo canes. With growing alarm, Imtiaz noted a Pakistan Army jeep parked on the far shoulder of the road, and a handful of soldiers with automatics watching everything attentively.

Three policemen wielding canes boarded the bus. Starting from the front, they began making detailed enquiries of each and every traveller, and to Imtiaz's relief, their language of choice was Urdu. They seemed particularly keen on knowing if there were any passengers on board travelling in groups, and one group of three villagers was asked to get off the bus and had to surrender to a detailed grilling at a makeshift office set up on the side of the road. Imtiaz observed that one of the policemen was carefully scrutinizing all the bags stowed in the overhead racks, demanding that the larger ones be opened for inspection.

Finally, the policeman reached the row that Imtiaz was seated in. Catching sight of the khaki haversack on the rack, he pointed to it with his cane.

'*Yeh kiska hai?*' he demanded, looking around. When Imtiaz raised his hand signalling ownership, the policeman motioned with his cane. '*Utaaro.*'

Imtiaz complied, taking care to see that his body language didn't rouse any suspicions. He couldn't afford to be overenthusiastic or cocky, but neither could he be uncooperative or meek and supplicating. The trick was to strike the right balance between the assurance that stems from innocence and the deference that authority naturally demands.

Rifling through the contents, the policemen chanced upon the passport. Opening it, he studied it in the light for a moment, even as one of his colleagues joined him.

'Where are you going?' the first policeman asked.

'Huzoor, Karachi.'

'*Aur yeh?*' the cop asked, waving the passport.

Imtiaz explained that he was going to Karachi in the hope of getting a Turkish work permit.

'Turkey!' the cop snorted derisively. 'The Turks themselves are busy getting out of Turkey and migrating to Europe and America to do the shittiest jobs they can get. And this man wants to go to Turkey to do the shittiest jobs he will get there. Live peacefully in Pakistan, chacha.'

The policeman's words drew disproportionate laughter from his co-passengers, and Imtiaz smiled and looked suitably embarrassed.

The second policeman, who seemed untouched by the amusement, looked at Imtiaz shrewdly.

'You live in Gultari. Why are you going all the way to the Turkish consulate in Karachi when you can easily go to the Turkish embassy in Islamabad? That is so much closer.'

'Huzoor, my uncle knows a travel agent in Karachi whose cousin works in the Turkish consulate in Karachi. I am hoping this cousin will recommend me and the embassy will grant me a permit. Allah knows how desperately I need it.'

Imtiaz put his hands together, as if entreating his fate and his interrogators to cease harassing him. He looked every bit the poor villager struggling to escape the clutches of crippling poverty.

'Are you travelling alone or is someone with you?' the cop demanded.

'I'm alone, huzoor,' Imtiaz looked around at his co-passengers, as if expecting them to vouch for him.

The policemen handed back the passport, and promptly lost all interest in him.

It was nearly 4.30 when the bus finally left the check-post. As the vehicle began weaving through the mountainous terrain, the passengers slowly settled back into sleep, the diversion at the checkpoint quickly forgotten.

Imtiaz, though, was wide awake.

What he had witnessed was no routine procedure. The Pakistani authorities were looking for something and they were acting on specific information or knowledge. And while he had no way of knowing what they were looking for, this could mean encountering many more such checks en route to Karachi.

He wondered if he would be able to clear all of them with as much ease.

22 July. Makran Coast, Balochistan

Rafiq sat near the gunwale of the high performance rigid-inflatable boat, peering into the night. The boat was well inside Pakistani territorial waters, the tiny coastal village of Malan just four kilometres to the north. They had successfully evaded the Pakistani Coast Guards to get to this point, but here onwards he would have to go it alone, first swimming to land, then walking through the southern fringes of the Hingol National Park before meeting the Makran Coastal Highway connecting the western port of Gwadar to Karachi.

Switching on a small, hooded pencil torch, Rafiq quickly checked to see if he had everything he needed for the journey. Not that there was much in the slim watertight bag which he would strap on over his black wetsuit—a black cotton shalwar-kameez, a white taqiyah, a tattered wallet containing Pakistani currency, a cheap digital watch, a small bottle of water and a pair of brown sandals. A small zip, however, was attached to the inside of the bag, and Rafiq unzipped it and flashed the beam into the compartment.

A small box, not more than five inches in length and two-and-a-half inches in depth lay in the pocket. Unlike the rest of the contents of the bag, the box hadn't been issued to Rafiq at the Unit Kilo base in Chandimandir Cantonment. In fact, those at the Unit Kilo base would have been very surprised to learn of the box and its contents.

Rafiq didn't open the box. He didn't need to, for he knew what was inside—a Thuraya SO-2510 satellite phone and a customized charger dock, sealed in thick polythene. The phone had come with explicit instructions on when and where it needed to be used.

Rafiq quickly zipped the pocket and the bag. A minute later, seated on the boat's gunwale, he looked at the shadowy figures of the two other men in the boat, both MARCOS commandos entrusted with the job of dropping Rafiq into Pakistani waters. Both men raised their hands and made 'thumbs-up' gestures, and Rafiq responded with one of his own.

Turning around, he quietly slipped into the cold water and kicked away from the boat.

23 July. Sukkur Airport, Sindh

'For the kind attention of all passengers, Pakistan International Airlines announces the departure of flight PK-539 from Sukkur to Karachi. All passengers travelling on flight PK-539 are requested to proceed towards the gate for boarding.'

As the sterile, pre-recorded message was repeated over the public address system in Sindhi and Urdu, roughly sixty people seated in the airport lounge got up and began filing towards the single gate. Outside, not far from the terminal, the Boeing 737-300 which was to ferry the passengers to Karachi could be seen, its baggage hatch open like the maw of some ravenous metallic beast.

Shamsheer, who had been sitting in one corner of the lounge, casually folded the copy of the *Nawa-i-Waqt* that he was reading and rose from his seat. Picking up a small leather suitcase, the kind businessmen take on overnight trips, he sauntered over to join the queue, making sure that he was somewhere in the middle of the concourse. It was a known fact that people found it easier to remember faces at the beginning and the very end of queues. For added precaution, he kept on the Ray-Ban Aviators he was wearing, the blazing mid-morning outside providing a reasonable excuse.

The boarding pass that he presented for validation identified him as Shamsheer Bux, a name that was also printed on the driving licence and MasterCard tucked inside his wallet, as well as on the leaves of the Habib Bank cheque book inside his suitcase. The driving licence and the chequebook, like the name they bore, were completely fake. The global credit card was authentic, though, and had been issued to a Shamsheer Bux in Riyadh fourteen months ago. The card was among the many that Unit Kilo routinely procured and maintained, and one of the things that Shamsheer had had to learn in Panchkula was to forge the signature on its back.

It was a good ten minutes before Shamsheer was on the plane, seated at a window towards the rear. As the aircraft began taxiing for take-off, he settled down in his seat and opened the newspaper, using it for flimsy recreation and even flimsier concealment.

The last two days had, quite literally, passed in a blur. From Jaisalmer, Shamsheer had headed in a northwesterly direction and crossed over to Pakistan near Gatwala, a feat achieved with the aid of Saadat Fakih's associates who still plied their illegal trade between the neighbouring countries. Once inside Pakistan, Shamsheer had been smuggled to Rohri, the ride in a dilapidated jeep through tortuous desert roads being anything but pleasurable as his handlers were eager to quickly rid themselves of their human contraband.

On reaching the safe house on the outskirts of Rohri the previous night, Shamsheer had undergone a remarkable transformation. He had exchanged his villager-on-the-run image for one of a prosperous but provincial Pakistani businessman, and it was this persona that had presented itself at Sukkur Airport earlier that morning. The visiting cards in his wallet proclaimed him to be the owner of El Grande Fashions & Hosiery, and the purported reason behind the trip was a meeting with a Karachi-based shipping agency to negotiate a big export deal.

Now, as the 737 lifted into the sky, Shamsheer glanced at his watch, a chunky gold-plated Rolex that complemented the gold rings adorning his middle and ring fingers. Though a fake, the Rolex was priceless on account of the GPS tracking unit embedded in it. The watch showed the time to be 10.20.

Shamsheer looked out of the tiny window. Down below he could see Sukkur, with the ribbon-like Indus flowing through it. Further away were the flat desert plains that characterized the topography of the region. A curtain of hot haze hung towards the horizon, obscuring virtually everything. He thanked his stars that he was flying to Karachi. Not only did flying help him get to his destination faster, it helped him beat the torrid summer heat. It also increased the odds of him reaching Karachi undetected—because, for some reason, no one expected infiltrators to travel around a country on commercial airlines.

If everything went according to plan, in an hour he would be at Jinnah International Airport. In two hours, he would meet Saadat.

23 July. Makran Coastal Highway, Balochistan

Rafiq sat in the shade of a huge bluff and surveyed the breathtaking scenery that lay in front of him. For almost as far as he could see, row upon row of craggy massifs rose out of the flat sandy earth, the rock a uniform chalky grey against a pale blue sky. Far to his left, the land fell away in rolling ochre-coloured dunes, beyond which, in the distance, he could make out a patch of the blue-grey waters of the Arabian Sea. Apart from a few dusty scrubs growing in the lee of the boulders, there was hardly any sign of vegetation.

The harsh sun was almost directly overhead. Rafiq opened a small bottle with less than a centimetre of water splashing inside. He had been rationing the water all morning, but now he was free to drink the last drop. For the two-lane, east-west highway to Karachi snaked away to his right, and even though the road marred the rugged, pristine beauty of the landscape, it meant both civilization and water were close at hand.

The swim from the boat to land had taken Rafiq the better part of the night, and it was almost dawn when he had hauled himself onto the shore. Without delay, he had buried the wetsuit and bag deep in the sand under a large boulder, before setting out in search of the coastal highway.

Before long, he had figured out that he had missed his landing point near the hamlet of Malan by a wide mark, probably on account of the darkness and the strong currents. He was nowhere near any human habitation and had walked all morning, fighting thirst, hunger and exhaustion, till finally, ten minutes earlier, he had turned the corner of a cliff to find the strip of macadam with the yellow-and-white markings.

He sat quietly in the shade for a while, letting the sweat dry off his kameez and his exposed arms. Two minibuses, half a dozen cars and some fifteen trucks went by. At last, as the creeping sun began encroaching the shade in which he sat, Rafiq stood up and clambered down the pebbled slope to the road below.

The first vehicle to come along was a jingle truck, slowly lumbering down the road, the sun glinting off its bright red bonnet and the elaborate metal and mirror-work that it was festooned with.

Rafiq raised his hand, signalling it to stop.

CHAPTER 6

23 July. Nushki, Balochistan

Hossam Al-Kamil took off the black qaraqul he was wearing and rubbed his scalp, feeling the short fuzz of his closely cropped hair tickle his large, calloused palm. He was staring down at the surface of the rough wooden table in front of him, his thoughtful eyes tracing the patterns made by the whorls in the dark wood.

Replacing the cap carefully on his head, he looked up at the man sitting opposite him. Farez Nizamuddin was in his late thirties, lean in build, his face covered by a straggly beard and moustache. At that moment, Nizamuddin was tugging nervously at his beard as he pressed a sat-phone to his right ear. After a while, he put the phone down and looked at Al-Kamil with anxious eyes.

'I'm just not getting through to Istanbul,' he said in Arabic, shrugging in helplessness.

Al-Kamil grunted, folded his hands, sucked his teeth and looked impatiently out of the small window to his left.

The two men were seated in a room on the second floor of a house on the western outskirts of the town of Nushki, roughly 120 kilometres to the southwest of Quetta. Out of the window, the flat Balochistan desert could be seen stretching towards the north and west into Afghanistan. A cool desert wind blew in from the window, blunting some of the dry, mid-afternoon heat. From where he sat, Al-Kamil could see nothing move in the bright sun outside.

'It's usually never so difficult... I don't know today... why...' Nizamuddin mumbled and apologized.

'It doesn't matter. Stop whining and just keep trying,' said Al-Kamil, his voice hardening.

He stood up abruptly, walked to the window and looked out towards the northern horizon. Nizamuddin, meanwhile, got busy with the phone again. After a few attempts, his eyes suddenly lit up, apprehension giving way to relief.

'*As-salāmu alaikum, sheikh sahib.*' Nizamuddin nodded eagerly a couple of times, before extending the phone to Al-Kamil. 'Please talk,' he said.

'*As-salāmu alaikum,*' Al-Kamil spoke into the phone.

'*Wa'Alaikum as-salām,*' Zawawi's voice came through clearly. 'Farez must have given you the news, right?'

'Yes. Is this thing about these Indian commandos true?'

'I can't say. Even the ISI doesn't know for sure. But they aren't taking any chances and neither are we.'

'So...what are we to do now? If Irshad Dilawar is in Miramshah or Parachinar, we can still get him.'

'No, don't do that,' Zawawi's voice was sharp. 'He might be in Saidu Sharif, for all we know. The ISI has planned to keep moving him around, so you'll be wasting your time chasing him.'

'So you're saying we call the whole thing off?' Al-Kamil didn't relish the prospect of giving up the hunt midway, and the disappointment was obvious in his voice. 'We have travelled many long days to get here... Now we abandon everything just because of some Indian commandos?'

'I said nothing about calling this off...'

Al-Kamil's ears pricked up. 'So?'

'You are to leave for Karachi immediately.'

'Karachi?'

'In four days, Dilawar will visit Karachi to meet some of his business partners from Saudi Arabia.' Al-Kamil could tell that Zawawi was smiling. 'That's where you will kill him.'

'Are you sure about this Karachi plan of his?'

'Absolutely.'

'And the ISI will allow him to travel to Karachi?'

'He's going to be there for only three days, so it fits in with their current plan of moving him around Pakistan.'

'What about these Indian commandos?'

'What about them? It's none of our business whether they are caught or killed by the Pakistanis. You and your men just have to be a bit more careful, that's all. The good part is that right now, the ISI is focused on Quetta, Miramshah, Parachinar and Saidu Sharif. They aren't thinking about Karachi yet. That gives you time to get there and hunker down.'

'I meant the Indians are also coming here for Dilawar.' Al-Kamil spoke softly, his face grim.

'So? If they do manage to kill Dilawar before you do, it's all the better for us. Now listen to me carefully about Karachi…'

Nearly half an hour later, Al-Kamil stood staring out of the window once again. Hands locked behind him, he thrust his chest out and he breathed in deeply. The scent of blood was back in the air. But this time there was another set of bloodhounds on the same trail.

Al-Kamil's face grew dark at the thought of the Indian commandos competing with him in this hunt. Perhaps it was fine with Musa Zawawi if the Indians got Dilawar first, but Al-Kamil didn't find the idea the least bit appealing.

Irshad Dilawar was his game, and if the Indians crossed his path trying to snatch his prize, he'd make them pay dearly.

23 July. Fatima Jinnah Road, Karachi

The third-floor office of Pentagram Travels was almost entirely dark. In fact, there were hardly any lights showing in any of the windows of the four-storeyed building, which housed a number of offices and business establishments. The only lights visible from outside were those of a Habib Bank ATM on the ground floor, and the glow signs of Pentagram Travels, and another establishment that simply went by the name of The Gallery.

Although the lights in the main office and lobby had been turned off, a small shaded lamp burned in one inner room of Pentagram Travels. The room was typical of most travel agencies, with the logos of a variety of airlines and posters of famous holiday destinations splashed across every conceivable surface. On one wall, amidst pictures of the Swiss Alps, the Eiffel Tower and the Singapore Merlion, was a mantelpiece. On it stood four trophies and a large photograph of a scrawny walnut of a man being felicitated by erstwhile Pakistani Prime Minister Nawaz Sharif.

An older version of the man in the photograph was, at that moment, seated in a high-backed swivel chair, facing a computer. He had a pair of headphones over his ears, the slender stem of the integrated mike jutting out in front of his mouth. The glow from the monitor lit his dark, wrinkled face, and the monitor's screen could be seen reflected in the round spectacles he wore. The eyes behind these glasses raised themselves apprehensively towards the closed door every now and again.

Saadat Fakih wasn't timid by nature, nor was he easily frightened. But this latest business that the colonel had embroiled him in had rattled him. Spying for the Indians was one thing. Harbouring Indian commandos inside Pakistani territory and supplying them with arms and logistical support was another. The former was decidedly dangerous; the latter was downright suicidal.

Despite his aversion for Irshad Dilawar, when Colonel Mohan had first told him about his role in Project Abhimanyu, Saadat had flatly refused to get involved. The colonel had repeatedly raised the price of his cooperation, and Saadat had repeatedly declined. Finally, Colonel Mohan had turned to blackmail and told him that he could either help the Indians, or he could sit back and wait for the Pakistanis to learn about his years of treachery. Saadat had considered informing the Pakistanis about Project Abhimanyu in lieu of amnesty, but he knew he couldn't bet on Pakistani gratitude. And, of course, the Indians would eventually come after him.

Left with no choice, Saadat had cursed the bullying colonel and rued his decision to work for the Indians.

Now, as he waited for the connection to get through, he cursed Colonel Mohan again. This stupid plot could jeopardize the twenty years of hard work he had put in to build Pentagram Travels and Jahangir Shipping into fine businesses, and move from the far fringes of respectability to the epicentre of social acceptability. If anything went wrong, he was certain to lose his livelihood and freedom. He knew he would be lucky if that was all he ended up losing.

The headphones crackled to life and Saadat could hear a phone ringing at the other end. After three rings, a voice spoke cautiously into his ear.

'Hello.'

'Afzal Enterprises?' he asked.

'*Ji haan.*'

'Achcha… Can I speak to Shahnawaz chacha?'

'Who's calling?'

'Murtaza from Karachi.'

'I'm afraid Shahnawaz chacha is asleep. He has a bad cold.'

'I see. Tea with ginger and cinnamon will do him good. Also a bit of Vicks massaged on the forehead.'

There was a moment's pause at the other end. Then the voice spoke.

'*Zara rukiye.* I think Shahnawaz chacha has woken up.'

His identity having been established through a chain of passwords, Saadat could hear a faint hum as his call was patched through to Colonel Mohan, somewhere in India. He was using Secure Voice over IP to file his report, and the connection was completely encrypted to defend against Pakistani packet sniffers. His conversation with the colonel was virtually unbreakable.

'*Boliye Saadat mian, sab khairiyat toh hai?*'

Saadat couldn't help scowling on hearing Colonel Mohan's voice. The man was hauling him to the slaughterhouse, yet he had the gall to enquire about his well-being.

'*Bas janaab, sab aap hi ki duaein hain,*' he answered, hoping that the sarcasm would hit home.

'Good. Now give me the news.' The colonel made no acknowledgement of the barb.

Saadat quickly briefed Colonel Mohan about his meeting with Shamsheer earlier in the day. He explained that he had had the captain transferred to the safe house, and had ensured that everything the captain needed had been placed at his disposal.

'Excellent. What about the computer that Rafiq will need? And the news van and the minibus?'

'All three have been tested and are ready, colonel sahib.'

'Weapons, ammunition, camera, laptop…?'

'Everything is ready.'

'Good. I assume the weapons, camera and laptop have been transferred to the apartment?'

'Huzoor.'

'I'm glad you found an apartment in time. I hope it is as good and safe as the first one.'

'It is. Your Imtiaz sahib shouldn't have any problem with this one.' There was a hint of sarcasm and disgruntlement in Saadat's response. After a pause, he asked, 'Waise, when are the other two expected here?'

'Rafiq reached Karachi a little while ago. I suppose he will get in touch with you tomorrow morning. Major Imtiaz is also making steady progress towards Karachi. He should also be establishing contact sometime tomorrow.'

'Okay. I shall call you tomorrow evening to give you an update.' Saadat was eager to terminate the conversation.

'One more thing,' Colonel Mohan said quickly.

'Yes?' Saadat's voice was strained with nervousness and exasperation.

'What is the general scene with the security in Karachi?'

Saadat wasn't sure what the colonel meant. 'You mean… the security in the city? You already have all the reports on the kind of arrangements the local police have…'

'No, no. That's not what I meant. I mean, have you sensed any change in these arrangements recently? Any sudden increase in patrolling or new roadblocks being put up, any signs of surveillance being stepped up?'

Saadat was silent for a while as he considered this.

'No… I haven't noticed anything out of the ordinary.'

'Are you certain?'

'Yes. But why do you ask?'

'I just want to be absolutely sure the Pakistanis aren't on to us, that's all.' After a slight pause, the colonel said, 'And you're positive that there are no changes in Dilawar's plans of coming to Karachi?'

'None that I have heard of,' Saadat answered a trifle wearily. 'Had there been any, I would already have told you, huzoor.'

'Fair enough. Call me tomorrow once Rafiq and Imtiaz are with you. *Khuda hafiz.*'

'*Khuda hafiz.*'

Ten minutes later, a Toyota Camry pulled out of the empty parking lot and turned into Fatima Jinnah Road. Saadat, sitting in its back seat, looked up at the Hotel Avari Towers, its huge glowing signage lighting up the face of one side wall. But for the cars entering and exiting the hotel's gates, the locality was devoid of activity. Even the Chinese fast food joint in the corner was shutting down for the night.

As the car approached the arterial Shara-e-Faisal connecting the city airport to downtown Karachi, Saadat peered out of the windows. There weren't any indications of increased police activity anywhere. Not yet.

24 July. ISI Headquarters, Khayaban-e-Suhrawardy, Islamabad

'I don't know whether to treat this as good news or bad.'

Lieutenant-General Rehmat stared across the table at Brigadier Razavi, Major-General Dar and Lieutenant-General Niazi, and it was hard to say if he was being sarcastic or whether he was simply stating a fact.

Less than a minute had elapsed since their conversation with Haider Nazir in India, but the silence that had prevailed ever since gave the impression of time having slowed to a crawl. The three junior officers fidgeted in their chairs, acutely aware of the tension smothering them in its heavy embrace.

'On the one hand, it is nice knowing that we have a little more information to work on. Very little, actually, but anything is better than nothing. We now know that we have to look for three Indian commandos who have crossed over to Pakistan to kill Dilawar.' The ISI director gave a theatrical pause as he surveyed the other three men.

'But what's appalling is that these men have already successfully entered Pakistan. That makes our job a lot harder. If we were not able to apprehend them when they were getting in, I'm afraid finding them inside Pakistan will prove to be a lot tougher. And honestly, the sloppiness we have displayed so far doesn't instil in me a lot of faith in our ability to ferret them out.'

A brief silence followed as the men digested the director's critique. At last, Major-General Dar spoke. 'It doesn't help that apart from a few basic facts, we have very little information to work on, sir.'

'That's right.' Lieutenant-General Niazi pounced at the chance to make a point. 'This Haider Nazir hasn't been particularly good at gathering information. All he's given us so far are some sketchy details. He can't even tell us from where and how these three Indians entered Pakistan.'

'Our agents are not trained to speculate idly,' Lieutenant-General Rehmat reminded his colleagues. 'They are trained to only pass on whatever information they have collected. That's the only way this business works the world over. Otherwise every country's intelligence would be running off on wild goose chases all the time. Haider has come across information that is obviously highly classified, so it is natural that we will have little to work on. Let's not make a scapegoat out of him.'

'You're right, sir,' acceded Major-General Dar. 'It's because of him that we know something of the plot to kill Dilawar. But the point is, what do we do next?'

'First, the police force across the country must be put on a state of high alert. They are to tap every source they have, check and recheck every little thing that looks mildly suspicious. Next, I want a directive issued to the Pakistan Telecommunication Company and all other private telecom operators to open their networks for the monitoring of all telephone conversations. Get our people hooked on to the networks immediately. If the Indians so much as sneeze over the phone, I want to know of it. I also want increased vigilance on all the Indian embassies and consulates in Pakistan, as well as on all businesses and organizations that are known to have dealt with or are dealing with India in some way or the other. Lastly, send out a communiqué to the Intelligence Bureau, Military Intelligence and the army to help wherever possible. Every bit of support would be welcome.'

'Right, sir,' said Major-General Dar. 'But I must add that when I spoke to a couple of army commanders yesterday, they told me that they are quite pressed themselves. The Americans are pushing against the Taliban and the al-Qaeda, and the army has apparently been asked to work with the American forces.'

'Nonsense!' snorted Lieutenant-General Niazi waspishly. 'Imagine helping these stupid Americans against our own people! Our government's policies are getting all warped. These civilians don't know a thing about what's good for Pakistan.'

Ignoring the retired veteran, Lieutenant-General Rehmat looked at Major-General Dar. 'I am aware that the army is dealing with other pressures, but let them know we would be happy to have their help, wherever possible.'

'I shall, sir. But I think it would be a good idea if you also spoke to some of the senior officers personally. That would carry more weight.'

Lieutenant-General Rehmat nodded in agreement and made a note in a small diary.

'Sir, wouldn't it also help if we told the Intelligence Bureau, the army and Military Intelligence about the exact nature of the threat? When they know who the Indians are targeting, they will see why it's important for them to help us.'

The director reflected on the proposal for a bit. 'You have a point, Dar sahib. Inform the Intelligence Bureau and Military Intelligence about the plot. But keep it from the army and the police. I don't want too many people getting to know of the details. As long as the intelligence guys know of it, they will put the necessary pressure on the army and the police.'

Major-General Dar nodded. There was a faraway expression on his face which showed that he was preoccupied with something.

'Sir, do you think Haider Nazir is right when he says that just three Indian commandos have entered Pakistan? You mentioned that if you were to mount such an operation, you'd pick a team of at least eight to ten men. Don't you think three men are too few for such a big job?'

'It is, and it bothers me too,' admitted Lieutenant-General Rehmat, his eyes narrowing suspiciously. 'I wonder if the Indians are actually sending two or maybe three different teams to carry out the assassination. It's logical. If we do bust one team, the other can still carry on. After all, if we catch one group, it is natural for us to drop our guard on the assumption that the plot has been foiled.'

The men shifted restively as this unsettling possibility took root.

'It means our job is a lot more complicated than we imagined,' said Major-

General Dar. 'We are like a blind man in a dark room looking for a black cat—when in reality, two black cats exist.'

'Black cats... That's what those NSG commandos are called in India. Though my suspicion is the chaps who have slipped in belong to the Marine Commandos. Either way, you are right. If we assume that there is more than one group of Indian commandos in Pakistan, our job just became that much harder.'

The director turned to Lieutenant-General Niazi, who was looking distinctly uncomfortable. 'I will not tell you what to do because you very well know what the situation demands. All I ask of you is to keep me posted on Irshad Dilawar's whereabouts. I personally think he is safest close to the Afghan border. Though I must add that in these times, safety is at best relative.'

'Janaab, I shall do everything to protect the man. Irshad Dilawar has done more to further Pakistan's interests than most. We have to keep him away from the Indians.'

Lieutenant-General Rehmat looked at the retired soldier, clearly understanding everything that was being implied.

'We will, Niazi sahib. You already have my word.'

25 July. Clifton, Karachi

The CNBC Pakistan news van was parked discreetly on a leafy side road, approximately three hundred metres from the palatial house adjacent to the Saudi Mosque. Traffic on the road was sporadic, and even the few passers-by barely took any notice of the van with the international news channel's multicoloured peacock logo emblazoned on its sides. There was nothing remotely novel about a news van belonging to a business channel in a financial hub like Karachi.

It was a different matter that the staffers at CNBC Pakistan's Karachi office would be hard-pressed to identify the two men inside it as their colleagues. For neither of the men had ever been to the news channel's Karachi headquarters located in the Techno City Corporate Tower. And as for the vehicle, before being modified into a news van a week earlier, it had served as a bus ferrying Pentagram Travels' patrons to and from the airport.

Shamsheer was sitting at the wheel reading a copy of *Daily Jang*, a slightly bored expression on his face as he idly turned its pages. He looked up distractedly every now and then, using the newspaper to drive away a pesky fly. A small Bluetooth headset adorned one of his ears, although the only connection it was capable of making was to the man in the van's trailer. A press card that dangled prominently around Shamsheer's neck proclaimed him to be a driver with CNBC Pakistan.

The ennui that manifested itself in the van's front was conspicuously absent in its covered trailer, where Rafiq sat hunched over a laptop, tapping furiously on its keys. Wires ran all over the trailer's floor, one set connecting the laptop to the antenna that thrust itself out of the van's roof, the other set linking the laptop to a small server. A camera and a few cables occupied the rest of the space, though they were completely useless except as props to lend authenticity to the news van.

'All okay outside?' Rafiq spoke into the mike that was connected to the headphones he had on.

'Yes, all clear,' he heard Shamsheer mumble back. 'Don't worry. You just focus on your job and make sure you download the right pictures.'

'*Pictures nahin, mian. Image files kahiye,*' Rafiq corrected, playful amusement showing in his voice.

'*Haan, haan, jo bhi,*' Shamsheer said indulgently. '*Bas Pamela Anderson ki tasveerein mat utaar lena. Nahin toh Major saab tumhaari kaafi kuch utaar lenge.*'

Rafiq merely laughed in reply, his eyes drawn to the images that had just appeared on the laptop's screen. They showed the insides of a house, captured using digital video cameras connected to a digital video recorder.

The images that Rafiq was viewing belonged to the house next to the Saudi Mosque, the one that Irshad Dilawar stayed in whenever he was in Karachi. And the images were being accessed from a server that lay somewhere inside the same house. Barely half an hour earlier, Rafiq had successfully hacked into the server, bypassed two fairly secure firewalls, and isolated ninety-three image files. He was now looking for sets of images that showed the house as it looked at night.

Rafiq methodically went through each stored file, seeking images from each and every one of the eight cameras installed inside and outside the house. He found MPEG-4 files of the gate, the walls and the open lawn, the front and back doors, the corridors and stairways inside, as well as those of individual rooms, including the one used for monitoring the video cameras. Many of the files had shots of security personnel and household staff moving around the house, but even though he looked hard, none seemed to have the man they had come to hunt down.

Making sure that he picked only those files which were recorded after midnight, Rafiq began downloading them on to the server in the van.

On the night of the attack, he would upload these images back on to the server in the house, and using customized software that he had partially developed, he would rig the system to display only these images on the monitors inside the house.

'It's fairly simple, as long as I am able to get the right images,' he had assured Imtiaz, Shamsheer and Colonel Mohan during one of the briefing sessions at Chandimandir Cantonment. 'If the images look the way the house would look at the time of the attack, those monitoring the video cameras won't be able to tell the difference and we can make our entry without being observed on camera.'

Of course, entry into the house would not be achievable without first disabling the intruder alarm systems which were installed along the high wall surrounding the house. And they also needed access codes to get past the many doors inside.

Disabling the alarms and getting the access codes were both jobs for Imtiaz, the former as late as on the morning of the day of the attack. As he watched the files download, Rafiq wondered what kind of progress the major had made with the latter.

25 July. Ancholi, Gulberg Town, Karachi

It was nearly eight o'clock when the city bus drew up to the bus stop near the junction of Shah Jehan Avenue and Samnabad Road. Six passengers got off the bus, Imtiaz being the last one to disembark. He stood back for a moment, courteously waiting for people to board the bus, before making his way forward. His eyes, though, rarely left the tall man who had got off the bus ahead of him. The man, who was in his late forties, had already started walking away from the bus stop. Leaving enough distance between him and his target, Imtiaz began tailing the man, careful not to lose him among other pedestrians, many of whom were returning home from work.

Imtiaz had been following the man ever since he had emerged from the gates blocking the entrance to the heavily-guarded house earlier in the day. From Clifton the man had first travelled to Firdous Colony in Liaquatabad Town, where he had visited a real estate broker. After nearly an hour, he headed for the nearest bus stop and caught a bus to Ancholi, where Imtiaz knew he lived. In fact, having reconnoitred the locality the previous evening, Imtiaz even knew which house the man stayed in.

According to the information provided by Saadat, the man's name was Ibrar Abidi, and he had been an ISI underling who had opted for voluntary retirement a couple of years earlier. Thereafter, he had somehow been put in charge of managing the safe house in Clifton, and from what Imtiaz understood, Abidi's role was that of a glorified housekeeper. Not that it really mattered to Imtiaz. As far as he was concerned, Abidi played a critical but very small part in this grand plan.

Abidi walked at a brisk pace and it soon became obvious to Imtiaz that the man was indeed homeward bound. As Abidi turned a corner into a side street, Imtiaz increased his pace. Reaching the corner, he spied Abidi walking down the road, but instead of following him, Imtiaz kept going straight till he reached a street running parallel to the one taken by Abidi. Imtiaz, who was virtually jogging by now, went down this street till he came to a quiet road that ran perpendicular to both the streets. Straight ahead was a fairly large park with huge trees running along its perimeter. The trees cast deep shadows on the far side of the road.

Picking his spot for the ambush, Imtiaz waited in the shelter afforded by the shadows. A minute passed before Abidi appeared at the end of the road. It was with both satisfaction and relief that Imtiaz watched him turn, cross the road and head his way. The road was deserted, except for a few cars that whizzed by.

When Abidi was roughly fifty metres away, Imtiaz stepped out of the shadows and began walking towards the man, his eyes carefully measuring the rapidly narrowing distance between the two of them. The two came face to face under a huge banyan tree, its roots hanging down and adding to the shadows cast by the sodium vapour street lamp overhead. Imtiaz had drawn a piece of paper from his pocket, and as he approached Abidi, he swerved towards the man, holding the paper out.

'Janaab, can you kindly tell me how to get to this address?'

It was the oldest trick in the book, and Abidi fell for it. Reaching for the piece of paper, he turned it towards the orange light. The address, scrawled untidily in Urdu, was that of a shop roughly two hundred metres away. Abidi promptly began giving directions, and Imtiaz followed them with some confusion, seeking clarifications now and then. His eyes surveyed the road for passers-by who could potentially interfere with his plan. Fortunately, the coast was clear.

Pretending to have grasped what Abidi had told him, Imtiaz took the paper back gratefully.

'*Shuqriya, janaab. Meherbaani aapki.*'

Abidi nodded, and the men turned to begin walking in opposite directions.

However, they had barely separated when Imtiaz turned, his body poised, his weight shifted to his left leg.

'Huzoor, one more thing…' he addressed Abidi from behind.

When Abidi turned, he fleetingly saw Imtiaz's right leg swinging upwards towards his face. He flinched and began raising his hands in defence, but it was too late. Imtiaz's foot landed on his jaw, the heavy boot smashing into his face, jerking his head back. Bolts of pain shot up the left side of his face, his knees buckled and he slumped forward, blood gushing out of his nose and split lips.

Imtiaz deftly caught Abidi before he hit the ground, his right hand grabbing the man's throat, his thumb ready to apply pressure on the windpipe at the first sign of resistance. There was none. Abidi had been knocked cold.

Imtiaz hauled his victim's limp form behind the banyan tree. He scanned the road once to check for any passers-by. Having ascertained that he wouldn't be observed, he took a pencil torch from his pocket and set to work.

He went through Abidi's shirt and trouser pockets, which yielded little besides a slightly dated Motorola mobile phone. Imtiaz switched the phone off and thrust it into his jacket pocket. He then turned the inert form on to its stomach and pulled Abidi's wallet free from his back pocket.

Opening the wallet, he quickly rifled through it. It held one thousand-rupee note and three five-hundred rupee notes, apart from quite a few notes of smaller denominations. Imtiaz stuffed all the money into the inside pocket of his jacket. He then checked the compartments that held plastic, and was immediately rewarded with the sight of a credit card. Peeking behind the credit card, Imtiaz saw another card made of hard plastic, having the same dimensions as that of the credit card. Pulling both cards free, he threw aside the credit card and the wallet.

The second card was plain, with just a picture of Abidi and the man's name and signature on its grey face. Imtiaz flipped the card around. Its back was much the same plain grey, except for the magnetic strip running horizontally across its top half. Imtiaz reached into his jacket and pulled out a portable access card reader. He pointed the reader to the magnetic strip, and the reader let out a short beep as the card's number registered on the reader.

Shoving the reader back into his jacket, he flung the card beside the wallet and the credit card. He then shone the torch on Abidi's right hand and two rings glinted dully in the yellow light. Imtiaz recognized one of them as being of gold, and he reached over and pried it free off the finger. He dropped the ring into his pocket, switched off the torch and stood up cautiously. Stepping out from behind the tree, he walked away, keeping as much to the shadows as possible.

Three minutes later, Imtiaz was crossing a huge, open ground, which he suspected was used for offering prayers. The ground was ringed with brightly lit shops, but its centre was dark. Halfway across the ground, Imtiaz reached into his jacket and pulled out Abidi's mobile phone. Ensuring he wasn't being observed, he flung the phone into the darkness in front of him.

He didn't need the phone. He didn't need the money or the gold ring he had taken from Abidi either. But the attack on Abidi had to look like a normal robbery, and no robber would be foolish enough to lose all his booty half a kilometre from the place of attack. And unlike the phone, the chances of the money and the ring being traced were less than minimal.

What Imtiaz had really wanted from Abidi was the access code to the house in Clifton. He hoped that the access card reader had read Abidi's card number properly, and that Rafiq would be able to decode the number rightly.

25 July. Fatima Jinnah Road, Karachi

'…done, major… I think phase… without a hitch and…'

Imtiaz pressed the headphones to his ears, straining to hear Colonel Mohan's voice. Saadat's darkened office inside Pentagram Travels was cloaked in sepulchral silence, yet the static in the air was drowning out much of what the colonel was saying. Imtiaz had disconnected and redialled the number twice, but on the third try he had given up, reconciling himself to listening to snatches of coherence over a sea of white noise.

'I'm sorry, sir. Can you repeat that?'

Extraordinarily enough, the colonel was able to hear him quite clearly, so Imtiaz had to consciously try and keep his voice down.

'I said, well done. You're on schedule and… sign of any problems.'

'No sign of any problems, sir. Thank you,' said Imtiaz, hoping he had understood the colonel.

'Good. What… recorded images… Rafiq manage getting…?'

'Yes, sir. Rafiq and Shamsheer got the images of the house this afternoon. Rafiq has already started picking the right ones and piecing them together in sequence for uploading.'

'…your part…'

Imtiaz winced as a particularly loud burst of static obliterated most of what Colonel Mohan had said. He instinctively leaned closer to the computer.

'I beg your pardon, sir, but I didn't get any of that.'

'…how did it…'

Saadat, who was seated next to Imtiaz wearing another set of headphones, pushed away from the table and shook his head in exasperation.

'I'm telling you, this is not working. There's a problem with the stupid connection.'

Saadat had been fretful ever since they had discovered that the static was making conversation difficult, and his expression clearly suggested that he would have liked Imtiaz to terminate the call so that they could clear out of his office.

Imtiaz took his headphones off and stared at Saadat with mounting irritation. 'I can see there's a problem, but the colonel can hear us. So let me talk, okay?'

As Saadat took refuge in grumpy silence, Imtiaz put the headphones back on.

'Sorry, sir. There is just too much disturbance on this side.'

'I can see that.' Colonel Mohan's voice came through in a surprising burst of clarity, his tone sardonic. 'Saadat mian seems quite pissed off with us, eh? Let him know that the more he cooperates, the sooner he will be rid of us.'

Saadat, who could hear what was being said, refused to respond to the rebuke. He just sat glowering at the PC's screen.

'Sir, you asked me something?'

'I asked whether you got the access card… of any use?'

'I got the access number, sir. Rafiq will decode it tomorrow.'

'Good. Major, I hope there… anywhere in Karachi? You might have…'

'Sorry, but what in Karachi?'

'Security, security… increase over the…'

'You're asking if there's an increase in security inside Karachi?'

'Yes.'

'Not that I have noticed. Just the usual, routine stuff… Everything appears normal here.'

Imtiaz raised his eyebrows at Saadat as if seeking an endorsement of his statement. Saadat merely nodded his head.

'Even Saadat hasn't noticed any change, sir.' Imtiaz added. 'Nothing out of the ordinary, I'd say.'

'…Clifton area?'

'Increased security in the vicinity of Clifton, sir?'

Whatever the colonel said was completely inaudible in the static. Imtiaz, who was also tiring of the conversation, assumed the colonel had answered in the affirmative.

'No, sir. Rafiq and Shamsheer didn't mention anything about it either. Shamsheer would definitely have observed such a thing.'

'That's nice.'

A brief, static-filled silence followed. Imtiaz, who wasn't sure if the colonel had posed a question, finally asked, 'Anything else, sir? Or is that all?'

'No, I… for now… me tomorrow… detailed progress… that clear?'

'I'll call you tomorrow with a full progress report, sir.'

A few minutes later, Imtiaz and Saadat quietly made their way out of the building and walked towards the lone Toyota Camry standing in the basement parking lot. It was ten past midnight, and apart from a stray cat that had been lying curled up at the foot of the stairs on the ground floor, they had encountered no living being.

Having disposed of his driver for the day, Saadat walked around the car and inserted the key into the door. As he slid behind the wheel, Saadat was—for probably the first time—relieved to see that there were no security guards lurking about the place. However, as they drove out of the parking lot, the car's headlights picked out a guard squinting at the moving car, trying to make out who its occupants were.

Saadat cursed violently. The guard would, in all probability, remember the car, and also recall that it was usually never found in the building's premises so late at night.

Imtiaz, who sensed that Saadat was highly strung, spoke softly.

'Relax. We won't be using your office from tomorrow.'

Saadat merely shook his head regretfully, gripped the steering-wheel tighter and looked straight ahead.

'*Yeh saraasar zyaati hai*,' he exploded suddenly. 'I do so much for the colonel, yet he treats me like shit. What if I get caught? *Woh mere janaaze pe maatam manaane aayenge kya?*' After a moment's pause, he mumbled in a self-chastising tone, 'I'm a fool to have fallen for this nonsense…'

As Saadat lapsed into silence, Imtiaz looked at him thoughtfully for a while. He then turned to stare out of the window as the car cruised down Ghazi Salahuddin Road, heading in a northwesterly direction towards the tenement in Paposh Nagar.

26 July. Chanakyapuri, New Delhi

The Toyota Corolla speeding down Ring Road was touching the 130 kmph-mark and could easily have attracted the attention of any Delhi Traffic Police unit stationed at hand. But Haider Nazir knew that the diplomatic plates and the Pakistani flag on the car's mast offered him considerable immunity.

There was also the minor matter of it being past three o'clock at night. Traffic on the Ring Road was at a minimum, and there were no traffic policemen patrolling the area.

The car slowed down marginally as it reached Moti Bagh, but as soon as he swung into Shanti Path, Nazir pressed the accelerator to the floor. His mind barely registered the line of embassies and consulates that lay on both sides of the wide avenue, all his faculties focused on the call he had received from his contact half an hour earlier.

He finally had something concrete for his bosses to work on. Islamabad would be pleased with him.

Once the Corolla entered the gates of the High Commission of Pakistan, Nazir parked quickly and almost jogged towards his office, a corner room on the first floor of the building. Entering his office, he bolted the door, ran to his desk and pulled out a Thuraya SO-2510 sat-phone from the bottom drawer. He punched in a code before dialling a number.

'Echo Oscar one, receiving.'

'Three eighty November, reporting, sir.'

'Proceed with your report.'

'It's about the planned attack on Irshad Dilawar, sir.'

'Okay. What's the update?'

Nazir drew a deep breath, savouring the moment. 'The three Indian commandos who have entered Pakistan, sir... At this moment, all three of them are in Karachi.'

CHAPTER 7

26 July. ISI Headquarters, Khayaban-e-Suhrawardy, Islamabad

Lieutenant-General Rehmat glared at Lieutenant-General Niazi, his face flushed with anger.

'For the last *five* days we have been sitting in this room and running around in circles over this planned attack. But not once, not *once*, did you utter a word about the fact that Irshad Dilawar is scheduled to go to Karachi tomorrow. This, despite my repeated requests to keep me updated on everything. Had it not been for Haider Nazir's call informing us that the Indians are planning to get him in Karachi, I and General Dar would have been oblivious to everything, right?'

Lieutenant-General Niazi squirmed uncomfortably in his chair. '*Aisi baat nahin hai, Tauseef mian...* I was about to tell you about it.'

'Now why would you have bothered? After all, you have independently taken the decision to clear this trip to Karachi.'

'He needs to go to Karachi for a business meeting,' the retired general mumbled. 'He'll be there only for two-three days, so I figured it fitted in nicely with our plan of moving him around the country.'

'It also fits in nicely with the Indian plan of attacking him there,' the director muttered through clenched teeth. He paused, then threw up his hands in exasperation. 'Imagine, the Indians know where Irshad Dilawar will be tomorrow, but the director of the ISI doesn't. *Subhan'Allah, kya security hai hamaari!*'

Lieutenant-General Niazi stared down at his clasped hands and said nothing. The director leaned forward and propped his elbows on the table.

'Thanks to your cavalier attitude, this could end up as the biggest fuck-up in our careers. You have retired and have little to lose, but Dar *sahib* and I are still in service. Don't jeopardize our careers because of your arrogance and stupidity.'

The awkward silence that followed was broken by a discreet knock on the door. The director took a sip of water from the glass resting near his elbow and composed himself as the door opened to admit Major-General Dar and Brigadier Razavi. The director hurriedly motioned both men to their chairs.

'So what more do you have on this?'

Major-General Dar cleared his throat, a serious expression on his large leathery face. 'Sir, we have received confirmation that the server in the house at Clifton was hacked into yesterday afternoon, and copies were made of seventeen MPEG-4 files of the video camera recordings stored in the server.'

'Copies were made of video camera recordings?'

'Yes, sir, CCTV images. All the copied files were of video recordings of the house at night.'

'Somebody wants to see what the house looks like at night,' Lieutenant-General Rehmat heaved a sigh and frowned.

'Sir, our tech guys are already on the job of trying to trace the IP connection that was used to breach the system and locate the exact spot from where the system was hacked.'

'Okay, but if you ask me, I don't think that will get us far,' Lieutenant-General Rehmat sounded tired. 'I suspect the Indians used some sort of a mobile platform, maybe a car of some sort, and a one-time-use connection and a dispensable computer to hack into the server. While I'm hoping they slipped up somewhere, it is unlikely they would have left a clear trail of any sort. Anything else?'

'Yes, sir.' Major-General Dar's expression turned a shade gloomier. 'We don't know if there is a connection here, but the manager of the Clifton house was attacked not very far from his home in Ancholi last night.'

'Ibrar Abidi?' Lieutenant-General Niazi raised his eyebrows. 'Who attacked him? What would anyone want from Ibrar? He's an insignificant housekeeper.'

Major-General Dar shrugged. 'All Abidi can say is that he was attacked by a stranger—who knocked him unconscious.'

'Oh!' The director considered this, before adding doubtfully, 'It could have been anyone. Some personal enmity, a robber...'

'The attack looks like a mugging with the motive of robbery,' Major-General Dar conceded. 'His mobile phone was taken, and some money and jewellery, nothing else. But the doctor who treated him says that the nature of the injuries Abidi has sustained points to a level of professional training that most normal robbers aren't exposed to.'

'Strange. But putting two and two together, I am inclined to believe that we have a situation on our hands.' The head spook fixed a cold eye on Lieutenant-General Niazi, and the latter quailed in his seat.

'Kyun Niazi sahib, you see the problem here? So much has happened and you did nothing to inform us about this Karachi trip. Please don't treat Dilawar's security as your personal fiefdom. It's our collective responsibility to protect the man.'

'*Ji janaab*,' the other man said weakly, dropping his eyes.

Lieutenant-General Rehmat looked at the three glum faces around him. He realized that he couldn't afford to have his men feeling dejected.

'Three Indian commandos don't have much of a chance against the kind of forces we can marshal,' he said, forcing brisk confidence into his voice. 'And we must remember that we now know exactly where they are and what their plan is. That gives us a distinct edge.'

He turned to Brigadier Razavi. 'I want you to call the Inspector General of Sindh Police...' He paused and looked at Major-General Dar. 'Is Baba Gafoor still the IG of Sindh?'

'He is, sir.'

'Good. So inform Gafoor about this business. I want you to impress upon him the fact that the threat to our security is very real. I want roadblocks set up on all roads leading into Karachi from Jamshoro and Thatta districts. Attention has to be paid to all vehicles entering and exiting the city. Ask him to start monitoring railway stations as well, and set up checkpoints along all the highways. Also tell him that I have specifically requested him to speak to the police commissioner of Karachi about the threat.'

'Yes, sir.' The brigadier was about to rise from his chair, but the director waved him down.

'Wait, I'm not done. Next, inform the coast guards to keep a sharp eye out for any suspicious boats in and around Karachi. Extra caution must be paid to all speedboats and high performance rigid-inflatable boats docked or moored in the vicinity of Karachi. Then inform all the telecommunication companies that we expect their continued cooperation in monitoring all telephone conversations on their networks. And inform our monitoring department to now focus on Karachi alone.'

'Yes sir.' Brigadier Razavi looked expectantly at the director to issue more orders.

'Now don't just sit there, young man. Go!'

Once the brigadier had left the room, Lieutenant-General Rehmat pressed the red button on the black two-speaker phone on his table. Immediately, a subaltern came on the line.

'Huzoor.'

'Get me Karachi CCPO Qasim Raja on the line.'

26 July. Clifton, Karachi

Shamsheer was the first to notice the car.

He was sitting on the sidewalk next to the ambulance, idly observing the road leading up to the house when the car caught his attention. It was a dark brown Suzuki Cultus, well past its best years. There was nothing remarkable about the car itself, but the manner in which it was being driven down the road got Shamsheer's antennae up.

Forty-five minutes earlier, he and Rafiq had driven the ambulance down the road when, a hundred metres from the house, they had conveniently discovered that the vehicle had a flat. They had pulled the ambulance over to the curb, taken out the jack and the spanners, and set to work changing the tyre. However, halfway through the job, they had found that the spare tyre was faulty as well.

Rafiq had hailed a passing cab and left to get the two tyres repaired, leaving the broken-down ambulance under Shamsheer's supervision. Rafiq would not return for another hour-and-a-half, giving Shamsheer ample opportunity to keep a watch on the house without raising any suspicions. By the time the ambulance was once again roadworthy, Imtiaz would have taken over the vigil.

Shamsheer was smoking his second cigarette when the Cultus went by slowly. He barely noticed it at first, the road being fairly busy with a steady stream of cars, buses and two-wheelers. However, when he glanced towards the house, Shamsheer sensed that this particular car had almost slowed down to a crawl in front of the house's gate, before gathering speed once again and disappearing round the bend. There really wasn't much to it, but some tiny bell sounded an alarm in his mind.

Nothing happened for the next ten minutes and Shamsheer had virtually forgotten about the car when he saw it reappear and make its way back down the road. Just as it passed the house, he again felt it decelerate a bit.

Shamsheer walked over to the driver's side of the ambulance, opened the door and pulled out a rag from under the seat. Closing the door, he began dusting and cleaning the ambulance, pretending to put the time he had in his hands to good use. As the Cultus approached the ambulance, Shamsheer casually glanced at it before returning to his chore.

That one glance had been enough for him to read the car's licence plate and memorize the licence number.

For a couple of minutes Shamsheer kept up his pretence, giving the ambulance a vigorous rubdown. Not that the vehicle needed one. Its life as an ambulance for the non-existent Pakistan Aid & Relief Fund was anyway going to be short-lived. By the end of the day, the revolving blue light on its roof, and the 'PAARF' and 'AMBULANCE' stickers adorning its body would have been removed, its false licence plates replaced. By the next morning, the vehicle would once again be just another minibus plying on Karachi's roads.

Having cleaned the ambulance to his satisfaction, Shamsheer got back into the driver's seat and plugged in a Walkman. As he pressed the 'play' button, his eyes switched between the far end of the road, where the Cultus had turned off, and the rear-view mirrors, which afforded him a view of the house.

Before the first song ended, the Cultus swung back into view. Restraining the instinct to stare at the approaching car, Shamsheer closed his eyes and swayed his head, as if locked in a state of trance. But through the slits of his eyes, he carefully watched the car.

The Cultus was almost upon the ambulance when Shamsheer opened his eyes and looked at it, his expression one of vapid curiosity. From where he sat, he could see the driver and the man riding shotgun. The driver was a gaunt man of about forty, with a thin moustache and a pointed goatee. He resembled a ghoul in some fairy tale.

It was the other man, however, who made a stronger impression on Shamsheer. There was something chillingly barbaric about the man's face, and his cold eyes were focused straight ahead, probably on the gates of the house. Shamsheer also took in the man's swarthy, bearded face, atop which sat a black qaraqul, the hair under it cropped very close.

On the back seat of the small car, Shamsheer was able to make out the dark shapes of two more men, but he couldn't make out their features. As the Cultus swept by, he tried to look into its back seat, but the car's tinted side windows were rolled up. Shamsheer resisted the urge to turn around and take a peek at the car's rear windows.

Instead, he watched the rear-view mirrors of the ambulance carefully. The Cultus went up the road at a steady pace, but just as it neared the house, it slowed down imperceptibly. In fact, had he not been anticipating the drop in the car's speed, Shamsheer was certain he would have failed to notice it. Unless someone in the house had also observed the car doing its pendulum-like transit on the road, no one would have found anything amiss about it.

Once the car crossed the house, it gathered speed and disappeared round the corner. That was the last Shamsheer saw of the Cultus.

26 July. ISI Headquarters, Khayaban-e-Suhrawardy, Islamabad

'It is imperative for us to capture these Indian commandos, so I want you to launch a manhunt in Karachi right away, Raja sahib.' Lieutenant-General Rehmat delivered his instructions in an even, clear voice. 'Mobilize thorough search operations across the city, question anyone moving around suspiciously. Anyone who cannot provide satisfactory bona fides is to be apprehended immediately. But let me warn you that the Indians may be armed, so let your men be prepared to shoot if necessary. Though, personally, I would like at least one of them being taken alive. Am I clear?'

'Yes sir.'

Karachi CCPO Qasim Raja had been at his obsequious best all through the conversation, yet the lieutenant-general believed he'd detected a hint of hesitation in the police commissioner's reply.

'So I understand that you shall deploy your police force to the singular task of nailing the Indians hiding in your city. And I have your assurance that your men will be up to this task.'

The way the two statements had been put left hardly any scope for negotiation, but the lieutenant-general decided to leave zero room for manoeuvre or misinterpretation. 'I must add that even the slightest bit of slackness on the part of the police force will be dealt with severely,' he added bluntly.

'Well, sir...actually...there's a small problem,' Commissioner Raja sounded genuinely apologetic.

'Problems are what policemen are trained to deal with,' said the director with growing irritation.

'Yes, sir. Absolutely. I agree, sir,' the policeman's words came out in a tumble. 'It's just that my force is already stretched to the limit and almost all my men are already working round the clock. I don't have enough men to spare, and I don't see the situation improving over the next two days, sir.'

'Why's that?' the lieutenant-general asked sharply.

'Sir, I'm sure you know about the MQM rally that's happening in Karachi the day after. We estimate that some seventy to eighty thousand MQM party workers and supporters will be attending the rally, many of whom will be travelling to Karachi from other parts of Sindh. My men are already neck deep in work, maintaining law and order and ensuring that there's adequate security in Karachi till the rally ends. You know how bad things are these days.'

Lieutenant-General Rehmat sighed. He knew exactly how bad things were, and he suddenly understood the police chief's predicament. Political rivalries in Pakistan had always been bloody affairs, but of late, the violence had taken a particularly severe turn, with ruthless vendetta killings of politicians and party workers becoming increasingly common. Karachi was one of the worst affected, with the rivalry between the MQM, the PPP and the ANP spiralling into drive-by shootings, assassinations and riots. Just last month, in the wake of a huge rally organized by the PPP, thirty-six people had been killed in Karachi, the bulk of them MQM workers. The upcoming rally could present MQM supporters with an opportunity to unleash a round of reprisals.

'I know what you mean and I appreciate the fact that your hands are full with keeping Karachi secure. But I must insist that getting the Indian commandos is high priority as well. They are as much a threat to Karachi's security.'

'Yes sir.' Qasim Raja's voice lacked conviction, and the lieutenant-general paused, as if making up his mind about something.

'Okay, I shall speak to Inspector General Gafoor and ask him to send additional police forces from Jamshoro and Thatta as backup for your men. And I'll get the Sindh Rangers to allocate more men to Karachi. They can help with the rally. But I will need you to divert some of your forces into hunting down the Indians. Your men know Karachi like the back of their hands; the Rangers and the cops from Jamshoro and Thatta don't.'

'Sure, sir,' Raja sounded relieved. 'As long as I have enough policemen for the rally, there won't be a problem deputing some of my men to go after the Indians. I shall start work on this immediately, sir.'

The director disconnected the call and looked at the two men across the table. Major-General Dar grimaced and shook his head.

'These rallies will be the end of Pakistan… The hunt for the Indian commandos is bound to get hampered.'

Lieutenant-General Rehmat nodded. The more he thought about it, the more he was convinced that their best bet of nabbing the Indians was when the commandos attacked the house. And that had given him an idea.

'Let us go through the security arrangements at the Clifton house. I want you to ask our tech guys to monitor the server in the house round-the-clock for any more breaches. I don't think the Indians will try and hack into it again, but if they do, I want us to know of it in thirty seconds flat. And Qasim Raja and his men should know of it in the next thirty, so that they can swoop down on the Indians. Next, I want an immediate increase in the number of security personnel guarding the house, and I want better surveillance of the area around the house.'

Lieutenant-General Niazi, who had been sitting quiet as a dormouse, looked at the director curiously. 'Surely we aren't going to let Dilawar go anywhere near that house, are we?'

The lieutenant-general stared evenly at the retired officer, his gaunt face showing no emotion.

'Now that you're once again concerned about his security, the answer is no. Forget the house, we aren't letting Dilawar go anywhere near Karachi. I don't care how important this business meeting might be, I want you to cancel all his engagements in Karachi right now. Dilawar is not to venture anywhere out of Parachinar. Do I make myself clear, Niazi sahib?'

The retired general, who was staring absent-mindedly in front of him, started and nodded. 'Yes, yes. But then why are we increasing security and surveillance at Clifton?'

'Because the Indians don't know that Dilawar will not be coming to Karachi. They must stay under the impression that everything is going according to plan. The additional security at Clifton will be proof of that.' As he spoke, a wicked gleam appeared in the director's eyes. 'In fact, I want you to send Dilawar's limousine along with a full security motorcade to the house tomorrow, as per schedule. I'm sure the Indians will be watching the house—let them believe that their target has reached Karachi.'

'This is good,' Major-General Dar beamed brightly for the first time since morning. Turning to Lieutenant-General Niazi, he asked, 'For how many days was Dilawar supposed to be in Karachi?'

'Three.'

'And was he scheduled to leave the house anytime during those three days?'

'No. All his meetings were to be at the house.'

'Okay. That means we will also have to ensure that the house receives dummy visitors and guests during those three days.'

'Wonderful, Dar sahib.' Lieutenant-General Rehmat liked the way the idea was catching on, sparking reactions all around. He rubbed his hands and looked at the two men.

'The Indians are bound to make a move in the next three days. Let us set a perfect trap and invite them into our little parlour. Let us give them such a welcome that the thought of such misadventures never occurs to them again.'

26 July. Sector E-7, Islamabad

Lieutenant-General Wajid Ali Khan Niazi stared at the green slopes of the Margalla Hills through the heavy drizzle. He was standing at a large bay window on the first floor of his palatial bungalow in what was one of the toniest localities in Islamabad. To the left, the thin, pencil-shaped minarets of the Faisal Mosque could be seen through the trees, while somewhere to the right, high in the hills, nestled the picturesque Daman-e-Koh.

The retired officer had neither inherited nor married into old money, which could have explained a bungalow of this size in a locality such as this one. And ordinary military men simply didn't pull in enough every month to be able to afford houses like this. But then, Lieutenant-General Niazi wasn't an ordinary military man—even though he had started his career as one.

Life for the lieutenant-general had changed the day US President Jimmy Carter had taken an executive decision to bankroll the Afghan mujahedeen in their war against the Soviet Army. The US had relied extensively on the ISI to distribute funds to the Afghan resistance, and small but significant portions of this money had slipped through the cracks—straight into the pockets of men like Lieutenant-General Niazi.

To be fair to the lieutenant-general, despite siphoning off their money, he had given back to the Americans in spades. As one of the lynchpins of the ISI during Operation Cyclone, Lieutenant-General Niazi had helped the Americans set up and run recruitment and training camps on both sides of the Afghan–Pakistan border. He had also worked closely with CIA officers in distributing weapons to the mujahedeen, and training them for use against the occupying Soviets.

That was how Lieutenant-General Niazi had first met Zeb Kirkland in Peshawar.

The lieutenant-general and the CIA operations officer shared a common interest in making money on the sly, and soon they were diverting weapons meant for the mujahedeen into the illegal arms trade. This brought Lieutenant-General Niazi into contact with Musa Zawawi, who shipped illegal arms across the Middle East and Africa.

It was around this time that the CIA came up with the clever but twisted idea of using drug money to finance the mujahedeen. The hills in Afghanistan were conducive for cultivating and processing heroin, which had a huge and lucrative market the world over. All that was needed was a conduit to smuggle the contraband.

Lieutenant-General Niazi, who was part of this secret plan, had come to know of Mumbai-based gangster Irshad Dilawar whose underworld network was rapidly expanding into the Gulf and Europe. In less than a month, the CIA, the ISI and Irshad Dilawar had entered a pact whereby Dilawar's network would smuggle and distribute the heroin that the Americans had produced in Afghanistan.

Over the years, the business association between Dilawar and Lieutenant-General Niazi had blossomed into a thick friendship, and when the gangster had fled India and sought refuge in Pakistan, the lieutenant-general had lobbied hard with the Pakistani government and the army to grant Dilawar asylum. And once he'd retired, Lieutenant-General Niazi had been the obvious choice for overseeing his friend's security.

But all that had changed following the al-Qaeda's 11 September attack on the USA.

Overnight, Osama bin Laden became the most wanted man on the planet, and everyone associated with him was immediately downgraded to pariah status. This included Irshad Dilawar. And as if that wasn't bad enough, murmurs that the American government may be sympathetic to India's demand to have Dilawar extradited for trial surfaced in Islamabad and Washington.

'You people have to protect me. If I fall into Indian hands, I swear I won't go down alone. I will expose every one of you and tell the world everything that you guys and the CIA did in Afghanistan. *Aap meri baat samajh rahein hain na, Wajid mian?*'

As he stood watching the rain clouds amass on the tops of the Margalla Hills, Lieutenant-General Niazi recalled the threat that Dilawar had issued eight months ago. The lieutenant-general had immediately spoken to a couple of his trusted friends in the Pakistani Army and the ISI—people who had a lot to lose if Dilawar carried out his threat. Zeb Kirkland, in the meantime, had sounded off some of his equally vulnerable bosses in the CIA.

Together, they had come to the conclusion that there was no guarantee that the Pakistani government would not crumble under sustained US pressure and agree to turn Dilawar over to the Indians. And in the absence of such a guarantee, the only option left was to eliminate Irshad Dilawar.

Lieutenant-General Niazi reached into his pocket, pulled out a Thuraya sat-phone and dialled a number. The phone rang just once before it was answered, Zawawi's shrill, nasal voice echoing in the lieutenant-general's ear.

'*As-salāmu alaikum, Loya sahib.*'

No one remembered exactly how Lieutenant-General Niazi had got the name Loya Pathan, but it probably had its genesis in one of the mujahedeen training camps that the soldier had helped set up in the hills around Zhawar in the early 1980s. The hardworking, Soviet-hating Pakistani officer had clearly caught the imagination of the Afghan cadre, and someone had decided to term him the 'grand Pathan'. The nickname had stuck, and those who knew him from those days continued to address him by that name.

'Musa, we have a problem again. Irshad Dilawar is not going to Karachi.'

'What the hell!' Zawawi sounded incredulous and exasperated. 'What's happening there?'

Lieutenant-General Niazi briefly told Zawawi about all that had come to light since that morning. The Algerian listened quietly, and when the lieutenant-general had finished, he cursed effusively.

'These bloody Indians have screwed up everything!' After a pause, he asked, 'Now what are we to do?'

'We need to think. But first, Hossam has to be told about this. He mustn't attack the house in Clifton. It's too dangerous, and it'll also be useless.'

'I can't do that.'

'What do you mean you can't do that?' the lieutenant-general demanded irritably.

'I can't get in touch with Hossam. He insisted that he shouldn't be contacted.'

'What nonsense is this?' Lieutenant-General Niazi could feel the anger mounting. 'You got in touch with him the last time...'

'I got in touch with my man in Nushki, and he gave Hossam the information. Once you and Mr Kirkland had cleared Karachi, I gave Hossam and his men the green signal to leave Nushki. Now, there's no way I can contact him.'

The lieutenant-general's heart sank. 'Oh, damn!'

'Have you spoken to Mr Kirkland about this yet?'

'No.' The soldier had hoped he could activate damage control before calling the CIA man.

'You should call him, Loya sahib. He would want to know about this.' Lieutenant-General Niazi sensed a hint of schadenfreude in Zawawi's tone. 'When you do, tell him that while Mali was my mistake, I have nothing to do with this goof-up of yours. *Ma'a-as-salāma*.'

Disconnecting the call, the lieutenant-general looked out of the window gloomily. He didn't relish the prospect of talking to Zeb Kirkland.

26 July. Astoria Gardens, Clifton, Karachi

Had the heavy velvet drapes not been drawn across the big windows, Shamsheer would have been accorded one of the most stunning views of downtown Karachi. The room he was in was huge, its south-facing windows, nineteen storeys high, overlooking a broad swathe of Clifton and the Arabian Sea beyond. Of course, the waters of the bay were now in darkness, but the twinkling lights of Clifton stretching away on both sides would still have been immensely pleasing to the eye.

The Indians, however, hadn't opened the drapes even once since the time they had stepped into the apartment earlier that evening. They had been chauffeur-driven through the gates of the posh Astoria Gardens in a Lexus RX 300, and when they had marched into the building's marble-and-glass lobby, their appearance and manner was that of globetrotting corporate executives—a dramatic makeover from the proletarian look they had sported in the middle-income neighbourhood of Paposh Nagar.

'For the first two days you'll stay in a working-class locality far from Clifton,' the colonel had explained back in Panchkula. 'You'll then be moved to an upmarket apartment close to Dilawar's safe house. This will give you better cover as it'll be hard for anyone to connect you guys to two places diametrically opposite to one another.'

The 3,500-square-foot apartment—which belonged to a non-resident Pakistani eye surgeon and had been leased by Jahangir Shipping for its guests from overseas—was ideal for Project Abhimanyu on three accounts. Astoria Gardens was barely 150 metres from the safe house which, from the accessibility point of view, would be critical on the day of the attack. Then, many apartments in Astoria Gardens had been leased out to multinational companies and the crowd that inhabited the complex was multi-ethnic, cosmopolitan and transitory in nature: new faces would hardly trigger neighbourly curiosity. The third and perhaps most important reason was that an apartment complex for the uber-rich was unlikely to be seen as a potential sanctuary for the Indian commandos.

'Masha'Allah, one can do so much with money! Honestly, I didn't want to get out of the Jacuzzi.'

Shamsheer, who was lounging on a white leather sofa, looked up at Rafiq. The lieutenant had walked into the sprawling drawing room clad in a pair of bright pink Bermudas and a black Iron Maiden T-shirt, his bare feet leaving a trail of wet prints on the white marble floor.

Staring at the opulence around him appreciatively, Rafiq walked over to the wall unit that housed a large plasma-screen Panasonic. A mantelpiece had been built into the wall unit, and on it were rows and rows of Swarovski crystals in various flower motifs. Scarlet poinsettias, wine red roses, deep blue forget-me-nots...

Reaching up, Rafiq gently lifted a purple geranium crystal out and turned it in his hands, marvelling at the exquisite craftsmanship. 'Amazing, yaar! *Kya banaate hain!*'

'Careful you don't drop it,' cautioned Shamsheer, glancing at his watch and rising from the sofa. 'Those things look damn expensive.' The captain called Rafiq over his shoulder. 'Come on... Major saab and Saadat are waiting. It's time to get in touch with Colonel Mohan.'

Inside one of the four spacious bedrooms, Imtiaz and Saadat sat at a table on which a computer had been rigged. Both men were wearing headphones, and as Shamsheer and Rafiq walked in, Imtiaz began dialling the colonel's number using Secure VoIP. Shamsheer and Rafiq picked up the two spare headphones lying on the table and put them on.

It took a minute for the connection to get through, and a couple more for them to confirm their identity through a password chain, before Colonel Mohan finally came on the line.

'Hello, Major. I hope you can hear me clearly today.'

'I can, sir. Very clearly.'

'Good. Yesterday was such a pain.'

'Yes, sir.'

There was a moment's pause. Then Colonel Mohan spoke again, 'Okay, so all of you have reached Clifton, I see.'

'Yes, sir.'

'Good. I hope the apartment is comfortable and fits your requirements?'

'It does, sir. Everything is in order and all the necessary arrangements have been made.' As an afterthought, Imtiaz added, 'All thanks to Saadat, sir.'

'Excellent.' The colonel took his cue from Imtiaz. 'Thank you so much for taking such good care of my men, Saadat mian.'

Imtiaz could sense Saadat straightening in his chair in response to the appreciation. 'Don't mention it, colonel sahib. They are my guests, and I'm only fulfilling my duty as a host.'

'Ah, that's why you made them stay in that hellhole in Paposh Nagar for two days.' Colonel Mohan chuckled, the humour in his voice unmistakable.

Seeing the others smile, Saadat laughed softly. 'Huzoor, I was merely following your orders. But they will agree that even there, I took as good care of them as possible.'

As everyone nodded and murmured their consent, the colonel sensed that the mood had lightened up. 'Chalo, it's good that everyone's happy. Now, what do you have to report?'

The conversation immediately turned businesslike. The colonel was pleased to hear that Rafiq had decoded the door access number obtained from Ibrar Abidi's access card, and that he had managed to stitch together the images that were to be uploaded back on to the server in the house.

'We're good to go once I've disabled the intruder alarm systems installed on the compound wall of the house. As planned, I'll do that on the morning of the day after, sir.'

'And you are putting up the camera tomorrow morning, right?'

'Yes sir. Early tomorrow morning,' replied Imtiaz.

'Do that. You won't be able to keep up physical surveillance of the house for much longer. I am sure security will be tightened around the house very soon. Speaking of security, do we have a final confirmation of Dilawar's arrival in Karachi tomorrow?'

Imtiaz turned to Saadat and raised an eyebrow.

'Yes, colonel sahib. I checked with my sources just two hours ago. They tell me that your man will arrive in Karachi tomorrow, as per schedule.'

'Are you absolutely sure of this?'

Imtiaz wasn't certain but he felt he heard an uncharacteristic strain in the colonel's voice.

'Well... No one can be absolutely sure until he actually arrives in the house,' said Saadat evenly. 'But my sources report that his trip is on schedule, which makes me reasonably sure.'

'That's fine then,' Colonel Mohan said abruptly.

There was a hiatus in the conversation and Imtiaz took advantage of it. 'Sir, there is one more thing to report. It may not be of any consequence, but I think it is important enough that you know.'

'Yes, Major?'

'This morning, when Shamsheer was keeping a vigil on the house, he happened to notice a car that was moving around the house in a suspicious manner.'

'Yes?' the colonel's voice rose, signalling his alertness and interest.

Shamsheer once again narrated the entire Suzuki Cultus episode, even going to the extent of describing the car's driver and the co-passenger to the best of his ability. Colonel Mohan listened to the account quietly, and when Shamsheer had finished, he was silent for a while.

'Sir, I have requested Saadat mian to try and help us in this, and he is already on the job,' said Imtiaz guardedly.

Ji huzoor, added Saadat, his voice now animated and eager to help. 'I have already put a call to a contact of mine in the transport registration department to try and trace the car's owner. Unfortunately, by the time I called him, he had left his office for the day, so he will be able to check and let me know only tomorrow morning. I shall let you and Imtiaz sahib know the moment I have something concrete.'

'Very good, Saadat,' the colonel spoke at last. 'We can only hope the license plates weren't fake.'

'Do you think this is important, sir?' asked Imtiaz.

'I don't know...' Colonel Mohan replied thoughtfully.

'I do think it strange that we have another carload of men doing a reconnaissance of the house exactly one day before Dilawar's arrival,' said Imtiaz. 'Also, the way Shamsheer describes the men in the car, it doesn't look like they were idle tourists. My gut tells me this can't be sheer coincidence. There's something going on.'

'You may be right, but it might be nothing very big either. I think you chaps just stay focused on the job ahead and don't worry too much. Anyway tomorrow we'll hopefully know more about the car's owner as well.'

'Right, sir. We shall talk again tomorrow.'

Once the call had been disconnected, Shamsheer, Rafiq and Saadat filed out of the room. It was well past dinner time and the rich aroma of Peshawari chicken filled the apartment. But Imtiaz's mind was not on dinner—it was on the Suzuki Cultus that Shamsheer had observed. He couldn't say why, but he knew that the men in the Cultus spelt trouble.

CHAPTER 8

27 July. Clifton, Karachi

The sun had been up in the sky for nearly three hours, but the roads around Astoria Gardens were still pretty much free of traffic. A few cars were pulling out of apartment complexes, and the odd school bus could be seen threading its way forward, but that apart, it didn't look like this part of Karachi was in any mood to jump-start another frenetic day of activity.

Imtiaz soaked in the morning calm as he cycled along the treelined avenue at a leisurely pace. Half a kilometre down the road was the safe house that he, Shamsheer and Rafiq were set to storm the next day, but looking at Imtiaz's nonchalance, no one could have guessed what was going through the major's mind.

As he rounded a bend and the safe house came into view, Imtiaz scanned the road intently for signs of security personnel. Except for a teenager walking two Labradors and a man carrying a pail of water and a scrubbing cloth towards a line of cars parked along the kerb, the road was empty. Imtiaz cycled past them, but roughly seventy metres from the house, not far from the point where Shamsheer had observed the Suzuki Cultus, he came to a halt.

Dismounting from his cycle, he lifted it onto the sidewalk and wheeled it to the base of three huge hoardings that stood at the edge of the road. Taking a toolbag from the cycle's carrier, he looked up at the hoardings.

One of the challenges that the commandos had been confronted with was finding a way of keeping round-the-clock vigil on the safe house before launching their attack. Mounting twenty-four-hour physical surveillance had been out of the question, and the solution had to involve the use of technology. Rafiq, expectedly, had come up with the answer.

Imtiaz studied the three hoardings briefly. The one to the extreme left had been rejected by Rafiq as being unsuitable for the task. The one in the middle was for a Nokia phone, while the third was an ad for Lux soap, featuring the huge, smiling face of Pakistani actress Reema. Rafiq had okayed the Nokia and Lux hoardings, but on making a few phone calls, Saadat had discovered that the contract on the former had expired, which made it a liability. The latter, however, was not due for renewal for another forty days, which meant that the company owning the hoarding was unlikely to check on it. Not in the next two days, at least. That was all the time they needed.

Imtiaz, who was wearing a soiled brown T-shirt with the logo of SIGNature, a hoarding company, printed on the sleeve and back, began climbing the hoarding's scaffolding. With the toolbag slung over his shoulder, he looked like an employee of SIGNature entrusted with the routine maintenance of the hoarding.

At the top, he harnessed himself to the scaffolding using a thick cable. He reached into his toolbag, produced a screwdriver-cum-tester and began checking the lamps above the hoarding, one by one. As he worked, he kept a watch on the road below and the gate of the safe house. He just hoped that some genuine employee from SIGNature didn't happen to pass by and notice him.

Having reached the end of the hoarding, Imtiaz slowly slid behind it. Propping himself carefully, he pulled out a camera from the toolbag. He didn't know much about technology nor did he care, but from what Rafiq had told him, Imtiaz understood that he was holding an AXIS 211 network camera, designed for security surveillance and remote monitoring.

Rafiq had already hooked the wireless camera on to a network video recorder, and using a secure connection, he was able to access live video streams from the camera on his laptop. Imtiaz's only job was to fix the camera the hoarding and ensure that it was pointed in the right direction.

Imtiaz lashed the camera in place behind one of the hoarding's lamps, taking care to see that the camera was hidden from sight while, at the same time, ensuring that its lens had an unobstructed view of the house. Once the camera was in place, he pulled out a cheap Chinese mobile phone from his pocket, switched it on and dialled a number. His call was answered in one ring.

'Yes.' Rafiq's voice came through.

'Okay?' asked Imtiaz.

Rafiq, who was seated in the Lexus RX 300 about two hundred metres away, was staring at his laptop. Images streaming in from the camera filled the laptop's screen.

'Left,' Rafiq said.

Imtiaz turned the camera's lens slightly towards the left.

'Left, left. Okay. Hold. Up.'

Imtiaz tilted the camera upwards.

'Up. Left… Down, down. Okay. Hold.'

Rafiq now had the house in full view. He stared at the images for a while, just to be certain that the camera had the gates and the house's main entrance covered. Having satisfied himself, he spoke into the phone one last time.

'Final okay.'

Imtiaz disconnected the call, switched off the phone, pulled off the battery cover and yanked out the phone's battery. He dropped the lifeless phone and its battery into the toolbag. He knew that Rafiq would have done the same with the phone he had just used.

As per the original plan, they were never to use mobile phones to talk to one another in Pakistan. However, the installation of the camera required it, so Saadat had procured two cheap, unbranded Chinese mobile phones from somewhere and bought two prepaid connections. Both phones had been activated only for the duration of that one call. Now, both phones would be cast away, virtually untraceable through their IMEI numbers—which, in all likelihood, were fake anyway—and inactive SIM cards. The only record of the call would be that one-minute conversation which, minus its context, would amount to little more than gibberish. And as the call had been made and received out in the open, getting the mobile service provider to trace the call wouldn't prove very helpful either.

Imtiaz scaled down the scaffolding, wound the cable and thrust it into the toolbag. As he began stuffing the screwdriver and tester into the bag, he casually looked in the direction of the house. A police van had appeared at the end of the road, and a posse of policemen was putting up a roadblock about fifty metres from the house's gate.

Mopping the sweat off his brow, Imtiaz walked over to the cycle, pushed it off the stand and wheeled it to the road. He then hopped onto it and rode away without a second glance at either the house or the hoarding.

27 July. Malir Cantonment, Karachi

Being a late riser, Saadat rarely had the luxury of reading the newspaper at home. He generally forced himself out of bed around 8.30, and spent the next forty-five minutes getting ready to leave for work. Breakfast was hurriedly crammed down the throat, and it wasn't until he was in his car, heading for office, that he managed catching up with the news.

As the Toyota Camry nosed down Malir Cantonment Road towards Jinnah Avenue and Shara-e-Faisal, Saadat settled down in the back seat and picked up the day's edition of *Nawa-i-Waqt*. He skimmed through the front page briefly and was about to turn to the sports section when a small headline at the bottom of the page caught his eye. As he read the story, his face grew anxious and he furtively peeked at his driver's face in the car's rear-view mirror. The driver's eyes were fixed on the road as he manoeuvred the car through the increasing traffic.

The sketchy news report was about the Karachi police looking for three Indian RAW agents who had reportedly slipped into Karachi to execute a series of terror strikes in the city. The journalist had quoted an unnamed source in the police department who had confirmed that the Karachi police had received intelligence about the presence of the Indians in the city. The story also quoted Karachi CCPO Qasim Raja as saying that the Karachi police was equipped to handle any threat posed by terrorists, even as he urged citizens to be alert to anything that looked suspicious.

Saadat closed and folded the paper and looked out of the window, squinting in the glare of the bright morning sun. He could sense a hollowness building in the pit of his stomach and he felt his shallow breath catching at his throat. The car had slowed down to a crawl, and all around him he could hear vehicles honking impatiently. He needed to get to office fast. And Imtiaz and his men needed to be warned.

'How come the traffic's so slow?' he asked his driver, trying to keep the quaver out of his voice.

'Some sort of a jam ahead, huzoor,' the driver shrugged dispassionately. 'Perhaps an accident... Or the police might have set up a roadblock.'

Saadat sank deeper in his seat. He didn't like the way things were going.

27 July. Mohajir Camp, Baldia Town, Karachi

The two rooms that Al-Kamil and his men had rented were situated on the first floor of a three-storey building, directly above a shop specializing in metalwork and immediately below an optician's store bearing a signboard that said Nabeel Optics. The neighbourhood was cramped, with shops, eateries, schools, mosques and residences all jostling one another for precious space. The narrow roads were full of people from every conceivable ethnic group in Pakistan.

Mohajir Camp wasn't one of the most scenic spots in Karachi, but it was a place where eight strangers to the city could easily lose themselves. It was for this reason that Al-Kamil had picked the predominantly low-income Baldia Town as a base of operation.

Al-Kamil and two of his men were seated at a tea-stall located diagonally across the street from their rooms. Two other members of his team were staking out the safe house in Clifton, while the remaining three were still fast asleep inside, even though it was nearly ten in the morning. While his partners at the tea-stall were engaged in a heated discussion about the American and Pakistani joint operation against the Taliban, Al-Kamil was immersed in a copy of the *Ummat*.

Turning the pages of the paper, he came across something that grabbed his attention. He began reading the piece, but the din all around distracted him. He quickly drained his glass of black tea and stood up. He crossed the busy road, sidestepped a couple of men hammering an iron grille into shape and mounted the narrow stairway to the rooms above. Entering one room, Al-Kamil closed the door to shut out the noise and sat down on the bed.

Opening the newspaper, he rapidly scanned the pages till he came upon the news item he was searching for. In a slow measured pace he went through the story, pausing now and then to assimilate what he was reading. At last, he put the paper aside and looked out of the lone window in the room. Save the flaking yellow wall and drainpipe of the neighbouring building, he could see nothing.

'*Yebnen kelp!*' he cursed under his breath.

RAW agents in Karachi—just when he was closing in on his target!

As he considered this, the thought of the Indian commandos who had supposedly entered Pakistan to kill Irshad Dilawar crossed Al-Kamil's mind. He wondered if the two were somehow connected. Not that it made a difference. Either way, security measures in Karachi would be increased.

Cursing the Indians again, Al-Kamil reached into his pocket and withdrew an unbranded Chinese mobile phone. His men in Clifton needed to be informed about this new threat immediately.

27 July. ISI Headquarters, Khayaban-e-Suhrawardy, Islamabad

'Are you out of your mind? How can you be so irresponsible? Don't you have even an ounce of sense in you?'

Major-General Dar and Lieutenant-General Niazi sat in silence as Lieutenant-General Rehmat roared into the speakerphone, his face contorted in rage. Copies of the Karachi and Lahore editions of *Nawa-i-Waqt* and the Karachi editions of *Ummat* and *Pakistan* lay scattered on the table, the news reports on the RAW agents circled with a red marker pen.

'When the reporter called you to check on facts, instead of making some inane statements, the first thing you should have done is disconnect his call and talk to me. This is a matter of Pakistan's security, and if you have been briefed by the Directorate for Inter-Services Intelligence, *everything* connected with the matter should first be reported back to the Directorate. Don't you know that, smarty-pants?'

'Sir, I was thinking that maybe...' Police Commissioner Qasim Raja's voice quavered over the line.

'Maybe *what*?' Lieutenant-General Rehmat thundered. 'That if the press wrote about this, the people of Karachi would come out and help you hunt down the Indians? Well, the only thing you have achieved is to alert the Indian commandos about the fact that we know they are in Karachi. In one stroke of overwhelming stupidity, you have squandered the element of surprise we had over the Indians.'

'I'm really sorry, sir,' the CCPO mumbled.

'Spare me your apologies. First you stick your head up your backside and then, you expect me to come and pull it free for you. Not possible. You've dug your own grave, so be...'

'Sir, please...' Raja sounded panicky, horribly aware of the fact that virtually all doors to respectability, money and power were beginning to shut permanently in his face. 'Sir, I shall talk to the newspaper editors immediately and get them to...'

'You will do absolutely nothing,' the director emphasized each word for effect. 'Just sit tight and pray that your men catch the Indians for you. That's your only hope. And if anyone mentions the Indians again, call me.'

'Yes, sir.'

'And find out who gave the press this story. Obviously someone in your department loves hobnobbing with the media. I want him suspended in twenty-four hours.'

Without waiting for Raja's answer, Lieutenant-General Rehmat disconnected the call and looked at the men across the table. 'The system leaks like a sieve. The only time people shut up here is when they have to tell *me* something.' Lieutenant-General Niazi dropped his eyes and studied his fingernails.

'We can only hope that the Indian commandos can't read Urdu. Or that they somehow missed seeing these news reports.' Major-General Dar didn't sound too hopeful.

'That's not good enough. The TV channels could pick up the story any minute. And the English press will want to do a follow-up story tomorrow. So get our media department to call the editors of all newspapers, radio stations and news channels, and have a statement issued denying any intelligence about suspected Indian activity in Karachi. Tell everyone that the news reports are false and the story is not worth pursuing. I suspect the damage has already been done, but let us look at containment, wherever possible.'

Once the major-general had left to act on the order, Lieutenant-General Rehmat looked at Lieutenant-General Niazi. 'What news at the house in Clifton?'

'All security arrangements are in place,' the older soldier replied. 'The Karachi police have set up roadblocks on both ends of the road leading to the house. Also, as recommended by you, I have had new access cards with new access codes issued to everyone authorized to enter the house. The security system has been reset, so the old access numbers won't work.'

'And the dummy limousine and motorcade...?'

Lieutenant-General Niazi looked at his watch. 'Arrival is in fifteen minutes. Around noon, I was told.'

The director nodded in satisfaction and turned his attention to a diary lying open in front of him. He began checklisting entries methodically, and silence enveloped the room.

Get them to move him out of Pakistan. Once he's out, we'll figure out a way of taking him down.

Zeb Kirkland's words, delivered over the phone the previous night, echoed in Lieutenant-General Niazi ears as he sat fidgeting in his chair, watching the chief spy scribbling in his diary. A minute passed, and Major-General Dar let himself back into the room. The director raised his eyebrows enquiringly.

'They've already started calling the editors and news bureaus, sir.'

As Major-General Dar settled into his seat, Lieutenant-General Niazi took a deep breath. Crossing his fingers, he spoke in a flat monotone.

'I think we will have to transfer Irshad Dilawar out of Parachinar.'

A momentary silence followed as the other two men processed the statement.

'Why?' the director asked sharply.

'Huzoor, the Americans have begun mounting operations against the Taliban all along the Afghan border, and the entire region is crawling with Pakistani and American forces. I fear that Dilawar's safe house in Parachinar might accidentally come under attack. And if some American happens to recognize Dilawar and reports back that he is indeed in Pakistan, the pressure on our government to hand him over to India will only increase.'

Lieutenant-General Rehmat leant forward on the table and considered this. He instinctively understood that Lieutenant-General Niazi had a point. The fugitive gangster could well become collateral damage in this war against the Taliban. And it would be a pity if, after having done so much to shield the man from the Indians, everything ended up exactly the way India wanted it.

'I would agree with Niazi sahib,' Major-General Dar said. 'There is a degree of risk involved in keeping Irshad Dilawar in Parachinar.'

Lieutenant-General Niazi looked at the director, his face expressionless. This was going nicely.

'Hmmm… So where do we move him to?' the director rubbed his chin. 'If the border with Afghanistan is unsafe, we have to overrule Saidu Sharif, Miramshah and Quetta as well. Even Peshawar could be perilous. We can't risk Murree as it's too close to India-controlled Kashmir, and Karachi is already out.'

Lieutenant-General Niazi curbed the temptation to speak up. He had to time this right.

'Why don't we move him to Islamabad or Rawalpindi?' Major-General Dar suggested. 'He'll be closer to us and we can protect him better.'

'Yes, but he'll also be a lot closer to the political establishment, and if they come to know he's here, they'll raise a stink. Also, the United States' national security advisor's visit to Islamabad is just round the corner. I won't take that chance. Dilawar has his uses, but he can be quite an inconvenience to the government.' The director scowled. 'I don't want any more heartburn from these politicians.'

'How about taking him out of the country?' Lieutenant-General Niazi shrugged in an offhand manner, hoping he hadn't sounded too eager with the proposal. 'Either to Nepal or to one of the Gulf nations? Sharjah and Bahrain might be risky, but I don't think Ras al-Khaimah or Doha should pose any problems.'

'Nepal is out,' countered the ISI director. 'The RAW has recently increased its presence there, and anyway, as far as the Nepal government is concerned, one can never be sure of their intentions. They have no allegiances and are simply playing everyone against everyone. The sooner we and India and China realize it, the better. The Gulf is a possibility, but again, there's only so much we can do to protect him there without attracting too much attention. No, our best bet is to keep him inside Pakistan.'

Lieutenant-General Niazi swallowed hard and tried his best to conceal his disappointment.

'That only leaves us with Panjgur and Gwadar,' said Major-General Dar. 'Both are quite far from the Afghan border, which is good.'

'No,' Lieutenant-General Niazi shook his head vehemently. He could feel the pulse pounding in his temple. 'Neither Panjgur nor Gwadar have good safe houses. The one in Gwadar is half-decent, but Panjgur…' He shook his head dismissively again. 'Just not safe enough.'

'Well then, for better or worse, it'll have to be Gwadar,' said the director with finality.

'Magar huzoor…' Lieutenant-General Niazi argued, looking and sounding disconsolate. 'I still think he's safer abroad.'

'Niazi sahib, the Gwadar safe house may not be the best we have, but we can always add more security personnel. And as long as the Indians think Dilawar is in Karachi, he'll be safe in Gwadar.' Lieutenant-General Rehmat suddenly peered at the retired soldier. 'Or is there some other problem?'

'Nahin.' The retired soldier blinked and shook his head hastily. 'Just the safety aspect…' His shoulders drooped. He knew he had gambled and lost. Kirkland wouldn't be happy.

At that moment, a phone tinkled softly. Lieutenant-General Niazi pulled out his mobile phone and pressed it to his ear. He listened for barely five seconds before disconnecting.

Looking from Lieutenant-General Rehmat to Major-General Dar, he said, 'Irshad Dilawar's motorcade has reached the Clifton safe house.'

27 July. Astoria Gardens, Clifton, Karachi

Imtiaz put aside the copy of *Nawa-i-Waqt* that he had been reading and considered Saadat, whose face seemed to have added five years overnight. Shamsheer sat back with folded arms in one of the sofas, grimly staring at the newspaper Imtiaz had put down. The only one missing in their company was Rafiq, who was in one of the bedrooms, monitoring the images from the network camera on his laptop.

'Is this the only paper to report the story?' Imtiaz asked.

'I don't know,' Saadat shrugged miserably. 'It's the only one I saw. Maybe the others also have it.'

Imtiaz stood up, thrust his hands into the pockets of his jeans and began pacing the room. 'What are the chances that we are the three Indians who have been mentioned in the story?'

'It says that the three Indians are RAW agents who have entered Karachi to trigger terror strikes,' Shamsheer offered. 'We're neither from the RAW nor here to engineer terror, but still…'

Imtiaz nodded slowly as he walked to the end of the room. Suddenly, he stopped and turned to address Saadat. 'Have you noticed a sudden increase in security across Karachi?'

'Yes, there are more roadblocks and a lot more policemen everywhere.But that could also be in preparation for the MQM rally that's happening the day after. I'm sure the police expect some violence during and after it.'

'Okay, but does security around the safe house in Clifton increase every time Dilawar comes to Karachi?'

'It's natural for security to be increased when…' Saadat began, but Imtiaz interjected.

'I understand that. What I meant is, is it normal for the Karachi police to set up roadblocks on both ends of the road on which the house is situated?'

'Roadblocks? On both ends of that road?' Saadat weighed this for a moment before slowly shaking his head. 'No, never a Karachi police roadblock. It's never happened before. If it had, my reports to colonel *sahib* would have definitely mentioned it.'

'Yes. During our briefing in India, there was no mention of police roadblocks near the house. But this morning, I saw the Karachi police setting up roadblocks fifty metres from the house.' He looked at the two men expectantly.

'Two police roadblocks that have never been put up before when Dilawar was visiting, and a newspaper report about three Indians entering Karachi,' Shamsheer said slowly. 'Unless the roadblocks also have something to do with the political rally, I'm afraid the three Indians in the news story are you, me and Rafiq.'

'Oh no,' groaned Saadat and buried his head in his hands. 'I'm finished.'

'Relax. It's not as if the three of us have been arrested and are on the verge of giving you away.' Imtiaz gave Saadat a withering look.

'Sir, what if all this actually has something to do with the men in the car I saw yesterday?' Shamsheer asked suddenly.

Imtiaz pondered this for a while. 'There's always a possibility,' he said, at last. Turning to Saadat, he asked, 'Did your friend in the transport registration department find out anything about the car?'

'Arre haan, I completely forgot. The Cultus apparently belongs to a retired college professor, and it seems it had been stolen from Dadu district a couple of days ago. The professor had even registered a police complaint in Dadu town on the day of the robbery.'

'Dadu... Where's that?'

'250 kilometres from Karachi,' Saadat pointed northwards. 'But what's interesting is that the car was found abandoned in Baldia Town last night. The remarkable thing is that the car was found intact. Even its music system had not been removed, and its petrol tank was nearly full. The police believe that as nothing was taken from the car, transportation was the only motive behind the robbery.'

'And the police haven't been able to find any clues from the car?'

'About the people who stole it?' Saadat's eyebrows shot up in disbelief. 'Kahaan sahib! A car is recovered four days after it was stolen in perfect condition, with possibly more petrol in it than at the time when it was taken. Everyone just thanks their good fortune and moves on.'

Imtiaz nodded quietly. Car recovered, case closed. He understood the mindset of the subcontinent.

'So that's a dead end. We aren't any wiser about the men in the Cultus, and we can be fairly certain that the Pakistanis probably know something about us. Damn!'

'Well, at least there's one piece of good news,' said Shamsheer. 'We know that Irshad Dilawar is finally in Clifton.'

'I'm not so sure about that.'

Imtiaz, Shamsheer and Saadat turned sharply towards the door. They hadn't noticed Rafiq as he had quietly made an appearance in the room.

'What did you say?' Imtiaz asked sharply, his eyes appraising Rafiq for any telltale signs of the young lieutenant's juvenile sense of humour.

Rafiq looked back at Imtiaz, his face serious. 'Sir, you might want to come in and look at what I've found.'

* * *

'Play it once again. From the beginning,' Imtiaz ordered.

The three commandos and Saadat were huddled around the computer they had used the previous night to talk to Colonel Mohan. Rafiq had made a copy of the recording of Irshad Dilawar's motorcade arriving at the safe house, and it was this loop that the four men were peering at on the monitor.

For the fourth time, Rafiq replayed the seven-minute recording.

The recording began with the first vehicle in the motorcade, a black jeep, stopping outside the main gate. Four men with Kalashnikovs got out of the jeep and took defensive positions around the gate as a fifth man went up to the security cabin and spoke to someone inside. He then got back into the jeep, and the gates opened to admit the vehicle. As the four armed men kept watch, a white SUV trailed the jeep inside. Next, a black limousine with darkened windows entered the gate, closely followed by another SUV. A second black jeep brought up the rear, and as it swept through the gate, the four men with Kalashnikovs jumped on board. The gates swung shut almost immediately.

At this point, Rafiq clicked on an icon marked '1/2' on the screen, and the video slowed down to half its normal speed. The men in the room watched closely as the limousine drew up to the portico of the house. Meanwhile, the other four vehicles fanned out along the driveway and stopped, disgorging armed men in jerky slow motion.

Imtiaz stared intently at the limousine which, by some quirk of fate, had been parked in a manner that offered the camera a clear view of each of its four doors. Shamsheer, on the other hand, kept a close eye on the men who had got out of the other vehicles in the motorcade.

For a full three minutes, the limousine just stood in the portico. None of its doors opened to let anyone out, and no one from either inside the house or from the motorcade approached it. At the end of three minutes, the limousine slowly drove away from the portico towards a chain of garages that were outside the camera's range of vision.

The four men in the room looked at one another in mystification. Irshad Dilawar's motorcade had reached the safe house, but they had seen no evidence of the gangster being part of it.

'Sir, if Irshad Dilawar arrived by that limo, why didn't he get out?' Rafiq finally broke the silence. 'And no one came to the car from the house either, which is strange. Someone should have come out to welcome Dilawar. He is, after all, an important guest of the Pakistani state.'

'Rafiq is right, sir,' said Shamsheer. 'Also, all the alertness and vigilance that the security personnel displayed outside the house vanished once the cars entered the compound and the gates were shut. Everyone just slacked off. The whole thing almost looked like a mock drill.'

Imtiaz nodded thoughtfully before turning to Saadat. 'Are you certain there is no hidden passage from the garage to the house? Some sort of a tunnel or something?'

'Nahin sir. The man who drew the plan for me knows each and every corner of the house. There is no secret entrance to the house from anywhere.

There's one entrance from the front portico, and one from the back, which is used by the domestic staff. That's all.'

'I don't see Dilawar using the back entrance, and he definitely didn't use the one in front. So, what we just saw can mean one of two things. That Irshad Dilawar's welcome committee was in the garage, and that's where he intends to stay, or…' Imtiaz didn't complete what he was saying.

'Or that the whole motorcade was a sham, put on to deceive someone into believing Dilawar had reached the house,' Rafiq spoke categorically. 'The behaviour and body language of those security guys was a dead giveaway, sir. Dilawar can't be under that roof.'

'Good job, lieutenant,' said Imtiaz, admiration showing in his voice. 'But I want to be absolutely sure about this.'

Pointing to Shamsheer, he said, 'Please go through everything that the camera has recorded from the time I installed it up to now. Make note of even the smallest thing that proves or disproves Dilawar's presence in that house. And Rafiq, you will immediately start monitoring the live feeds and will look for anything that either supports or debunks your theory.'

Shamsheer looked from Imtiaz to Rafiq. 'Rafiq has already hacked into the server in that house. Why not hack into the system once again and access today's video recordings stored in the server? Maybe we can even get live pictures from the video cameras installed in the house. That will tell us whether Dilawar is actually there or not.'

'No,' said Imtiaz decisively. 'If Irshad Dilawar is not in that house, and that dummy motorcade was meant to fool someone, those in charge of his security could be tracking every entry point into the house. That includes the server. Hacking into the system might expose us.'

'We're supposed to hack into the server tomorrow night to upload the doctored video files,' Rafiq grimaced. 'If they're monitoring the server, it would become a problem for us, sir.'

'It would, and we'll have to think of a solution for that. But first, we need to establish without doubt whether or not Dilawar is in that house.'

Shamsheer nodded and looked to Rafiq. 'Chalo, let's start working on the recording.'

Imtiaz turned to Saadat. 'Meanwhile, will you please use your good offices to find out if Dilawar came to Karachi this morning? And if he did, whether he is in that house?'

Saadat stared at Imtiaz, his eyes wide with fear. 'Imtiaz sahib, I have helped you as much as possible, but this is now getting very dangerous…'

'Saadat mian,' Imtiaz interrupted. 'I am grateful for all the help you have given us—without that, we wouldn't be so close to our target. But you must understand that everything now depends on our knowing Dilawar's exact whereabouts. Tomorrow night, the three of us are scheduled to enter that house. We must know if Dilawar is there. I see no point in putting lives on the line trying to achieve something entirely pointless. Please.'

Saadat stared at the floor as he mulled over Imtiaz's entreaty. Finally, he looked up. 'Theek hai, let me try and see if I can find something out.'

'Thank you. Thank you so much.'

Once Saadat had left, Imtiaz walked over to the huge drawing room windows. The velvet drapes were still drawn firmly together, but through a small crack he could see the sweep of the Arabian Sea, its waters glinting like molten gold in the late afternoon sunlight.

He thought about the newspaper report, the police roadblocks put up around the safe house, and the limousine that hadn't transported Irshad Dilawar to Clifton. It all added up. Somebody had tipped the Pakistanis off about Project Abhimanyu. Now a trap was being laid for him and his men… He wondered who had betrayed them.

27 July. Sector 2, RK Puram, Delhi

The special cell maintained by the Intelligence Bureau was situated hardly a hundred metres from the famous Ayyappa Temple in RK Puram, partially concealed behind a transformer and a public urinal. A weather-beaten signboard, riddled with splotches of rust and dirt, hung above the office's dungeon-like entrance, the words 'Department of Telecommunications—Subdivisional Office, Government of India' barely legible, even in broad daylight. Now, with dusk having settled over Delhi, it was hard to even make out the signboard.

The office, which employed a staff of about twenty, functioned as one of the IB's surveillance cells specializing in the monitoring of telephonic conversations involving almost all foreign embassy personnel in Delhi. Tapping the phones of diplomatic staff was a clear violation of the Vienna Convention on Diplomatic Relations, but maintaining a log of calls made and received by embassy personnel fell into a grey area. So, the twenty people in that building merely tracked each and every phone conversation, making note of who had called whom, plotting and analysing numbers and conversations for trends and patterns, and keeping their eyes open for anomalies.

One such anomaly had been brought to the notice of Assistant Central Intelligence Officer Binoy Verghese the previous day, and he had been intrigued enough to ask his subordinates to get him more information. The anomaly pertained to a call that Pakistani press attaché Haider Nazir had received on his mobile phone on the night of 25 July. Nazir had been under routine surveillance since the day he had come to Delhi, and the IB office had a map of all the numbers from which calls to him were made regularly.

There were two things about the call that Nazir had received that night which had caught the attention of Verghese's junior.

Nazir rarely ever received calls late in the night, and even on the two previous occasions that he had, the conversations had barely lasted more than a minute. On the first occasion, the call had been made by a Pakistani student studying in Jamia Millia Islamia, while on the second, it had been from a public phone booth in Karol Bagh. Both calls had been made well over a year ago, and the IB had not been able to establish any patterns.

However, the call on the night of 25 July had been made very late—at almost 2.30, which technically made it the morning of 26 July—and it had lasted a full three-and-a-half minutes. That, in itself, might not have raised any suspicions. What alerted Verghese's junior was the fact that the call had been made to Nazir from Dehradun.

Preliminary enquiries about the number in Dehradun had provided intriguing results. The call had been placed from the residence of Parthoprotim Lahiri, a teacher of humanities at the Rashtriya Indian Military College in Dehradun. Verghese immediately marshalled resources to check if there was any previous association between Lahiri and Nazir, but all efforts at finding a link drew a blank. Verghese then called a friend in the IB and asked if the bureau had a file on Lahiri. His friend assured him that he would rustle something up in a day or so.

The file on Lahiri had been emailed about an hour earlier and Verghese had decided to go through it straightaway, passing up a colleague's invitation to step out for a couple of drinks. However, as he sat hunched in front of the computer reading about Lahiri, Verghese began feeling he would have been better off downing his favourite rum-and-cola. There was practically nothing shady or dubious about the teacher's past, and everything pointed to impeccable rectitude.

Yet, the three-and-a-half-minute phone call was a nagging reality.

Verghese scrolled down the file, reading through every line in the hope that something would help explain the phone call to Nazir. Having almost reached the end, Verghese had nearly given up when he saw a small piece of information tucked under Lahiri's personal details.

Sitting up in his chair, Verghese read an annotation on Lahiri's marriage and family. The teacher was married to a woman named Nandini, from whom he had a son and daughter. The son was an IT professional, married and settled in Atlanta, while the daughter was married to a teacher in Doon School and lived in Doon Valley, not far from her parents' house. What interested Verghese, however, was Lahiri's wife's maiden name. And the name of the person written next to it.

The intelligence officer stared at the two names with wide eyes. He knew it might amount to nothing, but it was also possibly the missing piece to the puzzle of the mysterious phone call to Haider Nazir. He also realized that if he intended following this up, he would have to refer the case to his superior for clearance.

Investigating powerful, senior-level Government of India officials without authorization was way above his jurisdiction.

CHAPTER 9

27 July. Mauripur Road, Kiamari Town, Karachi

A sizeable crowd of onlookers hung around, craning their necks to catch a glimpse of the two dead bodies lying on the road next to the blue SUV, which was wedged on the road divider. Three police jeeps and two vans formed a rough protective circle around the bodies and the SUV, and policemen with batons were pushing back those who stepped too close to the cordoned off area. Three television news vans stood just outside the barricades that had been erected down the road, and cameramen were trying to sneak in shots of the bodies, even as the reporters jabbered away excitedly into their microphones.

One enterprising reporter from Geo News had managed to collar one of the onlookers, who claimed to have witnessed the entire incident from beginning to end. The TV camera panned on this lucky soul, giving him his three minutes of fame on national television.

According to the man's voluble account, the SUV had come tearing down the road from the direction of Jinnah Bridge, chased by two police jeeps. The road ahead, however, had been heavily barricaded, and probably seeing this, the SUV's driver had tried to take a U-turn by cutting across the concrete road divider. The divider, though, had proved to be too high, and the SUV's undercarriage had got stuck on it, rendering the vehicle immobile. With the police jeeps bearing down on them, two men had jumped out of the SUV and tried to make good their escape. One of the men had a pistol and had fired three rounds at the jeeps as he ran. The cops had immediately returned fire and both men had gone down.

What the witness couldn't tell television audiences was that the chase had actually commenced outside Bahria College on MT Khan Road, and that the men lying on the street were dead only because, earlier in the day, they had unwittingly stolen a vehicle belonging to the son of an influential PPP politician. The politician had made a few phone calls, and the Karachi police had instantly launched a hunt for the electric blue Kia Sportage. The men in the SUV had been driving back from Clifton towards Baldia Town with the intention of abandoning the car somewhere on Mauripur Road, but unfortunately for them, the police had spotted it. The men had been asked to pull over at a roadblock, but in a fit of panic they had hightailed away, setting up the chase down Jinnah Bridge.

An ambulance made its way down the road and drew up beside the SUV, its blue light revolving eerily in the pale orange glow of the streetlights. As a doctor and couple of medical assistants got out of the ambulance, two policemen sauntered over to the Sportage. Producing flashlights, they began inspecting the vehicle's dark interior. Almost immediately, one of the policemen noticed the flashing light of a mobile phone lying on the SUV's floor, next to the accelerator pedal.

Using his handkerchief, the policeman delicately fished the phone out of the car. Cradling it gingerly in his hands, he took it across to his superior, who was standing by one of the jeeps talking to the doctor. The two cops stared at the instrument as it buzzed and flashed silently in the dark. It was clear that they didn't know what to do next.

The phone, a cheap Chinese model, stopped ringing. The senior policeman quickly pressed a couple of buttons and the phone's screen lit up. The display showed that there were three missed calls, all from the same number. Undecided about what to with the phone, the policeman was about to hand it over to his junior for documentation when it once again came to life in his hands. The flashing screen revealed that the call was from the same number.

The two cops looked at one another. Then, acting on sheer impulse, the senior cop pressed the 'Answer' button and lifted the phone to his ear.

'Hello,' he said cautiously.

The caller disconnected immediately and the line went dead.

27 July. Mohajir Camp, Baldia Town, Karachi

Al-Kamil disconnected the call and stared at the phone he was holding, his eyes wild and glassy in the dim light of a naked 60-watt bulb dangling from the ceiling.

He had ordered the two men he had posted at Clifton to return to the rooms by sundown, so that all eight of them could go over the plan one final time. After all, the attack was due for launch in less than twenty-four hours. He had waited all evening with growing anxiety, and when the two failed to make an appearance by nine o'clock, he had risked calling them on the mobile phone.

Three times he had called, and all three times the phone had kept ringing. Then, on the fourth attempt, his call had been answered.

'Hello,' the person on the other end had said. The word and the voice confirmed Al-Kamil's worst fears.

The eight of them had made it a habit of speaking to one another in Arabic, and his men would have answered his call with either 'marhaban' or 'ahlan'—not 'hello'. And there was no question of the men having lost the phone and some stranger having found it and taken the call. The phone and the pistol were the two things his men would never have misplaced. Both were the only insurances they had against getting out of tight situations.

A stranger had taken his call. It meant his men had gotten into some sort of trouble.

Al-Kamil took two strides to the door and opened it. He marched down the first-floor veranda overlooking the narrow street, which was still teeming with people. Reaching a door, he rapped on it sharply. The door opened a crack and one of his men peered out warily.

'Something has happened to Tabarek and Jamal,' Al-Kamil growled softly in Arabic, his voice conveying urgency. 'Change in plan, so pack everything immediately. We leave this place in five minutes.'

Returning to his room, he pulled out a large bag stowed under the bed and began flinging his belongings into it hurriedly. In less than a minute, he was through. The only thing that remained was his mobile phone.

Al-Kamil walked over to a wooden table in a corner of the room. On the table were an earthenware pot half full of drinking water and a steel tumbler. Al-Kamil lifted the lid off the pot and dropped the phone through its mouth. He heard the phone plop into the water before sinking silently to the bottom. These were cheap, unbranded Chinese phones, virtually untraceable owing to their fake IMEI numbers, but Al-Kamil wasn't taking any chances.

He picked up the bag and walked out of the room, switching the light off on his way out.

27 July. Astoria Gardens, Clifton, Karachi

'There is absolutely no doubt about this, huzoor. My contacts have re-confirmed that Irshad Dilawar did not leave from Parachinar this morning. He is still there—not in Karachi.'

Saadat and Imtiaz were seated on the chairs in front of the computer, headphones strapped over their heads. Rafiq, also wearing headphones, sat cross-legged on the bed, listening quietly to the conversation, chewing assiduously on gum.

Colonel Mohan was quiet for a moment. 'Yet his motorcade arrived, and security in and around the safe house has been increased,' he said finally.

'Dilawar did not show up at the house, but the Pakistanis want to give the impression that he did,' Imtiaz spoke tightly. 'It's a trap, sir.'

'Are you still keeping a watch on the house?'

'Yes, sir. Shamsheer is watching it right now. We have been taking turns all through the day. Nothing indicates that Dilawar is there, sir.'

'That newspaper report you mentioned... it says the Karachi police confirmed that some Indians are in Karachi?'

'Yes sir. *Three* Indians. Saadat says that similar stories appeared in two other papers as well. And a few hours ago, the Karachi police shot dead two unidentified men somewhere near Karachi Dockyard. It's all over the TV news channels. The men were apparently trying to escape in a car, and died in an exchange of fire with the police. The news anchors are speculating that the dead men may be the RAW agents the papers reported about this morning.'

'Has the speculation been confirmed by the Karachi police?'

'No, sir. In fact, they seem to be consciously underplaying... even *denying* any Indian connection.'

'I see.'

'I find this very interesting, sir. First, the police here confirm news of Indian agents in Karachi. But now, even after killing two unknown men in a gun battle, the Karachi police aren't raising the Indian bogey.'

'Yes, that would be the natural thing to do,' the colonel conceded.

There was a moment's silence before Imtiaz spoke, 'Sir, could the newspaper reports be right? Have any more of our people slipped into Karachi?'

'No,' Colonel Mohan was categorical.

'That means we are the Indians in those news reports. The Karachi police had confirmed information which the press got hold of, but now the police are denying it to make everything appear normal. This proves that the Pakistanis know of our plan and are setting a trap for us.'

Saadat looked at Imtiaz, his eyes round with fear. Rafiq gazed down at the chequered bedspread with unseeing eyes, his lower jaw working mechanically on the chewing gum. Imtiaz just stared at the computer screen.

'Sir, someone has leaked the whole plot to the Pakistanis, severely compromising us and Project Abhimanyu.'

'You are right, major,' the colonel's voice sounded distant and weary.

'How many people know about Project Abhimanyu, sir?' Imtiaz asked.

'Sadly, enough for the system to have sprung a leak,' Colonel Mohan's answer was diplomatic. 'It could have happened at many places and will need to be thoroughly investigated.'

The silence that followed was broken by Rafiq. 'What do we do next, sir?'

'Well, with Dilawar not in Karachi, there's obviously very little we can do now. We are left with no choice but to abort Project Abhimanyu.'

A grave stillness descended on the room as the three men took in the import of the colonel's words. Finally, the major leaned forward in his seat. When he spoke, his tone was heavy with disappointment, but his words still hopeful.

'Do we have to abandon the operation entirely? I'm sure there has to be another way around this.'

Saadat stared open-mouthed at Imtiaz, refusing to believe that the major could still be considering the possibility of completing the mission. Rafiq also paused chewing for a fraction of a second as he sized up the major with narrowed eyes.

'I know this feels terrible after all the effort we have put in,' said Colonel Mohan soothingly. 'But let's face it. Irshad Dilawar is not in Karachi, and the chances of his coming there now are next to zero. And thanks to a traitor in our midst, you chaps are at great risk. Project Abhimanyu has to be aborted.'

'Perhaps all we need to do is be patient and formulate another plan,' Imtiaz protested. 'The Pakistanis don't know that we know about the trap they have sprung for us. While they wait for us to strike…'

'Be realistic, major,' the colonel cut in sharply. 'If the Pakistanis know about Project Abhimanyu, they will be on their guard. Never underestimate the enemy. The three of you cannot hope to pull this off now. And it's too dangerous for you chaps to be in Pakistan much longer. You will have to get out of there quickly.'

'Sir, I think we should just continue our surveillance of the house for a day or two longer. Meanwhile Saadat can find out more about Dilawar's exact whereabouts…'

'No, no. I am not doing…' Saadat, petrified, began objecting to whatever role he was being assigned in this caper when the colonel's voice cut both him and Imtiaz short.

'That's enough, major,' the colonel was curt. 'I am not prepared to risk your lives chasing a mirage. Abort Project Abhimanyu. That's an order.'

Imtiaz sighed and leaned back in his chair.

'I want you to pull the plug on all surveillance of the house,' Colonel Mohan continued. 'The three of you are to stay put in the apartment and not step out. Catch some sleep and recharge your bodies. Now that the Pakistanis have been alerted, you will not be able to leave Karachi as we had originally planned. Let me think of a way of getting you out of there. You shall call me tomorrow at noon, India time, and I will have a plan ready for you.'

A minute later, the colonel signed off. Saadat, who looked distinctly relieved now that the operation had been officially called off, stood up.

'I'll take your leave, major sahib,' he said. 'I shall be back tomorrow. Perhaps colonel sahib will have some job worthy of me... *Khuda hafiz.*'

Imtiaz nodded. '*Khuda hafiz.*'

Rafiq noticed the sour look on Imtiaz's face as he watched Saadat walk off, the spring in his step barely contained. As the front door of the apartment slammed shut, the major rose and marched stiffly out of the room. The lieutenant got off the bed and followed him.

Shamsheer needed to be told about the fate of Project Abhimanyu as well.

* * *

The muted television showed canned footage of the shooting on Mauripur Road, cutting intermittently back to the newsroom where the anchor went through the same threadbare facts over and over again. The words 'Breaking News: RAW in Karachi?' flashed on the screen now and then, and a clip of Karachi CCPO Qasim Raja came on, where he refused to speculate on the identity of the dead men.

Imtiaz wasn't even looking at the TV any longer. He just sat on one of the drawing room sofas, hands locked behind his head, legs splayed wide, staring up at the ceiling. He had barely spoken after the call to India, and after a quick dinner, Shamsheer and Rafiq had retired to bed, knowing that the atmosphere wasn't particularly conducive to conversation.

'Project Abhimanyu is the most critical operation undertaken by Unit Kilo so far. I'm not exaggerating when I say that the fate of Unit Kilo will depend greatly on its success.'

As he sat looking up at the bevelled edges of the false ceiling, Imtiaz recalled the discussion he'd had with Colonel Mohan in one of the rooms in Chandimandir Cantonment. 'There are people who are envious of what Unit Kilo is trying to achieve, and they will seize any opportunity to discredit us and have the unit disbanded,' the colonel had spoken in sombre tones. 'We can't let that happen.'

'I understand, sir,' Imtiaz had responded.

'Remember that as the leader of this team, a lot depends on you. We have picked the best men for this operation, but ultimately, it's your leadership that will count. The decisions you take will determine whether the mission fails or succeeds.'

Imtiaz reached for the remote control lying on the coffee table and switched off the television. Rising from the sofa, he walked over to the switchboard on the wall and flicked three switches. The room instantly went dark. Picking his way carefully through the room, he walked to the curtained windows, pushed one of the drapes aside, opened one window and stepped onto the small balcony outside. He breathed in deeply, feeling the salty tang of the sea in his lungs, letting his mind clear.

After a couple of minutes, Imtiaz turned to look in the direction of the safe house. He couldn't see it, of course, but he knew where it was. He also knew that the man he had come in search of was not in that house—and probably wouldn't be coming there in a long time.

That knowledge didn't bother him any longer, now that he had made up his mind. He would hunt the man down, wherever he was hiding.

As far as he was concerned, Project Abhimanyu was still very much on course.

* * *

Rafiq lay in the dark, listening for sounds from the drawing room. He knew that Imtiaz had turned off the drawing room lights a while ago, but he hadn't heard the major go to his bedroom, the one at the end, furthest from the main door. He wondered what the major was doing in the darkened drawing room.

Ever since Colonel Mohan had called off the operation, Rafiq had been silently observing Imtiaz. The major had hardly exchanged a word with him or Shamsheer, and during dinner, he had picked at his food distractedly. Yet, Rafiq had discerned an unnerving intensity in Imtiaz's gaze, and his instinct told him the major was up to something.

Then, all of a sudden, he recalled what Shamsheer had said about Imtiaz that day in the deer park in Panchkula.

Once he makes up his mind about a job, he will get it done, somehow or the other.

Now as he lay in his bed, his ears trying to pick up noises from the drawing room, Rafiq tried to fathom what was simmering in the major's mind. It had to be something to do with Project Abhimanyu.

But that wasn't good enough. He had to find out exactly what it was.

28 July. ISI Headquarters, Khayaban-e-Suhrawardy, Islamabad

'What do we know about the dead men so far?'

'Not much, sir. The section head of our Karachi bureau and his men have started working on this with the Karachi police. They are trying to get as much information as soon as possible. I have instructed Brigadier Razavi to bring us their reports as he gets them.'

Lieutenant-General Rehmat shook his head in frustration. 'I wish there was something to tell us if these men are the Indian commandos we're looking for?'

'It's hard to say, sir,' answered Major-General Dar. 'The problem is that nothing was found on them to suggest who they were. It's possible that they are our own jihadis—we have enough of them crawling all over the place. And we cannot rule out the possibility of them having something to do with the upcoming MQM rally.'

'Gangsters from Lyari hired to stir up political trouble?'

'Hired or simply loyal to one party or another,' the major-general nodded gloomily.

'Nothing in the SUV?'

'No, sir.'

'And the pistol?'

'Smith & Wesson Model 910. Fairly common. We've sent it for analysis, but the truth is one of them can be procured almost anywhere in Pakistan. They can be bought in bulk in Peshawar.'

'So all we're left with is the mobile phone,' Lieutenant-General Rehmat sighed.

'Yes, but unfortunately, it's one of those cheap Chinese models with a fake IMEI number. So the service operator doesn't have any call records, nor can a live trace be made to the place the call was made from. However, we have the number from which the call was made to the phone. The Karachi police are trying to trace the number. Hopefully, we'll soon have something concrete there.'

The major-general had barely finished when there was a rap on the door, and Lieutenant-General Niazi entered. Two steps behind him stood Brigadier Razavi.

'*As-Salāmu Alaikum*,' the retired soldier greeted the director.

'*Wa'Alaikum As-salām. Baithiye*,' Lieutenant-General Rehmat replied, pointing to a chair. He then looked at the junior officer.

'Yes?'

'Sir, the police have been able to trace the purchase of the phone connections to Mohajir Camp.'

'Baldia Town? That's good.'

'Two days ago, a shopkeeper in Mohajir Camp sold two prepaid connections to someone. The numbers of the two connections are that of the phone the police recovered from the dead men and that of the mystery phone that was used to call them.'

'Nice,' said the director. 'Have we got the shopkeeper's statement?'

'Yes, sir. Based on his description...' Brigadier Razavi stopped abruptly, interrupted by a phone ringing softly.

'Excuse me, sir. It's mine,' Major-General Dar said apologetically. Pulling out the phone, he looked at the screen and said, 'It's from Mir Mohammad Elahi, our Karachi section head.'

Seeing Lieutenant-General Rehmat nod, the major-general put the phone to his ear. 'Bataaiye, Elahi sahib...'

As he listened to the section head, the major-general's eyes lit up. 'That's very good. Zara hold keejiye...' Covering the mouthpiece, he said, 'Sir, they have found the phone. It was found in...'

Lieutenant-General Rehmat raised his hand. 'I want to speak to him. Tell him we shall call him back on his mobile from my direct line.'

Thirty seconds later, they could hear Elahi's phone ringing over the speaker.

'Hello,' the section chief's voice was thin but clear.

'This is Lieutenant-General Rehmat speaking. You were saying the phone has been recovered?'

'Ji janaab. It was found in a room in Mohajir Camp. In a pot of water.'

'Inside a pot full of water?'

'Yes, sir. The ID of the SIM card in the phone matches one of the connections sold by a shopkeeper...'

'Okay, okay. Got it,' the director interrupted Elahi. 'Good that you've got the phone. You guys had just got the information from the shopkeeper, so I must say that was quick.'

As it turned out, the discovery of the phone had had nothing to do with the shopkeeper's statement to the police, or the latter's alacrity thereafter. It transpired that the owner of the tenement had woken up in the morning to discover that her tenants had quietly vacated the premises the previous night. On going through the rooms, she had found the mobile phone dunked in the pot of water. Unable to make anything of it—and surprised that her tenants had left, even though they had paid a full month's rent in advance—she had begun gossiping about the matter.

The woman's account had reached the ears of a policeman who lived in the locality, and he happened to idly mention the incident to a colleague. The colleague, who had some knowledge of the hunt for a phone in Mohajir Camp, put two and two together, resulting in the police getting their hands on the discarded phone.

'Has the landlady's statement been recorded?' the director pressed eagerly.

'Sir, she says that she rented the rooms out to a man three days ago,' explained Elahi. 'The man apparently gave his name as Khalil Abdali. He rented two rooms as there were eight of them.'

The eyebrows of the three serving officers shot up at the section chief's words. 'Is she sure there were *eight* of them?' Lieutenant-General Rehmat asked.

'Yes, sir. She is positive.'

Lieutenant-General Niazi felt his lips go dry. He averted his face and coughed into a handkerchief, trying to regain his composure.

The director paused to think, and then asked, 'Did she find out who they were and why they had rented the rooms?'

'She says that Khalil Abdali was the only one who dealt with her, and that he spoke in broken Balochi. He apparently seemed more comfortable in Pashto, which she doesn't understand. So she wasn't able to find out much about them. She anyway says that the locality has a huge migrant population, so one has simply stopped asking questions and seeking credentials. She did confirm that the men had big bags with them—which isn't unusual among migrant labourers. The interesting thing is that she claims to have overheard some of the men conversing in Arabic.'

'Okay,' the director absorbed the flood of information slowly. 'Till what time were these men in the rooms? What do the neighbours say?'

'It seems they were definitely there till around dinner-time. No one actually noticed them go, though. The place is pretty densely populated, so it's easy to lose oneself in a crowd.'

'What about the phone that was found?'

'By the looks of it, it spent the entire night submerged in water. The police have taken it to the lab for testing and our men will also have a look at it there. But right now, it is next to useless.'

'Was anything else found in the rooms?'

'No, sir. Not a scrap. The landlady swears that was the way she found it.'

'Okay. Record the statements of the neighbours as well and see if we get any clue about where these men came from and where they might have gone. Get the landlady to describe Khalil Abdali and let the police make a sketch. See if she can also describe some of Khalil's associates. And ask the police to immediately launch a hunt for the six men.'

'Yes, sir…' Elahi hesitated for a moment. 'There is one thing which might be of importance. There is a tea-stall opposite the rooms, and it seems Khalil and his men frequented it quite often. The police have questioned the tea-stall owner, and he remembers Khalil having spoken to him on the first day the men arrived in the locality. It seems Khalil was keen on knowing the easiest way of getting from Mohajir Camp to Clifton.'

So complete was the ensuing silence that the sound of the split air conditioner was clearly audible.

'Interesting,' Lieutenant-General Rehmat finally breathed out.

Unsure about how to respond to his boss's ambiguous observation, Elahi kept shut.

'Okay, I have already told you what needs to be done. Now just do everything at double the speed. Statements, sketches, manhunt… all double fast. Tell CCPO Raja that his men are doing a good job, so can he please press more policemen into the hunt. Tell him it is my personal request. And keep Major-General Dar informed about your progress. *Khuda hafiz*.'

The director reclined in his chair and smiled at the men across the table. 'We've come quite a distance from where we started this morning. But the question is—are Khalil Abdali and his men the Indians we have been looking for?'

'They can't be,' said Lieutenant-General Niazi, clearing his throat. 'Haider Nazir had mentioned that there were three Indians. This group has eight members. We're chasing the wrong people.'

'Maybe,' admitted Lieutenant-General Rehmat. 'But I have always said that an operation of this scale needs eight men at least. It's possible that Nazir got his facts wrong. And we can't forget the fact that Khalil asked the tea-stall owner for directions to Clifton. It's the most critical thing in this affair.'

'But these men were speaking Arabic, and this Khalil speaks Pashto,' Major-General Dar pointed out.

'I wouldn't expect the Indians to be talking in Hindustani or Bengali or Madrasi inside Pakistan. And the fact that Khalil Abdali speaks Pashto is important. The Indians have been meddling around quite a bit in Afghanistan. Maybe one of their men who was there is now part of this operation.'

'The only way we'll know for sure is by catching Khalil or one of his men alive,' said the major-general.

'Precisely. So let's hope Qasim Raja's men show some initiative. In fact, I suggest we depute some more of our men to Karachi immediately. Inform Elahi about this as well. Now that we have a clear trail to follow, let's go after Khalil and company like bloodhounds.'

As Major-General Dar rose to carry out the orders, the director turned to Lieutenant-General Niazi and was surprised to see that the colour had drained from the old soldier's face.

'What happened, Niazi sahib?'

'Nothing. Just a bit tired. I haven't been sleeping well... because of all this,' Lieutenant-General Niazi smiled weakly.

The director nodded thoughtfully. 'What news of the man who has been giving all of us so many headaches and sleepless nights?'

'He will be moved to Gwadar this afternoon.'

CHAPTER 10

28 July. Astoria Gardens, Clifton, Karachi

The muffled noise of car horns on the streets far below barely penetrated the hush of the bedroom. The bright morning sun, which had been streaming into the apartment an hour ago, had been eclipsed by a thick bank of clouds, but the humidity was still pretty high.

Shamsheer was sitting on the edge of the bed, legs crossed, staring blankly in front of him. Rafiq sat a little to his left, his back to the bed's headboard, a sheet of bubble wrap in his hands. He pressed and popped one bubble after another absent-mindedly.

Tup, tup… tup, tup…

Shamsheer turned towards Rafiq with a frown. '*Mat karo, bhai.* It's irritating,' he snapped.

The lieutenant looked up in surprise, then put the bubble wrap down on the pillow beside him. He considered Shamsheer for a while in silence.

'What major saab is suggesting is not just dangerous, it's also a clear case of insubordination,' he said at last, keeping his voice low. 'Colonel saab will be furious when he hears of this.'

Shamsheer glanced at Rafiq briefly, but said nothing.

'Even you are worried about this, aren't you?' Rafiq persisted.

'No, I'm not *worried*. I'm just thinking.'

Rafiq waited for an elaboration, but when he saw that Shamsheer wasn't going to oblige, he asked, 'But why is the major so obsessed about this operation? Why is he prepared to cross any line in pursuit of Dilawar?'

'You heard him. He doesn't want Project Abhimanyu to fail.'

'Yes, but the decision to abort this operation was not his. And Project Abhimanyu didn't fail because of him, so he's not going to be blamed for it.'

Shamsheer opened his mouth to say something, but changed his mind. Shaking his head, he said, 'It doesn't matter. As far as the major is concerned, this operation cannot fail, and now there's nothing you and I or Colonel

Mohan can do to make him think otherwise. If he has decided that he's not returning to India without completing this operation, that's it.'

'This is going to get us in trouble.'

Shamsheer looked at Rafiq with narrowed eyes. 'Get this straight. Major saab has made a decision and he has only *informed* us about it. He has not involved either of us in that decision in any way, so I don't see the need for *you* to worry about its consequences. Your job is safe and secure, so I suggest you sit quietly and wait for Colonel saab to get us out of here.' Shamsheer's tone left no doubt about what he thought of Rafiq's opinions.

Taken aback by the bluntness of Shamsheer's words, Rafiq fell into momentary silence. When he spoke, his tone was conciliatory. 'No disrespect, sir. It's just that this has come as a big surprise to me. But how is he going to get Dilawar all by himself?'

'I have no idea. All I know is that now that he's made up his mind, he will find a way.'

'With Saadat's help?' Rafiq asked doubtfully, gesturing towards the bedroom across the hall where Imtiaz had been billeted with Saadat for the last fifteen minutes.

Shamsheer merely shrugged.

'I don't even know if we should trust that man anymore,' Rafiq argued. 'How do we know he isn't the one who has been informing the Pakistanis about our operation? He's been in Pakistan for years, so it's natural for him to have built friendships and loyalties here. And at the end of the day, his business interests are all here. Siding with the Pakistanis will always work to his advantage.'

Shamsheer shook his head. 'If Saadat was the traitor, he would have exposed us long ago. He had all the information about Project Abhimanyu from the very beginning. He knew when we were coming here and how. We have been at his mercy ever since we entered Pakistan. He could have had us arrested in Paposh Nagar. He could have directed the cops to this apartment. Yet, we're still here, unharmed. Saadat may not like us because we're a threat to his safety, but he isn't the one who has been sharing secrets with the Pakistanis.'

The brief silence that followed was broken by the lieutenant. 'Shouldn't we try and talk the major out of his decision?'

'It won't work,' Shamsheer was categorical. 'And anyway, I think his reasons for continuing with the mission are absolutely valid. We are already inside Pakistan, and if we turn back now, we may never get another opportunity to come back and kill Dilawar. I'm beginning to see the major's point clearly.'

Rafiq studied the captain's face. Then, as the significance of Shamsheer's words dawned on him, his eyes narrowed suspiciously. 'Are you saying that…?'

Shamsheer nodded. 'Yes. Major saab won't be alone when he goes after Dilawar. I will be with him.'

Rafiq stared back at Shamsheer in stupefaction, his lips working silently as he struggled to form words. 'You… can't be… you must be joking?'

Seeing Shamsheer shake his head gravely, the lieutenant swallowed hard. 'But… why? Your entire career…'

'I know,' Shamsheer interrupted calmly.

'So?'

'A soldier's duty first lies with the men he works with and the man who leads him. I may have been put on this operation by Colonel Mohan, but my leader is Major Imtiaz. Colonels and generals can give orders, but it is the leader at the battlefront who knows what best to do. Major saab is working to make this operation a success, and he is the one who has our best interests in mind. That's the only reason why he has chosen to go after Dilawar alone, instead of seeking our assistance. As a soldier, it is my duty to respond to my leader's decision and help him achieve his objective.'

As Shamsheer stood up, Rafiq looked at him in bewilderment. The captain stared back, before giving a shrug and walking out of the room. Rafiq sat on the bed, looking down at the white and pink floral pattern on the bedspread, listening to Shamsheer's footsteps receding into his bedroom.

Once he was certain that Shamsheer wouldn't be returning, Rafiq got off the bed, rummaged through his bag and pulled out the Thuraya sat-phone. It was time to place another call.

* * *

Saadat sat slumped on the chair opposite Imtiaz, his thin shoulders drooping, his dour face showing no trace of the relief that had manifested the previous night, once Project Abhimanyu had been called off. The only thing animated about Saadat was his eyes, which cast about the room anxiously. He reminded Imtiaz of a mouse that was desperately looking for a way to get out of a mousetrap.

'What you ask for is… very…' Saadat trailed off weakly, almost as if he dreaded even contemplating the consequences of what was wanted of him.

'And what have I asked for?' Imtiaz reasoned calmly. 'I have not put a gun into your hands and ordered you to come with me to find and kill Dilawar. I have not asked you to loan me one of your travel agency buses, so that I can drive around Pakistan looking for his whereabouts. All I want from you is that you use your contacts to find out where Dilawar is right now. Once I have that information, I shall walk out of here and never bother you again. That's a promise.'

Saadat shuffled his feet uncomfortably. 'You know how dangerous all this is for me. I have to live in this country. If I'm caught...'

'You have risked a lot to help us, and I can't thank you enough for that. But huzoor, that is why I implore you to help me one last time. You are the one man I can trust to take me that extra mile.'

Saadat heaved a deep sigh. 'There is also Colonel sahib. If he comes to know that I have been helping you behind his back, he will make life hell for me. He only needs an excuse to start harassing me.'

'He will come to know only if one of us tells him,' Imtiaz countered.

'They might tell him,' Saadat jerked his thumb in the direction of the other bedroom.

'I shall tell Shamsheer and Rafiq not to mention it to the Colonel. And anyway, you can pin all the blame on me. You can always say that I threatened you into parting with the information.'

Saadat stared at the floor morosely. 'Why do you want to risk your life like this? Colonel sahib himself said it is far too dangerous to go any further. Why are you pushing yourself when even your superiors don't think it's worth the effort?'

'Because I haven't come so far just to fail. Mian, you have risked *your* safety to make this operation a success. I can't let all your efforts—all our efforts—go to waste. I can't allow Project Abhimanyu to be held to ransom by a traitor whose only intention is to see all of us fail. I'm doing this for each and every one of us.'

Saadat looked at the major's honest face for a few moments. 'Huzoor, I admire and respect your determination. But your decision is a terrible one. I honestly don't think you stand a chance all by yourself.'

'Perhaps you're right, but there's no harm in trying. *Himmat-e-mardan, madad-e-khuda.* I need to know where to find Dilawar. The rest I shall leave to God.'

'I shall try, major sahib.' Saadat got up from his chair and made his way to the door. 'But there is no guarantee I'll be able to find the information you want. Pakistan may not be as big as India, but it is still a large country. Irshad Dilawar could be anywhere.'

'*Shukriya, Saadat mian*. Help me find the man who is responsible for so many deaths, including that of your younger brother. Help me for your sake and mine and your younger brother's.'

Saadat paused for a fraction of a second, his hand on the doorknob. Then, without uttering a word, he opened the door and walked out of the apartment. Imtiaz glanced at his watch. It was just past 11.30—which meant twelve noon in India. It was time to inform the colonel about his decision.

28 July. Bahadur Shah Zafar Marg, ITO, Delhi

The two-storeyed building was situated in a lane a stone's throw from the office of the University Grants Commission. The building's façade was fairly decrepit, paint peeling off the woodwork and large splotches of damp making grotesque patterns on the walls. By the looks of it, the building's windows were rarely opened to admit fresh air and sunlight, and the sole entry into the building was a small aluminium-and-glass door, accessed from one side. A big signboard outside announced that a company by the name of Vaishnav Traders occupied the premises, but there was nothing to say what exactly the establishment traded in.

Inside, past a small reception area guarded by a formidable Punjabi matron who kept salesmen and other unwanted visitors out, was one of the field offices of the Intelligence Bureau. And in one corner of the bustling office sat Assistant Director Abhay Shankar Pasricha, a small man with stooping shoulders and a studious face—one that would have looked perfectly at home on a university campus. In fact, Assistant Director Pasricha had been a senior research scholar studying environmental security and terrorism at Jawaharlal Nehru University before he was recruited into the Intelligence Bureau more than a decade earlier.

The assistant director was, at that moment, looking impassively at Intelligence Officer Binoy Verghese as the latter explained the broad details of the case, beginning with the log that was being maintained on Haider Nazir, and the mysterious three-and-a-half minute telephone conversation that the Pakistani had had on the night of 25 July. Now and then, the assistant director glanced at a file that Verghese had presented him. The file lay on the table, unopened.

When Verghese reached the point where he had initiated an enquiry on Parthoprotim Lahiri in Dehradun, he paused. 'Unfortunately, there was nothing in Lahiri's file that was even remotely suspicious. I admit that I was literally chasing my own tail over the matter when I chanced upon a small factoid on Lahiri's family.'

Assistant Director Pasricha remained silent, but his eyes showed a spark of interest.

'It was Lahiri's wife's maiden name that gave me the vital clue,' said Verghese. 'Before marriage, his wife's name was Nandini Dixit.'

'What's your point?'

'Nandini Dixit is the younger sister of Major-General Tushar Dixit.'

The assistant director scrutinized the junior officer narrowly. Verghese could sense that what he had just revealed was being processed rapidly, and that the outcome of that evaluation would determine the fate of the investigation he was proposing.

Assistant Director Pasricha shook his head. 'That doesn't mean anything, Verghese. You cannot launch an investigation on someone of Major-General Tushar Dixit's rank and stature just because he happens to be the brother of someone from whose house a mysterious phone call was made. You'll have to do better than that.'

'But sir, the call was made to a Pakistani embassy staffer...'

'Agreed, but don't put the cart before the horse. First investigate and establish who made that call. It could have been anybody. No, there is no way I can clear your request to open an investigation on Major-General Dixit.'

From the very beginning, Verghese had known that he was working on a tenuous premise, one that was unlikely to cut any ice with Assistant Director Pasricha. He had realized that getting an authorization to investigate Major-General Dixit on the basis of one small fact was out of the question. Which was why, after getting home the previous night, he had decided to stick his neck out and make a couple of phone calls to two of his Delhi Malayalee Association friends working in the Defence Ministry.

One of them had called back in the morning with the information he had wanted.

'Sir, I know this is a breach of protocol and you're not going to like it,' Verghese pressed. 'But as I suspected there may be something very complicated going on, I used certain unofficial channels to find out a few things about Major-General Dixit.'

The assistant director's expression instantly turned to one of disapproval, but Verghese chose to ignore it. 'While most of the things I wanted to know were either unavailable or of no use in this matter, there's one critical thing that could change your decision about giving me the authorization.'

'Let's see,' Assistant Director Pasricha was noncommittal.

'I have irrefutable evidence that Major-General Dixit was out of Delhi on the night of 25 July. In fact, he was in Dehradun that night, staying over at his sister and brother-in-law's house.'

The assistant director raised his eyebrows. 'Are you sure?'

'Yes sir. Major-General Dixit was in that house when the call to Haider Nazir was made.'

28 July. Astoria Gardens, Clifton, Karachi

Imtiaz sat on one of the drawing room sofas, staring at Shamsheer. The captain looked back at the major, waiting for him to respond to the offer that had just been made. Rafiq stood to one side, his eyes watching Imtiaz and Shamsheer as he tried to assess what the outcome of Shamsheer's proposal would be.

'Do you understand what it means to challenge the order of a colonel of the Indian Army?' the major finally broke the silence by addressing Shamsheer. Imtiaz remembered what Colonel Mohan had told him just half an hour earlier while trying to persuade him to change his mind, and he figured those were very good arguments to sway the captain's resolve. 'It means a court-martial and a very high possibility of being dismissed from service. It means a life of disgrace. Why do you want to destroy what you have worked so hard and so long to achieve in a moment of rashness?'

'Sir, this is not a rash or impulsive decision,' Shamsheer countered. 'I have thought about this all morning. Yes, I am risking everything by choosing to come with you. But then, I risked everything the day I entered Pakistan for this operation. Actually, maybe the day I signed up to join the army. It's the same with you and Rafiq, sir. We have already put our lives on the line. Once that's been done, there's nothing more to risk.'

Imtiaz pondered this for a while before speaking. 'For a soldier, there is one thing more precious than life, and that is honour. That must never be risked, and your decision puts your honour at stake. There is no honour in being court-martialled and dismissed from service, captain.'

'But sir, you are taking that risk as well. There has to be a reason why *you* are prepared to stake your honour, and if you can do it, so can I.'

'I am doing this because I don't want this mission to fail. As the leader of a mission that is falling apart, I am trying to redeem my honour by making the operation a success.'

'If you have your honour to redeem, I have mine, sir,' Shamsheer argued stubbornly. 'After all, I am also a part of this failed operation. If his leader chooses to stay and fight, it is a soldier's duty—and his *right*—to stay and fight alongside his leader. By asking me to leave you to fight alone, you are not giving me an opportunity to redeem my honour. Is that fair?'

Imtiaz considered Shamsheer silently for a moment. At last, turning to Rafiq, he spoke, 'The captain and I have worked together quite a few times in the past, and we go back some way. Would you mind if I talked to him in private?'

'Absolutely not, sir,' Rafiq answered. He turned to leave the room, but Imtiaz stopped him.

'No, no. I didn't mean you should leave the room. I meant that the captain and I will go out for a small walk. Sitting inside all day can get tiresome anyway.' Noticing the look of alarm on Rafiq's face, he quickly added, 'Don't worry. I don't disagree with Colonel Mohan on everything. We won't be going out of this apartment complex. There's a nice garden outside and we'll just be taking a walk around it.'

Though not very big, the garden was spacious enough to meet the requirements of the residents of Astoria Gardens. Lined on all sides by decorative palms, the garden had a nice broad walking path that ran around the sprawl of lawn in the middle. Rose shrubs dotted the lawn, while four gulmohar trees spread a canopy overhead.

Imtiaz and Shamsheer had barely entered the garden and walked twenty feet when the latter spoke. 'I'm sorry if I said something that was improper, sir. I sincerely apologize for that. It's just that I want to come...' He stopped on seeing the major raise a hand.

'There's no need to apologize. You said nothing that I wouldn't have said, and I do not for a minute doubt your intentions.' Imtiaz surveyed Shamsheer for a moment, before smiling softly. 'I want to thank you for offering your help. It is welcome and I accept it.'

Shamsheer's face brightened with relief instantly. 'Thank you, sir. Thank you so...'

Imtiaz had raised his hand again. 'You can thank me once we have finished what we are setting out to achieve,' he said, his face once again serious. 'But first tell me... when did you decide to come with me?'

Shamsheer looked slightly perplexed at the question, but he still cast his mind back. 'Some two hours ago...'

Why are you and Shamsheer behaving like cowboys when you should be behaving like mature commandos?

'And before you told me of your decision, did you tell anyone else about it?'

'Yes, sir. I told Rafiq, sir. After you told us about your decision, we were talking about what to do next, and I told him I had decided to join you.' The captain looked at Imtiaz apologetically. 'I am sorry I did that, sir. I know I should have told you first…'

'No, I'm glad you told him. It clears a lot of things.'

'Like what?'

'Like… what a rookie like Rafiq Mehmood is doing in this operation, and why the colonel insisted on sending him instead of a more senior and experienced commando.'

Shamsheer stared at the major, mystified.

'Let me explain. Before you came and told me about your decision, I was talking to Colonel Mohan about *my* decision.'

'I know, sir,' the captain interjected. 'And immediately before that you were with Saadat. That's why I couldn't tell you about my decision earlier.'

'Right,' Imtiaz nodded. 'The colonel was horrified and furious when I told him what I intended to do, and he spent a long time trying to brainwash me out of pursuing Project Abhimanyu. He threw everything he had at me. Court-martial, promotions, more opportunities to lead Unit Kilo operations… But that's not important. What is, is the fact that, while trying to convince me, he said something that, at that time, sounded very bizarre—he asked me why the two of us were behaving like cowboys when we should be behaving like mature commandos. He asked me what *we* hoped to achieve by going after Dilawar like this.'

'You and me?' Shamsheer was astonished.

'Yes. He mentioned you by name. I found it strange because, at that time, all I knew was that I was going alone. You were nowhere in the picture. Yes, it's possible that the colonel could have assumed that I had somehow convinced you and Rafiq to come with me. But if that was the case, why did he name only *you* and not Rafiq? It's because he knew you were coming with me… while Rafiq wasn't.'

'You mean…'

'Yes, the colonel knew of your decision to join me *even before* I knew of it. How do you think that happened?'

'Through the only other person who knew of my decision,' said Shamsheer quietly.

Imtiaz nodded. 'Unfortunately for Colonel Mohan, he did not know that you had not found the time or the opportunity to tell *me* about your decision. He simply assumed that you had already told me about it as well.'

The two soldiers walked in silence for a while. The clouds that had been gathering over Karachi since morning now hung heavy and grey over the city. Rain was imminent.

Suddenly, Shamsheer turned to Imtiaz. 'Sir, that means Colonel Mohan must also have known about *your* decision to go after Dilawar before you called him. But you said that he sounded shocked when you told him. So he must have been pretending...'

'Yes, he was,' agreed Imtiaz.

'But how did Rafiq tell the colonel?'

The major shrugged. 'That doesn't matter. The point is Rafiq has been spying on us for the colonel. So question number one: why was Rafiq sent to spy on us? Two: why is the colonel enacting such a big charade? Three: what is happening here that we both know nothing about?'

As the two officers reverted to pensive silence, the first few drops of rain began falling haphazardly over Clifton.

* * *

Imtiaz folded his arms across his chest and considered Rafiq thoughtfully. The lieutenant shifted from one foot to the other, unnerved by the major's piercing gaze. He stole a quick glance towards Shamsheer, who was seated on a sofa looking up at him, then turned back to the major.

'Are you absolutely sure about this?' Imtiaz finally asked, cocking his head to one side.

'Yes, sir,' Rafiq answered quickly.

'I'd like to know why?'

'Sir, I have had some time to think about this, and everything that the captain said makes sense. A soldier's duty towards his leader... his honour... the fact that we may never get another chance to kill Dilawar... I realize what he is saying is right. And if he's right, there's really only one option in front of me—helping you in hunting down Irshad Dilawar.'

'You know that volunteering to come with me has some very serious implications for your career,' Imtiaz looked at the lieutenant evenly. 'You could really get shafted.'

'I know, sir. You explained that to Shamsheer. But if it doesn't matter to him, it doesn't matter to me.'

Imtiaz heaved a doubtful sigh. 'I don't know...'

'Sir, please let me come with you,' Rafiq spoke entreatingly. 'It would be a disgrace to me if the two of you went without me. I want to help... Sir, *please*.'

The major appraised Rafiq for a moment, then looked at Shamsheer, a smile playing at the corner of his lips. 'Your stubbornness is spreading like a virus.'

'I beg your pardon sir, but you started it,' Shamsheer smiled back.

Imtiaz turned to Rafiq. 'I tried my best to convince the captain not to do this, but it was of no use. So I'm not going to waste more time trying to convince you. One more person in the team is always welcome.'

Rafiq's face lit up. 'Thank you for accepting me, sir. Really, I'm honoured...' As the major nodded politely and turned away, Rafiq asked, a bit too eagerly, 'So what's the plan now?'

'The plan...' Imtiaz paused and looked the lieutenant in the eye. '...is to wait for Saadat to get us Irshad Dilawar's exact whereabouts. We then figure out how to get there and kill him.'

28 July. Chandimandir Cantonment, Panchkula

General Dixit stood in the midst of a group of fellow army officers, a glass of Johnnie Walker Black Label in his hand. He nodded and shook his head distractedly as the officers around him debated the merits of including three spinners in India's upcoming tour of Australia, but every now and then, he glanced at his watch impatiently.

Just his bloody luck that Project Abhimanyu had to get out of hand on the *one* day he was out of Delhi! And just when he'd thought the colonel had everything under control.

The general had barely landed in Panchkula that afternoon when Colonel Mohan had called him and broken the news about Imtiaz and Shamsheer's mutiny. Unfortunately, the general was attending an important commemoration ceremony at the Western Command headquarters, which was to be followed by a formal dinner—neither of which he could afford to skip. So he had sat through the commemoration, chafing inwardly, wondering how things could have gone so wrong, so suddenly.

Under the pretext of checking for missed calls or messages, General Dixit pulled out his mobile phone and once again checked the time. It was just past eight. Dinner wouldn't be served for another forty-five minutes, and he'd be lucky to be on board the Dhruv by 9.30. Even then, he wouldn't be able to talk to the colonel as he'd have the voluble Lieutenant-General Sherawat of the 22 Infantry Division for company all the way back to Delhi.

He hoped the colonel would call with an update soon.

'What do you think, Dixit saab?' The general looked up to see Lieutenant-General Sherawat address him. 'I say we should have Harbhajan and one more spinner. That's all.'

Before the general could form an opinion, another officer answered on his behalf. 'Lekin Harbhajan's form is the problem. He's not getting wickets these days.'

'That's why I say our attack must focus on pace,' Lieutenant-General Sherawat countered. 'Why carry excess baggage when spin anyway doesn't work on Australian pitches...'

At that moment, General Dixit's phone rang. Excusing himself, he walked hurriedly on to the manicured lawns surrounding the officer's club. Once he was out of earshot, he took the call.

'Yes. Tell me,' he said brusquely.

'Sir, as per my instructions, Rafiq has volunteered to join Imtiaz and Shamsheer,' Colonel Mohan's voice came through clearly.

'They've accepted his offer?'

'Yes sir.'

'Good. Bloody bastards!' General Dixit paused, then spoke again. 'So has he found out what their plan is?'

'Sir, they are going to Parachinar.'

'*What*? Damn, how did they come to know he's there?'

'Saadat visited the apartment this evening, sir.'

'He's helping them?' Conscious that his voice had risen sharply, the general looked around, hoping he hadn't attracted any attention and wasn't being overheard. He covered his mouth with his hand to muffle his voice. 'Once this is over, Saadat will have to kiss his scrawny, dried-up ass goodbye,' he growled. 'Fuck!'

'Saadat probably didn't have a choice in the matter, sir. Imtiaz might have arm-twisted him in some way...'

'Fuck!' General Dixit cursed again. 'They're going to *Parachinar*!'

'That's actually not a problem, sir.'

'Colonel... Are you kidding me?'

'Dilawar was moved out of Parachinar this afternoon, sir. Apparently the ISI think Parachinar is unsafe because of the Americans cracking down on the Taliban.'

'So... where is he now?' the general whispered.

'At the Gwadar safe house, sir.'

'Oh!' The general could feel the relief flooding through him. 'So our major Rambo is on the wrong trail. That's good.'

'Sir, what do we do about Imtiaz and Shamsheer now?'

'Screw them!' The general spoke with feeling. 'When are they leaving for Parachinar?'

'Tomorrow night, it seems,' the colonel replied. 'Rafiq says they're going to start planning the details tomorrow morning. Imtiaz has asked Saadat to get him maps of Parachinar and the safe house there.'

'That gives us time to think. I'm boarding the helicopter in an hour or so, but it will be late by the time I get to Delhi. So let's meet first thing tomorrow morning. My place... not later than eight o'clock.'

29 July. Astoria Gardens, Clifton, Karachi

Rafiq depressed the lever on the cistern and knotted his pyjamas, his eyes struggling to keep themselves open. Exiting the bathroom, he fumbled with the light switch and was about to turn back into bed when he realized that his throat was parched.

Bleary-eyed, he shambled out of his bedroom, switched on the light in the hall and made his way to the kitchen. Opening the refrigerator, he pulled out a bottle of water and drank a few gulps before replacing it. He was about to switch the hall light off and return to his bedroom when something in the periphery of his vision caught his attention.

The light from the hall fell on a portion of the darkened drawing room—the portion closest to the main door of the house. And in this half-light, Rafiq noticed a pair of shoes arranged neatly by the main door. His shoes.

The presence of his shoes by the door didn't surprise him. What did, however, was the absence of more shoes. There should have been *three* pairs—his, as well as those belonging to the major and the captain.

Rafiq's eyes flew open instantly, every muscle in his body taut. He jerked his head around and looked at the door leading into the major's bedroom. It was closed—something that the major never did.

Rafiq cursed. He turned the other way and looked at Shamsheer's bedroom on the far side. It was closed too.

Quickly but softly, Rafiq opened the door to Imtiaz's bedroom and looked in. It was empty. He checked the attached bathroom to see if it was occupied. It wasn't. With rising panic, he rushed to Shamsheer's bedroom, but even before he got to it, he knew it would be empty. For as he passed the main door, he noticed that the latch and chain used to fasten the door from the inside were undone—even though he had seen Shamsheer latching and bolting the door before they had retired for the night.

A minute later, Rafiq was sitting on his bed, fully alert. As he cradled the Thuraya sat-phone to his ear, he heard the bell ringing at the other end.

'Hello.' Colonel Mohan's voice was thick and heavy with sleep.

'Sir, Rafiq here.' The lieutenant waited for an acknowledgement, but when there was none, he spoke urgently. 'Sir, the house is empty.'

'Which house?' The colonel sounded disoriented.

'This one. I mean Astoria. The major and the captain are not here.'

A fraction of a second later, Colonel Mohan's voice came as a whip-crack. '*What?*'

Rafiq quickly told the colonel how he had discovered Imtiaz and Shamsheer's disappearance. The colonel listened quietly before exploding with frustration.

'Oh goddamn it… Damn, damn, damn,' he shouted. There was a brief pause, and then he spoke again. 'Listen carefully, lieutenant. When did you last see them?'

'Sir, just before we retired to bed, about…' Rafiq glanced at the bedside clock. It was nearing four o'clock. 'About four hours ago. Just before midnight, sir. We finished dinner and watched some TV…'

'Okay, okay,' the colonel cut in. 'Did you check their bedrooms to see if their personal belongings are still there.'

'I already did, sir. Their bags are missing, and although some clothes are lying around, most of it isn't there.'

'What about the weapons? Have they been taken as well?'

'Two combat knives are missing, sir. But all the weapons are here.'

'Okay. So they have gone,' Colonel Mohan spoke with a finality that left little room for doubt. After a short pause, he spoke again. 'You didn't notice any change in their behaviour, I assume.'

'No, sir. Everything was very… cordial. The major even discussed some routes we could take to reach Parachinar. I didn't get the impression that they suspected anything.'

'Never mind, lieutenant.' Rafiq heard Colonel Mohan sigh. Then, as if making up his mind, the colonel spoke again. 'Now I want you to stay on standby. Scan the whole apartment for any evidence of where the major and the captain might have gone. If you find something, call me immediately. Otherwise, wait for my instructions.'

'Yes, sir.'

'One more thing. When Saadat came there last evening, did all of you meet him?'

'No, sir. Only the major did.'

'So it was Imtiaz who told you that you'll all be going to Parachinar next?'

'Yes. He told me and Shamsheer. Saadat brought the information that Dilawar is in Parachinar.'

'But you didn't hear Saadat say that, did you?'

'No sir. It was the major who told us.'

29 July. Hauz Khas Enclave, Delhi

'I tried everything to convince him to change his mind. I coaxed and cajoled him, I promised that we would revive Project Abhimanyu as soon as the environment was conducive; I offered him a deal of leading the next three Unit Kilo operations, and I threatened him with court-martial and dismissal. Nothing worked, sir. He was adamant that he would complete this operation.'

'Hmph!' General Dixit snorted. 'I always thought he was a pig-headed bastard.' The general scowled and took a large gulp of black coffee as if to soothe some nagging pain.

The general and Colonel Mohan were in the drawing room of the former's house, not far from the busy intersection of Outer Ring Road and Aurobindo Marg. Although daybreak was still an hour away, the distant noise of early morning traffic filtered into the room through the open bay window that overlooked a small neighbourhood park. While the colonel sat on a rattan chair, the general stood leaning against a mammoth bookcase, its shelves filled with rows and rows of books. Tracer, the general's pet Labrador, blind in one eye and fairly advanced in years, lay snoozing on the carpet.

'The worst part is that Imtiaz has decided to cut all lines of communication with us.' The colonel looked morose. 'As he was convinced that the plot to kill Dilawar had been leaked to the Pakistanis, he didn't want to jeopardize his plans any further by sharing them with anyone.'

'And now that it's obvious that he suspects Rafiq of something, my guess is he has his suspicions about us as well. Definitely you…' General Dixit took another sip of coffee and shook his head ruefully. 'Too smart for his own good. We shouldn't have picked him for this mission. Poor judgment on our part.'

'Both him and Shamsheer, sir.'

The general nodded. 'Old cronies, both of them. Clever of you to have sent that lieutenant along to keep tabs on Imtiaz. You didn't envisage the possibility of Imtiaz rebelling like this, did you?'

'I didn't, sir. But something told me that we might need to keep an eye on him. And Rafiq is the only one I could trust to do the job. No other commando in Unit Kilo would have agreed to spy on Imtiaz. They all respect him too much.'

General Dixit walked to the window and looked at the darkness outside. A steady drizzle had started, the sound of raindrops on the leaves muffling all other noises. 'That's all very well, but now that Rafiq is no longer in a position to spy on Imtiaz and Shamsheer, what next?'

'We have to somehow stop them from getting to Dilawar.'

General Dixit turned and looked down at the junior officer. 'If we knew precisely where Imtiaz and Shamsheer are at this moment, we could pass the information on to the Pakistanis through our friend Haider Nazir,' the general's voice was cold and calculative. 'But then, we don't know where they are, so that won't work. So the next best thing is to warn the Pakistanis that these two are on their way to Parachinar. We can only hope that the Pakistanis will figure out a way of nabbing them when they get there.'

'Sir, they are good soldiers,' Colonel Mohan spoke pressingly. 'I think we should find some way of intercepting them...'

'Intercepting them? Why?' The general's voice rose by a note. Tracer lifted his head and looked at his master dolefully, then put his head back on his paws.

'I wasn't the one to challenge orders and hatch this rabid plan of chasing Dilawar all over Pakistan,' General Dixit dropped his voice, but not his vehemence. 'I wasn't the one to cut all lines of communication. Those were Imtiaz's decisions. They might be good soldiers, but right now our only concern must be Dilawar's safety—nothing else should matter. As long as Dilawar is safe in Gwadar, I don't care what happens to Imtiaz and Shamsheer in Parachinar.'

'Sir, when I spoke of intercepting them, I was thinking of Dilawar's safety.'

There was something in the colonel's voice that made General Dixit stop and take notice. 'What do you mean?'

'I mean Imtiaz and Shamsheer may actually be heading towards Gwadar instead of Parachinar.'

Seeing the confusion on the general's face, Colonel Mohan continued, 'Sir, we are assuming that they are going to Parachinar because that's what Imtiaz told Rafiq yesterday. But from the manner in which they have disappeared, we can now guess that something gave Rafiq away to Imtiaz and Shamsheer. If that's the case, how can we be sure that Imtiaz wasn't feeding Rafiq with wrong information?'

'Bloody hell!' General Dixit's lips moved in a silent whisper at the possibility.

'Sir, Saadat is supposed to have given Imtiaz the information about Dilawar being in Parachinar. My point is that Saadat has built an extremely effective and reliable network inside Pakistan. With such a strong network, chances are that Saadat would have known that Dilawar has been shifted from Parachinar to Gwadar, and *this* is the information that he would have given Imtiaz. After all, he doesn't need to mislead Imtiaz.'

'But Imtiaz instead told Rafiq about Parachinar to throw him off track,' the general surmised. 'Hmm… We could be wrong, of course. Perhaps they know nothing of Gwadar.'

'My guess is they do, sir. But even if they don't, it's a possibility that we cannot afford to overlook.'

'Damn! We must take Saadat to task once this thing is over,' General Dixit growled. 'But first, we must do everything in our capacity to stop Imtiaz and Shamsheer.'

'We don't have too many options, sir,' Colonel Mohan looked at the general unhappily.

'We have one—the option of eliminating them altogether. Activate Lieutenant Rafiq Mehmood immediately.'

Colonel Mohan shifted in his chair unhappily. 'They are both very good men, sir,' he repeated stiffly.

'Then it becomes even more imperative to have them removed before they can get to Dilawar,' the general spoke icily. 'Activate Rafiq with the objective of eliminating them.'

Instead of responding, the colonel sat pensively in his chair. Tracer yawned, stood up and walked stiffly out of the room.

Noticing the colonel's reticence, General Dixit said, 'Come on, Mohan. There is no room for sentimentality in our trade. Imtiaz and Shamsheer may be really good soldiers, but right now they pose a serious threat to us. There is only one way to stop them now.'

Colonel Mohan sighed and looked at the general. 'I shall activate Rafiq, sir. But to be totally honest, if Rafiq has lost Imtiaz's trust, I don't think he will be able to stop them.'

'Why not?' General Dixit stared in surprise. 'Rafiq is supposed to be one of the best men we've got in Unit Kilo.'

'He is, sir. But he's not good enough to stop Imtiaz. Not when Imtiaz's guard is up. He and Shamsheer will keep a lookout for Rafiq and will always be two steps ahead of him. I've trained and worked with Imtiaz long enough to know how his mind works.'

'Are you implying that Imtiaz is unstoppable?' There was an uneasy edge in the general's voice.

'Well, the only person who can counter him now is someone who knows how he thinks and acts. And someone he doesn't expect to be in the picture. There's only one such person I can think of—me.'

General Dixit stared into his empty coffee mug for a while. Then, placing the mug on an ornate wooden cabinet that housed a minibar, he looked at the colonel quizzically.

'So you will go into Pakistan to stop him?'

'It's the only way.'

'But you will still activate Rafiq. I don't want to take any chances. I want to put in action everything that can stop Imtiaz, and the truth is that Rafiq has a lead over you. Activate him immediately.'

'Yes, sir,' the colonel answered thoughtfully. 'I'll talk to Rafiq right away. As a starting point, I'll ask him to speak to Saadat when he comes in later this morning. I'm sure if we apply enough pressure, Saadat will give us some critical leads. I'll also ask Rafiq to keep me informed on the progress he makes. Here onwards, the two of us will have to work in tandem.'

'When do you plan to leave for Pakistan?'

'Today. As early as possible, sir.'

'And what's your plan to enter Pakistan and track Imtiaz and Shamsheer down?'

'None at the moment, sir,' Colonel Mohan replied candidly. 'But in an hour or so, I'll have a plan ready.'

PART THREE:
THE GREAT GAMBLE

CHAPTER 11

29 July. Mubarak Village, Kiamari Town, Karachi

The three hutments were located deep inside a small but dense mangrove forest, approximately three kilometres north of the picturesque Mubarak Village, which lay on the western extremity of Kiamari Town. The east-west road connecting Mubarak Goth to Hawke's Bay ran a kilometre to the south of the mangrove forest, but the vicinity was largely uninhabited.

Al-Kamil and his men had chanced upon the forest the morning after their run from Mohajir Camp, and Al-Kamil had instantly realized that it offered them a nice hideaway. While scoping it out for shelter, they had come across the three shanties which were inhabited by two families of vagabond Balochi tribesmen. The mercenaries had stormed the huts, taken the nine Balochi villagers hostage, and herded them into one of the huts where they now lay—bound, gagged and beaten into submission.

Al-Kamil emerged from the largest of the huts, his head bent as he squeezed himself out of the low, narrow door. Outside, one of his men was minding the hut holding the captive Balochis, while another was busy cleaning his Kalashnikov. The remaining three had been posted as guards on the western, southern and northeastern fringes of the forest to watch out for any sign of approaching danger.

Striking a westerly direction, Al-Kamil walked through the mangroves, till he reached a narrow stretch of sandy beach separating the forest from the sea. The bright, blue morning sky was cloudless, and the clear sea water rolled serenely onto land, wave after wave. The beach itself was completely deserted.

Al-Kamil strode on to the wet sand and simply stood for a while, staring out at the sea, his dirty brown shirt billowing in the wind. Then, snapping out of a reverie, he unbuttoned his breast pocket and pulled out a folded sheet of paper. Opening it, he looked at the map drawn on it with a blue ballpoint pen.

Tahir Shawqat wasn't much of a cartographer or an artist, but Al-Kamil knew that the rough drawing the crippled Syrian had made the previous evening was going to prove invaluable in his hunt for Irshad Dilawar.

Al-Kamil and Tahir Shawqat had known one another from the time they had trained young Hezbollah recruits for combat in South Lebanon, during the mid-nineties. Shawqat had been a junior officer of the Shu'bat al-Mukhabarat al-'Askariyya, or the Military Intelligence Service of Syria, which coordinated the war activities of the Syrian and Lebanese forces that were fighting the Israel Defense Forces in Lebanon. Al-Kamil and Shawqat had worked together for almost two years when, in April 1996, Israel launched Operation Grapes of Wrath to counter the shelling of Northern Israel by the Hezbollah.

At the time Israel commenced the operation, Al-Kamil and Shawqat were in the Beqaa Valley in Lebanon, training a group of fifty cadets in a waterworks installation that had been converted into a Hezbollah training centre. On the morning of the third day of Operation Grapes of Wrath, the waterworks installation came under heavy artillery fire. Al-Kamil, who had gone for his early morning run, escaped the attack, but on returning, he had found the camp in shambles.

Ploughing through the ruins, he discovered Shawqat lying semi-conscious, his right leg mangled under the impact of one of the shells. Al-Kamil freed Shawqat from under the debris and carried him to the nearest hospital five kilometres away, where, over the next seven months, the Syrian slowly regained partial use of his leg. On being discharged from hospital, Shawqat was incapable of returning to the Syrian army, and thereafter, he had just disappeared from Lebanon.

Al-Kamil had all but forgotten Shawqat when, three years ago, the Syrian had suddenly called on him at his house on the outskirts of Beirut. Al-Kamil learnt that Shawqat had somehow ended up in Karachi, where he was involved in a money laundering and cricket match-fixing racket. Apologetic about having gone away without saying goodbye, Shawqat was eternally thankful to Al-Kamil for having saved his life. As a token of gratitude, he had told Al-Kamil that he would repay him in any way possible, should Al-Kamil ever need help in Syria or Pakistan. He had also given Al-Kamil his phone number in Karachi.

Three years after coming into its possession, Al-Kamil had finally dialled that number from a public phone booth outside Mubarak Village the previous afternoon. He needed to find out what had happened to Jamal and Tabarek, and the Syrian was the only one he could trust to help him in Pakistan.

'Is it really Katzav, the butcher of Beirut?' Shawqat had sounded overjoyed over the phone. 'You're in *Karachi*? Come home, my friend... come...'

Two hours later, sitting in the drawing room of Shawqat's house in Qasba Colony in SITE Town, Al-Kamil learnt about the death of two unidentified men in a police encounter on Mauripur Road. Shawqat managed to procure a picture of one of the dead men, whom Al-Kamil instantly identified as Tabarek.

'Can you help me find two men to replace them?' Al-Kamil had asked.

The Syrian, who had listened to Al-Kamil with rapt attention, sighed. 'Difficult at such short notice, but let me see what I can do for an old friend.' Asking Al-Kamil to make himself at home, he had limped out of the room.

After nearly an hour, just as Al-Kamil had begun having grave misgivings, Shawqat had returned. Lowering himself stiffly onto a divan, he had asked, 'Who told you Irshad Dilawar is in Karachi? In Clifton, to be precise?'

'A contact of mine,' Al-Kamil answered, his eyes narrowing in suspicion.

'Then your contact is wrong, commander. The man you are looking for is not in Karachi. He's in Gwadar.'

Shawqat had watched as Al-Kamil's face clouded over in a mixture of rage and frustration. Then, as Al-Kamil sat staring at the floor, the Syrian spoke again. 'I'm afraid I can't get you the replacements for the dead men immediately. But if you give me another hour, I'll get you Irshad Dilawar's exact location in Gwadar.'

Folding the map, Al-Kamil thrust it back into his pocket, his vision going out towards the sea. Somewhere straight ahead, far away across the water, was the town of Gwadar. At nightfall, they would kill the nine Balochi hostages before crossing over from Sindh into Balochistan province. Once inside Balochistan, getting to Gwadar wouldn't be a problem.

As he turned back towards the hutments, Al-Kamil fleetingly wondered if he should call Musa Zawawi and let him know about his decision to go to Gwadar. He rejected the idea almost immediately. From Quetta to Karachi, the men who had hired him had proved to be highly undependable in providing him with Irshad Dilawar's correct whereabouts. Their sloppiness had already cost him two men, and almost got the rest of them killed as well. Musa and his bunch didn't deserve to be kept updated.

He would tell them about Gwadar once he had killed Irshad Dilawar.

29 July. Astoria Gardens, Clifton, Karachi

'But I didn't have a choice in the matter, Colonel sahib. Believe me, I didn't *want* to help him.'

Saadat was seated in front of the computer, headphones strapped over his head, looking miserable. Rafiq sat beside the old spy, listening quietly as Colonel Mohan probed and prodded for answers.

'But you did help him,' the colonel's voice was flat and matter-of-fact. 'As far as I'm concerned, that's what matters.'

'Huzoor, what could I do? That mad man kept threatening to expose me. One call, he kept saying... *one* call to the Pakistanis is all that's needed to nail me. And he's right. All he needs to do is tell them about Paposh Nagar or this apartment, and I'm finished. I never wanted to be part of any of this... I'm happy he has gone and I don't have to deal with him anymore. Now I request you and Rafiq mian to also leave so that I can live peacefully.'

A brief silence followed. 'You could have called me and let me know that Imtiaz was threatening you.'

'What good would that have done, huzoor? *India se fauj bhej dete meri hifaazat ke liye*? Had he come to know that I had complained to you, he'd have made life even worse for me.'

'So you told him about Parachinar.'

'Yes.'

'And he was happy with that?' the colonel asked pointedly. 'He didn't ask you for more help?'

'Of course he did, sahib,' Saadat was indignant. 'Can I arrange for transport? Can I arrange a place for them to stay... he just kept demanding one thing after another. In fact, he insisted that I bring him some maps of Gwadar, which is why I came here this morning.'

For a fraction of a second there was dead silence. 'Maps of *Gwadar*?' the colonel asked sharply.

Saadat went pale and swallowed. 'I meant Parachinar, sahib. *Woh yunhi zubaan fisal gayee*... The maps are of Parachinar. Rafiq can see them.'

'Yes sir. I have three maps here. All of Parachinar,' the lieutenant confirmed.

'Hmm...' Colonel Mohan sounded thoughtful. 'Mian, where do you think Imtiaz and Shamsheer could have gone so late at night? Other than you, they don't know anyone in Karachi. Who could they have turned to for help?'

'*Kya pata, huzoor*,' Saadat shrugged.

'I think it's strange that the major chose not to take your help and just disappeared quietly,' the colonel persisted. 'I mean he was pressuring you for assistance, so why did he suddenly decide he didn't need your help?'

'I don't know… Maybe he realized that if he took my help, I would know precisely what he was planning, and that I would tell you what he was up to? Maybe he didn't want to take that chance? I really don't know where they could have gone. I mean, forget me… they didn't tell Rafiq sahib here anything and he's their friend. So why would they trust me?'

As the colonel mulled this over, the lieutenant fixed a cold eye on Saadat.

'Okay, so it's obvious they have gone to Parachinar,' Colonel Mohan spoke at last. 'Chalo Saadat mian, that will be all for now. You may go.'

'Ji huzoor,' Saadat paused. 'Would you… want me to do anything for you?'

'Umm… I shall let you know if I do.'

Saadat pulled off the headphones and rose from his chair. He motioned to Rafiq with his hands, indicating that he was leaving, and walked out of the room. On reaching the main door, he opened it and let himself out. He glanced at his watch. It was a quarter past ten.

Rafiq heard the main door shut and spoke into his microphone. 'He's left, sir.'

'Okay. Now I want you to prepare for an immediate departure to Gwadar.'

'Gwadar, sir?' Rafiq looked and sounded confused. 'But they've left for Parachi…'

'Parachinar was a red herring,' Colonel Mohan interrupted. 'Imtiaz was sending us on a false trail. I suspected as much, and Saadat confirmed it when he accidentally said 'Gwadar' when referring to the maps…'

'That means he's been helping the major and he may know a lot more, sir,' the lieutenant growled. 'We should have questioned him some more. I could have encouraged him to talk…'

'That would have been a waste of time. We know where Imtiaz and Shamsheer are heading—that's all we need to know. Now listen carefully. Here's the plan…'

29 July. ISI Headquarters, Khayaban-e-Suhrawardy, Islamabad

Lieutenant-General Rehmat leaned back in his chair, closed his eyes and gently massaged his forehead and temples. A small jar of Vicks VapoRub sat on the table to one side, and the room was redolent with the smell of the mentholated balm. Sniffling heavily, he slowly sat up, wiped his fingers on a handkerchief, and opened a file that lay in front of him. Flipping through it, he came to a page with a pencil-and-ink sketch of a bearded man with a heavy face. The man was wearing a black qaraqul, and the name 'Khalil Abdali' had been pencilled at the bottom.

Through watering eyes, the lieutenant-general studied the police sketch. The man in it could have resembled just about anyone on Pakistan's streets, and the sketch didn't inspire much confidence in the director. Snapping the file shut, he stared truculently at Lieutenant-General Niazi across the table.

Nothing was going right with this investigation!

It had been more than thirty-six hours since the two men had been shot dead on Mauripur Road, yet little had been achieved in terms of establishing their identity or that of their associates who had fled from Mohajir Camp. The phones and the pistol that had been recovered had yielded no useful information, and the dragnet that had been cast to nab Khalil and his men had caught nothing. And even though the Karachi police had received five calls from people who claimed to have seen the men, all the calls had proved to be false leads.

To add to the problem, owing to the MQM rally, Karachi was witnessing a huge influx of people from all over Sindh—which was making the police's job harder and preventing CCPO Qasim Raja from pressing more of his men into the manhunt.

'What time does this rally end today?' Lieutenant-General Rehmat asked General Niazi.

'It's supposed to finish at around five in the evening. *Lekin aapko toh pata hai*... these things never start and end on time.'

'Just our goddamn luck,' the director grimaced.

The only silver lining—if it could be called that—was the fact that the dead men's fingerprints did not match any of the police records in Karachi, Lahore, Islamabad, Rawalpindi and Peshawar. If criminal records of the men did not exist in Pakistan, it only strengthened the possibility of them being Indian commandos. Somehow, it made the situation seem less hopeless in the director's mind.

'What news in Clifton?'

'Nothing, janaab,' the retired soldier answered.

'No sign of an attack, no more attempts to hack into the server?'

'No.'

The director was about to speak when the door opened abruptly and Major-General Dar walked in, his face animated. 'Sir, we've just got an ID on one of the dead men. His fingerprints were on record in Nowshera.'

'Nowshera…' Lieutenant-General Rehmat frowned. 'Who is he?'

'Jamal Qayyum Khan, an ex-soldier of the Afghan mujahideen from Kunar Province. The Nowshera police had his prints because he was arrested in connection with a kidnap-and-ransom bid five years ago. We still don't have all his details, but it seems he had become a hired killer after leaving the mujahedeen.'

The other two men digested this information in silence. 'An Afghan mujahedeen… So these guys aren't the Indian commandos after all,' Lieutenant-General Rehmat breathed out finally, his face glum as the prospect of closing in on the Indians crumbled. He fumbled with his handkerchief, covered his mouth and nose, and sneezed violently.

'But sir, Khalil did ask that tea-stall owner about Clifton,' Major-General Dar reminded him.

'A coincidence,' the director shook his head. 'These guys are hired killers. Probably here to stir up trouble during the rally. Shit!'

As the major-general stood uncertainly, Lieutenant-General Niazi spoke. 'Tauseef mian, if Khalil and his men are not the Indian commandos, why haven't the Indians still attacked the house? We've done everything to give the impression that Dilawar has been there for the last two days, yet…'

The director nodded. 'It can only mean that someone or something has put them on their guard or that, for some reason, they aren't able to carry out their plan.'

'You mean they have abandoned their plan? Perhaps we overplayed our hand by adding too much security around the house,' the retired soldier said pointedly. 'It might actually have deterred the Indians.'

The director sniffled. He knew the other man could well be right, but he was loath to admit it. 'I don't think that could be a reason. I'm sure they would have come here expecting high security… There is a third possibility—they are just *waiting*.'

'For what, huzoor?'

'An opportunity to strike at the right moment—a moment closer to the arrival of the United States' national security advisor in Delhi.'

The other two officers looked at one another in incomprehension.

'What if the Indians believe that they cannot convince the national security advisor about Dilawar's presence in Pakistan? What do they do then? Stage an attack on Dilawar and try to kill him when the US national security advisor is in Delhi. Think of the media coverage the attack would get—in India, in Pakistan and in America. In one stroke, the Indians would have proved his presence in Pakistan, and succeeded in discrediting us before the western world. Even if they failed to kill him, their purpose would be achieved.'

Lieutenant-General Niazi tugged at his goatee nervously. 'And we'd then be forced to extradite him.'

The director inclined his head. 'I'm glad we came to know of this plot and decided not to send Dilawar to Karachi. Now the Indians can attack the house whenever they want.'

An uneasy silence engulfed the room.

'But the threat still exists, janaab,' Lieutenant-General Niazi said plaintively. 'The Indians may still be able to convince the national security advisor to lean on our President and Prime Minister to extradite Dilawar. The battle is won only if we stand firm and don't let that happen. Please talk to the wazir-e-azam about this. Tell him about the Indian plot to kill Dilawar, and why it is important not to allow his extradition.'

'I will,' Lieutenant-General Rehmat said. 'I'm just hoping that by tomorrow morning we can somehow nab one of the Indians. If we do, not only will I talk to the wazir-e-azam, I will also blow the reputation of the Indians sky high. Their plan was to discredit us. I'll pay them back in the same coin.'

'But what if we can't get our hands on the Indians by tomorrow?'

The director considered this for a moment before shrugging. 'Then we'll tell the Prime Minister that the two men who were killed on Mauripur Road *are* the Indian commandos who had come into Pakistan to kill Dilawar. We'll just have to manufacture some evidence to prove it.'

As Lieutenant-General Niazi and Major-General Dar exchanged glances, the director reached for the jar of Vicks.

'In fact, I've already briefed the relevant department heads to start working on this.'

29 July. Malir Cantonment, Karachi

The digital clock on the dashboard of the Toyota Camry read 12:03 as Saadat eased the car through the heavy wooden gates of the bungalow. On one of the pillars supporting the gate was a black granite plaque, the words 'Aayat' and 'Plot No. 43' inscribed in gold lettering. The posh bungalow was one of many that lined the quiet road, 2.5 kilometres from Cantt Bazar.

Saadat parked outside the bungalow's garage, picked up a briefcase lying on the seat next to him and stepped out of the car. He walked briskly to the main door of the large two-storey building, and rang the doorbell three times in quick succession. Then, fumbling in his pocket, he extracted a key and, inserting it into the door, let himself in.

As Saadat shut the door behind him and turned, he saw a figure wearing a light grey shirt and blue jeans standing at the head of a centrally-located stairway leading up to the first floor.

'Aadaab, mian,' said Shamsheer, glancing at his watch. 'You're late. Was there a problem?'

Saadat shook his head as he began mounting the stairs. 'Just the traffic—it's getting worse by the day. And because of the rally, many roads have been blocked. I had to take two detours. All okay here?'

Shamsheer nodded as the two men made their way towards one of the upper storey bedrooms. Pushing the door open, Saadat entered the room, followed by Shamsheer. Imtiaz, who was sitting on the huge double bed, hunched over a large map, looked up and straightened.

'Come, come,' he said, folding the map carefully. He waited as Saadat placed his briefcase on a dressing table and sat down on the lone chair, then pressed forward. 'So tell us the news.'

'The news is that Colonel sahib is quite pissed with both of you—*and me*. He has strong suspicions that I have played some part in your sudden disappearance from Astoria. I admitted that I helped you a bit after you threatened me, but I assured him that I know nothing about your disappearance.'

'What else?'

'Colonel sahib and Rafiq are planning something.'

The major and the captain exchanged glances. 'What?' Imtiaz asked.

'I don't know. They didn't mention anything specific... I just felt it.' Saadat paused briefly before continuing, 'Before leaving, I asked Colonel sahib if he wanted me to do something for him. His answer was very vague. It was as if he had decided his next course of action, and he didn't see the need for any assistance from me.'

Imtiaz pondered this for a moment. 'They're probably trying to figure out a way of stopping us from reaching Parachinar.'

Shamsheer nodded. 'Your idea of sending Saadat to the apartment with the maps of Parachinar must have helped.' The captain turned to Saadat. 'You told them you'd brought the maps, right?'

The older man wondered if he should tell the commandos about the slip he'd made, and decided against it. 'Ji... huzoor,' he dropped his gaze. 'Whatever it is they're planning, the two of you should be on your guard.'

Imtiaz sighed. 'We always are. Now, did you manage to get the other things organized?'

Saadat reached for his briefcase, opened it and extracted two rolls of white satin cloth, each attached to a wooden stick. He handed both to Imtiaz. The major unfurled the rolls and inspected them.

Each piece was roughly 12 inches in width and 8 inches in height. A thick, broad red stripe ran vertically down the left of each cloth, followed by a slightly narrower stripe in dark green. The red-and-green stripes accounted for exactly half the area of each cloth, leaving the right half pure white. Imtiaz picked up the two pieces of cloth by the sticks and waved them above his head.

'Perfect, huzoor,' said Saadat with a smile. 'As long as you and Shamsheer sahib keep waving these MQM flags enthusiastically, no one will suspect that you're not MQM supporters attending the rally.'

Imtiaz smiled and threw one of the flags to Shamsheer, who caught it deftly. The captain then walked over to a wall-mounted mirror, held the flag up and admired himself.

'*Subhan'Allah, kisi ki nazar na lag jaaye,*' Saadat chuckled playfully. 'Captain sahib, you don't really need that flag to look like a rabid party activist.'

Shamsheer grinned broadly and returned the flag to the major. Rolling the two flags and setting them aside, Imtiaz looked at Saadat. 'What about your friend in Gwadar?'

Saadat reached into his briefcase once again and extracted a slip of paper. 'This is Shihab Perwaiz's address and contact number,' he said, handing it to Imtiaz. 'Please memorize it and destroy the paper.'

'He will arrange for everything we need?'

'He has already started making the arrangements, huzoor. Your stay, guns, transport if needed... Everything will be ready by the time you reach Gwadar. If there's something you need that I have overlooked, just ask Perwaiz *mian*. He will try and get it for you.'

'How do we pay him? We are not carrying much money.'

'Just give him this,' Saadat extended an open hand. In his palm lay a thick gold ring, heavily inlaid with a bright blue opal, flecked with rose pink streaks and swirls. 'It is both proof of your identity and payment for whatever you may need.'

The major picked up the ring and weighed it thoughtfully. 'This must be very precious for Perwaiz to accept it as payment.'

'Yes, but not as precious as Saadat Fakih's word.'

Imtiaz nodded as he put the ring into his pocket. When he spoke, his voice was solemn. 'Saadat mian, I don't know how to thank you for everything you have done. I had only asked you for help in locating Dilawar's whereabouts. But you have gone out of your way to…'

Saadat raised a hand and interrupted the major. 'Don't thank me, huzoor. By the grace of Allah, this house of mine was lying vacant. If this house hadn't been there, I couldn't possibly have taken you to the house I stay in, and that's where the matter would have ended. And had I not known Perwaiz mian in Gwadar…' Saadat threw up his hands and shrugged expansively.

'True, but you needn't have done even this much. It was not expected from you, and for that I am thankful.'

'Major sahib, you are a man with honest intentions and great determination. I helped you because I saw that your own people were working against you. Not all of us have the good fortune or courage to do what is right. The least I could do was to help someone who has that courage and determination.'

29 July. Fatih, Istanbul

Musa Zawawi stared intently at his laptop for a few moments, then raised his eyes and looked at Zeb Kirkland. The Algerian nodded once and leaned towards an encrypted speakerphone lying on his desk.

'Yes, Loya sahib. That does look like Hossam.'

Earlier that morning, Lieutenant-General Niazi had managed to mail the police sketch of Khalil Abdali to Zawawi. Now the Algerian and the ex-CIA officer were seated in a poky office overlooking the Golden Horn, holding a conference with the lieutenant-general about their next course of action.

'And one of the men who came with Hossam was Jamal Qayyum Khan?' Lieutenant-General Niazi's voice sounded tremulous over the phone.

'One of them was named Jamal Khan, though I can't say about the Qayyum bit. He was one of the Afghan mujahedeen in the team.'

'Well, your Jamal Khan is certified dead, and there's a manhunt on in Karachi for Hossam,' the Pakistani spoke bitterly. 'Newspapers in Karachi are carrying his pictures. If he's caught, we're all in hot water.'

Zawawi looked at Kirkland, who shifted his massive weight from his right buttock to his left and stared meditatively out of the window. In his plaid khaki short pants, yellow bush shirt and open sandals, he looked like an overweight American tourist.

'How could you have agreed to Hossam's condition that he was not to be contacted?' Lieutenant-General Niazi screamed over the phone. 'That was so stupid!'

'Don't try to shift the blame on me, Loya sahib,' Zawawi spoke hotly. 'Every assassin has his own way of working. Those were Hossam's terms and I had to respect them. And anyway, none of this would have mattered had your intel on Dilawar been better.'

'What do you mean by that?' The Pakistani officer's voice rose by another note.

'First, you set Quetta as the target, then suddenly, you shifted it to Karachi,' the Algerian turned the screws on the lieutenant-general. 'I was able to redirect Hossam to Karachi, but then you guys changed the plan again and sent Dilawar to Gwadar. I can't be blamed for the goof-ups that have happened at your end.'

'Those weren't my decisions,' Lieutenant-General Niazi contested. 'Lieutenant-General Tauseef Rehmat made them and I cannot challenge him.'

Kirkland suddenly leaned into the phone, his tone tough. 'Loya, you once told me you were in a position to influence decisions taken by the ISI. I didn't see you pulling much weight this time.'

'I tried, Kirkland sahib,' the lieutenant-general wailed. 'It's just that these Indian commandos messed everything up…'

'That's it. None of us could have factored the Indians in, so I see no point in blaming anyone here.' The American paused. 'And anyway, why are we making such a big deal of Hossam? What's the worst that will happen if he's caught? He was hired by Musa—he knows nothing of you and me or why we want Dilawar out of the way. And you Pakistanis can do nothing about Musa. Our real problem is how to get someone to eliminate Dilawar in Gwadar.'

Kirkland raised an eyebrow at Zawawi. The Algerian shook his head. 'Not possible at such short notice. Everyone will want time to plan an attack.'

'Anyone inside Pakistan, Loya?' the American demanded.

'No, Kirkland sahib… It's too risky to get someone locally. In Pakistan, it's hard to tell the ISI's friends from its enemies.' Lieutenant-General Niazi paused before slowly adding, 'Besides, we might not need to kill Dilawar after all.'

Kirkland sat upright and stared intently at the speakerphone. 'Enlighten me, please.'

'Well… General Rehmat is planning to plant evidence on Jamal Khan and the other chap, and pass them off as two of the Indian commandos. He plans to place this… *evidence*… before our Prime Minister, and convince him not to agree to any extradition demands made by India.'

'Cool.' The CIA man sounded genuinely impressed. 'When does your general intend to meet the Prime Minister?'

'In the next day or two.'

'Okay. Keep me informed. If this plan works, our boy gets to stay in Pakistan and all of us have nothing to worry about.'

29 July. Gutter Baghicha, SITE Town, Karachi

The epicentre of the MQM rally had been the large, open ground opposite the Mazar-e-Quaid in central Karachi, but Imtiaz and Shamsheer, who had no direct interest in the rally, had bypassed the iconic mausoleum entirely. Instead, they had gone straight towards Gutter Baghicha to the northwest, and had simply hung around in the old park's vicinity till they saw groups of MQM workers and supporters returning from the direction of Mohammad Ali Jinnah Road.

The two commandos made a beeline for the long row of buses, vans and jeeps parked along Manghopir Road, waiting to ferry party members back to wherever they had come from. Mingling carefully with the boisterous MQM loyalists, they then walked to the section of the road where, according to Saadat, the vehicles bound for the Karachi–Lasbela border were supposed to halt.

After watching a dozen of the Lasbela-bound buses and jeeps depart, Imtiaz and Shamsheer ventured on to the road. Prominently displaying their MQM flags, they approached a group of bus drivers and requested them for a lift back towards Lasbela. Their story was that they were forced to hitch a ride back as their own bus had somehow left without them.

One driver, a hefty man with thick glasses, listened to their tale, nodding sympathetically all along. '*Hota hai, hota hai,*' he said, when Imtiaz finished his narration. Then, slapping a downcast Shamsheer heartily on the shoulder, he added, 'Never mind, brother. We'll find place for both of you.'

Forty minutes later, the bus's engine came to life amidst much cheering, sloganeering and flag-waving. As the vehicle pulled out of its place in the queue and made its way down Manghopir Road, Imtiaz and Shamsheer, seated on the roof of the bus, joined in the infectious merrymaking.

The bus wound its way through peak-hour traffic, heading in a northwesterly direction towards N25. The road was packed with cars, taxis, two-wheelers and buses, and Imtiaz could see many of these vehicles bearing MQM supporters home. He also noticed with great satisfaction that posses of

Karachi policemen were working to get the vehicles carrying MQM supporters out of city limits as quickly as possible.

'Rallies like this are known to result in political violence, and Karachi has suffered much. So the police is usually keen to get rid of those who come to attend these rallies,' Saadat had explained late the previous night. 'And no policeman in his right senses will stop and check buses full of zealous party workers. So once you're in an MQM bus, you'll be out of Karachi without too much trouble.'

Thanking Saadat silently once again for all his help and ingenuity, Imtiaz looked at his watch. It was nearing half past seven. He hoped they would be on the Makran Coastal Highway by midnight.

CHAPTER 12

29 July. Madinat Al Sultan Qaboos, Muscat, Sultanate of Oman

The man seated opposite Colonel Mohan picked up the buzzing mobile phone and pressed it to his ear.

'Salaam,' he said tentatively.

On hearing the voice at the other end, the man's face brightened, and he relaxed. '*Ana bekhair, shokran*,' he said, smiling genially. '*Hal beemkanek mosa'adati*?'

He listened to the caller attentively for a while, his brows knitting in concentration. '*Addesh...? Hada shay'un Jameel... Na'am*,' he nodded vigorously a few times, then shot a brief glance at the colonel and gave him a thumbs-up.

'*La taqlaq! Shokran... shokran jazeelan*,' he said finally, and put the phone down. The relief on his face was palpable.

As Colonel Mohan raised his eyebrows, the man leaned back on his sofa and grinned, his white teeth in sharp contrast to his dark face, which was just a shade or two lighter than the thick black moustache overhanging his upper lip.

'It's done, Mohan ji,' he said, speaking in a pronounced South Indian accent. 'We've finally found a boat that's ready to take you.' Pointing his index finger heavenwards, he added, 'See, I told you... just keep faith in God.'

The colonel shook his head and smiled. 'I prefer keeping faith in you, Swamyji.'

T.P. Doraiswamy—or Swamyji, as he was called by his close friends and associates—was a bundle of infinite resourcefulness, and the colonel knew that had he been dealing with anyone else, he wouldn't have made as much headway. It wasn't without reason that Doraiswamy was one of the top handlers for Unit Kilo in the Middle East.

It had been less than twelve hours since the first call had gone out to Doraiswamy, asking him to make a series of arrangements for Colonel Mohan's excursion into Pakistan. The Tamilian had promptly stepped into action, and by the time the Sultanate of Oman's embassy in Delhi had opened for business, he had faxed and emailed the colonel fake letters, purportedly from the Oman office of Telecommunications Consultants India Ltd., requesting the colonel's urgent presence in Muscat to troubleshoot an ongoing project. Doraiswamy had also pulled a few strings in Oman, and the embassy had issued a fast-track visa to telecom engineer Surinder Mohan, who had then caught a mid-afternoon Air India flight from Delhi to Muscat.

The Airbus A319 had touched down at Muscat International Airport around four o'clock, and thirty minutes later, Doraiswamy had driven the colonel to a penthouse in the posh residential locality of Madinat Qaboos. It was in this house that the two men had spent the last couple of hours.

'Are you sure this boat can get me to the Pakistani coast before daybreak?' Colonel Mohan asked.

'If you leave by eight tonight, you will be in Pakistan before dawn.' Seeing the doubt on the colonel's face, Doraiswamy added, 'Don't worry, Mohan ji. The men who operate these boats regularly smuggle illegal Pakistani immigrants into Muscat. That's how they make a living. And you can't smuggle boatloads of illegal immigrants in daylight, can you? Everything has to happen between nightfall and sunrise.'

The colonel nodded and looked at his watch. It was 6.50. 'How far is the boat from here?'

'Approximately five kilometres away... Not far from Muttrah harbour.'

'So what if we leave now? The boat can depart at around 7.30 instead of eight. That way I'll reach Pakistan half an hour earlier.'

Doraiswamy stood up, walked over to a window, pushed the curtains aside and peered out. While large parts of the sky had turned a dark greyish-purple, its western fringes were still vividly streaked with yellow and orange. The light outside was adequate for Doraiswamy to see the other penthouses in the neighbourhood, and by craning his neck he could clearly make out the Western Al Hajar Mountains rising darkly along the city's northern coastline.

'No,' Doraiswamy turned back. 'It won't be dark enough to set sail by 7.30. Eight o'clock is perfect. And there's no point in your reaching the boat early. You can't simply hang around there. You'll attract too much attention, and the men who are taking you will be uncomfortable. We'll leave in half an hour.'

Colonel Mohan sighed. Then, looking up at the Tamilian, he asked, 'Is it always so difficult commandeering a boat in these parts? I would have thought it a lot easier, considering this is their livelihood.'

'It never was so hard,' admitted Doraiswamy, sitting down on the sofa. 'But from what I've gathered, the boatmen have suddenly become extremely wary of "private enquiries" such as ours. It seems they are reluctant to accommodate such requests out of fear.'

'What do they fear?'

'It seems about twelve days ago, a fishing trawler was hired near Ras al-Khaimah to take eight men to the Iran–Pakistan border. The rumour doing the rounds is that one of the eight men was Hossam Al-Kamil.'

'Is he some sort of a pirate?'

'No, no... He is a bit of a folk hero in these parts. He was a Hezbollah commander who apparently was a terror for the Israelis and the South Lebanon Army in Beirut. Anyway, the point is that since the day this fishing trawler set sail, it hasn't been seen or heard of. Nothing is known about the whereabouts of the boat and its crew. The boat's owner is convinced that its disappearance has something to do with the eight men who travelled in the boat. The news has spread, triggering fear among all the boatmen.'

The colonel shrugged. He didn't really care enough about the matter. Then, as a thought crossed his mind, he said, 'This trawler was bound for the Iran–Pakistan border? But why would a Hezbollah commander head for that part of the world? And why would he take the sea route?'

It was Doraiswamy's turn to shrug. 'God knows. Besides, this Hossam is no longer with the Hezbollah. He's apparently turned mercenary and has become a specialist in assassinations.'

'Assassinations...' Colonel Mohan uttered the word slowly. 'Very interesting.' He leaned forward, his face suddenly alert.

'Yes. According to the grapevine, Hossam has assassinated more than a dozen people after leaving the Hezbollah,' said Doraiswamy, studying the colonel's face.

'Who does he work for?'

'For anyone who will pay. It's speculated that the Turkish government hired him to assassinate three top members of the Turkish mafia in Odessa two years ago. It's said that a betting syndicate paid him to murder a scion of one of the most influential families in Jordan last year. They say he killed a well-known Saudi Arabian businessman for defrauding a Saudi minister in an elaborate property scam. Then there's the death of two American engineers in a car accident in Kuwait last month... The rumour is that the Americans were undercover CIA operatives, and that Hossam engineered the crash at the behest of the Iraqis. As you can see, he has no loyalties and is prepared to work on either side of the law—for individuals, groups *and* governments.'

'Do you have a picture of this guy?'

'Not right now, but I can organize one once I reach my office.'

'Okay. Please mail a picture of him to General Dixit as soon as possible, along with as much information you can get about him. It would be great if you found out exactly where Hossam was heading ten days ago, and who might be employing him currently. Tell the general that I shall talk to him about this soon.'

'Consider it done in the next two hours, Mohan ji,' assured Doraiswamy. 'But if I may ask, why this sudden interest in Hossam?'

'It pays to know what an ex-Hezbollah commander and professional assassin is doing in our backyard,' the colonel smiled, looked at his watch and stood up. 'I think it's time we made a move.'

Doraiswamy rose, walked over to a writing-table and opened a drawer. From inside, he pulled out a Beretta 92FS, a shoulder holster and three clips full of bullets. Next, he extracted a pair of Sunagor Compact Super Zoom binoculars and a fully-charged Thuraya SAT-phone.

'Everything you had asked for,' he said, depositing the equipment on a coffee table. 'When do you expect to be back?'

'I can't say.' Colonel Mohan inspected the Beretta closely, then proceeded to strap the shoulder holster in place. 'It may take a couple of days… maybe more.'

The colonel pulled a heavy black windbreaker over his shirt, and thrust the three spare magazines and the ultra-light binoculars into its inside pockets. Next, he picked up the Thuraya and dropped it into the outside pocket of the jacket. Zipping the windbreaker up to his chest, he looked at Doraiswamy.

'I'm ready,' he said.

30 July. Gwadar Town, Balochistan

Taking care to stay away from the window, Rafiq stood up and stretched. His back was stiff, his shoulders ached, and he could feel the exhaustion in his heavy eyelids. But sleep wasn't something he could afford to give in to just yet.

In all probability, Imtiaz and Shamsheer were already in Gwadar, and the colonel had asked him to be prepared to move at a moment's notice.

Rafiq's journey from Karachi to Gwadar had been extremely frenetic, and had begun right after Saadat had left the apartment in Astoria Gardens. The colonel had instructed him to get to the port town as quickly as possible and wait for further instructions, but immediately thereafter, the lieutenant had encountered a problem: he didn't have any money to travel to Gwadar.

For before making their escape, Imtiaz and Shamsheer had very cleverly emptied his wallet and pockets of almost all the cash he had, leaving him nearly broke and incapable of following them.

Rafiq had briefly considered tapping Saadat for help, but not only was that below his dignity, he knew he could no longer depend on the spy for assistance. After exploring an array of options, the lieutenant had finally reached Electronics Market in Saddar with two bags. The haversack on his back had a few clothes, his sat-phone, two Glock 17s and quite a few rounds of ammunition. The other bag held ten individual pieces of Swarovski crystals that he had swiped from the mantelpiece in the apartment. These he sold to a fat Sindhi pawnbroker, and raised fifteen thousand rupees.

Within half an hour of having disposed of the stolen crystals, Rafiq had boarded a bus from the central bus station in Saddar to Hub Chowki on the Karachi–Lasbela border. From there he caught a jeep heading for the coastal town of Gaddani. Disembarking at the turn-off to Gaddani, he befriended an elderly motorcyclist riding along N25 to Winder and talked the man into giving him a lift. But within ten minutes of leaving Gaddani, the lieutenant had relieved the biker of the Honda CG 125 at gunpoint, and driven swiftly away.

Riding virtually non-stop and halting just once to fill up some petrol, the lieutenant had driven all evening and night, traversing the same road he'd taken to come to Karachi just six days earlier. The 650-kilometre ride had been arduous, and it was past two o'clock when Rafiq finally approached the vicinity of Gwadar. However, instead of entering the town at night, he had stopped two kilometres outside town. Parking the Honda in a ditch, he had slept intermittently till daybreak. He then hid the two-wheeler behind a pile of large boulders, away from the road, and walked into Gwadar.

Ten minutes later, he found himself in front of the City Centre Lodge, where he had rented a room for the day.

Massaging his lower back with both hands, Rafiq looked around the room. If he'd had a choice, City Centre Lodge was the last place he would have wanted to be in. The building was a run-down, two-storey structure, with three shops occupying the ground floor, and the lodge directly above. The lodge itself comprised of rows of cramped, smelly rooms arranged on two sides of a dingy, narrow corridor, at the end of which was a yellowing washbasin, next to a bathroom and lavatory. City Centre Lodge's clientele was predominantly truck drivers who frequented the Gwadar Subzi Mandi situated nearby, a fact amply advertised by the pervasive stench of decaying vegetables. The plush comforts of Astoria Gardens seemed a universe away.

Stifling a yawn, Rafiq was considering stretching out on the rough, lumpy bed and resting his tired body a bit when he heard the muffled ring of his sat-phone. He rummaged through his haversack and pulled out the phone. He didn't recognize the number.

'Hello,' he said warily.

'Colonel Mohan here.'

'Yes, sir.' Rafiq was fully alert, all traces of fatigue gone in an instant. He listened to the colonel for a moment before speaking.

'I reached Gwadar about one-and-a-half hours ago, sir.' After another short silence, he said, 'A lodge, sir. City Centre Lodge... On the outskirts, just as you enter this dump from the eastern side.'

When the colonel spoke next, Rafiq's eyes opened wide in astonishment. 'You mean you're *here*... in *Gwadar*?' He shook his head, his expression one of wonder and admiration. 'No, sir. I haven't seen them. I haven't gone out of the lodge so far. I was waiting for your instructions.'

Rafiq listened as Colonel Mohan rattled off a list of orders. Finally, he said, 'Right, sir,' and put the phone down.

Walking to the window, he slowly peered out at the street below. But for the odd jeep and cyclist, it was practically deserted. Though it was nearing a quarter to nine, Gwadar hadn't fully woken up to a new day. And that was a problem. Until and unless there were enough townsfolk out on the roads, he couldn't venture out and start looking for the major and captain. If he stepped into those empty streets, they would spot him from a mile.

Provided they were already in Gwadar, that is.

30 July. Pishukan Village, Balochistan

Colonel Mohan lay flat on his stomach and peered through the Sunagor Compact at the house.

It stood virtually on the periphery of Pishukan, a small fishing village located approximately twenty-five kilometres due west of Gwadar town, at the very end of the sweep of Padi Zarr or the west bay of Gwadar port. The village was made up of some 350-odd buildings, but in terms of size and architecture, none of them quite compared to the house that the colonel was viewing. For that matter, the house stood out of its surroundings like a beacon, forcing the colonel to question the wisdom of those who had picked it as a safe house for Irshad Dilawar. It would have attracted the attention of even the most disinterested of passers-by.

Set roughly fifty metres off from the Pishukan–Gwadar road, the house was a modern, two-storey structure, with a huge portico jutting out in front. A large wooden garage stood to the left of the house, and the colonel was able to make out the shapes of two vehicles parked inside. In addition to those, an SUV stood in the shade of the portico. The house was protected by a seven-foot-high steel mesh that ran around the perimeter of the compound, with four strands of barbed wire forming a V-shape at the top of the fence. Floodlights were positioned on all four corners of the compound, which could be accessed only through a heavy wrought-iron gate manned by three men carrying automatics.

The colonel took his eyes away from the binoculars and surveyed the landscape in front of him. He was lying on an escarpment of Gard Koh, a small hill that rose dramatically out of the flat sandy earth north of Pishukan. The high cliff commanded a good view of the surrounding countryside and the coast, as well as the Pishukan–Gwadar road that ran barely five hundred metres from the base of the hill. The road was presently deserted, and the only human activity the colonel could perceive with a naked eye was along the distant waterfront of Pishukan.

The boat had left Muscat at eight sharp the previous evening, and after an uneventful journey, Colonel Mohan had been dropped in an empty cove ten kilometres inside the Pakistan border, just north of the coastal town of Jiwani. The colonel found the Jiwani–Gwadar road at daybreak, and after a short wait, hitched a ride east in a jeep till he reached the turnoff to Pishukan. Using the map he had memorized for directions, he had then arrived outside Pishukan, before climbing to the top of Gard Koh and calling Rafiq.

As the hot, early morning sun beat down on him, the colonel felt the sweat breaking out on his forehead and running down his cheeks. Pushing himself up on all fours, he crawled away from the cliff's edge and sought refuge in the shade of a pile of medium-sized boulders. Picking up his jacket from the ground, he withdrew a small hip-flask from one of its pockets and took two tiny swigs of water. He stared eastward in the direction of Gwadar. All he could see was the flat sea melting into a grey shimmering haze in the distance.

He wondered whether Imtiaz and Shamsheer were somewhere in the town, and if they were, whether Rafiq would be able to find them. With the governments of Pakistan and China funnelling billions of dollars into its development as a strategic port, Gwadar wasn't exactly a stamp-sized outpost any longer. It had grown rapidly into a bustling town, bracing itself for bigger things to come.

Locating two men in a town the size of Gwadar was going to be a challenge.

That's why, being where he was, Colonel Mohan believed he stood a better chance of catching sight of Imtiaz or Shamsheer or both. He knew that the two would need to reconnoitre the safe house at least once before launching their attack. And he knew that given the flat landscape around the house, the only way they could conduct a productive recce without raising suspicions was by actually walking or driving past the house a couple of times.

What the colonel was hoping and waiting for was to see one of them as they walked or drove down the road leading to Pishukan village.

Colonel Mohan's thoughts were suddenly disturbed by the sound of an engine. Screwing the flask's lid back on hurriedly and grabbing the binoculars, he scrambled to the edge of the cliff and peered down at the road. It was empty, but the engine's sound was unmistakable, steadily growing louder in the silence.

Then, the colonel picked up the shape of a small truck coming towards him in the distance. It was heading towards Pishukan. Pressing the Sunagor to his eyes, the colonel trained its sights on the approaching truck. Hardly breathing, he stared into the front of the truck, waiting for it to draw as close to the cliff as possible, so that he could get a better view.

The truck wheezed and grunted forward, and at last reached the point closest to where the colonel was lying. Squinting into the truck's cab, he studied the faces of the driver and the co-passenger. They weren't the men he was waiting for.

Although disappointed, Colonel Mohan waited for the truck to draw away from him, so that he could look into its back. When he saw that it, too, was empty, he lowered the binoculars and lay observing the vehicle. As it neared the safe house, he again raised the Sunagor to his eyes and watched to see if the truck dropped speed as it passed the house.

Nothing of the sort happened. The vehicle merely trundled on towards the village.

The colonel sighed, put the binoculars aside and wiped his brow. He could see that it was going to be a tiring, energy-sapping day full of such false alarms, one that demanded vast resources of patience—but he had bargained for that.

What worried him, however, was the fact that Imtiaz and Shamsheer had disappeared from the apartment in Karachi two nights ago. They had a head start over him, and there was always the possibility that they had already scouted the safe house to their satisfaction. That would mean this vigil of his would be entirely futile.

The colonel thrust the thought away before it could prey on him longer.

30 July. Gwadar Town, Balochistan

The most remarkable thing about Shihab Perwaiz was the manner in which he fitted the cultural and racial stereotype of an Afghan.

Standing six-feet-five-inches tall and built like a professional wrestler, Perwaiz had a rich, reddish brown beard and a large, hooked nose. Charcoal black eyes flashed under bushy eyebrows, and the man's face had a tan that could only have come from spending a lot of time in the scorching sun. To top it all, he had a deep authoritative voice, and his booming laughter tended to knock and bounce off the walls, as if looking for a way to escape.

Looking at the man, Imtiaz could hear the sound of hoofbeats and smell the gunpowder as the Afghans charged down the mountain slopes to battle the British Empire, more than 150 years ago. Perwaiz would have been perfectly at home in a nineteenth-century battlefield, smiting his enemies with a broadsword.

Now, of course, the giant had plumped for the calm of domesticity, and the only thing that his big hands wielded was a delicate cup and saucer made of bone china. He raised the former to his lips, poured the sugary liquid down his throat and grunted in satisfaction. Wiping his lips with the back of his hand, he leaned back on the richly brocaded divan and looked from Imtiaz to Shamsheer.

'The two of you must be quite tired. Why don't you rest for a while before proceeding? I have a spare bedroom upstairs that you could use,' he motioned with his hand towards the ceiling.

Despite being equally fluent in Urdu and Pashto, Perwaiz had made it a point to hold the conversation in Balochi. For even though he fit the Afghan stereotype, in reality, Perwaiz was a staunch Balochi nationalist of Iranian extract.

Imtiaz had to concede that Perwaiz's offer was extremely tempting. He and Shamsheer had spent the night hitching rides in trucks and jeeps as they had worked their way westwards, and exhaustion was fast catching up. Yet, he was also eager to get on with the job that had brought them to Gwadar.

'Thank you so much for extending us an invitation to rest under your roof,' Imtiaz replied, also in Balochi, making an effort to sound as graceful as possible. 'But I am afraid we will have to decline your hospitality, even though the gesture is greatly appreciated. While we have reached Gwadar by the grace of Allah, there's still a lot of work to be done. We cannot afford to rest.'

Perwaiz stroked his beard and nodded. 'As you wish,' he said, and drained his tea. He placed the cup on the saucer, and then put both down on the low table in front of him. When he addressed Imtiaz again, he dropped his voice a fraction. 'The abandoned house in Kuan Mori has everything you need. Food, water, clothes, soap, razors, jackets, blankets, lanterns, torches, kerosene, a stove... Saadat mian didn't tell me anything about mobile phones, so I haven't made any provisions for them. But if you need one, I can...' Seeing Imtiaz shake his head, he stopped.

'No, Perwaiz sahib,' said Imtiaz. 'It's fine. Do accept our most sincere thanks for everything that you have provided.'

'Oh, it is nothing,' replied Perwaiz with a wave of his hand. 'You are Saadat's friends, and it is my pleasure to be of assistance to you.' He paused, then sounding slightly apologetic, he added, 'You will have to forgive me if the guns I have got are not the best available in the market. But they are the best I could rustle up at such short notice.'

Imtiaz's heart skipped a beat. The guns were what he had been depending on Perwaiz for the most. Trying not to show his anxiety, he spoke aloud, 'I am sure you would have got us the best you could.'

'There's just one Kalashnikov, one Heckler & Koch submachine gun, and two pistols. And lots and lots of ammunition. Will that do?'

Considering he had been mentally preparing himself for rusty double-barrelled shotguns, the names that Perwaiz had just rattled off sounded like a veritable armoury to Imtiaz. He smiled softly, hoping his relief wasn't too obvious. 'A battle tank and a rocket launcher would have helped nicely, but we'll make do with what you've got for us.'

'I had ordered those as well, but it seems both are in short supply ever since the Americans started waging their war against the Taliban,' said Perwaiz, laughing loudly. Then he continued, 'I'm afraid I can't put a car or jeep at your disposal. That's because the house is in the hills and can only be accessed on foot. And in these parts, you couldn't possibly leave a jeep parked on the road. An unattended jeep would draw too much attention—so much that you wouldn't find it when you returned.' Perwaiz grinned and winked at the men meaningfully. 'But yes, there is an old bicycle in the house that you might want to use. Though I can't see what purpose it will serve, considering you'll have to carry it quite a bit to the highway. And I don't know of many instances where people went to war on cycles.'

The man erupted in laughter once again, as Imtiaz and Shamsheer smiled politely. He pushed a plate full of maize cookies towards them. Seeing them decline politely, Perwaiz picked up one, his face suddenly serious.

'The man you have come for... You do know where to find him, don't you?' He looked at Imtiaz evenly.

Imtiaz glanced at Shamsheer, but didn't provide an answer. A tense silence stretched through the room.

'Oh, don't get me wrong,' said Perwaiz hurriedly. 'All I meant was that the man you are hunting for is in Pishukan. I only meant to help you with that information, just in case Saadat mian hadn't told you everything, expecting *me* to tell you both. Such confusions do arise, you know.'

'Saadat told you who we are looking for?' the major asked slowly.

'Of course. Isn't it obvious?'

'Why is it obvious?'

'Because *I* was the one to tell him that the man you had been looking for in Karachi is now in Gwadar.'

Imtiaz stared at Perwaiz. 'So you are one of Saadat's contacts!' he exclaimed.

'Yes, though personally, I prefer the word "friend". We have been very good friends for a long time. He trusts me implicitly. And as his friends, so can you.'

Imtiaz bowed his head. 'I'm sorry. I didn't know. Do accept my apologies.' Looking up, he added, 'Yes, Saadat mian told us about the safe house in Pishukan. The cycle will come in handy for scouting the house.'

'There is one more thing that the two of you should know,' Perwaiz interjected. 'It will help you plan your attack better.'

The major looked at Perwaiz with interest.

'Gwadar is still a small town, and Pishukan is nothing but a village,' Perwaiz continued. 'There is little here in terms of entertainment—certainly nothing close to what the man you are after is used to in big cities like Karachi, Lahore and Islamabad. So it is natural for him to crave some... entertainment.'

Imtiaz and Shamsheer leaned forward, latching on to every word.

'That's why, every evening, your man and his friends visit the Zobair Continental Hotel in Gwadar, where they while away at least three-four hours of their time. Don't ask me what they do there, but the hotel is the nearest thing to luxury in Gwadar.'

'He goes there *every* evening?' asked Shamsheer.

'Yes. He usually reaches the hotel by seven o'clock, and is there at least till 10.30.'

'So he never gets back to the house in Pishukan before eleven o'clock,' said Imtiaz, nodding thoughtfully. He stood up, and Shamsheer and Perwaiz followed suit.

Looking up at their towering host, the major said, 'Thank you for everything you have done, Perwaiz sahib. With your permission, we shall now leave.'

'You have my phone number,' Perwaiz said, as he accompanied the two Indians into a small courtyard behind the house. 'Let me know if you need anything. If I can arrange it for you, I will.' Opening a small wooden door in the high compound wall, he ushered Imtiaz and Shamsheer out into a narrow back alley.

'Go straight till you reach the main road,' he pointed. 'Take a left and walk down the street till you come to a jeep stand at the junction. Jeeps and pickups heading for Jiwani, Pishukan and Pasni leave every fifteen-twenty minutes. Take a jeep heading for Jiwani, and get off at the stop for Kuan Mori. Then head in a northerly direction towards the hills. Use the map I've given you. Remember that the house is hidden in the hills, seven kilometres from the highway. You should be able to get to it well before noon.'

CHAPTER 13

30 July. Bahadur Shah Zafar Marg, ITO, Delhi

Assistant Director Abhay Shankar Pasricha closed the file he was reading, took off his glasses and looked at Intelligence Officer Binoy Verghese. 'Who is this T.P. Doraiswamy?' he enquired.

'A very remarkable and resourceful agent who, for some inexplicable reason, didn't go far in our intelligence structure,' answered Verghese. 'He was posted to the Middle East immediately after Iraq invaded Kuwait in 1990. He was sent to monitor the developments in the region, especially in the context of increased US influence throughout the Persian Gulf. He proved to be very good, and within a few years, he built a strong and reliable intelligence network for India in the Middle East. But six years ago, he was suddenly put in charge of tracking the narcotics trade in the region, while the intelligence network he had built and overseen was handed to someone else—a classic case of talent getting sidelined. Anyway, since then, Doraiswamy has been low on the intelligence radar.'

Assistant Director Pasricha put on his spectacles and opened the file once again. 'Interesting that General Tushar Dixit chooses someone like Doraiswamy to get things done for him,' he said slowly. Looking up at Verghese, he asked, 'This telephone transcript... when did this conversation happen?'

'Early yesterday morning, sir. The general called Doraiswamy from his cell phone.'

The assistant director turned a couple of pages. 'He asks Doraiswamy to arrange for this Colonel Surinder Mohan's illegal entry into Pakistan from Oman... Who is Colonel Mohan?'

'Other than the fact that he is General Dixit's trusted aide and was once involved in intelligence and counter-insurgency operations, nothing much is known about Colonel Mohan, sir.'

'And did this colonel leave for Oman yesterday?'

'He did, sir. He was issued a visa at the embassy of the Sultanate of Oman yesterday morning, and he left from Delhi to Muscat by an Air India afternoon flight. And it seems Colonel Mohan's visa application mentioned him to be a *telecom engineer*.'

Assistant Director Pasricha once again closed the file and removed his glasses. 'Maybe our boys in military intelligence are running some covert operation,' he said, leaning back in his chair. 'Perhaps there's nothing more to it.'

'Yes, but I checked with some of my contacts in intelligence. They tell me that Doraiswamy is no longer involved in operations. His role is limited to gathering intelligence on the movement of contraband, analyzing consignment shipment patterns, creating profiles of drug dealers... that kind of stuff. Doraiswamy is not authorized to do any of what the general asked him to do. Isn't that fishy?'

'You must remember that very often, the left hand has no idea what the right hand is doing. Sometimes it's by design, but very often, it's just the way things work in our line of business. Frankly, Verghese, on the basis of this transcript alone, I don't see a compelling case against General Dixit.'

'What about the Pakistani press attaché Haider Nazir, sir?' Verghese persisted. 'We have evidence that that phone call he received was from the house that belongs to the general's sister. And we know that the general was in that house when the call was made. And according to the report in front of you, Haider Nazir attended a party thrown by General Dixit in his house last year. Isn't that too much of a coincidence?'

'According to the same report in front of me, apart from Haider Nazir, there was another Pakistani embassy staffer at the party. And apart from the two Pakistanis, there were embassy staff from three other countries as well. Diplomatic courtesy, plain and simple. And as far as the phone call is concerned, unless we're able to get our hands on what was actually said, we have nothing to go on. The general and Haider Nazir know each other, so they decided to talk. That's it.'

'It's the first and only time they've ever spoken over the phone to one another. And when they did, it is long distance, late at night. Some friendship, I must say!' Verghese scoffed, his face flushed with frustration.

'You may be on to something, but don't you see that it's not strong enough to press charges?' asked Assistant Director Pasricha, shaking his head. Seeing the despondent expression on Verghese's face, he clucked sympathetically. 'I'm not asking you to give this up. Work on it. Get me something that is more... more *incriminating*. That's all I want, okay?'

Verghese had traversed only half the distance to the main door of the Intelligence Bureau office when his mobile phone started ringing.

'Hello,' he spoke into the phone as he continued towards the exit.

However, he had hardly taken half a dozen steps when he stopped walking. His face, which had been sullen just moments earlier, became bright and his eyes shone in excitement as he stood rooted to the floor. 'Are you hundred per cent sure about this?' he asked finally, a mild tremble in his voice.

Less than a minute later, he was back inside Assistant Director Pasricha's cabin, seated across the desk. The assistant director looked at him curiously.

'Sir, I had asked my men to do a background check on Haider Nazir,' Verghese began. 'One of them has just got something which I think is critical to this case.'

'Okay,' the assistant director leaned forward.

'Before being posted to Delhi, Haider Nazir was in the Pakistani embassy in Tajikistan. It seems that the Government of Tajikistan officially ordered Pakistan to have Haider Nazir removed from the embassy and recalled to Pakistan, as they had evidence of him spying in their country. My men have checked this with their contacts in the Tajikistan embassy in Delhi, and they have a confirmation on this.'

Assistant Director Pasricha considered Verghese quietly as the junior officer continued talking. 'Sir, here we have a professional Pakistani spy who gets a suspicious call from General Dixit late at night. Four days later, the general organizes a clandestine trip for one of his deputies into Pakistan. If this isn't incriminating, I don't know what is.'

Slowly, almost imperceptibly, the assistant director nodded. 'Put this latest bit on Haider Nazir down in a report immediately, with as much supporting evidence possible. We will need everything in writing.'

'That means you're referring the case to headquarters?' asked Verghese, his eyes hopeful.

'First, put everything down in writing,' the assistant director answered, a small smile playing on the corners of his lips. 'Meanwhile, let me talk to my boss and see what we can do. But to answer your question, yes, I think we finally have enough on Major-General Tushar Dixit to formally open a case.'

30 July. Kuan Mori, Balochistan

When Shihab Perwaiz had said that the house was hidden in the hills, he hadn't been exaggerating. In fact, it was so well hidden and camouflaged that despite Perwaiz having marked it out on the map, Imtiaz and

Shamsheer spent more than half an hour scouring the ridges and ravines before locating it.

Built almost entirely of mud bricks, the house was little more than a low-slung hut with a flat, rusted tin roof. It was located in the lee of a huge bluff, tucked away at the bottom of a narrow gorge. The lone door was covered by a heavy curtain made of gunnysack, while the solitary source of light and ventilation was a small, crude window set high on the far side of the wall. The hut had, in the not so distant past, clearly served as a makeshift shelter for goats and sheep, and the stale smell of livestock and animal faeces lingered in the air inside.

Imtiaz was sitting on the hut's uneven earthen floor, a map of Gwadar spread out in front of him. Shamsheer squatted beside the major, idly toying with one of the Czechoslovakian-made CZ 85B pistols that Perwaiz had procured for them. They studied the map in the light of a lantern, for although it was just past noon, being wedged between two steep cliffs, the hut was dark and gloomy from inside. The light through the curtains barely touched the two rough sacks and the old bicycle that were propped against the far wall.

'We are here,' Imtiaz said, pointing to a spot on the map roughly at the halfway mark between Gwadar town and Pishukan. 'And now that we have the additional information that Perwaiz gave us, we have the option of striking here *and* here.' The major tapped the map at Pishukan and at the hammer-head of Gwadar, where the Zobair Continental Hotel was situated.

'Or…' said Shamsheer, '…anywhere here.' His index finger traced the arc of the Pishukan–Gwadar Road.

'Yes, but finding a suitable place for an ambush in that 35-kilometre stretch of road won't be easy. There might be traffic, plus we might not find adequate place to hide. At the end of the day, there's just the two of us. Still, we must not overrule that possibility.'

'When do you think we should carry out the hit?'

'As soon as possible,' the major answered without a moment's pause. 'Ideally, by tomorrow night… Certainly in the next forty-eight hours. We must finalize our plan by noon tomorrow.'

'You think it can be done so soon, sir?' Shamsheer sounded doubtful as he stared at the map. 'It took us fifteen days to plan the strike in Karachi. We have been here barely five hours, and we still need to familiarize ourselves with the safe house and the hotel in Gwadar.'

'When we planned Karachi, we had the luxury of knowing exactly when and for how long Dilawar would be in the city. We have no such knowledge to work on now. I'm worried that the Pakistanis may move Dilawar out of here. Before he was supposed to come to Karachi, he was in Parachinar. Then suddenly, they moved him here. And if you remember, the colonel told us that the ISI keeps shifting him between safe houses. That's why we shouldn't delay the attack. We should plan and execute quickly.'

Shamsheer nodded silently. After a short pause, Imtiaz spoke again, 'The other thing that worries me is Rafiq.'

The captain looked up sharply. 'How can *he* interfere with our plans? If anything, he'll be on his way to Parachinar.'

'I know we did everything to give the impression that we're going there, but… the colonel cannot be fooled easily. That bothers me.'

Shamsheer thought about this a while. 'Sir, why is the colonel so intent on stopping us? Just because we challenged his authority and refused to follow his orders?'

Imtiaz stared grimly at the lantern's dull yellow flame. 'No,' his voice was emotionless. 'However unbelievable it may sound, it's because the colonel is also somehow involved in this betrayal.'

The two soldiers sat quietly for a while, till Shamsheer asked, 'So what do we do next?'

'Conduct a recce of the house and the hotel before the sun sets. See what the lay of the land is like, what kind of approaches they have, what the escape routes are like… You pick one, I'll take the other.'

'I'll go and check out the hotel.'

'Then I'll go to Pishukan. But first, let's have lunch.' Imtiaz folded the map, stood up, walked over to one of the sacks leaning against the wall and pulled out a can of tinned sardines. Lighting a kerosene stove, he set a pan over the fire and dumped the sardines into it.

Shamsheer pointed to the cycle. 'You can take that. I would look foolish riding up to the hotel on it.'

The major nodded. 'And I suggest you take that pistol with you. I'll take the other one. Who knows… we just might need them.'

30 July. Pishukan Village, Balochistan

Gnawing hunger in the pit of his stomach and a dry, burning thirst in the throat competed for Colonel Mohan's attention as he lay on top of the cliff, surveying the landscape. His last meal, comprising two loaves of home-made bread and some fried fish, had been on board the boat the previous night, and it was more than an hour since he had consumed the last of the water in his hip-flask. He was having trouble concentrating, and the monotony of the job wasn't helping a bit.

He realized that it had been a long time since he'd been in the field, and his advancing years and the full-time desk job had blunted his instincts.

Then, as the hunger pangs threatened to cross the threshold into intolerance, the colonel heard his sat-phone ring. It was General Dixit calling.

'Any news of our heroes?' the general asked tersely, without preamble.

'No sir, nothing so far. I'm still maintaining vigil near the safe house, and Rafiq is combing Gwadar.'

'Hmm,' the general grunted in obvious dissatisfaction. 'Okay, I have some news for you. There's an almost a hundred per cent chance that the chap Shamsheer saw in Clifton that day is Hossam Al-Kamil.'

'Really, sir?' the colonel asked eagerly. 'So I wasn't wrong after all.'

On a hunch, Colonel Mohan had asked Doraiswamy to mail the general some pictures of Al-Kamil, which the Tamilian had dutifully done. The colonel and the general had already discussed the possibility of Al-Kamil being the man whom Shamsheer had observed in the Suzuki Cultus in Clifton, and the general had agreed that Shamsheer's description matched Al-Kamil's pictures. However, as that wasn't conclusive, they had decided to wait for Doraiswamy to dig out more information about Al-Kamil.

'That's right. Swamyji has found out that this Hossam Al-Kamil was hired in Istanbul a month ago to kill Dilawar. Apparently a Turkish syndicate was also approached for the job, but finally, Hossam was given the contract.'

'Shit,' Colonel Mohan breathed out slowly. 'Do we know who hired him?'

'Well, it seems an Algerian contractor called Zarawi or something hired him.'

'An Algerian contractor... That doesn't make any sense, sir.'

'It doesn't,' the general conceded. 'Which, in all probability, means that he's hired Hossam on behalf of someone else.'

'Any idea who it could be, sir?'

'No. It could be any of the usual suspects.'

'Does the ISI know about this?'

'How would I know?' The colonel got the impression that the general's words were accompanied by a grimace and a shrug.

'Do we tip them off about Hossam and the plot?'

'We must, and quickly,' General Dixit answered. 'But before that, you and Rafiq must find and eliminate Imtiaz and Shamsheer, and get out of there. I don't want this affair to get any more complicated.'

'Yes sir.'

'And please hurry up,' the general snapped. 'I want Imtiaz stopped and stopped fast. Well before this Hossam becomes my next headache.'

It was a couple of minutes after the general had disconnected that Colonel Mohan spied a faint movement out of the corner of his right eye. Raising the binoculars, he saw two camels burdened with heavy bags walking sedately down the road. The beasts were led by two men, and immediately, the colonel stiffened. He peered at the mini caravan, waiting for it to draw closer so that he could make out the faces of the two men.

Pulling the Beretta out of the holster, he wondered what his course of action should be if they were, indeed, Imtiaz and Shamsheer. Every sinew in his body tense, the colonel watched the procession draw nearer. Finally, the men's faces came into focus, and the colonel relaxed. The man leading the camel in front was scrawny and bent with age, while the one behind was a young boy of about fifteen.

The colonel was on the verge of putting the Sunagor down when, almost as if directed by some sixth sense, he swung the binoculars a little to the right. Instantly, he was back on full alert.

A lone cyclist was about a hundred metres behind the camels, pedalling at a steady pace.

The cyclist looked like a local villager, but there was something about his bearing that caught Colonel Mohan's attention. As he observed the cyclist approach, then overtake the camels, he almost stopped breathing. At last, he lowered the binoculars and licked his dry lips.

Major Imtiaz Ahmed was in Pishukan.

Gripping the Beretta tightly, the colonel scanned the cycle for any sign of weapons. There were none, which could only mean that the major was merely conducting a recce. Just to be sure, the colonel rapidly searched the landscape for any sign of Shamsheer, but the captain was nowhere in sight.

As Imtiaz rode past the safe house and went on towards Pishukan, Colonel Mohan made a quick decision. There was no point in engaging the major right away—before confronting Imtiaz, he had to find out Shamsheer's whereabouts as well. There was no point in deactivating one if the other was still on the loose. And the only way he could trace Shamsheer was by following Imtiaz.

Here, the colonel was faced with a problem. Imtiaz was on a cycle, and no matter how quickly he moved, the colonel knew that keeping up would be difficult, especially as he had to stay unobserved. To compound the problem, he had no idea how far Shamsheer and Imtiaz's hideout was—if it was more than three kilometres from the hill, the chances of his finding it by tailing Imtiaz were very slim.

The only option he had was to try and move as far *ahead* of Imtiaz as possible, so that he could keep checking back on the major's progress through the Sunagor, even as he tried and stayed ahead.

Colonel Mohan thrust his pistol into the holster and scrambled up. He needed to get off Gard Koh and work his way back towards Gwadar *before* Imtiaz made a U-turn at Pishukan. Crouching low, the colonel ran to the pile of boulders where his jacket lay. Swooping up the jacket smoothly, he continued running towards the narrow path that led down from the hill.

As he shuffled and scurried down the steep incline, the colonel began pulling on his jacket. However, when he thrust his left arm into the jacket's sleeve and pulled the garment close, he heard a flat, plasticky clatter near his left foot. Stopping to look down, Colonel Mohan saw his satellite phone skim along the path towards the edge of a precipice.

The phone had accidentally fallen out of the jacket's pocket.

The colonel lunged forward, but before he could get his hands on it, the phone reached the edge of the precipice, where it teetered briefly. Then, slowly, it toppled into the thirty-foot-deep chasm. It caromed off a few rocks before hitting the bottom with a crash, spilling its digital guts in all directions.

'Fuck you,' the colonel snarled under his breath, staring at the smashed instrument in acute dismay.

Then, with a shake of his head, he stuffed the binoculars carefully into an inside pocket, and resumed his descent.

30 July. Gwadar Town, Balochistan

The mid-afternoon sun was blazing down on Gwadar, and Shamsheer, like everyone else out in the streets, tried his best to keep to the shade offered by the buildings and the trees. Walking casually through various lanes and side streets, he made his way towards the jeep stand from where he and Imtiaz had caught the pickup to Kuan Mori earlier in the day.

His excursion to the Zobair Continental Hotel hadn't taken very long, for the plain and simple reason that there hadn't been much for him to see and do there. He had spent the bulk of his time taking a hot and arduous walk up to the stunningly picturesque cliff of Koh-e-Batil, which overlooked the newly-developed port, the town of Gwadar and the blue waters of the Arabian Sea that virtually surrounded the cliff.

The three-star hotel was situated at one end of Koh-e-Batil, and looking at it the captain had realized that he was too shabbily attired to get past its gates, let alone be entertained by the staff within. So instead, he had focused on making a mental map of the hotel and its surroundings, taking special note of the hotel's main entry and exit points, its approach roads, the flow of traffic within its compound and the kind of security measures it had in place. He also observed the distances between the hotel and the nearest coastline, as well as the nearest inhabited buildings.

Then, left with little else to do, the captain had decided to explore Gwadar town. He knew it was important to get the lay of the land—that would be critical if they decided to launch the attack on the hotel, and needed to make a swift and clean getaway thereafter.

Reaching the end of a narrow alley, Shamsheer turned into a small street lined with shops selling a variety of goods. The street was full of people, and Shamsheer swam into the crowd. He crossed two shops selling clothes, a small emporium specializing in local handicrafts and a building housing a branch of the National Bank of Pakistan, before coming to a shop selling sweetmeats. The sign outside, which also bore the hand-painted logo of Pepsi, proudly proclaimed: 'Nagina Restaurant, Since 1991'. The aroma of fresh, barbecued chicken and mutton kababs wafted out of the joint.

Tempted, Shamsheer decided to stop for a bite. He entered the restaurant, picked a seat that afforded him a view of the street and sat down on a wooden bench. Having placed his order of mutton kababs and tea, Shamsheer looked into the street casually.

And he froze.

Diagonally opposite the restaurant was a grocery store. The shop was fairly crowded, but one of the men in the shop was, at that moment, looking out into the street, his face turned in Shamsheer's direction.

The captain instantly recognized the man. The cold, cruel face under the black qaraqul was unmistakable. It was the face that he had seen inside the Suzuki Cultus in Clifton.

As Shamsheer watched, the man handed the grocer some money and elbowed his way out of the shop carrying two heavy bags, one partially filled with vegetables. The man looked up and down the street once, then turned to his left and headed towards the main road leading to the jeep stand.

Without fully knowing what command he was responding to, Shamsheer got up from the bench, slipped out of the restaurant and began following the man, unmindful of the shouts coming from the restaurant's waiter, who had just brought a plate of warm, succulent kababs to the table.

* * *

Rafiq turned the corner of one of Gwadar's arterial roads and entered a side street with rows of shops on both sides. The street was bustling with people, and Rafiq wondered if he should retrace his steps and try another less-crowded one. There was no way he could possibly find either Imtiaz or Shamsheer in this throng. But then he had spent almost the entire day roaming around Gwadar without catching sight of the two commandos, so he decided that it really didn't make a difference. In fact, one part of his mind was already convinced that the colonel had been wrong, and that Imtiaz and Shamsheer were miles away from Gwadar—probably somewhere much closer to Parachinar.

So, shrugging inwardly, the lieutenant adjusted the haversack on his back and pressed into the crowd. He had walked barely fifty metres when his attention was drawn to a cry.

'*Huzoor… huzoor… O chacha!*'

Turning around, he noticed that the shout had come from an eatery located on the other side of the street. A young man of about twenty, presumably the restaurant's waiter, was standing at the door of the restaurant holding a plate full of food in his left hand. He seemed to be hailing someone in the street, an expression of surprise and annoyance on his face.

Wondering who the man was beckoning, Rafiq turned his head to follow the direction of the waiter's gaze. He was able to catch a glimpse of a tall, lean figure walking hurriedly away towards the main road, but before he could get a better view, the man was lost in the crowd. The waiter, too, appeared to have given up and had withdrawn into the restaurant.

Rafiq turned to continue on his way when something about the man struck him as being odd. He paused and turned once again, his brows knitted in thought… Then his face underwent a dramatic transformation as realization suddenly dawned on him. It was the man's long, loping strides that had been familiar. It was the gait of one of the men he was looking for.

Breaking into a run, the lieutenant cut across the street and began jogging in the direction the man had taken. He dodged and weaved through the crowds, craning his neck, but couldn't see his target. Then, looking across the road, he saw the back of the man as he turned left into the main road. Increasing his pace, Rafiq crossed the street once again, and swerved around the corner. He took three steps before breaking his run all of a sudden and stopping short.

Fifteen metres ahead of him stood Shamsheer, leaning against a hoarding for Nestlé's bottled water.

Rafiq quickly ducked into a nearby cigarette shop, hoping it would give him adequate cover. A couple of danglers advertising cigarette brands hung from the shop's awning, and the lieutenant positioned himself behind one of them, hoping it concealed his face. He then watched Shamsheer carefully.

The captain seemed to be hiding behind the wall and looking at someone or something further down the road. Rafiq tried to see what Shamsheer was observing, but from where he stood, all he could see was a busy road with lots of jeeps preparing to take people back to nearby villages.

A minute or two passed and Rafiq was debating his next move when Shamsheer suddenly stepped out from behind the wall. The captain took two steps on to the road and looked down it, before walking slowly towards one of the parked jeeps. As the lieutenant watched, Shamsheer went up to the jeep's driver and asked him something. He then climbed into the back of the jeep, which was already half full of people. A minute later, three more villagers got into the jeep, and the driver started the engine. Slowly, the vehicle lurched out on to the road and drove away.

Rafiq slipped out of the cigarette shop and quickly made his way to one of the jeeps parked on the road. Its driver, a stocky man with distinctly Oriental features, was busy enjoying a greasy mutton patty.

'*As-salāmu alaikum*,' Rafiq greeted the man. His mouth full, the man merely nodded in return. 'I need you to take me in your jeep,' Rafiq said in Balochi.

'I'm eating,' the driver answered, holding up the half-eaten patty as evidence. 'And anyway, it's not my turn. Those two are before me.' He pointed to two jeeps that had taken their places on the road.

'I can't wait,' said Rafiq. 'And I don't want to get slowed down by other villagers. I want to go quickly and directly.' He paused, then reached into his pocket and pulled out his wallet. 'I'm willing to pay.'

The driver looked at him silently, but with greedy eyes. Rafiq pulled two hundred-rupee notes out of the wallet and rubbed them slowly between thumb and forefinger.

The driver grinned and held up three fingers. The lieutenant nodded and extracted another hundred-rupee note. He thrust the three notes towards the driver, who immediately grabbed the cash and slipped it into his shirt pocket. Stuffing what remained of the patty into his mouth and wiping his oily fingers on his trouser leg, the driver slapped the empty seat next to him.

Once Rafiq was seated, the driver turned on the ignition and the engine roared. 'Where do you want to go?' he asked, as he threw the stubborn gearstick forward.

'I want you to catch up with the jeep that just left from here. Don't get too close. Just follow it at a distance. Stop when it stops, go when it goes. When I want to get off, I'll tell you. Understand?'

The driver looked across at Rafiq meaningfully and smiled a slimy, leering smile. 'Understood,' he said.

30 July. Constitution Avenue, Islamabad

Lieutenant-General Rehmat folded his arms and stared morosely out of the window of the Mitsubishi Pajero. To his right sat Lieutenant-General Niazi, who was looking out of the other window, while Major-General Dar sat in front, riding shotgun. The SUV reached the end of Khayaban-e-Suhrawardy and swung left into Constitution Avenue. Then, as it gathered pace and began devouring the intervening distance to the Prime Minister's official residence, the head of the ISI turned his attention back to the file that lay on his lap.

Inside were a dozen police, medical and forensic reports, and half-a-dozen pictures of Jamal Qayyum Khan and his yet-to-be-identified accomplice whom the Karachi police had killed. The lieutenant-general flipped through these without interest, till he came to a page on which a list of things had been itemized. The director ran his eyes over the list once again with a modicum of satisfaction.

While most of the inventory on that page pertained to articles actually recovered from the dead men, there were a few items, highlighted with a fluorescent marker, which had been planted there at the behest of Lieutenant-General Rehmat. These included an old pair of Indian-made Rupa Frontline briefs, supposedly worn by one of the dead men, and a cheap leather wallet purportedly recovered from the other. The report further noted that among other things, an old bus ticket issued by the Himachal Road Transport Corporation had been found inside the wallet, while the wallet's inner lining was fortified with strips of newspaper printed in Devnagari script.

On the basis of this circumstantial evidence, the suggestively worded report surmised that there was strong reason to believe that the two men who had been shot dead on Mauripur Road were connected with India. Importantly, while the file also contained Haider Nazir's initial reports of the Indian plan to infiltrate Pakistan, there was no mention whatsoever of Jamal Qayyum Khan by name, nor was there any reference to the fingerprint report generated by the police in Nowshera, which had helped identify the ex-Afghan rebel.

As the Pajero passed the Prime Minister's Secretariat, Lieutenant-General Niazi turned to the director.

'Janaab, do you think this would be enough to convince him?' he asked doubtfully.

Lieutenant-General Rehmat closed the file and sighed. So far, the Karachi police had made no headway in tracking the Indian commandos down, nor had they uncovered anything new about Jamal Qayyum Khan's associates at Mohajir Camp. And even though the trap had been set up at Clifton, there were no signs of an Indian attack in the offing.

'Yes, it should,' he answered, hoping his voice had carried as much conviction as his words.

Almost everything now depended on the outcome of the meeting with the Prime Minister. In ten minutes, they would have an audience with the man, and he had half an hour to sketch out the Indian plot, present all the cooked-up evidence in the file, and convince the Prime Minister not to buckle under pressure and surrender Irshad Dilawar to the Indians.

30 July. Kuan Mori, Balochistan

The moment the sun dipped behind the mountains, Rafiq felt the temperature drop by a few degrees. As if on cue, the weak breeze that had been blowing intermittently from the south strengthened, and the lieutenant shivered involuntarily as he huddled behind a cluster of rocks and observed the small hut hidden inside the mouth of the narrow gorge. He was certain he wouldn't have discerned the structure had Shamsheer not made a beeline for it.

Wondering whether the major was also inside the hut, Rafiq once again pulled out his sat-phone and dialled the colonel's number. From the time he had got off the jeep and had begun tailing Shamsheer on foot, he had been trying to ring the colonel to inform him of the sighting, and the fact that he was following his quarry. However, for some reason, the colonel's phone was unreachable.

For a full minute he kept the phone pressed to his ear, desperately hoping he would get through, but all he heard was silence, broken by the sound of the wind keening eerily down a gulch to his right. Shaking his head in mild frustration, he returned the phone to his pocket.

The light was failing rapidly, and even though a weak half-moon hung in the sky, the hut was now just a dark, squarish shape, jutting out of the deeper shadows of the gorge beyond. Although Shamsheer was inside, there was no sign of light coming from within. Soon, the hut and the gorge would be steeped in darkness, allowing his prey to slip in and out easily. Rafiq knew he couldn't let that happen. He had to take down Shamsheer—and hopefully, the major as well—as quickly as possible. That much was clear from the instructions he had received.

Opening his haversack, Rafiq quietly withdrew the two Glocks and checked to see if both were loaded. Then, zipping the haversack shut and slinging it on again, he picked up a pistol in each hand and began moving cautiously towards the building.

* * *

Shamsheer sat cross-legged on the floor, his back to the wall, the lantern burning low by his side. His eyes stared meditatively into the recesses of the hut, where the shadows shifted and jostled in a sinister half-light.

There was no doubt in his mind that the man he had seen in Gwadar town was the same person he'd seen in Clifton. He had had a good look at the man's face, and he was positive that he couldn't have been mistaken. What Shamsheer couldn't decide upon, however, was whether or not the man's presence in Gwadar was a coincidence.

Back in the apartment in Karachi, they had all agreed that the manner in which the Suzuki Cultus had driven past the Clifton safe house was suspicious. Then, Saadat had discovered that the car had actually been stolen, and later abandoned. And now, one of the men in that car was in Gwadar, thirty-odd kilometres from another of Irshad Dilawar's safe houses… It just couldn't be a coincidence.

But what if he had, indeed, made an error in identifying the man? It was easy to mistake people of similar racial extract, and the truth was that he had seen the man in Clifton just *once*, that too in a passing car…

As he sat and wrestled with these thoughts, Shamsheer heard a footfall outside and sighed. Imtiaz was obviously back from his visit to Pishukan, and he would tell him about the man in Gwadar, and see what the major made of it.

The captain was in the process of getting to his feet when a thought crossed his mind and he tensed. He realized that while he had heard a footfall, he hadn't heard even a faint jangle of the cycle, either being wheeled or being put down. It also suddenly occurred to him that the major always walked like a cat.

The footfall couldn't have been the major's!

His senses awakened to danger, Shamsheer reached for the CZ 85B tucked into his waistband. But halfway into the move, he remembered that after entering the shed, he had taken the pistol out and placed it with the other guns in the bag—which lay in the far corner of the room, a good fifteen feet from where he crouched.

Ruing his judgment, the captain was about to take a step towards the bag when, out of the corner of his eye, he saw the gunnysack curtain being whipped aside and a figure enter the room.

'Don't move,' the man barked. 'Raise your hands slowly and stand straight, or I will shoot.'

Shamsheer didn't need to see the man to know who he was. Raising his hands, he turned to face Rafiq. The first thing he noticed was the two pistols levelled straight at him.

CHAPTER 14

30 July. Badarpur Thermal Power Station, Delhi

As his Hyundai Accent pulled up to the main gate of the Badarpur Thermal Power Station, General Dixit peered out of the window at the twin chimneys towering into the night sky.

His chauffeur presented a few identity papers to the Central Industrial Security Force sentries manning the gate, and once the general's credentials had been satisfactorily established, the car was allowed to pass through into the power station's sprawling compound.

'General saab, believe me, this is important. It's too sensitive to share over the phone. So please come.'

Under-secretary Chandrakant Upreiti had been insistent when he had telephoned an hour-and-a-half earlier, and the general had had to give in, even though he'd planned on spending the evening with his daughter and son-in-law.

'Okay Upreiti saab. But where are we meeting?'

'At the Minars. See you,' Upreiti had signed off.

'The Minars' was a reference to the chimneys that the general had just been surveying, and served as a code for the Badarpur Thermal Power Station, which was one of the favoured locations for unofficial or quasi-official meetings between the top brass of the Joint Intelligence Committee, the RAW, the Central Intelligence Bureau and military intelligence. The fact that the Minars had been chosen as the venue instilled in General Dixit an immediate sense of urgency.

The Hyundai Accent traversed virtually the entire length of the power station's complex, before coming to a halt in front of a two-storey building at its northern periphery. As the general got out of his car, two burly men in civil clothes approached him and escorted him decorously into the building.

The conference room lay at the very end of a long corridor, its entrance blocked by a heavy wooden door with a 'Do not disturb' sticker pasted permanently on it. Knowing that the sign did not apply to him, General Dixit was about to reach for the doorknob when the door swung open inwards to reveal Upreiti's dark face framed in the doorway.

'Aaiye, General saab, please come. Come, come,' Upreiti twittered meaninglessly, stepping aside to admit the general.

The general walked in and, almost immediately, he stopped and stared, his eyebrows climbing upwards. 'Quite a gathering, I can see,' he said, looking at the men seated in the room.

'Yes, yes,' answered Upreiti, closing the door. Turning around, he added, 'Er, you probably know everyone, right?'

Apart from the under-secretary and the general himself, there were five people in the room, and General Dixit knew four of them. The man sitting closest to the door was a short, stout man with a thick black moustache and sad eyes. '*Namaskaar, dada. Bhalo?*' the general smiled as he addressed Principal Secretary Bimon Talukdar, Upreiti's boss at the Joint Intelligence Committee.

'*Nomoshkaar,*' the principal secretary mumbled dolefully.

The chair next to Talukdar was occupied by a wiry man with a thick mop of grey hair on his head, and a moustache of the same shade on his lip. His generous eyes twinkled in animation as he sized up the general, but the toothy smile that usually dwelt on his lips was missing. The general didn't notice this, however, as he stretched out his hand.

'Dhawan saab, long time! *Kya haal hain?*'

'All well,' responded Prathamesh Dhawan, a special director at the Intelligence Bureau, whose responsibilities included monitoring and countering Pakistani espionage networks operating inside Indian territory. He rose from his chair and shook the general's hand diffidently, before sitting down again.

The man sitting to the immediate right of Dhawan was slightly built with narrow stooping shoulders. The general, who had never met the man before, instantly decided that there was an air of academia about him. As the man showed no indication of rising to greet him, General Dixit merely smiled and bobbed his head politely before turning to the uniformed man sitting at the far end of the room.

'Good evening, sir,' said the general, straightening and saluting the man, even as he wondered why Under-secretary Upreiti had spent time persuading him to come for this meeting, when *this* man was anyway in attendance. Lieutenant-General Parashuram Bhonsle was the head of Indian military intelligence, northern sector, and if a senior officer of the Indian military intelligence was attending a meeting, protocol demanded that General Dixit also be present.

'Good evening,' said Lieutenant-General Bhonsle stiffly. The usually affable officer didn't bother returning the general's salute, and it was then that General Dixit first sensed the frostiness in the air.

The general turned to the fifth man in the room—Inspector General Jagdish Rawat of the RAW. 'Hello, sir, good to see you,' said General Dixit, his mind already racing as it tried to fathom the purpose of the meeting.

'Good to see *you*,' smirked Inspector General Rawat. The general didn't miss the intonation in the RAW officer's voice.

Licking his lips nervously, General Dixit turned towards Upreiti, who came hurriedly to his side. 'And *this* is Assistant Director Abhay Pasricha of the Intelligence Bureau.'

The general turned back to see the small, professorial man stand up and quietly proffer his hand. As the general took it, Special Director Dhawan looked at the general apologetically.

'Sorry, I should have introduced the two of you. My colleague Pasricha… and this is Major-General Tushar Dixit.'

The general finally took his seat, and following a moment's awkward silence, asked, 'So what are we here for?'

Looking at the faces around him, the general saw a mixture of diffidence and discomfiture in the way the men looked from one to the other, as if expecting the question to miraculously answer itself. Inspector General Rawat was the only one who looked decidedly happy.

'Oh, we just have to wait a bit,' trilled Upreiti at last. 'Mr Seshadri and Vashisht saab will be joining us as well.'

'Seshadri saab?' asked General Dixit, raising his brows. Seeing Upreiti nod, he settled back in the sofa, trying to work out what this meant. YV Narayana Seshadri was the Director of RAW, while Satyendra Vashisht was the agency's additional director. Once the two men were in the room, some of the biggest names in Indian intelligence would be under one roof.

'Seshadri saab and Vashisht saab will be here any moment,' said Upreiti, glancing at his watch. Then, in an attempt at injecting conversation into the room, he smiled and added, 'We can say that they are both fashionably late.'

The under-secretary's stab at forced gaiety fell flat, as everyone merely smiled weakly and nodded. Inspector General Rawat, however, picked up the baton after a short pause.

'Sure, they are a bit late,' he said, speaking for his superiors. 'But then they are busy outsmarting the Pakistanis. And these days we find Pakistanis in the unlikeliest of places, don't we?'

General Dixit looked across at the inspector general, taking in the man's condescending tone and the air of smug superiority. He then noticed the others in the room as they exchanged glances at the end of Inspector General Rawat's little speech.

That's when, in a sudden stroke of clarity, all the chips fell into place in the general's mind. He understood why some of the most powerful names in Indian intelligence were sitting around him. He understood why the head of the RAW and his deputy were expected, and why Inspector General Rawat was being so cocky about everything. Above all, he understood the purpose behind Upreiti's niceties and the contrasting undercurrent of hostility in the room.

Somehow, the men in the room had come to know about Haider Nazir!

As waves of dismay and helplessness crashed over him, the general bit his lip and looked down at the carpet. At that moment, the door opened and in walked the director and the additional director of the RAW.

30 July. Kuan Mori, Balochistan

'Where is the major?'

Rafiq stood just inside the hut's door, his guns pointing unwaveringly at Shamsheer. Although the captain couldn't see Rafiq's eyes clearly in the half-light, he sensed a deathly calm in the young man's countenance.

'Do you know what you're doing?' Shamsheer asked slowly.

The lieutenant didn't reply.

'You're pointing a gun at a colleague and fellow commando,' Shamsheer answered his own question in the hope of drawing the junior officer into a debate and buying time. 'As a Unit Kilo commando, this conduct should make you feel very proud of yourself.'

'You wouldn't be talking about a commando's conduct if *you* were the one holding these guns, would you?' said Rafiq, his voice sardonic. 'And where was this conduct when you and the major walked out of the apartment in Karachi? I don't remember any friendly farewells that night.'

Shamsheer was silent for a moment. 'That's because you didn't cover yourself in glory by snooping on me and the major, and reporting what we were doing back to the colonel.'

'I was simply following orders,' the lieutenant said bluntly.

'The way you're following them now?'

Rafiq chose not to reply.

'And these orders include killing your fellow commandos?'

'They include stopping you and the major from doing what both of you have set out to do.'

'And how will you stop us? By killing us, right? Shouldn't you be questioning the motives of those who have given you such orders?'

'Unlike you and the major, I do not question the decisions and orders issued by my superiors,' the lieutenant's tone was biting. 'As soldiers and commandos, we are trained to always, *always* obey orders. If a soldier can question one order, he can question a hundred. And sooner or later, he will question the decision to go into battle. No army can afford such questions. Or such soldiers.'

'Not all decisions that are made are right or good. History is full of...'

'By themselves, decisions are neither good nor bad,' the lieutenant cut in. 'If something works, it becomes a good decision. If it doesn't, it becomes a bad one. It's only the consequences that make decisions look good or bad. But none of this really matters, so let's not waste time over it. You still haven't answered my question: where is the major?'

Quickly thinking of how he could prolong the conversation, the captain replied, 'He is scouting the safe house in Pishukan.'

'So when is he returning?'

'He won't be back till tomorrow morning,' answered Shamsheer, raising the pitch of his voice a few decibels. 'He is mounting surveillance on the house through the night.'

Although he wasn't sure, the captain thought he had just heard a pebble roll somewhere outside.

Rafiq considered this for a moment before speaking. 'How come you aren't with him?'

'Because I need to sleep as I'm supposed to relieve the major tomorrow morning,' the captain answered, hoping Rafiq would not notice the increase in the volume of his voice. 'We're surveying the house round-the-clock, and I have duty all day tomorrow.'

'That's strange. If you're taking turns at monitoring the house, what were you doing in Gwadar this afternoon?'

'We started our surveillance from this evening. And I was in Gwadar to arrange for transport out of this place once we're done.'

Rafiq chewed on this for a while. 'That means the major won't come here till you report there tomorrow morning, right?' he asked finally.

'Correct.'

'What will he do if you don't show up in the morning?'

'I don't know. We didn't discuss that possibility, so you'll have to ask him.'

'You don't have any mobile phones to talk to one another, do you?'

'No. As you can see, we are still treating the operation very seriously.'

Shamsheer could see that his ruse had worked and that the lieutenant was clearly at a loss. Rafiq had the choice of either killing him or holding him hostage, and waiting for the major to eventually return. But then Shamsheer also knew that Rafiq had no guarantee that the major, suspecting the worst, would ever come to the hut if Shamsheer didn't turn up at the appointed hour. Rafiq also had the option of ordering the captain to take him to Imtiaz, but that line was fraught with risk and uncertainty.

'Where are you supposed to relieve the major, and at what time?' Rafiq asked suddenly.

Shamsheer, who had no idea of what the safe house and its environs looked like, was taken aback. He had no way of telling whether or not the lieutenant knew anything about the safe house and its vicinity.

'There's an old, run-down shed, not very different from this one, pretty close to the house,' he hazarded an answer. 'It's what we're using for our surveillance. I'm supposed to meet the major there at eight in the morning.'

'A shed like this one,' Rafiq said thoughtfully, and Shamsheer winced inwardly. However, what the young commando said next put him slightly at ease. 'Is it the only building near the house?'

'No, there are a few other huts nearby. Pishukan is a full-fledged village,' said the captain, trying to sound confident and authoritative.

Rafiq nodded slowly, thinking about how he could pass this information on to the colonel, whose sat-phone was unreachable.

Looking at the faraway expression on the lieutenant's face, a new thought suddenly crossed Shamsheer's mind. He realized that the story he had just cooked up might well have presented Rafiq with a fresh option. Now, the lieutenant might just decide to kill him and try and hunt the major down based on his make-believe description. Unwittingly, his concoction might prove to be his undoing.

As an involuntary shiver ran down Shamsheer's spine, he decided to muddy the waters further by adding to Rafiq's confusion. 'By the way, I suppose you know that the major and I are not alone,' he said.

'What!' Even in the dim light, the captain could see Rafiq's pupils as his eyes flew open in surprise. 'Who's with you? Who is helping you here in Gwadar?'

'Rafiq mian, you can find friends in the strangest parts of the world.'

'So Saadat has been…' the lieutenant began, then stopped and stared at Shamsheer. His eyes suddenly narrowed and he raised his pistols towards the captain's head.

'I don't believe you. No, I don't believe *anything* you have said. If you really had friends here helping you and the major, you would never have told me about it. You would have kept it a surprise—not given it away like that. You're lying. You've been lying *all this while.*'

As Rafiq cocked his guns, he felt something cold and round press into the base of his skull, a couple of inches behind his right ear.

'Drop your guns now, lieutenant. Immediately,' Imtiaz's voice growled menacingly.

* * *

The cold wind that had been blowing from the south dropped suddenly, only to change direction and pick up a minute later. It now blew from the east, and Colonel Mohan had to turn up the collar of his windbreaker to keep the chill from getting under his shirt. The good part about this, though, was that the colonel could now hear snatches of conversation emanating from somewhere ahead.

Pressing himself to the mountainside, the colonel strained his eyes, trying to make out what lay in the shadows of the narrow gorge situated fifty metres from where he was hiding. All he knew was that Imtiaz had gone into the defile, and that the voices being borne to him by the wind also appeared to be coming from the general direction of the gorge.

The chase from Pishukan had been frantic, and there had been moments when the colonel was certain he would not be able to keep pace with Imtiaz. For not only did Imtiaz have an edge on account of his cycle, the flat open landscape offered very little concealment, severely hampering Colonel Mohan's movements. In fact, the colonel had virtually reconciled himself to losing Imtiaz when, in the most fortuitous manner, the chain of the major's cycle had snapped, forcing the major to dismount and wheel the bicycle the rest of the way.

The odds having been considerably evened, Colonel Mohan had followed Imtiaz off the highway, through the desert and into the hills. Although the dim moonlight proved adequate for tailing Imtiaz across the hills, the colonel had begun wondering how much longer the chase would last when the major had suddenly lowered the cycle to the ground and crouched.

Peering through his Sunagor, the colonel had observed Imtiaz move surreptitiously between boulders and outcroppings, before finally entering the dark gorge.

Drawing his Beretta out of the holster, Colonel Mohan darted to a small gully not far from the mouth of the gorge. Throwing himself into the gully, he sat up and peered out carefully, half-expecting a burst of gunfire. There was none. Bracing himself, the colonel broke cover again, this time running towards one of the cliffs adjoining the gorge. Flattening himself, his back to the rock-face, he waited for a while before slowly inching forward.

Reaching the mouth of the gorge, Colonel Mohan took two tentative steps into the darkness when there was a sudden glow of a light fifty feet ahead. The colonel froze and stared as the cliff-face on the far side was lit briefly by a rectangular patch of yellow light. The light went out almost immediately, as if something heavy had been dropped across it, but in that brief burst of incandescence, the colonel had noticed the squat contours of a building jump out of the surrounding gloom.

He had also seen the shadow of a man passing through and across the yellow rectangle. He knew that the light had come from a door as someone had pushed a curtain aside to enter or exit the building.

The colonel waited for a while, listening for voices, and he was rewarded with a murmur. He was certain it was coming from the building. Crouching low, gripping the Beretta tightly in his hand, he began shuffling forward slowly. Thirty seconds later, his groping hand touched the side of the building. Pressing his back against the wall, the colonel straightened.

'I asked you to drop your guns immediately.'

Imtiaz's voice came through clearly, startling the colonel. A moment later, he heard the cocking of a gun, followed by the major's voice. 'For the last time, I say—drop your guns.'

It took a moment for Colonel Mohan to realize that the major's command had come from somewhere inside the building, and was not directed at him. Puzzled, the colonel moved quickly to his left and peeked around the edge of the building. Immediately, he saw the door, barely ten feet away, a thin sliver of light pouring out from underneath it. He also saw a shadow falling on the heavy curtain that was drawn across the door.

'Sir, I have the captain in my sights. I can shoot him as quickly as you can shoot me.'

Colonel Mohan's eyes widened with alarm as he recognized the second voice. Creeping swiftly to the door, he peeped in through a narrow chink between the doorway and the curtain. From the angle he was in, the colonel could see Imtiaz holding a pistol to Rafiq's head. The lieutenant, for his part, was pointing two guns at someone who was out of view. Both Imtiaz and Rafiq had their backs to the door.

'Go ahead and shoot him,' the major spoke gruffly. 'But before the captain's body hits the ground, it will be covered with pieces of your brain. And after I have killed you, I will go after Dilawar, and you still won't be able to stop me. So be sensible and put your guns down.'

Rafiq didn't answer, but the colonel could see that the lieutenant wasn't planning to lower his pistols.

'You have one last chance. Then I shoot,' the major ordered.

Moving swiftly and silently, Colonel Mohan swept the curtain aside, stepped into the hut and pointed his Beretta at the back of Imtiaz's head.

'Don't shoot, major. Don't do *anything* stupid.'

There was complete silence in the room as all four soldiers stood motionless, as if part of some grotesque tableau.

'Please don't shoot, major,' Colonel Mohan said again. 'And that applies to you as well, lieutenant. In fact, I want you to lower your guns now, Rafiq.'

'Sir…?' Surprise and suspicion mingled in Rafiq's voice.

'Yes, lower your guns. It's an order. There will be no shooting here tonight.'

The lieutenant slowly lowered his arms, his eyes on Shamsheer.

'Good. Captain, now you may lower your hands.'

As Shamsheer slowly dropped his stiff hands, Colonel Mohan continued speaking, 'Now as evidence of my good faith, I shall lower *my* gun first, major. The captain can see what I am doing, and you can obviously trust him.'

Seeing Shamsheer nod, the colonel carefully brought his Beretta down and cautiously walked in front of Imtiaz and Rafiq. 'Now I want both of you to also put your guns away. Like I said, no one is shooting anyone here.'

It was almost a full minute before all the weapons were lowered and stowed away, and the four men stood facing one another uncertainly. For a while, no one spoke.

'Thank you for listening to me,' the colonel said finally, relief flooding his voice. Looking from Imtiaz to Rafiq to Shamsheer, he added, 'It would have been a very sad day if the three best men I ever had, had ended up killing one another.'

The three commandos nodded, but the confusion and mistrust was plain on their faces. 'What's happening here?' Imtiaz asked finally, his voice still edgy. 'What are you doing in Pakistan?'

'Like Rafiq, I also came here to stop you. But my objective was to take you back—alive. All three of you.'

'But… why is it so important to stop us?' asked Shamsheer.

'I'll explain everything. But first, do you have some food here? I've eaten nothing all day.'

A minute later, the stove had been lit. Imtiaz emptied three tins of sardine and two of beans into a large pan and set it to fry, as the others sat in a circle and watched him. The lantern's wick had been turned up, and almost miraculously, all the pent-up strain and nervous tension in the room began ebbing, as if driven out by the lantern's cheery glow.

Turning on his haunches, the major looked at Colonel Mohan. 'This will take some time to cook, sir. Why don't you start telling us what this is all about?'

The colonel sighed and turned to Shamsheer. 'The reason why it was so important to stop you is because the man you have come to kill is actually India's most precious asset in Pakistan. The Pakistanis like to believe that Irshad Dilawar is *their* trump card, but the truth is that he is *our* best kept secret.'

Rafiq, Shamsheer and Imtiaz stared at him blankly, then as the colonel's words hit home, they looked at one another in stunned silence. Pausing briefly for effect, Colonel Mohan looked at the faces around him and nodded.

'Irshad Dilawar is India's number one spy in Pakistan.'

CHAPTER 15

30 July. Badarpur Thermal Power Station, Delhi

Narayana Seshadri folded his arms and solemnly studied the faces of the seven men sitting around him. Finally, the director of the RAW turned to Special Director Dhawan of the Intelligence Bureau.

'As you were the one to first call me about this, I take it that you took the initiative of inviting everyone else as well?' he asked.

'Sir, I had informed only you, Talukdar saab and General Bhonsle about it,' answered the special director, spreading his hands as if to absolve himself of everything else. 'And of course, I also asked Pasricha to attend as it was his department that presented me with the report on General Dixit. I don't know about the others.'

The RAW director nodded. It was only natural for the IB officer to inform the heads of the RAW, the Joint Intelligence Committee and military intelligence about what he had learned. But that didn't explain the presence of Upreiti and Inspector General Rawat.

'Sir, I was the one to involve Upreiti in this meeting,' said Principal Secretary Talukdar softly. 'As you know, Upreiti has been working closely with General Dixit on an ongoing operation, so I thought it was important for him to know about the matter. What the IB has discovered might have serious implications on the operation.'

'Yes, sir,' Upreiti spoke up. 'And I asked Rawat saab to come as he is also a member of the core group behind the special operation.'

Before Seshadri could acknowledge either of the bureaucrats of the Intelligence Committee, Lieutenant-General Bhonsle leaned forward in his seat, a severe expression on his face.

'What is this special operation that's being spoken about?' he demanded acidly. 'The RAW and the JIC seem to know of it, but how come I, one of the senior-most officers at military intelligence, know nothing of an operation involving a major-general of the Indian Army? I insist on a full explanation.'

The director of the RAW sighed and exchanged a small glance with Additional Director Vashisht, before turning to the man in the vortex of the storm.

'Can you see the amount of fuss a bit of carelessness on your part has created, Dixit *saab*?' he asked. 'Do you think explaining all of this will be easy? Do you think we can keep everything to ourselves any longer?'

General Dixit, who had been sitting quietly staring at the floor, looked up at the RAW director. 'No, sir,' he said, shaking his head apologetically. 'I'm sorry about the whole thing.'

Seshadri shook his head ruefully, leaned back in his sofa and addressed the men gathered around him.

'Gentlemen, I wish none of this had ever happened. I wish General Dixit had never made the call to Haider Nazir, which alerted the Intelligence Bureau. I wish the IB had done nothing about it, and I wish none of you had come to know of any of this. But now that you have learnt some half-truths, I think it's time you got to know the whole truth. A truth that only three people in this room know of—I, my deputy Vashisht and General Dixit here.'

The director paused and looked at the faces staring at him intently. 'But first, I want a solemn promise from all of you that what you are about to discover will not be discussed or disclosed to anyone outside. I am talking about extremely classified information pertaining to India's security interests.'

Everyone in the group nodded, signalling their intent to keep silent.

'Fine,' said Seshadri. Turning to General Dixit, he said, 'But before I begin, can I have some clarity on Project Abhimanyu? Do you have any update on your two maverick commandos?'

'Sir, Colonel Mohan is in Pakistan. He has promised to take care of them before they get to Irshad Dilawar,' the general answered.

As the others looked from the general to the director, startled and confused, Seshadri pursed his lips. 'I hope he does,' he said. 'We can't afford to let two commandos undo all the hard work we have put in all these years.'

30 July. Kuan Mori, Balochistan

The sound of the wind blowing outside and the faint sizzle of oil on the frying pan were the only sounds to be heard as Imtiaz, Shamsheer and Rafiq gaped at the colonel in amazement.

'I don't believe this, sir,' Rafiq finally broke the stunned silence, shaking his head. 'You're saying the one man everyone in India has come to *detest* is actually working in our country's interests? It's... just not possible.'

'I know what I'm saying is very hard to believe. But that is precisely the result of years of systematic propaganda and disinformation that *we* have been putting out to keep anyone from sniffing out the truth.' Colonel Mohan smiled. 'I must admit we have done a damn good job of convincing the world into believing our version of the truth.'

'So everything we know about the man is one big lie? A cooked-up story?' Imtiaz asked incredulously. 'His rise in Mumbai's underworld, his bitter rivalry with gangsters like Vasantrao Guru and Babloo Kasim, his role in the Royale Cinema bomb blast... All that has to be true—it's all been very well documented.'

'You're right,' replied the colonel. 'Everything that you know about Irshad Dilawar up to the Royale Cinema blast and his permanent relocation to Sharjah is true. But nearly everything anyone has heard *after* that is false.'

'But how did India's most wanted criminal become our top agent in Pakistan?' asked Shamsheer.

'See, once Dilawar moved to Sharjah and started establishing his base there, the Indian government began trying its best to get him extradited, so that we could proceed with his legal persecution. Following the Royale Cinema bomb blast, India redoubled its efforts to bring him back, but Dilawar, who had the backing of the Pakistanis, was influential enough to keep avoiding the extradition process. It soon became obvious to everyone that getting him back wouldn't be an easy task.'

'Now, one of the things that few people know about is that after Dilawar fled to Sharjah, there were two attempts on his life, both by his rivals. One of them, in fact, was a very close call, and Dilawar's escape was providential. It was around this time that the RAW devised a top-secret master-plan of recruiting Dilawar as an Indian agent against Pakistan.'

'I don't get the logic, sir,' Rafiq interjected. 'Of all people, why recruit Dilawar as an Indian spy?'

'Dilawar had the complete patronage of Pakistan,' Colonel Mohan explained. 'He was clearly seen as anti-Indian, he had big contacts in the Pakistani military establishment, his underworld network was fairly strong in the country, and he was also friendly with many Pakistani politicians. What that essentially meant was that he would always be welcome in Pakistan, and that he would be free to do as he pleased. We just decided to use all that to our advantage.'

'And Dilawar agreed to do something like this, just like that?' the major asked, his expression overtly sceptical.

'No, no. He needed a lot of... encouragement,' answered Colonel Mohan. 'There had already been two assassination bids on him, and we engineered a third attempt—a mock attack to demonstrate that no matter where he went, he would never be safe from us. Also, even though he was out of the country, Dilawar had vast business interests in India, not to mention an extended family. We made it evident that we would shut everything down and make things very hard for his kith and kin in India. We then assured him that if he cooperated with us, we would de-fang his rivals and do everything to protect him and his interests. In return, all he had to do was endear himself even further to the Pakistani establishment, and pass on whatever information he gleaned from his ISI friends.'

'You mean he wasn't left with a choice,' said Rafiq.

The colonel nodded. 'He could either have accepted our amnesty and our offer, or have waited for someone to come after him, while everything he had in India just vanished into thin air.'

'But how could we cut a deal with someone as blatantly anti-Indian as him?', Imtiaz bristled with indignation.

'People like Dilawar can never be anti-anybody or pro-somebody, major,' the colonel explained patiently. 'They live for themselves and work only for money. The only things that concern Dilawar are his own safety and his business interests. He was never emotionally involved in the Royale Cinema blast—he was just carrying out Pakistan's terror agenda on India for a price. All we did was raise the price. Or, in this case, the reward for working for us.'

'Did we have any guarantee that he wouldn't align with the Pakistanis and double-cross us?' asked Shamsheer.

'In this business, you can trust virtually everyone and no one,' Colonel Mohan shrugged. 'So Dilawar's cooperation is constantly under review. Every promise of ours is based on the quality and consistency of information he delivers. We made it clear that the minute he double-crosses us, all the bets are off and we will cut him loose.'

'We shook hands with someone who has taken innocent Indian lives,' the major shook his head obstinately.

The colonel considered Imtiaz for a moment. 'Yes, but in the process we are now in a position to *save* countless Indian lives. From the information he's provided, we have learnt a great deal about the ISI's extensive operations in Afghanistan, Nepal, Bangladesh, Sri Lanka, Myanmar and the whole of the Middle East. We now know how the ISI has been working against Indian interests in this region, and how it has been channelling drug-money and arms into India. We have learnt a lot about how the ISI recruits and trains operatives for jihadi outfits from places as far and wide as Bangladesh, Saudi Arabia and even Sudan, not to mention Pakistan itself. We now know more about the connections between Pakistan and terror groups like the ULFA, the Bodo Security Force, the LTTE and the Naxalites. And based on the information we have got, we have successfully thwarted innumerable terror attacks on India by Pakistan-backed jihadi groups. All in all, our experiment has been quite a success.'

'What about the countless terror attacks that have actually been carried out on Indian soil?'

'Those have largely been our own intelligence failures,' Colonel Mohan admitted. 'Lax security, poor coordination between intelligence agencies and the police... The truth is that the foiled attacks vastly outnumber the ones that succeed, but it's the latter that naturally attract greater media attention.'

'And these news reports of Dilawar's network assisting Pakistan-sponsored terrorism in India?'

'What is seen, heard and read is part of the propaganda that we have been perpetuating about Dilawar, used to keep the farce intact.'

'So his criminal network in India doesn't exist?' It was Rafiq's turn to look sceptical.

'The underworld in India continues to exist, and Dilawar still controls large parts of it. It is part of the quid pro quo, our side of the bargain. And the truth is that Dilawar's network in India has to stay alive if this subterfuge has to work—the Pakistanis aren't exactly fools, and would become suspicious were the network to shut down suddenly. The network also serves our purpose of feeding Pakistan with the kind of information we want to plant.'

Shamsheer shifted in his seat. 'I still don't see why Dilawar agreed to do something as risky as this,' he said. 'Wasn't he safer just siding with the Pakistanis?'

'Look at it this way. Right now, because he is seen as being anti-Indian, he is Pakistan's darling and has this country's unadulterated patronage. All we have to do is make a few noises about him in the media and get our politicians to clamour for his extradition, and the Pakistanis immediately start lavishing attention on him. He's leading a pampered life here. At the same time, he has our guarantee of safety. Had he not accepted our deal, he would be spending half his time on the run, never knowing when someone would materialize with a gun or when a booby-trapped bomb would go off. Now, he has the best of both worlds.'

The three Unit Kilo commandos sat in silence, contemplating what they had just been told. The colonel looked at the three bowed heads and sighed, 'I understand that all this is terribly hard to believe, but if it isn't true, how come Irshad Dilawar is still alive today?'

Looking from Shamsheer to Imtiaz, he spoke again, 'You are just two commandos, but look at what you've achieved. You are barely twenty-five kilometres from your target. And you, major... You were fifty or hundred metres away from Dilawar when you cycled past the safe house this afternoon—that close! If Irshad Dilawar wasn't our man, couldn't we have killed him whenever we wanted to?'

Imtiaz looked at the colonel and nodded. Then, taking a deep breath, he asked, 'If Dilawar is so important to us, why were the three of us sent into Pakistan with instructions to kill him? What was the objective behind Project Abhimanyu?'

Aware that Rafiq and Shamsheer's eyes were also upon him, Colonel Mohan spoke in measured tones, 'Project Abhimanyu was meticulously drawn up to *protect* Irshad Dilawar—not kill him.'

30 July. Badarpur Thermal Power Station, Delhi

Upreiti's jaw dropped as he stared at Seshadri. 'You mean... Project Abhimanyu was a smokescreen?' he blurted out.

'Yes,' the director nodded. 'It was a hoax, a red herring, a bluff operation. A decoy to fool the enemy.'

Principal Secretary Talukdar coughed politely into his hand. 'So what was its true purpose?'

Seshadri cleared his throat a couple of times. 'Dixit saab, my throat is dry from all this talking. Would you mind taking over?'

'Sure, sir.' The general leaned forward and looked at the ring of curious faces. 'So, as Seshadri saab just explained, our gamble to enlist Dilawar as a spy paid off, and things have been going rather nicely for us. But of late, there have been certain developments that threaten to jeopardize the status quo.'

Pausing briefly to collect his thoughts, General Dixit continued. 'As you all know, a leopard can't really change its spots. So while Dilawar has been acting out his charade in Pakistan and cooperating with us, he has also been busy growing his underworld empire in other directions. And that brought him in contact with elements in the Taliban, and later, the al-Qaeda.'

'You must understand that we have no direct control over who Dilawar chooses to dine with,' the director of the RAW butted in. 'On the positive side, this gave us access to some information about the Taliban and the al-Qaeda.'

'Right,' agreed General Dixit. 'Anyway, none of this was much of a concern for us till the September 11 attack on the United States. The al-Qaeda immediately became the world's biggest villain, and everyone remotely associated with Osama bin Laden fell afoul of the US administration. As a result, Dilawar was designated as a global terrorist by the United States Department of Treasury, and his assets were frozen. When this happened, our overzealous politicians instantly saw a great opportunity to start demanding Dilawar's extradition from Pakistan—and this time there were a lot more sympathetic ears all around.'

'Now though Pakistan has kept denying that they have anything to do with him, there's a growing lobby within Pakistan that believes that Dilawar is increasingly becoming a liability,' Seshadri took up the thread of the narrative once again. 'This lobby believes that with more and more American and British policymakers buying India's point of view and tilting towards India, it's time Irshad Dilawar was made persona non grata in Pakistan.

'The tipping point—and the genesis of Project Abhimanyu—was another assassination bid on Dilawar in the Republic of Mali in early May. Dilawar had a narrow escape, and we still aren't sure who was behind the attack, but it was clear that the Pakistanis had let their guard down and weren't investing enough in protecting Dilawar. And as if that wasn't bad enough, last month, the Indian home ministry asked the RAW to work with the Intelligence Bureau in putting together a fresh dossier on Dilawar. The Indian Government intends to present this dossier to the United States' national security advisor during his upcoming visit to India.'

'I am aware of this dossier,' said Special Director Dhawan of the IB. 'From Delhi, the US national security advisor is going to Islamabad, and the dossier is meant to demonstrate Dilawar's role in terror activities in India, and get America to lean on Islamabad even harder. There is a strong feeling in South Block that this time Washington will prevail upon Pakistan to turn Dilawar over to India.'

'You begin to see our problem?' the director of the RAW looked at the gathering. 'Now you see the need for a Project Abhimanyu?'

Lieutenant-General Bhonsle looked at Seshadri shrewdly. 'The Pakistanis are being lax about Dilawar's security, plus now there is a real threat of them handing him over to India. Everything that we have planned and worked towards can come to a premature end.'

'And we can't let that happen, can we?' Seshadri pointed out. 'That's why General Dixit hatched Project Abhimanyu.'

'We realized that the stronger our attempts to get Dilawar, the more the ISI would resist and the tighter they would hold on to him,' the general explained. 'So we created the mirage of India launching a secret commando operation to assassinate Dilawar. We wanted to have our commandos infiltrate Pakistan and get within striking distance of Dilawar before the US national security advisor landed in Pakistan. We would then abort the operation, and wait for the ISI to dig its heels in when the debate to turn Dilawar over to India surfaced in Islamabad.'

'How come the Joint Intelligence Committee doesn't have any knowledge of this dossier that is being handed to the American national security advisor?' Principal Secretary Talukdar asked with a touch of irritability.

'I apologize for having kept it from you,' said Seshadri, looking genuinely contrite. 'If the JIC had come to know of the home ministry's request for the dossier, you and Upreiti would have vetoed General Dixit's proposal to send commandos into Pakistan to kill Dilawar. You would have preferred waiting to see if the dossier did the trick for India. But we had to act *before* that dossier left India.'

'So that meeting which Dixit saab and the colonel held with me and Rawat saab in that farmhouse—that was part of the sham.' Upreiti appeared slightly upset at having been taken for a ride.

'It was and my apologies to both of you,' said General Dixit. 'But for the plan to work, the operation had to look authentic at every given point in time—otherwise it wouldn't have washed with the Pakistanis. That meant our best commandos had to actually cross the border and reach Karachi, and that wouldn't have been possible without Unit Kilo getting a formal go-ahead from the two of you.'

'What's Haider Nazir's role in all this?' asked Assistant Director Pasricha suddenly.

'He is a known ISI agent in the Pakistani embassy,' explained deputy Vashisht.

'You mean he's a double agent, one of our people?'

'No, he's a 24-carat ISI agent, and a decent one at that. But we uncovered him last year. We had the choice of registering a formal complaint and having him recalled to Pakistan. Instead, we thought it smarter to use him to plant information inside the ISI.'

'Disinformation, actually,' Seshadri corrected.

'Yes, actually,' Vashisht smiled. 'General Dixit is his contact, and he was our conduit to let the ISI know about our planned attack on Dilawar.'

'Why that phone call from Dehradun?' Pasricha looked at General Dixit quizzically. 'That wasn't very smart.'

'It was a desperate attempt at sending a message across to Pakistan,' the general answered, looking sheepish. 'We were afraid that the Pakistanis were not taking the threat posed by Project Abhimanyu seriously enough, so we needed to plant some more information about the operation. Unfortunately, I was in Dehradun that day attending a family function, and as I am Haider Nazir's only contact, I simply had to call him. I never expected my sister's number in Dehradun to be traced back to me.'

'So how do we know whether Project Abhimanyu served its purpose?' Lieutenant-General Bhonsle asked.

'It has, to the effect that the Pakistanis took the threat to Dilawar's life seriously. They didn't let him come to Karachi,' replied General Dixit. 'The real test, though, will be seeing what happens after the United States' national security advisor leaves Islamabad for Washington.'

'Yes, but the threat to Dilawar's life still exists,' the RAW director interjected quickly. 'We are yet to rein in your two commandos. And we have to quickly inform the Pakistanis about the assassination plot hatched in Istanbul. To my mind, this Hossam Al-Kamil spells big trouble.'

30 July. Kuan Mori, Balochistan

Dinner was done, and the colonel stood by the hut's door, watching the three Unit Kilo commandos sitting in contemplative silence, processing the flood of information that he had loosed upon them. Imtiaz, in particular, appeared to be brooding over something, and the colonel slowly walked over and sat down beside him.

'What are you thinking about?'

'Saadat,' the major replied, keeping his eyes averted.

As Shamsheer and Rafiq turned towards them, the colonel looked at Imtiaz curiously. 'Saadat… What about him?'

'Whatever he did for me, he did because he believed we were going after Dilawar to kill him. But now Dilawar isn't going to die, so the promises I made to Saadat have become empty and meaningless.' The major shook his head in bitterness.

Colonel Mohan chewed his upper lip pensively before speaking. 'Saadat helped you because he believed you were doing what you thought was right.

At that time, killing Dilawar was the right thing to do. Now that you know the truth, protecting him is.' After a short pause, he added, 'God willing, one day you will get the opportunity to sit down and explain everything to Saadat. He will understand.'

'Sure,' snorted Imtiaz, a sour smile playing on his lips. 'Till that happens, he can keep thinking of me as the man who failed to repay his trust.'

The colonel considered Imtiaz solemnly for a moment. When he spoke, his tone was calm and matter-of-fact.

'I remember once telling you that this is a thankless job with no room for public honour,' he said. 'In Unit Kilo, the only thing that matters is achieving the objective, major. Project Abhimanyu achieved its objective the day the Pakistanis realized the threat to Dilawar's life and decided not to let him come to Karachi. You have played a very important part in achieving that objective. As a Unit Kilo commando, what more could you ask for?'

'I wish you hadn't deliberately misled us—none of this would have happened had we known the truth,' the major said levelly. 'And I wish you had trusted me more instead of getting Rafiq to spy on me and the captain. It nearly cost the lives of one or two Unit Kilo commandos today.'

The colonel dropped his gaze and nodded. 'Those were mistakes and I'm sorry for that.' Then, raising his head, he looked Imtiaz in the eye and shrugged. 'Maybe I shouldn't have lied to any of you about this operation. I just did what I thought was right. I realize I was probably wrong.'

For a while, the men sat immersed in silence.

'It's okay, sir,' Imtiaz said finally. 'I'm also sorry for having taken this so personally. I guess it's the price we pay for being in a dark and secretive business.' The major's tone implied that the matter was settled as far as he was concerned.

The colonel nodded. 'At least I'm thankful we timed Project Abhimanyu just right. Who knows what would have happened if Dilawar had actually come to Karachi four days ago and the Pakistanis had been as lax about his security.'

'You mean if our operation hadn't happened at all?' asked Rafiq curiously. Seeing the colonel nod, he asked, 'Why? What would have happened then?'

'We have just discovered that a contract to kill Dilawar was drawn up sometime last month. An Arab mercenary named Hossam Al-Kamil has been picked for the job, and we know that he, along with a group of men, travelled from Ras al-Khaimah to Pakistan about ten days ago. In fact, we are fairly certain that one of the men Shamsheer saw in the car in Clifton was—what happened?'

The colonel looked at Shamsheer, who was staring wide-eyed into space, his mouth partly open. The captain looked at the three faces turned towards him, shut his mouth and swallowed hard.

'In all this confusion, I completely forgot,' he spoke in a rush. 'The man I saw in Clifton... I saw him again. This evening. In Gwadar market.'

'What?' The colonel fixed an intense gaze on Shamsheer.

'Yes. I've tried to tell myself that I may be mistaken, but I know I'm not. It was the same man.'

Colonel Mohan sat upright, his mind on the house in Pishukan. 'If Hossam Al-Kamil is in Gwadar, Irshad Dilawar's life is in grave danger.' Turning to Rafiq, he extended his hand. 'I've lost my sat-phone... I need yours. General Dixit must be informed about this immediately.'

Three minutes later, the colonel re-entered the hut and looked at his commandos. 'Okay, we have ten minutes to clear out of here. We have to head for the Iranian border as quickly as possible.'

'But... what about Hossam?' Shamsheer asked slowly.

'The general is passing on all information we have on Hossam Al-Kamil to Haider Nazir right away. Haider is our Pakistani contact in Delhi... In less than half an hour, Haider Nazir will deliver that information to his ISI bosses. We can expect the Pakistanis to launch a massive search operation for Hossam in and around Gwadar in no time.'

The colonel flicked his fingers to signal urgency. 'It's a long way to the Iranian border. We must move fast to escape that dragnet.'

30 July. RAW Headquarters, Lodhi Road, Delhi

'Where are you guys?'

General Dixit leaned over a two-way speakerphone that lay on a large mahogany desk, his face tense, knuckles white as he gripped the edge of the table tightly. Additional Director Vashisht sat hunched in a sofa beside the general, his brows furrowed with anxiety. Seshadri, meanwhile, walked the length of his large but spartan office, his hands clasped behind him, head bent in thought.

'In the hills, sir...' Colonel Mohan's voice sounded metallic as it crackled over the phone. 'A few kilometres off the Makran Highway, heading west for the Iranian border.'

'Have you contacted Swamyji yet?'

'No, sir. As you had instructed, I planned to call him after…'

'Then don't call him,' General Dixit interrupted. He looked up at Seshadri briefly, and the director nodded. The general turned back to the phone.

'Colonel, listen to me carefully. There's a change in plan. Haider Nazir cannot be contacted as he's been hospitalized for acute appendicitis.'

'In hospital? Shit,' the colonel said in dismay.

'I know. It's quite sudden. It seems he was admitted to AIIMS late this afternoon, where he's now in intensive care. The surgery is scheduled for tomorrow morning, so there's no way we can pass on the news about Al-Kamil's presence in Gwadar to the Pakistanis.'

'Damn!' The concern in Colonel Mohan's voice was clearly audible. 'What do we do now, sir?'

Drawing a deep breath, the general once again glanced from the RAW chief to his deputy. 'We need the four of you to keep watch over Dilawar and prevent him from coming to any harm.'

30 July. Kuan Mori, Balochistan

Colonel Mohan huddled into a crevice to cut the sound of the wind as he strained to hear the general. Imtiaz, Rafiq and Shamsheer stood around him, listening intently to what the colonel was saying.

'I don't know, sir,' the colonel shook his head. 'We have no idea how long Hossam has been in Gwadar. God forbid, he might have planned an attack *tonight*… It's a possibility… Imtiaz tells me an attack could be staged at the hotel in Gwadar town as well… No, sir…'

The colonel listened to the general for a while before speaking. 'Sir, we are a lot closer to Pishukan than to the hotel. Also, it's nearly 10.30… If Hossam has picked the hotel to launch his attack, we'll never get there in time. I suggest we head for the safe house instead—that will be a lot quicker. Plus, if Hossam has already attacked the hotel, we'll know by just observing the activity at the safe house.'

When the general spoke next, Colonel Mohan nodded a couple of times. 'I understand, sir… If the attack has already occurred, we withdraw quietly. Otherwise, we watch for any sign of Hossam and his men, at least till daybreak. Right, sir… Right… We have our pistols with us… Yes, sir. We will.'

The colonel put the phone away and turned to the major. 'Okay, we're going to Pishukan. There's a hill opposite the safe house… It offers a good view of the surrounding desert. I used it all day while waiting for you or Shamsheer to show up. That's where we set up our stake-out.'

'What happens if we observe Hossam and his men near the house?' Rafiq asked. 'Do we attack?'

'It depends... We'll try not to engage Hossam directly. The safe house is well guarded, so if we spy an attack, we will raise an alarm by firing our guns in the air. Hopefully, Dilawar's guards will respond to the alert.'

'Still, if Hossam's men gain the upper hand?' Imtiaz pressed.

When Colonel Mohan spoke, there was firm resolve in his voice. 'We will have to step in and neutralize Hossam's attack.'

CHAPTER 16

31 July. RAW Headquarters, Lodhi Road, Delhi

The early morning stillness was broken by the raucous cries of parakeets on a gulmohar just outside the open window. The noise woke General Dixit from a shallow sleep, and the general blinked a couple of times as he established his bearings. He had dozed off sitting at a large, glass-topped conference table that occupied a third of the room's floor space.

He glanced at his watch—twenty minutes past six. Springing up from his chair, he made for the closed door, but even as he reached for the doorknob, the door opened to admit Seshadri. The head of the RAW was holding a cup of thin, anaemic tea in one hand.

'Any news from your colonel?' the director asked without preamble.

'None so far.'

'We can interpret that as good news, I suppose... These all-night affairs are no longer easy,' he said sourly, as he lowered himself into a chair and stretched his long legs out. 'What lousy timing for Nazir to have his bloody appendicitis.'

General Dixit nodded. 'Where is Vashisht saab?'

'He's talking to our section head in Abu Dhabi, trying to get something more on Al-Kamil if possible. Anything to help the colonel and his men when they call...'

As if on cue, General Dixit's mobile phone rang. 'It's Mohan,' he announced, before accepting the call and switching on the speaker phone. 'Yes colonel... I have Seshadri saab here with me. What's your report?'

'Sir, we have spent the last five hours in Pishukan and everything is normal here,' the colonel's voice was faint but clear. 'There was no attack on Dilawar last night.'

'That's good,' said the general, smiling at Seshadri in relief. 'And there's no immediate threat of an attack?'

'No sir. The sun is almost up, and there's sufficient light all around. The approach to the safe house is open on all sides, so I don't expect an attack here before sundown.'

'Good.'

For a moment there was silence as the general and the director considered one another.

'Mohan... as you know, Haider Nazir is going to be out of bounds for some time,' General Dixit ventured slowly. 'And unfortunately, we can't suddenly use any of our other contacts to inform the ISI about the threat to Dilawar's life without raising suspicions in Pakistan. You get what I'm saying?'

'Yes, sir.'

'Now, even though there appears to be no immediate risk to Dilawar, the fact remains that Al-Kamil is somewhere in Gwadar. He is bound to make a move without much delay. My guess is probably sometime tonight.'

'It is a strong possibility, sir,' the colonel conceded.

'I know what I'm going to say next is not going to be easy, but Irshad Dilawar's safety now rests solely in *your* hands, colonel.' General Dixit paused briefly to clear his throat. 'I don't know how the four of you are going to do it, but it's up to you chaps to somehow foil Al-Kamil's plans.'

'We realized as much, sir,' the colonel's voice was calm and reassuring. 'In fact, a solution has already crossed the major's mind.'

Seshadri looked at General Dixit, eyebrows raised in surprise. The general smiled back broadly, a proud father basking in the light of a child's brilliance.

'Wonderful,' said the general. 'So what does he propose you do?'

'We have to figure out Al-Kamil's exact whereabouts, sir,' Colonel Mohan replied. 'We can't just sit here assuming that Al-Kamil will attack the safe house. He might choose to atttack Dilawar at the hotel in Gwadar—it's more risky but, for the same reason, more unexpected as well. Also, as Shamsheer points out, Dilawar's motorcade could be ambushed anywhere between Gwadar and Pishukan. The only way of stopping Al-Kamil is by taking the fight to his doorstep. We have the entire day to do that.'

'But Gwadar covers a very large area. Do you have any ideas about where you can begin looking for Al-Kamil?'

'Well, sir, Imtiaz does,' answered the colonel. 'He says he knows a man who can help us.'

31 July. Gwadar Town, Balochistan

The only sound in the darkened living room was the low, hollow bubbling of the hookah as Shihab Perwaiz lounged on the divan, eyes closed. Imtiaz sat on a cushioned stool opposite the divan, studying the reclining figure patiently. Finally, after a couple of minutes of silence, the Balochi opened his eyes and considered the major.

'Do you realize that the description you have given me can apply to half the population of Gwadar?' he asked. 'Dark rugged face, thick black beard, sharp eyes, short hair... I can line up fifty people from this neighbourhood alone who answer to that description.'

'He is also known to wear a black qaraqul and is heavily built. Not very tall, though,' offered Imtiaz.

'That's better,' Perwaiz smiled sarcastically. 'Now the number gets reduced to twenty.'

Seeing his guest's face fall, the Balochi relented. 'Isn't there something more you can tell me about this man you are looking for?'

'His name is Hossam Al-Kamil, and he is neither Balochi nor a Pathan. He's an Arab. And there are seven or eight men with him. That's all I can say.'

'You are certain he's in Gwadar?'

Imtiaz could tell that Perwaiz's curiosity had been piqued, and that he would have liked to know why the major was interested in finding this man. 'Yes,' he replied. 'He was definitely in Gwadar town yesterday, and I am certain he is still in the vicinity.'

Perwaiz propped himself up on one elbow. 'I will make some enquiries and see if I can find anything out.' Judging from the tone of his voice, the big man didn't seem very hopeful, though.

'Maybe you could ask some of the jeep drivers if they know anything,' said Imtiaz slowly. 'One of them might have ferried these men either into or out of Gwadar.'

'Ah yes,' said Perwaiz, cocking a calculative eye at the major. 'Maybe they will know and remember something.'

'Yes, huzoor. We could even reward those who remember well.'

'Yes, yes. Why not?' Perwaiz agreed, interpreting the major perfectly. 'Let me see what comes up.'

'Thank you,' the major bowed. 'I wouldn't know how to repay you for your help.'

'Tcha!' the big man brushed off the major's words. 'Saadat mian's friends don't need to repay me. Now what was the second thing you wanted?'

'I need a vehicle.'

Seeing Perwaiz's eyes narrow, the major added, 'I know you explained that there were some problems involved. But you have my word... I shall not let the vehicle come to harm, nor will I use it in a manner that draws attention to you.'

The Balochi evaluated this request before asking, 'Will you need a driver as well?'

'No huzoor. Both Shamsheer and I are proficient drivers.'

'Then it won't be so much of a problem,' said Perwaiz, looking slightly relieved. After a short pause, he added, 'You will find an empty Willys jeep with a flat tyre on the highway near Kuan Mori around noon today. The spare tyre will be in the back of the jeep, hidden under a tarpaulin. Just make sure you get to the jeep before someone else does.'

'I will,' said Imtiaz. 'What about Al-Kamil?'

'Call me around one o'clock. Hopefully I'll have some news for you about him.'

31 July. Koh-e-Mehdi, Balochistan

Al-Kamil looked solemnly at the faces of the four men around him.

'Brothers, the time has come to avenge the loss of Jamal and Tabarek,' he said, addressing them in Arabic. 'The time has come for us to be rewarded for our patience and perseverance. By the grace of Allah, tonight we shall finally accomplish what we had set out to achieve.'

The five men were sitting in a tight circle in the middle of a room that had once served as the heart of a brick kiln. The rough cement floor of the room was still covered with a fine, greyish-white dust which also hung in the air, the suspended particles dancing in the light of the late afternoon sun that streamed in through the solitary open window. In direct contrast to the pool of bright light in the middle, the room itself was largely in shadow, the huge gaping maw of the firing oven barely discernible in the gloom.

'When do we launch our attack?' asked one of the men, licking his lips in anticipation.

'Tonight, the moment our target's car leaves the Zobair Hotel's gates to return to the house in Pishukan,' answered Al-Kamil. 'Now let me explain the plan to you. Ask Saddiki to join us here. He can continue keeping watch from the window.'

As one of the mercenaries departed to fetch Saddiki, Al-Kamil turned to the oldest man in the group.

'Make sure that everything we need is stowed in the jeep, and that the jeep is ready for departure,' he ordered. 'Irshad Dilawar comes out of the hotel around 10.30 every night. If we are to be ready for him, we should be in our positions by ten. So we must leave for Gwadar by nine.'

July 31. Kuan Mori, Balochistan

'Major... major...'

Imtiaz heard the voice cut through his sleep even as his mind registered the pressure of a hand shaking him persistently by the shoulder. Forcing his eyes open, he saw the hut's mud walls and black ceiling swim into focus.

'Major... It's nearly five o'clock.'

Turning his head sideways, Imtiaz saw Colonel Mohan crouching beside him, Rafiq's sat-phone in one hand.

'Get up,' the colonel sounded on edge. 'It's time to call Perwaiz again.'

The major threw aside the blanket, stood up and accepted the Thuraya. He looked groggily at Shamsheer—the captain was sitting against one wall, shaking a leg in nervous impatience. Rafiq wasn't to be seen, but Imtiaz knew the boy was guarding the jeep that Perwaiz had placed at their disposal.

'I hope Perwaiz has found something useful at last,' muttered Colonel Mohan. 'We're seriously running out of time.'

Imtiaz didn't reply. This was the third time he was calling Perwaiz that afternoon—on both the previous occasions he'd drawn blanks, the Balochi having failed to unearth any information on Al-Kamil's whereabouts. Pushing aside the gunnysack curtain, the major walked out of the hut to make the call.

The colonel stretched himself out on a blanket, crossed his hands under his head and studied the hut's ceiling with worried eyes.

'Sir, was Al-Kamil also behind the attack on Dilawar in Mali?' The captain's voice disturbed the tense silence.

'Maybe, but we can't say for sure. What we do know is that one of the attackers was a fairly well-known Algerian contract killer. Dilawar's guards killed him. And it seems Al-Kamil was also hired by an Algerian.'

'But why would any Algerians want to kill him?'

'I really wish we knew. My guess is that the Algerians are working for someone else.'

'Who? His rivals in Mumbai's underworld?'

Colonel Mohan propped himself on one elbow and looked at the captain. 'There are many who would also like to see the last of Irshad Dilawar... Dilawar's underworld rivals aren't just in Mumbai. He has made enemies in the Israeli mafia, the Turkish syndicates and the powerful Russian mafia. Then, it could even be the CIA.'

Seeing the captain's eyebrows shoot up, Colonel Mohan nodded. 'Dilawar has helped the CIA in many ways. Smuggling heroin that helped the CIA fund the Afghanistan mujahedeen. Providing their agents information and protection in the Middle East during the Iraqi conflict... Laundering their dirty money... He knows too many secrets that, if revealed, can be quite embarrassing to the CIA and America.'

As Shamsheer stared in amazement, the colonel continued, 'These attempts might even have been masterminded by some Pakistanis. Dilawar has lots of businesses in Karachi and Sindh that clash with the commercial interests of many Pakistani politicians and businessmen. So there's a high level of resentment towards him *within* Pakistan. For the last three years, one prominent Pakistani minister has been lobbying privately to have Dilawar extradited to India. Can you beat that?'

Before the captain could respond, the curtain swished aside to let Imtiaz in. 'It looks like Perwaiz mian has finally found Al-Kamil,' he announced.

'Great!' The colonel sat bolt upright. 'Where is he?'

The major pulled out the map of Gwadar from one of the bags and spread it on the blanket. Colonel Mohan and Shamsheer huddled around him.

'Here,' he said, pointing to a spot to the northeast of Gwadar, at the apex of the curve of the east bay of Gwadar port. 'This is Koh-e-Mehdi, a huge hill with sharp, vertical cliffs, very close to the bay. It seems Al-Kamil and his men have been seen near an abandoned brick kiln close to the foot of Koh-e-Mehdi on the northern side. The kiln is about three kilometres from the coastal village of Sur Bandar.' Imtiaz drew a circle on the map, covering the area between the eastern flank of Koh-e-Mehdi and Sur Bandar. 'They are somewhere here.'

'Is Perwaiz certain that they're the men we want?' asked the colonel.

'Well, the group consists of six men, all strangers to these parts. And it seems one of the men answers to the description of Al-Kamil.'

Colonel Mohan nodded and looked at his watch. 'This place is roughly twenty-five kilometres from where we are, and it's nearing 5.30.' Rising to his feet, he walked to the hut's door, pushed the gunnysack curtain aside and assessed the amount of daylight left. 'If we move quickly, we can conduct a thorough recce of Al-Kamil's base by sundown. And once it's sufficiently dark, we can attack him before he puts his plans into operation.'

He looked from Imtiaz to Shamsheer for a moment before smiling tightly. 'Let's go, boys. Let's take Al-Kamil down and make sure Project Abhimanyu remains a success.'

CHAPTER 17

31 July. Koh-e-Mehdi, Balochistan

The dark, ridged heights of the Koh-e-Mehdi towered above the quiet desert landscape, chalky grey in the dull moonlight. The night air was still, though a gentle breeze blew occasionally, kicking up small clouds of dust that danced, wraith-like, before subsiding. The only sound that broke the silence was the sporadic noise of vehicles motoring down the Makran Coastal Highway a kilometre away.

Imtiaz lay half-buried in the sand, virtually immobile, watching the brick kiln and the two sentries standing guard beside the jeep parked outside. The kiln, which was hardly sixty metres away, its back to the Koh-e-Mehdi, had already been surrounded by the four Unit Kilo commandos.

Finding the kiln had been surprisingly easy. Shamsheer had spotted it through the Sunagor Compact as they had driven down the Makran Highway, and following a quick recce on foot, he had made a positive identification of both Al-Kamil and the driver of the Suzuki Cultus standing outside the kiln.

Planning their assault, however, had proved to be far more complicated, as the approach to the kiln was completely flat and open on three sides. The only cover available was a small copse of acacia and dwarf palm, seventy metres from the kiln. With no way of storming the building without being observed by the two lookouts, the only option for the commandos was to try and close in from the sides, using the ridges and ravines of the Koh-e-Mehdi for cover.

To compound the problem, Al-Kamil and his men had the protection of the building, and the commandos didn't possess the weaponry needed to force the mercenaries out into the open. And, of course, the question of a long-drawn stand-off didn't arise. Theirs had to be a swift strike, followed by a clean getaway—before the local authorities got wind of it and came investigating.

As they had been grappling with this, Rafiq had observed the mercenaries loading guns into the jeep and readying for departure. Realizing that Al-Kamil was planning his attack for later that night, Colonel Mohan had quickly sketched out a plan of ambushing them as they left the kiln.

Imtiaz slowly turned his head to his right and looked at the small grove of acacia and palms. He knew that Rafiq was hiding behind one of the trees. Slowly, he turned back towards the two guards watching the desert. Even if they looked in his direction, all they would see in the half-light was a motionless mound of sand. With satisfaction he noted that the sentries didn't think it worth their while to watch the hillside. It was just as well—the colonel and Shamsheer were hiding in the shadows of the Koh-e-Mehdi, barely thirty metres from the kiln.

The minutes passed slowly and wisps of clouds scudded steadily in from the south, obscuring the quarter moon now and then. Imtiaz was beginning to wonder how long their wait would last when the door of the kiln opened and a man's silhouette appeared. One of the guards immediately walked over to the door. As the major watched, the man and the guard conversed briefly, before the former turned back inside. Meanwhile, the guard hailed the second sentry in Arabic.

'Saddiki… It's time to go.'

The guard by the jeep immediately unslung and stowed away his weapon, before climbing into the driver's seat.

In less than thirty seconds, four men emerged from the kiln and walked to the jeep. While one of them went around to the front, the other three got into its back, one after the other. They were joined by the guard, and a fraction of a second later, the jeep's engine sprang to life. A moment later, the vehicle's headlights were turned on, its yellow beams lighting up the side of the house.

Imtiaz darted a quick glance towards the copse where Rafiq was hiding. As he and the lieutenant were the ones with the assault rifles, it was up to them to launch the fiercest part of the attack and inflict as much damage on Al-Kamil's team as possible. Colonel Mohan and Shamsheer were expected to provide only diversionary fire with their pistols—though with some luck they would also help mop up the mercenaries.

The driver threw the jeep into gear and the vehicle lunged forward. The major, every sinew in his body taut, immediately shifted his attention to a small shrub about twenty metres away from where he was lying. By observing the tyre treads in the mud, the commandos had concluded that whenever the mercenaries departed, they would drive past the shrub. The plan was to simultaneously open fire on the jeep the moment it crossed the shrub.

As the jeep lurched and bounced across the uneven ground, Imtiaz slowly pushed himself up on to his knees. Then, just as the jeep reached the shrub, he propped himself on one knee and raised the Heckler & Koch to his shoulder.

Taking a second to aim at the moving vehicle, he pressed the trigger.

* * *

Rafiq peeked around the trunk of the large acacia that he was hiding behind, his eyes narrowing in the glare of the approaching jeep's headlights. He looked at the shrub, its dry brambly branches sticking out in the light of the headlamps. Quickly assessing the distance between the jeep and the shrub, the lieutenant crouched back into the shelter of the tree. Hoisting his Kalashnikov in both hands, he looked up at the sky and murmured a short prayer. He then turned and stuck his head out once again to look at the jeep.

Two seconds later, the jeep crossed the shrub. Stepping out of the tree's cover, Rafiq pulled the Kalashnikov's trigger.

Nothing happened.

As Rafiq's mind registered the fact that the gun had failed to fire, a burst of gunfire rent the night air, masking the sound of the jeep's engine completely. Almost immediately, a flock of birds roosting in the branches above took flight, startling the lieutenant. He looked up, then quickly returned his gaze to the jeep, which was now weaving about drunkenly.

Raising his Kalashnikov, he frantically pressed the trigger once again. Again, the gun jammed.

A second, longer burst of gunfire ripped the night, and this time Rafiq heard the sound of bullets thumping into metal, and glass being smashed. He thought he also heard someone cry out in pain.

Rafiq stared open-mouthed as the jeep suddenly jerked to a standstill, its engine dying abruptly. One of its headlights had gone out, hit by a bullet. A third round of gunfire opened to his left, while a series of gunshots came from the direction of the kiln.

The lieutenant lifted the Kalashnikov once again and pressed the trigger for the third time. But the stubborn weapon refused to respond.

His lips dry, the tremor in his hand distinctly noticeable, Rafiq stared at the jeep. The driver was slumped over the steering-wheel, but the man sitting next to the driver was trying to open the door and get out.

As the man swung the door open, Rafiq ducked behind the tree, dropped the Kalashnikov to the ground, reached into his waistband and pulled out one of the Glock 17s.

Peering out, the lieutenant saw a bulky figure step out of the jeep. The man immediately turned, raised a gun and fired three rounds in the direction of the kiln. As the man's back was to him, Rafiq stepped out from behind the tree and ran towards the jeep in a crouch, his pistol levelled as he tried to aim for the man's head.

When he was reasonably sure he had the man covered, the lieutenant pulled the trigger.

However, just as he fired, the man dropped down on one knee. The shot missed the man's head by inches, and he immediately whirled around and fired at Rafiq. The lieutenant ducked and quickly fired two rounds back at the mercenary, but as the man's bulk was now behind the jeep's open door, both bullets thudded dully into metal. At that moment, someone in the back of the jeep began shooting, and Rafiq heard retaliatory gunfire from his left and from the direction of the kiln.

Acutely aware that he was standing in the glare of the jeep's headlamp, Rafiq decided that he needed to kill the light immediately. Swinging around in a small, tight arc, he aimed the Glock at the lone, burning headlight and pulled the trigger.

At the same moment, out of the corner of his eye, he saw the man step out from behind the open door and fire at him.

There was hardly a fraction of a second's difference between the two discharges, and for all practical purposes, the two shots sounded as one to Rafiq's ears. He watched the headlamp shatter, shards of glass flying in all directions as the Glock's bullet wrecked the fragile bulb inside.

He also felt his right shoulder being slammed back. Immediately, a searing heat shot up the right side of his neck and coursed down his hand and torso. The Glock slipped out of his powerless fingers.

Then, as an inky blackness replaced the light, the lieutenant slowly keeled over and hit the ground.

* * *

The moon had slipped behind a huge bank of clouds and the darkness was absolute.

Imtiaz lay in the sand, hardly breathing, as he tried to pick up sounds of movement coming from the direction of the jeep. There were none.

Slowly, he raised his head and peered into the darkness, looking for anything that showed that the mercenaries were moving around. But all he could make out was the shape of the jeep, that too, barely. There was no sign of the colonel, Shamsheer or Rafiq either.

The commandos had decided that once Al-Kamil and his men had been brought down, each one was to quietly withdraw and make his way to the Willys jeep that was parked in a ravine about 500 metres away, in the direction of Gwadar. Stressing that the attack had to be brutal but short, the colonel had made it clear that it didn't matter if the mercenaries weren't all dead.

'We just have to hit them severely enough for Al-Kamil's plan to get *completely* screwed. Shoot and scoot before anyone realizes what's happening. The Pakistanis can pick up the pieces later.'

Imtiaz gingerly pushed himself on to all fours. Then, very quietly, he stood up, his rifle ready to shoot at the slightest sign of trouble. For a while, he just stood silently, making sure that the coast was clear. At last he began his walk towards Perwaiz's jeep.

* * *

'It's nearly fifteen minutes since we reached,' said Colonel Mohan, looking at his watch impatiently. 'Where is he?'

Neither Imtiaz nor Shamsheer answered. The three men were standing next to the Willys jeep, their eyes scanning the desert in the direction of the brick kiln. The colonel periodically turned towards the Makran Highway and raised the binoculars to his eyes. A few vehicles had already stopped along the highway, and the commandos could only guess that the gunfire had attracted the curiosity of the motorists.

'I hope he gets here soon,' said the colonel anxiously. 'If any of those motorists is a law-abiding citizen, the local police will be here before we know it.'

'Maybe the lieutenant doesn't remember where the jeep is parked and is still looking for it,' said Shamsheer, without much conviction.

'He's too well trained for that,' said the major flatly. 'And how difficult is it for anyone to find their way here. All one has to do is walk along the foot of Koh-e-Mehdi.'

The tense, uncomfortable silence that followed was broken by Colonel Mohan. 'Damn!' he snarled, peering through the Sunagor. 'I can see a red light flashing on the road. It's either an ambulance or the police.'

'It can't be an ambulance, sir,' said Shamsheer. 'We haven't heard a siren.'

After a pause, the colonel spoke grimly. 'You're right. It isn't an ambulance. So it has to be the police. Great! Soon they'll have checkpoints set up on the roads.'

As the two junior officers exchanged worried glances, the colonel lowered the binoculars. For a while, the three men stood staring at the flat expanse of the desert.

'This isn't looking good… dammit!' Colonel Mohan said.

'I'll go and look for him, sir,' said Imtiaz suddenly. 'Give me ten minutes.'

Without waiting for an answer from the colonel, he pulled the Czech pistol out of his waistband and broke into a run, heading back towards the kiln.

* * *

Imtiaz picked his way cautiously towards the clump of trees, his eyes scanning the ground ahead for movement. The faint moon was out once again, and the major could make out the kiln and the jeep, the latter with one of its side doors open. He could also see three bodies lying on the ground, one approximately fifteen feet behind the jeep, the other close to the open door. The third body lay roughly halfway between the jeep and the copse.

As the lieutenant had been stationed among the trees, the major decided to first check there. But a quick scan revealed the copse to be empty. Imtiaz then turned towards the dark form lying between the trees and the jeep. He approached the prone figure carefully, eyes darting all around, pistol levelled to shoot at the slightest hint of trouble.

The inert form was lying face down, and Imtiaz stretched one foot and prodded the body a couple of times. Getting no response, the major extracted a small pencil torch from his pocket, flicked the switch and pointed it at the man's face. He drew his breath involuntarily.

Rafiq's face was completely drained of blood.

The major crouched and placed two fingers on Rafiq's neck, checking for his pulse. For a moment he felt nothing. Then, as he pressed his fingers deeper, Imtiaz sensed the beat of blood coursing through the vein. Relieved, he placed the torch on the ground. Thrusting his pistol into the back of his waistband, he gently turned the lieutenant on his back and immediately felt the sticky wetness of blood on his right hand.

Checking quickly, he discovered that one side of Rafiq's shirt was covered in blood from the bullet wound near the right shoulder. Even in the dim light of the torch, the major could see that the injury was fairly deep, the damage quite severe.

Stealing a quick glance towards the red flashing light on the highway, Imtiaz switched off the torch and slipped it back into his pocket. Next, he propped the lieutenant to a sitting position, then, bracing his legs, he first pulled Rafiq gently to his feet, before expertly hoisting him over his shoulder.

As he adjusted the dead weight, the major noticed the red light of the police jeep slowly begin moving in his direction. It was hard to judge distances in the dark, but there seemed to be enough time for him to carry Rafiq away from the spot.

That's when he heard the low, angry grunt.

It came from directly behind him, from the direction of the jeep.

Even as he turned, Imtiaz's hand flew to his waistband—but with Rafiq's dead weight across his shoulder, he wasn't fast enough. Out of the corner of his eye, he saw a dark, bulky figure rush towards him. A split second later, the man hurled himself at the major with a ferocious growl.

The man's weight and momentum threw Imtiaz completely off balance, and he went crashing down with Rafiq on top of him. As he hit the ground, face forward, Rafiq landed heavily across the lower half of his body, pinning the major to the desert floor.

Imtiaz twisted around, desperately trying to get back to his feet, but the lieutenant's unconscious body severely hampered movement. And before he knew it, the major felt his assailant clamber on top of him, and a pair of rough, heavy hands grabbed his throat and began choking him.

Imtiaz's head began reeling. Fighting off panic and forcing himself to think clearly, the major employed a classic Krav Maga technique to break the stranglehold. He threw his hands at his attacker's open wrists, slapping both hands away from his windpipe. The relief was momentary, but before his attacker could exert pressure again, Imtiaz landed a palm-heel strike on the man's lips and nose. Then, before the man could recover, the major raised his shoulders off the ground and swung his left elbow at the man's face. The blow landed on the side of the man's head and he rolled off the major.

Imtiaz scrambled up as quickly as possible, his hands running along his waistband, searching for the pistol. But the gun wasn't there. It had been dislodged in the melee, and now lay somewhere in the darkness of the desert floor.

Turning around, the major saw his assailant regain his feet with amazing speed. Instantly, he banished the thought of the pistol from his mind. This would now have to be settled the old-fashioned way, the major realized.

Both men stood in the dull light, heads bent low and fists up, facing each other in a deadly duel. They circled one another cautiously, the attacker feinting with his left hand a couple of times. Imtiaz watched as the man then feinted with his right.

A second later, he realized it hadn't been a feint. His attacker had flung a handful of sand at his face.

The major blinked and instinctively took evasive action. Seizing the opportunity, the man drove a powerful kick into Imtiaz's stomach. The major doubled over. The man immediately swung his left knee at Imtiaz's head—but the major had anticipated this and blocked the attack. Then, seeing Imtiaz bent before him, the man raised his hand to strike the back of the major's exposed head.

The hand descended rapidly, but at the last moment, Imtiaz raised his left hand and fended off the blow. Simultaneously, using his entire body for momentum and speed, the major counter-attacked. Moving close, he first slammed a fist under the man's sternum, then scythed his left elbow across his face. As the man staggered back, the major kicked him savagely in the groin, before smashing his boot into the face.

For two seconds, the man swayed uncertainly. He then fell flat on his back and lay still.

Breathing heavily, Imtiaz looked towards the highway. The red light was much closer now. Hurrying over to Rafiq, the major bent down and carefully lifted the lieutenant onto his shoulders again. He then began trudging back towards the Willys jeep.

But he had only taken a few steps when he heard a guttural curse issued in Arabic.

'*Yebnen kelp!*'

Imtiaz turned slowly and stared at his attacker kneeling in the sand fifteen feet away, pointing a pistol at him.

'*Kul khara we moot.*' Even in the shallow light, Imtiaz could see the man's triumphant smile as his finger began pulling back the trigger.

In the stillness of the night, the gun's roar sounded incredibly loud. The major winced and closed his eyes, waiting for the bullet to crash into him.

Nothing happened.

That's when it struck Imtiaz that the report had come from his left, and not from directly ahead, where the man had been kneeling. Opening his eyes, the major looked briefly at the crumpled figure lying on the sand. He then turned to his left.

At first, he could see nothing but pitch black. But as he strained his eyes, a figure materialized out of the darkness like an apparition.

It was Shamsheer, approaching cautiously, his arms raised, the CZ 85B he held pointing straight at the dead man.

'Are you okay, sir?' the captain asked, slightly out of breath. His eyes stayed on the man on the ground.

'I'm fine,' the major answered, conscious of the mild tremor in his voice. 'You got him.'

Shamsheer finally lowered his pistol and looked at Imtiaz. 'Then let's go, sir. The police are almost here. They're bound to have heard the gunshot.'

The police jeep was now less than 200 metres away, its headlights arcing up and down as it bounded forward.

'Yes, but first, I want to know who this guy was.'

Adjusting Rafiq's weight on his shoulders, Imtiaz walked up to his dead assailant. Pulling the torch out of his pocket, he shone the light on the man. Shamsheer joined the major and looked down at Hossam Al-Kamil's bruised and battered face. Even in death, those blank, sightless eyes staring up at the torch seemed to retain their harsh cruelty.

'Now let's please get out of here, sir,' said Shamsheer, shivering slightly.

EPILOGUE

13 August. Solang Valley, Himachal Pradesh

Imtiaz breathed in the fresh, moisture-laden morning air and soaked in the stillness of the hills as he walked slowly up the narrow trail that wound through the cedar and pine forest. The valley below him was cloaked in mist, the Beas flowing at its bottom, hidden from sight. Even the trees ahead and above him were engulfed in a uniform diaphanous whiteness.

Cresting the hill, the major shrugged off his backpack and leaned it against a tree. He then walked a couple of yards to the edge of an open, grassy bluff and stared out at the higher peaks of the Pir Panjal range. Somewhere to his right, down by the river, was the village of Palchan. Far to his left and behind him was his destination—Beas Kund, the source of the Beas.

Thrusting his hands deep into his parka, the major smiled to himself, conscious of the calm that he felt.

At that moment, his cell phone rang. Surprised that his phone was still receiving a signal, Imtiaz pulled the instrument out of his pocket. He didn't recognize the number on the screen.

'Hello.'

'Hello sir. I hope I didn't wake you up.'

Recognizing Shamsheer's voice, the major smiled. 'No, no. It's fine. I have been up since six o'clock. How're you?'

'I'm fine, sir. I just called to tell you that I went to see Rafiq at the Army Hospital yesterday. You know that he came out of coma three days ago, don't you?'

'I know,' said Imtiaz, 'Colonel Mohan had called to tell me. He said the lieutenant was out of danger, but was still in the ICU under observation. How's he now?'

'Weak. You know he lost a lot of blood. And the collarbone will take quite some time to mend.'

'Right,' Imtiaz nodded. 'It was completely smashed by the bullet.'

'They also have to remove a few more bone fragments lodged in his neck and shoulder, so he'll have to undergo another surgery in a while. But he'll survive. He sounded pretty cheerful—he says he can't wait to return to Unit Kilo.'

'He's a spunky chap,' the major sensed a smile behind Shamsheer's words, and he smiled too. 'He'll bounce back.'

'Yes sir. He was asking about you. I told him you're on leave, hiking in the Himalayas.'

'I shall visit him as soon as I'm back in Delhi,' the major promised.

'He specifically asked me to convey his thanks for what you did that night. He can't believe you went back for him—especially after everything he had done to stop us from getting to Dilawar.'

'He was only following orders,' answered Imtiaz. After a pause, he added, 'Speaking of thank-yous, I never got the opportunity to thank *you* for helping me that night. If you hadn't arrived in time, both Rafiq and I would have been buried in Pakistan. That was some shot you fired. How did you get Hossam at that distance in the dark?'

'I guess I was lucky, sir,' said Shamsheer bashfully. '*Waise meri ammi hamesha kehti hain ki meri nazarein ulloo ki hain.*'

'*Aapki ammi ko meri umar lag jaaye,*' answered the major.

Less than a minute later, Imtiaz disconnected the call. As he was stowing the phone away, he heard voices from down the trail. Turning around, he saw three hikers approaching. He recognized the group from the hotel he had been staying at in Manali. While one was a brown-haired Briton, the other two were a middle-aged Bengali couple.

The major turned back and began surveying the valley when a sudden breeze carried the Bengali gentleman's words to his ears.

'...Indian government is completely incompetent. They make fools of themselves begging and grovelling to get Irshad Dilawar back.'

Imtiaz stopped breathing, all his faculties focused on the hikers.

'Incompetence is the bedrock of all governance,' the Englishman chuckled back.

'True, but our government wears it like a medal,' the Bengali said indignantly. 'You read what our honourable Home Minister had to say in yesterday's papers... It seems he's *disappointed* with Pakistan's response. Disappointed... Hmph!'

Imtiaz understood what the man was talking about—an interview with the Indian Home Minister, which had appeared in the previous day's edition of the *Hindustan Times*. The Home Minister had reacted to the Pakistani Prime

Minister's much-publicized interview on CNN a couple of days earlier, where the Pakistani Prime Minister had flatly denied Irshad Dilawar's presence in Pakistan, rubbishing it as a 'figment of India's fermented and frustrated imagination'.

'Well, to be fair to your Home Minister, I can't see what else he could have said,' the Englishman offered. The group was now close enough for Imtiaz to overhear every word. 'I take it your government has done everything in its capacity to get the US to pressure Pakistan into turning Dilawar over. What more could they do?'

'That's the problem,' the Indian seized on his friend's opinion argumentatively. 'Like crybabies we go running to America for everything. The American president, vice-president, some advisor... Whoever comes here, all we do is just complain. Pakistan is supporting terrorism, Pakistan is not cooperating, Pakistan is this, Pakistan is that... And in return, all we get is some sympathy and some meaningless promises.'

'So what would you like your government to do instead?' the Briton asked as they passed Imtiaz.

'We must solve our own problems,' the answer came readily. 'Why can't we send our army commandos into Pakistan to kill Dilawar or some of those jihadis in those training camps? I'm sure it can be done. All it needs is political will...'

As the group picked its way downhill, the voices faded. Imtiaz continued observing the heavy mist rolling up the valley. It now clung to the treeline twenty feet from where he stood. Everything beyond was firmly opaque and white.

13 August. The High Commission of Pakistan, Chanakyapuri, New Delhi

Haider Nazir sat upright in his chair, eyes wide open, as he carefully went through a sheet of paper in his hands. The paper, which had been delivered to him earlier that morning through one of General Dixit's couriers, contained a list of names and places, as well as specific dates and flight details between Istanbul, Amsterdam, Bamako and Islamabad.

The information that Nazir now held was a summary of the efforts that TP Doraiswamy and various RAW section heads and operatives had put in to uncover as much information as possible on Hossam Al-Kamil and Musa Zawawi. The RAW investigation had made slow progress till an operative based in Kuwait had chanced upon a link between Zawawi and Zeb Kirkland. Following that lead, the agency's section head in Paris had learnt of the American's visits to Zawawi's Amsterdam apartment, which had then brought Lieutenant-General Niazi to the RAW's notice.

Delving deeper, the intelligence agency had discovered that the retired Pakistani general had made a couple of trips to Istanbul and Bamako earlier in the year—all of which tied up neatly with the two attempts planned on Dilawar's life. After debating the findings extensively and concluding that both the bids were connected to the CIA, it had been decided that the best option was to gift-wrap the information selectively and let Islamabad deal with the messy affair.

Nazir once again looked at the name at the top of the page—Retired Lieutenant-General Wajid Ali Khan Niazi. It didn't make sense. The man was an ISI veteran, and he had been entrusted the task of shepherding Irshad Dilawar because he was close to the gangster. So why would he be part of a plot to kill Dilawar?

For money of course, the press attaché surmised grimly.

Opening his drawer, Nazir reached for the Thuraya sat-phone, taking great care so that his stomach muscles, still tender from the appendectomy, weren't strained in any way. In his book, there was no mercy for greed and treachery.

As he dialled Lieutenant-General Tauseef Rehmat's telephone, Nazir decided this would make a nice Independence Day present for the ISI chief.

13 August. RAW Headquarters, Lodhi Road, Delhi

'*Aadaab arz hai, Dilawar mian.*'

'*Aadaab, Seshadri saab. Sab khairiyat mein?*'

'*Bilkul.*'

Seshadri and Additional Director Vashisht sat in a small, soundproof room deep in the basement of the RAW Headquarters, headphones strapped over their heads. The conversation they were having was completely encrypted, and once they were done, the only evidence of it would exist in a digital recording stored in two coded hard disks that were secured in a vault at the end of the room.

'So what do you have for us today?' asked Seshadri.

'The ISI is preparing a plan to dispatch a group of thirty-forty jihadis into Kashmir from the east.'

'East meaning…?'

'From Aksai Chin or Himachal Pradesh… The entry into Kashmir valley is through Ladakh.'

'Aksai Chin?' Seshadri turned to Vashisht sharply. 'That means using China as a conduit!'

'Yes. China is the point of entry into Himachal as well.'

The RAW director paused as he took this in. 'Is this happening with Chinese approval?'

'I don't know. I just heard of this plan. I don't even know at what stage the plan is, but I thought you should know. I'll try and find out more, if possible.'

'Yes, thank you for this. Anything else?'

There was a short silence before the man at the other end spoke. 'Yes, one more thing. Though I believe this will be of greater interest and use to the Americans. There is a man, a Pakistani belonging to the al-Qaeda…'

13 August. Vasant Vihar, New Delhi

'The Pakistani's name is Abu Ahmed al-Kuwaiti, Mr Reiner,' said Seshadri.

The tall, craggy man seated opposite the RAW chief nodded, listening with keen interest. Hammond Reiner, station chief of the CIA in Delhi, had built his entire career out of listening intently to people.

'We're not sure if that's his real name, but that's the one he's known by,' said Seshadri.

'And he's high in the al-Qaeda hierarchy?'

'More mid-level. But apparently very loyal to the cause.'

Reiner nodded again. 'So what's so special about him?'

'He's one of the few people whom Osama bin Laden trusts completely.'

The station chief's eyebrows rose and he shuffled forward in his seat. 'In that case, we might already have a dossier on him.'

'It's possible,' the director of the RAW conceded. 'What I'm here for, though, is to tell you about a house that al-Kuwaiti owns. It's known as Waziristan Haveli and is located in Abbottabad. From what we've learnt, this house is a kilometre or so away from the Pakistan Military Academy.'

'And?' Reiner's instincts told him this was leading somewhere special.

'We may be wrong, but our guess is you may want to keep a close watch on al-Kuwaiti and his house in Abbottabad. We hear the house has some very fascinating tenants.'

'You mean Osama…?' The American's eyes widened in surprise. 'How reliable is this information?'

'I wouldn't be here if I didn't think it was reliable, would I?' Seshadri's eyes twinkled. 'And anyway, what's the harm in checking it out?'

'Yeah,' Reiner nodded. 'I'll get on the phone with Langley straightaway. Thanks you, Mr Seshadri.'

'My pleasure,' said the Indian, rising. 'Just one request. When you speak to Langley, tell them we'd like to be kept out of this completely. No mention of India anywhere, ever. Please.'

'Not even if we *do* find our man holed up in Abbottabad?'

'No,' Sheshadri smiled and shook Reiner's hand. 'You Americans have hunted him for years now—you deserve all the credit when you find him.'

ACKNOWLEDGEMENTS

I thank my parents Shama Nath and Jyoti Prasad Nath, for giving me the freedom to follow my heart. This book is just one of the happy by-products of that freedom.

My wife Pragya Madan, who has been the anchoring calm in my turbulent life, and my daughter Kaavya, whose faith in her 'Dada' is unshakeable.

My brother Murthy Sudhakar, whose none-too-subtle hints got me to seriously consider writing fiction. Your efforts paid off, bro!

Friend and ex-colleague Ravi Balakrishnan, for believing in this story more than I did, and keeping the fire going with his enthusiasm, encouragement and feedback.

Saurabh Garg, Hasmita Chander, Rajiv Narayan and Prathap Suthan, for ploughing through the clunky first draft and sharing their feedback. You've all made this a better read.

Madhu Ram and Dr Shankar Ayyappan Kutty, for their small but significant technical contributions. Madhu for the French, Shankar for the appendicitis.

My agent Kanishka Gupta, who agreed to represent me within an hour of seeing my manuscript. You were a great source of strength in those uncertain times.

My editor Rahul Soni, who edited the final draft with the precision and care of a gem-cutter. Your honesty and open-mindedness amazes and delights.

My publisher Ahmed Faiyaz and everyone else at Grey Oak and Rupa Publications. Thank you once again!

www.ingramcontent.com/pod-product-compliance
Lightning Source LLC
Chambersburg PA
CBHW031059020726
47495CB00007B/1951